C000270182

DON'T PASS ME BY

by

Julie McGowan

DON'T PASS ME BY

ISBN 978-1-909278-10-3

FIRST EDITION

Sunpenny Publishing - www.supenny.com

Printed and bound in England by CMP (uk) Limited

MORE BOOKS FROM JULIE McGOWAN:
The Mountains Between
Just One More Summer

MORE BOOKS FROM SUNPENNY LIMITED:
Blackbirds Baked In A Pie, by Eugene Barter
Breaking the Circle, by Althea Barr
Bridge to Nowhere, by Stephanie Parker McKean
Dance of Eagles, by JS Holloway
Far Out: Sailing Into a Disappearing World, by Corinna Weyreter
Going Astray, by Christine Moore
Loyalty and Disloyalty, by Dag Heward-Mills
My Sea is Wide (Illustrated), by Rowland Evans
Those Who Accuse you, by Dag Heward-Mills
Uncharted Waters, by Sara duBose

For Ann & Allan Wilkinson, in gratitude for
all the years of support, affection and fun.

*

With particular thanks to:

*My husband Peter and children Daniel, Catherine, Robert and
Elizabeth, and their spouses, for their
ever-present love and encouragement.*

*Emily, for being the most delightful distraction
when I need a break.*

Rosemary Johnson, for her persistent belief in me.

*Debbie and Georgia, Vi and Linda, for their
continuing support.*

*My great publishers, Jo and Andrew Holloway,
for their eagle eyes, their friendly approach, and their
ability once more to make this process so much fun.*

*And all the people who've taken the time and trouble
to contact me to tell me that they like what I do!*

1.

First, there was the blast. Then… silence. A complete and disturbing absence of any sound. No reassuring ticking of the clock that had kept Lydia company through many long evenings spent alone at the fireside. No creaking of floorboards. No whining of the cupboard door in the scullery as it swung back and forth on its hinges because it wouldn't close properly. Nothing.

As the first shock of the explosion began to recede, Lydia struggled to make sense of what had happened. She knew she had to move, although for the moment her brain felt too fuddled to work out why. There was just a need, an urgency that she couldn't identify. Tentatively she opened her eyes into the eerie quiet, forcing them to stay open against the grittiness of the brick dust that was swirling through the air as haphazardly as the confused thoughts swirling through her brain.

A huge orange halo lit the room from where the window, indeed the whole back wall, had been. It highlighted strange mounds of rubble and timber. Cold night air rushed in through the hole, aiding her return to consciousness. Into the silence came a thin, reedy, wail. Rescue workers, ambulances, perhaps.

She eased herself into a sitting position, wincing as her head made contact with the kitchen table. That must have been what saved her – she must have landed under the table as she fell. She winced again as she tried to push away some of the rubble around her feet. The wailing sound was increasing now, more insistent… more recognisable…

Grace! Grace was alive!

Suddenly Lydia was completely awake as the wailing turned into outraged howls. Her baby's need helped to push the pain away as she struggled to her feet, wincing this time from the sharp pain down her side.

She remembered now. It had nothing to do with the explosion.

"I'm coming!" she called, her voice croaky from the brick dust which had settled on the back of her throat. "I'm coming!"

As she began to clamber towards the front of the house, she found Billy lying immobile just a yard away from her, part of his body covered by fallen masonry. Perhaps he was dead.

The thought triggered no emotion. She forced her way into the hall.

The front part of the house seemed untouched apart from the layer of dust which had already penetrated everywhere. Grace was in her pram, unharmed, her limbs flailing in indignation that her demands were not being met with her mother's usual swiftness. "*Thank God,*" Lydia said of a deity she no longer believed in. "*Thank God.*"

She lifted the crying infant into her arms, wiping her reddened distressed face with the edge of her cot sheet. "Sssh, ssh, you must be quiet while I think what to do."

She lowered herself onto the bottom part of the staircase, the weight of the baby sending spasms of pain shooting from her side round to her back. The child's crying ended abruptly as she latched desperately onto the breast Lydia offered her, and while Grace sucked, Lydia tried to force her foggy brain to work.

It couldn't have been a bomb – there had been no air raid warning. She could only think of the gasworks in the next street. The surrounding houses would have taken the brunt of it, with the back of this house catching the tail end. Strange to think that they had all been waiting for the day when Hitler would send his bombs over and now their house – possibly their street – had been destroyed by what appeared to be an explosion at the gasworks.

The earlier part of the evening came back to her. Billy's anger. His army boots against her body as she writhed on the floor, crawling towards the shelter of the table for protection minutes before the blast. Ironically, it was that which must have saved her from further injury.

They must go, now, she knew, before the rescue workers arrived to deal not just with them, but with Billy also. But what if he was dead? Then there'd be no need for them to get away in a hurry. She had to check.

Soothed by her feed and tired from her prolonged bout of crying, the baby soon fell asleep. Lydia settled her in the pram and steeled herself to return to the back room, from where there had so far not been a sound.

Billy was lying in the same position. Very quietly Lydia moved towards him, stepping carefully so as not to dislodge the remnants of their home, lest she disturb him. There was a trickle of blood on his forehead, but otherwise his face was unharmed. Grey with dust, as was his hair, his relaxed features gave him an innocent, boyish look, belying her last sight of his face, contorted with fury. He looked as handsome as when they first met, when he had swept her off her feet.

She gave herself a mental shake. No time now for remembering. His left arm was lying free of the masonry which pinned his body to the floor. Gingerly she slid her hand around his wrist. There was a pulse. Faint, but steady.

At the same moment she thought she could hear voices shouting and she knew it wouldn't be long before helpers arrived, calling out for survivors, with torch-light playing around the desolation.

"Goodbye Billy," she whispered.

She made her way back past the sleeping baby and climbed the stairs. Her movements were deliberate, almost trance-like, as she forced to herself to think only of the immediate need to get away with Grace. What had gone before and where their future lay could not, for the moment, be considered.

As below, the rear bedroom was devastated, but the bag she had already packed was sitting on the double bed at the front. She picked it up and tiptoed back down the stairs. Lifting the baby up and wrapping her in a shawl, she quietly stepped out through the front door into the night.

2.

"They're coming! The car's just turned in at the gate!"

Rhian left her vantage point in the front porch and flew into the kitchen, where her older sister was buttering bread.

"How many?" Bronwen asked as she wiped her hands on an old towel.

"I couldn't see. *Come on.*"

The two girls stood on the porch steps as the car pulled up. In the front were their parents and in the back sat a thin, dark-haired figure.

"It's a boy!" Rhian exclaimed. "Mam said we'd have girls!"

Mam got out of the car. "Don't gawp, you two – he's feeling shy enough already. I hope that kettle's not boiling dry."

Bronwen scuttled back into the house, but Rhian stayed to watch her Dad pull forward the passenger seat and the young boy climb out. Her heart began to beat more rapidly. *A boy! I wonder if he'll play with me. Climb trees and make dams in the brook. And Dad will be pleased to have a boy around.*

"Alright lad?" Dad was asking in his firm voice as the boy straightened up and surveyed the girl as openly as she was looking at him. He was several inches taller than Rhian, wearing a crumpled school uniform with a cap which sat askew as if not strong enough to subdue the thatch of dark hair upon which it perched.

"This is my daughter Rhian, who's nine," Dad went on, "and the other girl, who's just gone inside is Bronwen, who's thirteen – so you see, you'll fit in very nicely with us."

Rhian said "Hallo" shyly, but he simply nodded slightly and looked about him as Dad lifted a battered cardboard suitcase and a gas mask out of the boot.

"Come on," he said, removing the cap and pressing it into the boy's hands. "You'll feel better when you get some of Mam's food inside you."

Rhian ran on ahead into the kitchen. Mam was talking to

5

Bronwen as she bustled round the kitchen with her usual swift movements.

"Mr. Owain Owen had said he'd try and make sure we'd have a girl – it would just be easier with the two of you – but Mrs. Owain Owen said that was all that was left – the girls had all been accounted for. I don't know why *Mister* Owain Owen is the Billeting Officer – he doesn't get a word in when that wife of his is around…"

Rhian and Bronwen exchanged quick glances at this, because their own Dad rarely said a word when his wife was in full flow, but that was because she was chatty in a friendly way, not downright bossy like Mrs. Owain Owen. Aware of footsteps behind her, Rhian said loudly, "Dad told us to come through."

She moved further into the stone flagged kitchen and indicated the boy standing in the doorway. Mam's eyes swept over him. Rhian hoped he didn't see the pity in Mam's eyes as she surveyed his bedraggled state.

"Why don't you show Arthur where he is upstairs," she told Rhian, in the kind voice she used when her children were feeling poorly. "Bronwen, tell your Dad that he'd better come in for his supper now as well, before he starts seeing to the animals, because I won't be doing it twice."

The boy followed Rhian up the steep staircase, his feet clattering on the polished wooden steps.

"You'd better wash your hands, Mam always checks," she said, showing him the small bathroom. She coloured slightly. "The… er… lavatory's next door, if you need to go first."

But the boy washed his hands quickly under the cold tap, dried them skimpily on the towel Rhian proffered and then turned to her.

"I'm not stopping," he said.

"I think you have to," she replied. "Look, this is your room – you can see right across the farm from here."

She opened a door opposite the bathroom. Inside was a bed with a candlewick cover, a narrow wardrobe and a dressing table. The boy followed her in, looked through the window and then sat on the bed. Rhian felt hot all over again; would he be able to tell that there was a rubber sheet underneath the cotton one? Mam had been to a talk on evacuees at the Red Shed. "They all wet the bed, apparently," she'd said on her return.

"What's your name?" Rhian asked the boy now.

"Arfur," he said. "But I'm not stopping – not once me Mum's better, anyway."

"What's wrong with her?'

"She got hurt in the black-out. Broke her leg. There was no-one else for me to stay with, but I'm going back soon as she's better."

She wondered if she should say sorry about his Mam, but he didn't look as if he wanted her sympathy.

"You sound odd," was all she said instead. "Where are you from?"

"Bermondsey," he answered. "That's in London," he went on when he saw the blank look on her face. "But it's not me that talks funny, it's you lot."

He looked out of the window again.

"Where's all the other houses?"

"In the village – you'll have passed them in the car. We're at the end. Because we're a farm. Only a small one though. Cows in the flat fields and some sheep on the high ones. And we've got a pig."

He didn't seem to be listening to her chatter, but continued to stare out of the window.

"Will you climb trees with me?" Rhian asked after a few moments.

He turned quickly back to her then.

"Girls don't climb trees!" he scoffed. "'Specially not little puny girls."

"Yes they do!" she cried hotly. "And I'm not puny! I'll show you!"

"No point," he said, "'cos I'm not gonna be stopping."

Bronwen was calling them from downstairs. But Rhian didn't hurry him out of the room. She surveyed him steadily instead, taking in his dark, hostile eyes, the hair that was now flopping over his forehead and the shabby pullover that looked too small for him.

Oh yes you are staying, she thought, with the same certainty that her Auntie Ginnie, once she had a small sherry and a Marie biscuit inside her, claimed to know things. One way or another, she knew he was going to stay in her life forever.

3.

The car bounced and bumped along the rutted road, but thankfully the baby still slept in Lydia's arms.

"It seems a bit of a long way in the car," the Billeting Officer's wife said from the front seat, as the road began to rise steeply on leaving the main street, "but it's easy by foot if you go through Amos's field – that's what the doctor usually does – on his bike most likely, whatever the weather – how he hasn't caught a chill I don't know…"

The woman talked on, whilst her husband concentrated on the lane which was taking them to goodness knows where. Lydia had little idea of where she was, except that it was hilly and remote, and at the moment she didn't care. She leaned her head on the back of the seat and hoped there would be time for a decent cup of tea before the baby woke demanding a feed. And perhaps something to eat – the sandwiches on the train seemed a long time ago.

It had been a long day. She had listened to the dawn chorus from a bench on the scruffy bit of waste ground which pretended to be a park some streets away from the night's devastation, before making her way to Sebastapol Street where the public baths thankfully opened early. The lady on the door had watched over the baby for an extra tuppence while Lydia bathed and changed into clean clothes. Then there had just been time for tea and a bun in a café before inveigling her way through the straggling lines of evacuees at the station and climbing unnoticed onto the train.

It had taken forever to reach Bridgend and then there'd been a wait for the change to a narrow branch line. Children were dropped off at various unpronounceable stops along the line, but Lydia had stayed put until they had reached this place and it was evident they were going no further.

The welcoming committee, consisting of a number of well-meaning ladies with sing-song voices, had put on quite a spread in the schoolroom, but the children had dived onto that, and Lydia had only managed a small piece of cake and a cup that was more milk than tea.

She was brought back to the present by the Billeting Officer, who rejoiced in the name of Owain Owen, clearing his throat preparatory to using a voice which probably didn't get much exercise when he was at home. He'd been efficient enough at the village school, though, dispatching the motley collection of children and the occasional mother to various houses and farms, ticking them off carefully on his clipboard. Until he came to Lydia, that is.

Then he'd resorted to checking through myriad forms and pieces of paper, muttering a few "I don't knows" before rifling through the papers again in the vain hope that they would, after all, throw up a solution for what to do with this young woman and her baby who were two bodies more than he'd been led to expect.

"I hope he's at home," he said now.

"He's at home," Mrs. Owain Owen said, with the satisfaction of one who knew the whereabouts of most of the locals at any given time. "Olwen Hughes saw him leaving the Matthews' house not half-an-hour since."

She swivelled her bulk around in the seat to address Lydia. "Terrible time Mrs. Matthews has been having with her old Dad – but the doctor's wonderful with him. Well, he's got a way with him – with almost everyone, the doctor has. Works ever so hard, he does – the only one here, now, see – even though he's got a dicky heart. That's what's kept him here, instead of joining up, but we're not complaining. He'll be very pleased that I've found him someone so soon – bit of a shock it was when his last house-keeper up and left. None of us knew she'd been at all close to her sister, but when the call came that she was sick, well, off she went, just like that. But then they do say blood's thicker than water, don't they? Chapel, are you?"

Lydia started at this abrupt non sequitur. "Er… no… um… C of E – I was brought up C of E."

Now was probably not the time to tell the woman that she never wanted to see the inside of a church again.

Mrs. Owain Owen sniffed and turned back in her seat.

"Ebenezer Baptist chapel most of us go to round here – but there's one or two that go to St. Paul's." The last two words were uttered in a way that gave a clear indication of the low opinion she had of those few foolhardy souls. Her voice brightened again as they pulled up in front of a square, stone-built house.

"There you are, Owain," she nodded at the light shining from a front window. "Told you he was in. Quiet man, he is – keeps himself to himself," she told Lydia. "Except when he's with his patients, that is. Different man, then."

"No blackout," her husband said as he opened the car door. "He'll have to be told, doctor or no."

"It's nowhere near dark yet, man, there's no need to be such a stickler – 'specially out here – who's to see?"

Lydia eased herself and the baby out of the back seat as they continued to bicker. A cool wind whipped through her thin summer dress, making her instinctively hold the baby closer. The light was just beginning to fade, and there was little sign up on this hillside of the hot sunny day through which they had travelled. She looked around at the raw beauty of the mountains which surrounded the village. There was a bleak majesty about their rounded tops rising above wooded areas here and there and fields which looked far too steep for man or beast to cope with. Barely a sound could be heard apart from the shushing of the wind through the trees at the side of the house. She shivered slightly and followed the Owens up the steps to the front door, where Mrs. Owen had already tugged at a large bell pull.

It didn't take long for the door to be opened by a tall gaunt man with a towel in his hands.

"Ah! Doctor Eliot!" Mrs. Owen beamed at him and hoisted her Welsh accent up a notch or two. "Sorry to trouble you when you're probably getting your supper, but I think you'll be pleased when you know why we're here. Brought you a new housekeeper we have – extra evacuee from London she is, sort of surplus to requirements, you might say – so as soon as Mr. Owen here told me there was a bit of quandary, I thought of you – killing two birds you might say…"

She stepped back with a flourish, narrowly avoiding her husband's feet, and flung her arms wide to indicate Lydia, like a conjuror producing a rabbit out of a hat. Or, thought Lydia more darkly, like a procuress eager to please some eastern potentate.

The doctor, looking anything but pleased at the sudden offering brought before him, frowned as he peered out into the gathering gloom.

"A baby," he said. "You've brought a baby here?"

Mr. Owen cleared his throat. "I know it's a bit irregular, sir, you not being on the list for an evacuee" – he indicated the clipboard under his arm – "but we've run out of billets, sir, at least for the time being, and as my wife says, you're looking for a housekeeper, so…"

The doctor ran his hand through his hair, glanced down at the towel in his other hand, and said (still frowning, Lydia noticed), "Well, look, you'd better come in. We can't sort this out standing on the doorstep, but really, I don't think…"

He'd already turned and was leading the way into the house. Mr. Owen stood back before his wife and Lydia as they trooped into the room with the lights on: a rectangular space, save for the bay window at one end, with a small welcoming fire in the grate. It was furnished with several comfortable armchairs and a sofa, but no little nick-nacks or personal touches from a feminine hand. A masculine room, Lydia decided, plain and a bit austere – rather like its inhabitant, from first impressions.

The doctor stood before the fire and motioned them to sit down, but Lydia stayed on her feet, rocking the baby backwards and forwards.

"I've already advertised for a housekeeper," the doctor said, looking directly at the Owens.

"I know you have," Mrs. Owen replied, "but in all honesty, Doctor, you're not going to find another Miss Williams in a hurry. Those that haven't got their own families to see to are stepping into the breach left by the menfolk being away. And you must be finding it a bit hard on your own, what with the hours you have to keep…" Her sharp button eyes surveyed the room, her fingers moving restlessly on her lap as if longing to wipe themselves across the layer of dust on the occasional table beside her to prove her point.

"Yes, but evacuees… children… I hadn't…" the doctor began, before Mr. Owen, slightly surprised at his own boldness, interrupted.

"Well, sir, I must tell you that if Miss Williams had still been here, I would have been obliged to place some evacuees with you, because of the space you've got. Not many houses of this size in the village, there aren't."

"The Joneses at Ton farm have taken four boys – all sharing one big bedroom," his wife added in impressed tones. "So a baby, with its mother to take care of it, shouldn't be any trouble."

It was at this moment, with the immaculate timing of the very young, that the baby decided to stir. Suddenly flinging out an arm, she gave a prolonged and lusty wail, her face reddening with the effort.

Unperturbed, Lydia sat herself on the sofa and unbuttoned her dress, turning away slightly until the baby was suckling. A strand of wavy brown hair fell across her face as she crooned gently to her child.

"Oh!" Mrs Owen said, shock at the brazenness of feeding one's child in front of others – in front of *men* – leaving her momentarily speechless, while her husband passed the rim of his hat through his hands, round and round, his gaze fixed intently on the fire-place.

"I'll draw your curtains, sir," he said, jumping to his feet at this solution to his embarrassment. "The blackout, you know – it must be lighting up time by now."

He moved swiftly round behind the sofa at the doctor's nod, easing the heavy curtains along their pole with consummate care and deliberation.

"Perhaps you'd like another room, my dear – the kitchen maybe?" Mrs. Owen asked, a hint of steeliness in her voice.

Lydia lifted her head, brushing the strand of hair away.

"No. Thank you. This is fine." She would have liked to ask for a glass of water because feeding the baby always produced a raging thirst, but she was aware of the need to impress upon this man that she was not going to be any trouble.

The doctor, apparently oblivious to the embarrassment felt by the other two, directed his gaze sharply towards her when he heard the low soft tones of her voice.

"Where are you from?" he asked.

"Bermondsey," she replied, her eyes back on the baby. "Our house was damaged by a gasworks explosion."

He frowned, his rather heavy dark eyebrows almost meeting. News of the explosion had been on the morning wireless. But he was surprised that she had been caught up in it. He'd met plenty of people from the East End when he'd been working in London, and this self-possessed young woman didn't sound like any of them.

"And your husband?"

"He's... he's dead... killed... abroad."

There was a moment's silence.

"I'm sorry," the doctor said, while Mrs. Owen tutted softly and looked sorrowful. "But do you have no other family? Isn't there someone you could have gone to?"

"There's no-one," she said, dropping her head again to look at the baby.

"Well, Doctor Eliot?" Mrs Owen asked. It was all very well showing respect for the dead, and she was very sorry that this child was going to grow up without a father, but she was also aware that her husband couldn't fiddle with the curtains any longer but had no intention of moving back into the middle of the room. "What are we going to do?"

"There isn't much *I* can do, is there, Mrs. Owen?" he replied, his tone conveying to Lydia at least that he had been placed in an impossible situation. "Mrs.... I'm sorry, I don't know your name?"

"Dawson," Lydia said. "I'm Lydia Dawson."

"Mrs. Dawson had better stay here for now – a trial period, perhaps, and we'll see after that."

"Thank you, Doctor." Mr. Owen skirted round the edge of the room and held his hand out. "I knew you'd be able to help out. Very grateful we are, very grateful. And I'm sure you won't be disappointed," he added, as if he'd just supplied the man with a new household appliance.

The two men moved into the hall. Before she followed them, Mrs. Owen leaned over Lydia, torn between sympathy for this young woman and a desire to do things properly.

"We usually show a bit more discretion – a bit of decorum, in these parts, you know – when there's a baby to feed," she whispered, the feather sticking out of the brim of her brown felt hat nodding in time with her head.

She moved back slightly at the challenging look she received from the girl's deep brown eyes. "I've shown more bosom than this in an evening gown," she said, "and all the men were happy to look then."

Mrs. Owain Owen pursed her lips until they were etched in small vertical lines. For one of the few times in her life she wondered if she'd made a mistake. Perhaps this young woman, whom she'd realised from the start was different from the rest of the recent arrivals, was more of a hussy than she'd thought. Evening gown indeed! In Bermondsey?

"I'll be along with my husband in a few days to see how you're settling in," she said now, her tone haughty and formal.

"Thank you," Lydia said simply. "I'm sure we'll be fine."

Mrs. Owen opened her mouth as if to say more, but the baby suddenly lifted her head and turned towards the woman, fixing her with intense blue eyes and bestowing upon her a wide milky smile.

"Oh! There now. There now," she said, her own features softening in response. "Isn't she a little beauty! "She stared at the baby for a few moments before abruptly turning way. "I must go. Mr. Owen will be wanting his supper."

"Well done," Lydia said to the baby, dropping a kiss on her silky head as the door closed. She was rewarded with a resounding burp.

She could hear more talking in the hall as she settled the baby on her other breast and it was several minutes before the door opened again. This time the doctor came in alone, bringing with him her large battered hold-all.

"Is this all your luggage?"

She nodded. "I got told off because it was bigger and heavier than we were supposed to bring, but I explained that all the baby's things were in it as well."

His frown, which seemed to be habitual, deepened. "No, I meant is this *all* your luggage? What about all the bits and pieces you need for the baby – I don't have anything here... cots and so on..."

Lydia transferred the baby to her shoulder, deftly buttoning her dress with her free hand, stifling a smile. He'd obviously never visited the East End and seen how few cots were about, even before the war began.

"Do you have a chest of drawers in your spare room?" she asked.

"Of course."

"And a bucket in the kitchen?"

"I should imagine so – Miss Williams was always mopping and cleaning."

"Then that's all the bits and pieces I need for Grace. Perhaps you could show me – the room?" she went on as he continued to look sceptical.

"Oh yes… yes of course… it's this way."

He picked up the hold-all again and led her up the steep staircase whose dark stained wooden banisters added to the feeling of gloom pervading the hallway as daylight began to fade.

"This is Miss Williams' old room," he said, opening a door to the left of the landing. "My room's on the other side, and there are two smaller rooms at the back – perhaps one would do for the baby… I don't know… and there's a bathroom at the back too – with a bit of a temperamental geyser for the hot water, I'm afraid…"

He stood aside to let her enter. After the tenebrous hall, she gave an involuntary gasp of pleasure as she stood inside the door. Immediately to her right was a wide, deep window with, through the lace curtains covering its lower half, the same view she had seen from outside. But from this height one could see all the way down the valley, with the very last of the evening sun glinting here and there on the river which wound its way between the rounded hillsides.

"Interlocking spurs," she said.

"I'm sorry?"

She turned to the doctor with a smile. "Interlocking spurs – the way the hillsides fit into one another – it's about the only thing I remember from school geography lessons!"

She surveyed the rest of the room. In front of the window was a small marble topped table with, next to it, a mahogany rocking chair. She had a fleeting mental picture of herself nursing the baby in this chair, a gentle breeze lifting the lace curtain through the open window. She gave herself a mental shake. *You're here to work as the housekeeper. There won't be much time for sitting in rocking chairs.*

16

The bed was high and iron-framed, with a small chest of drawers beside it. Along one wall was a cavernous wardrobe in which her few belongings would be lost, and, on the other wall, a taller, wider chest in burred walnut.

"Ah! This is what we need," she said, aware that the doctor was watching her solemnly and feeling a little foolish after his lack of reaction to her geography remark. Laying the baby down in the middle of the bed she stooped to pull out the deep bottom drawer of the walnut chest. As she did so a searing pain in her side made her cry aloud.

"What's the matter? Are you hurt?" He was beside her in a few strides, his frown this time one of concern.

She straightened up, her hand over her ribs, blinking hard to banish the tears which had sprung to her eyes.

"It's nothing... I was injured... when I went back into the house... something fell on me..."

"I'd better have a look. Undo your dress."

"No, really. It's a lot less painful than it was... it was just the drawer... it's a bit stiff."

He gave a small sigh.

"I should take a look as it's obviously painful. You've just sat and fed your baby in front of three strangers – I don't think now is the time for modesty."

It wasn't that. She opened her mouth to answer, but one glance at his face showed that he wasn't expecting any more resistance to his order. Reluctantly she unbuttoned her dress and slid it off her right arm, turning her head away as she did so. A large area of bruising, dark purple and slightly shiny, extended from below her armpit to her waist.

"Has anyone taken a look at this before?" The doctor's voice was harsh but his fingers felt cool and tender as they ran over the livid skin.

"There was no need – it's only some bruising. I told you, it's feeling better." She bit her lip to force herself not to respond as he pressed on a rib.

"Any trouble with your waterworks? Dark, cloudy urine, anything like that?"

She shook her head.

"I want to have a listen to your chest. I'll just get my stetho-

17

scope."

There was no point in arguing as he was already leaving the room. Lydia sat on the edge of the bed and looked down at where her baby lay cooing, oblivious to her mother's anxieties.

"We've got to make this work," Lydia leaned over and whispered to her. "I want to stay here – it feels alright. Even if he is a bit grumpy." The baby gurgled and reached out a dimpled hand towards the lock of hair which was dangling tantalisingly just out of reach.

He came quickly back. "I've brought you this," he said, handing her a glass of water. "You look a bit pale."

"I told you, I'm fine. But thank you for the water – I get really thirsty when I feed Grace." She took a long drink. The water was very cold and pure. The doctor stood motionless, watching as she drank.

"Right. I just want to sound your chest," he said, taking the glass from her as soon as she'd finished. "Lean forward please."

His tone remained professional, but there was something strangely intimate about sitting here in this unfamiliar room as he examined her. And comforting. That was it. Perhaps that was what Mrs. Owen meant when she said he was a good doctor. It certainly didn't come from any penchant for small talk.

He was listening intently, leaning over her so that she could hear his breathing, issuing instructions for her to take deep breaths, and listening again.

"I think you may have cracked a couple of ribs," he said at last as he straightened up. "And there's a raised imprint of something – how did you say you did it?"

"I went back into the house, after it was damaged – some masonry fell on me – bricks and so on – they've probably left their mark."

"Hmm." His expression was inscrutable, but she had the feeling he would like to say more.

"I'll strap it for you. It won't make it heal any faster, but it might feel a bit more comfortable," he said eventually. "Luckily there doesn't seem to be any lung damage but you need to take things easy for a while – no heavy lifting, that sort of thing."

Neither spoke as his cool hands applied the strapping. She forced a smile as she pulled her clothes back on. "Thank you, it feels better already. I think it was only that drawer – like I said, it was a bit stiff."

"Oh yes, the drawer…" He turned to look at it. "What are you intending to do with it?"

"Perhaps you'd move it – just here alongside the bed. Then I can put a folded blanket inside and it'll be perfect for the baby. An instant cradle – at least until she's sitting up and moving around."

He nodded and did as she asked. "I suppose I'd better show you around the rest of the house."

"Please." She picked up the baby, biting on her lip so that the doctor wouldn't see that it was an effort. "And you'd better tell me what my duties are."

He nodded again as they headed for the stairs.

"Your main duty," he said over his shoulder, "is to answer the telephone efficiently and keep any messages for me. It's been the biggest problem since Miss Williams left. The phone's here."

He showed her an alcove behind the staircase. "This notebook and pencil stays here all the time, and it's very important that you write every message down, so that no mistakes are made over patients. Most of them use the public telephone in the village and they can be a bit unsure of it." He gave the ghost of a smile, which lifted the heaviness of his brow. "There are any number of Joneses, Evanses and Williamses in these parts – it's very easy to get them muddled up."

She wanted to ask him if he was from these parts; he didn't sound like the few people she'd spoken to so far. But it seemed too personal a question, and anyway he was moving swiftly to the back of the house.

"This is the kitchen," he said, opening the door onto a large room with an old-fashioned looking range on one wall, in front of which were two battered armchairs. "Very much Miss Williams' domain – I still can't find everything, even though I've been on my own for the past week."

He ran his hand through his hair as he spoke, pushing it away from his face, which made him look younger and less severe.

She looked round the rest of the room. *Miss Williams' domain.* And evidently destined to be Lydia's. The demarcation between employer and employee had been subtly made. *Employer and servant* she told herself. Well, that would be different, anyway. She'd never been a servant before.

The doctor was watching her, evidently waiting for some reaction. Her eyes lighted on the square scrubbed table in the middle of the room, upon which was a loaf of bread and some tomatoes.

"We interrupted your supper."

"Oh – oh, um, yes. I was just about to make a start. I'm sorry – have you eaten – I didn't think…"

She preferred his uncertainty. It made her feel more equal to the situation.

"We were given sandwiches when we arrived. Most of the children were ravenous, poor things."

She shifted the baby's weight to her other arm. "Is there some sort of scullery through there?" she asked, nodding towards a door in the far corner.

"Yes, yes there is. And a larder – with a cold shelf, that sort of thing."

She nodded again and went through the door. The scullery held a stone sink, a couple of buckets and mops and, thankfully, a large, oval wicker wash basket. Picking it up with her spare hand, she went back into the kitchen. She placed the basket on the floor, added a cushion from one of the chairs and laid the baby in it with a swift kiss.

"I'll get your supper," she said, turning to the doctor.

The frown again. "You don't have to – you've only just arrived."

"It'll help me to find where everything is. Do you have a dining room where you normally eat? I could bring it through."

"No, no. That won't be necessary. The kitchen is fine – and, please, join me." He smiled properly for the first time that evening, transforming the severity of his face and showing strong white teeth. "Proficient in the dispensary, absolutely hopeless in the kitchen I'm afraid."

She smiled back, feeling her shoulders relax for the first time since her arrival. "I'll see what I can do."

She returned to the scullery and opened the larder door. "Oh!" Inside was a crock of eggs – real eggs! She'd already become used to seeing them just one at a time.

"You have eggs," she said, poking her head round the

doorway. "Can I use those – I mean, can I use two? You don't see as many in London."

"It's one of the advantages of being buried in the country. And having patients who might not have the money to pay you but are generous with what they have got. They were fresh from one of the farms this morning – I don't know how many Miss Williams usually got through in a week, but we haven't run short."

Scrambled, she decided. With the tomatoes and bread – and there was some butter on the shelf. Her mouth watered as she worked and despite her tiredness she couldn't help but smile to herself. How life had changed so – that now one could get this excited at the prospect of a scrambled egg.

Her sense of comfort didn't last long. She became aware of the doctor watching her as she moved around the kitchen, placing the kettle on the hob for tea and finding plates and cutlery. She wondered if some light conversation would be appropriate, but a sideways glance showed that his face was sombre again and she couldn't think of anything appropriate to say.

The baby had no such inhibitions though. As the adults ate, she fixed the doctor with an unblinking stare and made increasingly loud gurgling sounds to attract his attention. Eventually she succeeded and rewarded him with a gummy smile and a flurry of kicking legs and waving arms.

"How old is she?"

"Four months."

"She's very bonny. Did your – did her father see her?"

Lydia busied herself re-filling the teapot, concentrating on keeping her hand steady and allowing her sheet of hair to fall across her face. "Yes – yes, a couple of times."

The baby wasn't distracting him any more. Lydia could feel the full force of his stare on her. Then he placed a small bottle in front of her.

"Some aspirin – for those painful ribs. Take two now, and then you can have four doses a day, after meals."

"Thank you."

He continued to watch her as she swallowed the pills, and again she felt such a sense of comfort that she couldn't meet his gaze. It seemed a long time since someone had shown her any concern.

"You must eat well while you're here – however long that ends up being. We have plenty of fresh milk. It can't be easy in London, trying to feed a baby. You're very thin."

His tone professional now, she was able to lift her head. "Thank you. I appreciate your concern."

She began to clear the supper things away.

"You're not from Bermondsey yourself, though." It was more of a statement than a question.

"No. No – um, Home Counties. My husband is – was – from that part of London."

To her relief the telephone began to ring, which sent him out into the hall in a couple of long strides.

"I have to go out on a call," he said when he reappeared a few minutes later, his medical bag and car keys in his hand. "Miss Williams didn't used to wait up for me, but she left her door ajar slightly so that she could hear the phone. If anyone does call, record the message like I showed you, and tell them that I've gone to Pantyglas farm. Here – I've written it down. These Welsh names are the very devil to remember until you get used to them."

He handed her a slip of paper and with a nod was gone. Lydia swiftly cleared away the rest of the supper things, banked down the range fire and then, grimacing at the pain, picked up her daughter.

"Come on, let's get you changed, then one more feed and we can both sleep." The prospect of resting in a comfortable bed had never seemed so alluring. Not given to prayer, Lydia nevertheless sent up a wish as she climbed the stairs, to whoever might be listening, that this place would work out well for them both.

4.

D r. Eliot was already in the kitchen when Lydia went downstairs the next morning. Try as she might, she hadn't been able to stay awake to listen for his return the night before, and now she felt that she would be found wanting because she wasn't already busy preparing his breakfast. She was also aware that the bruising down her side was making her a lot stiffer today.

"I'm sorry," she said, plopping the baby down unceremoniously in the laundry basket and trying not to let her stiffness show. "Grace didn't wake as early as usual, and it's so quiet here I didn't stir."

"That's alright – you must both have been tired after yesterday, and I told you that you should rest until your ribs heal a bit. Tea and a slice of bread and butter I can just about manage. Please attend to yourself." His words were kind enough, but his face remained impassive. It was as if there was a shutter over his emotions. He was probably regretting already the position he'd been placed in.

Lydia poured herself a cup of tea from the pot he'd made and helped herself to some bread. After a moment or two he leaned across and filled a cup with milk from the jug.

"I also said you should drink plenty of milk while you're here."

She took the cup with a smile. "Do you always treat everyone as a patient?"

"I can't afford to have a housekeeper who's not able to do the work – or a baby in the house keeping me awake all night because she's hungry." This time there was a slight smile to soften the words.

"Your patient last night – was everything alright?"

"No – he died."

"Oh – I'm sorry."

The shutters were back down again. She didn't know what

else to say, so concentrated on drinking her milk.

When he spoke next his tone was brisk. "I'm usually in my dispensary by eight-thirty, because surgery starts at nine, although there are often people here before then, so I'd better show you that part of things."

They left the baby sleeping in the basket as he led her out into the hall and through a door at the opposite end, into a square room kitted out as a surgery.

"I like this room to be kept as clean as possible, for obvious reasons, and Miss Williams usually kept my desk sorted – prescription sheets and the inkwell topped up, that sort of thing. The patients wait through here."

A door on the other side of the surgery led into a long, low, single storey extension, with bench seating all around the edge. At the far end was a hatch for the dispensary.

"If patients come looking for me out of surgery hours, they press the bell outside here – it rings in the house, so there's no fear of not hearing it. If both of us are out during the day, then we pin a note on the outside door to tell anyone who comes where I am.

"You get into the dispensary through this door," the doctor went on, taking her through a third door from his surgery. "Mrs. Griffiths from the village comes in each morning and makes up any prescriptions from the night before that aren't urgent, and sees to the morning patients. Any urgent medicines at evening surgery I see to myself. Mrs. Griffiths keeps everything tidy in here and answers the phone during surgery, but you need to see to the floor – oh, and the floor in the waiting room needs mopping frequently, if the weather is bad.

"Look here –" He'd been looking around the room, but now he turned to her, the frown deep between his brows. "Do you think you're up to all this? With the house and the baby and everything?"

Lydia thought of the super-human strength she'd needed to stand up to the worst of Billy's drunken rages and wondered what this man would have thought of her if he'd been witness to some of those confrontations.

"I'm much stronger than I look," she said, raising her chin stubbornly. "I know you must feel more than irritated to have us both foisted on you like this, but like Mrs. Owen said last night, you could have had a houseful of East End kids if Miss Williams had stayed. So why don't we see how we get along, and if you think it's not working you can ask Mr. Owen to place me somewhere else?"

Her eyes held his for a moment before he said, "Very well."

Further conversation was interrupted by the sound of the waiting room door opening and a cheery voice calling out, "Hallo-o-o it's only me!"

A smiling young woman bounced into the room with a healthy exuberance that reminded Lydia of a golden retriever they'd had at home.

"Morning Doctor! I'd heard you had a new housekeeper, so I came a bit early so we could have a little chat – get friendly, you know, before it gets too busy. And you must be her!" She held out her hand as she spoke: "I'm Rita Griffiths – Oh!" She took in the nonplussed expression on Lydia's face that anyone could know of her presence so soon. "Our little paper boy I got it from – he'd heard from Joe Bevan, the milkman – all the evacuees are the talk of the village this morning, see?"

She gave a wink, "Like that round here, we are. Someone will work out they're related to you when you've been here a little while. Bit prettier than Miss Williams, isn't she, Doctor?"

Fortunately, before he could answer, she turned back to Lydia. "I've brought a list for you, of things I thought you should know about – you know what these men are like, they forget to tell you the most important things."

By this time she had taken off her jacket and hat and put on a pristine white overall.

"Alright if we go through so I can have a look at this beautiful baby I've heard about before surgery starts?"

Dr. Eliot wasn't actually smiling, but there was a twitchiness about his lips which indicated his amusement at his assistant's chattiness and the startled look on the face of his new housekeeper.

"Of course," he said gravely, and turned to his desk.

After exclaiming in whispers over the still-sleeping Grace, she handed Lydia a piece of paper torn out of an exercise book.

"I thought you might like an idea of Miss Williams' routine. Not that I'm saying you must do the same, mind, I just thought it would give you something to go on – oh, and the Doctor's ration paraphernalia is in the kitchen drawer."

"That's very kind of you, thank you Mrs. Griffiths," Lydia said as soon as the woman paused to take breath.

"Not Mrs. Griffiths – I'm Rita, except if we're talking in front of patients, when the Doctor likes it a bit more formal."

"And I'm Lydia – Lydia Dawson, or," Lydia gave a grin, "did you know that already?"

Dimples appeared in Rita's cheeks.

"No, I didn't actually – just a description. You'll be 'the posh lady from London up at the Doctor's house' for quite a while, or at least until the next new thing comes along! You and the evacuees are the most excitement we've had since the war began. Oh – while I remember – welfare clinic is at the Ebenezer rooms on Thursday mornings – so's you can get your cod liver oil and orange juice."

She put her head on one side and considered Lydia for a moment. "You'll be good for Dr. Eliot, maybe bring him out of his shell a bit. Miss Williams was seventy if she was a day and no more chatty than him – except when she was with her cronies in the village, and they'll be giving you the once over soon enough, so be warned. I know he seems a bit off-putting at first, but he's a pet really."

The 'pet' put his head round the door then to remind her a little testily that there were prescriptions to be made up from last night, but Rita took no notice of his tone as she made her happy way into the dispensary.

"Right," Lydia said to the baby as she began to stir, "time to prove my worth so you and I can stay here for a while. It could be just the breathing space we need."

The baby gurgled back at the sound of her mother's voice and Lydia thanked her lucky stars, not for the first time, that she had such an easy child. After swallowing a couple of aspirin to ease the nagging pain in her side, she set to. First, she found an old enamel bucket in which she could boil Grace's nappies, "to get them out of the way before he finishes surgery – so he won't think you're a nuisance!" She stopped to plant a kiss on the baby's cheek. How could anyone find her a nuisance? But then Billy hadn't been too taken with her, or the demands of fatherhood.

Then she consulted the list Rita had given her. Most of it was common sense but there was useful information about the shops in the village. She wondered how far it was to walk, and how she'd get there and back with shopping bags and a baby to carry, but decided she would worry about that later.

11a.m. Dr. comes back into house after surgery for quick cup of tea before doing his rounds, the list informed her. So she had two hours to make a difference. She looked round the kitchen. The range needed a good clean, but she could do that tomorrow. Everywhere else had evidently not seen a duster or a broom for some time, so she decided to work on that first.

By the time Dr. Eliot came through for his tea, the kitchen table, cupboards and dresser were gleaming, the scullery was washed through and tidy, and the kitchen floor swept and mopped. The nappies were blowing on the line in the back garden – which was rather overgrown except for a well-organised vegetable plot – and the kettle was singing on the hob.

Lydia, who had been pleased to sit down and feed and change the baby half-way through, to ease the pain from her ribs, pushed her hair from her face and tried to look welcoming as he came in through the door. She hadn't been prepared for just how much pain her injuries would cause when she tried to do physical work, and it seemed to get worse as the morning wore on, but she didn't want him to know that.

"Good timing – a cup of tea coming up," she said, trying not to wince as she lifted the heavy old kettle. She was also ravenously hungry and wished there was a cake or something, but the larder was fairly empty. She would evidently have to add baking to the list of chores.

"Thank you." He sat at the table and cleared his throat. "Um – I realised during surgery that we hadn't discussed money or anything –"

He was interrupted by a knock on the door and Rita once more bustling in.

"Sorry to intrude, but I forgot to give you these this morning." She proffered a bulging paper bag to Lydia. "Scones – yesterday's baking, but they'll tide you over for your elevenses till you get organised. Oh! There's a difference in here already, isn't there Doctor? Well, I won't keep you! See you on Monday."

And with that she was gone, before Lydia could thank her properly, and leaving the doctor surveying the kitchen in a slightly bemused way.

"I'm sorry," he said, rather stiffly. "I hadn't really noticed when I first came in, but yes, you have done a good job in here. Thank you."

"As long as I'm doing the work I'm supposed to do, there's no need to thank me." Lydia kept her tone formal too as she buttered two scones. Perhaps this was why Miss Williams had been quiet – gauging how to talk to this man was like walking through a minefield.

"I'm going to do the surgery and the front of the house after this cup of tea," she told him. "Then I do need to go to the shops this afternoon, if that fits in with your timetable?"

"I'll be here all afternoon, unless there is some sort of emergency, which there rarely is at that time of day."

"Oh, I see – because I was wondering if I could leave the baby here with you while I shop. She's usually very good – but I can't carry her too far at the moment – I'll be fine in a day or two, though."

"Hmm." The frown was back in place. He obviously didn't like his schedule to be disrupted. "I was going to suggest that you leave the surgery – Mrs. Griffiths has been keeping it clean – and that you rest for the afternoon – I can see you're in pain from the way you're moving. Perhaps I could do the shopping, if you tell me what we need?"

"That's the problem – I don't know what the village shops sell compared with London. And I'll need to register for my rations."

"Right. Well let's think about that after lunch. A simple meal of whatever you can find will do, by the way – I'm not too bothered about what I eat."

He stood up and handed her a piece of paper. "These are my home visits for today. There aren't many and they're all fairly close, so I'll use my bicycle, but if there are any urgent calls you'll have some idea to tell people where they might find me."

He made to leave, and then turned back. "Oh, and about money – I always left some cash for housekeeping in the drawer and topped it up when Miss Williams told me "

"That will be fine. Do you have a housekeeping book, or do I just give you receipts?"

He looked up sharply from checking his bag. "I prefer to work on trust."

"I'm very pleased to hear it. It won't be misplaced."

She could hear the cold formality of her own words – what was it about this man that made her react like this? She recalled Mrs. Owain Owen's words about him being good to his patients, and certainly when he showed concern for her wellbeing he sounded so different.

"And your pay – Miss Williams received £4 a month on top of her keep – but maybe you will need more, with the baby?"

"That's considerate of you – but I have the Forces' pension, so £4 will be fine."

Actually, she wouldn't be getting any of Billy's money now nobody knew where she was, but money was the least of her worries.

"Good." He nodded and gave a small smile. "I'm pleased we've got all that business out of the way. I should be back around one."

When he was gone she picked the baby up.

"What a funny man!" she told her daughter. "Not exactly Mr. Charm, is he?"

The baby gurgled back, blowing bubbles as she did so, making her mother laugh, which increased the aching in her side. "Whereas you are charming, charming, charming, aren't you? And you've been such a good girl we'll have a little playtime first before we get on with the chores!"

She carried the baby outside into the sunshine, to see what could be gleaned from the kitchen garden. The morning was warm now, with barely a cloud in the sky. The house was on a slight plateau so that the garden was relatively flat, with hillside rearing up beyond its low stone wall, to correspond with the hill-side opposite.

Lydia breathed in as deeply as she dared. The air was pure and fresh. There was no evidence that the war had touched this place so far. She'd got away from Billy and she and the baby were safe. Despite the uncertainty of the future and her rather taciturn boss, she allowed herself to grasp the first tentative strands of happiness and relief.

It was a little after one o'clock when the doctor arrived home, by which time a simple lunch of bread, cheese and fresh lettuce was on the table, the baby was asleep and Lydia was trying not to hold her side continually to ease the pain.

She heard him call from the hall.

"I've got this for you," he said without preamble, and pointed through the open front door to where, on the front path, stood a battered black pram.

"Oh!" exclaimed Lydia. "How did you come by that?"

"Well, I was thinking about how you couldn't possibly manage to carry the baby about everywhere, so I asked around and one of my patients came up with this. It's a bit old, I'm afraid."

"I don't care about that!" she said, moving it to and fro, "it's wonderful! Thank you so much! I'll be able to put Grace to sleep outside in the fresh air, as well as taking her out."

There was a bag attached to the pram handle which he now opened.

"The women round here are suckers for a new baby – when one of them saw me pushing the pram with one hand and my bike with the other, she asked who it was for and then gave me these. They're mainly clothes – oh, and this…"

He handed her a small, furry toy rabbit. Suddenly the kindness of complete strangers and the pain she was suffering were all too much for Lydia. She turned quickly away from him, but not before he saw the glint of tears in her eyes.

"If the baby will sleep in it this afternoon, then, like I said this morning I think you should rest as well," he told her, picking out another package wrapped in greaseproof paper from inside the pram. "There's ham here – another grateful patient – which we can have tonight, so you can go down to the village tomorrow. There's no need to try to get everything done at once."

The words were kind but his voice betrayed little emotion. Lydia nodded and took the packages from him. "I'm sorry," she said. "Difficult situations I can cope with – kindness, at the moment, I find a little harder… um… London hasn't been the easiest place…"

Her head was pounding now, in rhythm with the pain in her side. She bit down hard on her lip, to stop herself from dissolving completely into tears. But she couldn't stop the sensation that everything around her was beginning to swim.

What would he think? She had to show him that she was worth everyone's trouble. Perhaps after some food she would feel better, then she could think about the shopping... and sorting out the rest of the house... and Grace... and...

She turned to push the pram into the house, but as she tried to reach for the handle it seemed too far away... A wave of pain shot through her body as the ground appeared to come up to meet her.

The last thing she heard was the doctor's voice, harsh and impatient, "Oh! For the love of Mike!!"

5.

Amy let her breath out with a long sigh when a chink of early morning light peeped through the side of the blackout. She felt as if she'd been holding her breath for most of the night. At home her mother had put a little night light in her room when the blackout was brought in. But then her mother had known she was scared of the dark. The woman here – Mrs… what was her name? Something to do with churches… Priest, that was it. She didn't know anything like that about Amy and hadn't asked. Or smiled at her the way her mother would have done before kissing her goodnight. Not that she would have wanted Mrs. Priest to kiss her goodnight – she didn't have a comforting sort of smell like Amy's mother.

She wondered what her mother was doing now. She didn't know what time it was – perhaps her mother was sitting at their kitchen table having her breakfast, all by herself, before she hurried off to see to Gran and then dashed off to work.

The picture brought tears to Amy's eyes, but she swiftly wiped them away. She'd promised her mother she would try to be brave – like her namesake, Amy Johnson. "If she can fly across the world in an aeroplane, then you can be brave enough to go on a train journey without me," her mother had said.

"Can't I be brave enough not to mind if the bombs come and stay here with you instead?" Amy had asked.

Her mother had shaken her head, but Amy had seen the sadness in her eyes.

"You can't, love, it's too difficult – and you're all I've got with your Dad away – I can't risk something happening to you."

"Then come with me!"

But her mother had shaken her head again. "I can't – only mothers with very small children are being allowed to go." She'd smiled then. "And I know you're small, but not small enough I'm afraid – and besides, there'll be no-one else to look in on Gran. So there's nothing left for it but to be brave – like Daddy's being all the time he's away."

Amy had stayed close to her friend Maisie the whole time, in the hope that they would go to a house together. But Maisie's two older brothers had already been siphoned off with their class at an earlier village stop, so she had been intent on keeping her little brother with her, like she'd promised her mother. The funny little man with the clipboard had split Maisie and Amy up almost as soon as they'd reached the schoolroom.

Her thoughts were interrupted by a more urgent need. Mrs. Priest's house wasn't all that different from her own – in the middle of a long row, with a kitchen tacked on the back, and three small bedrooms upstairs. Amy was in a little bedroom at the back, just big enough for a bed to fit under the window, and space for a chair and a chest of drawers, where Mrs. Priest had put away Amy's clothes last night, with a lot of muttering over what she did or didn't have. Amy also knew it was like her house because the lavvy was out in the back yard, and that was where she needed to go now.

She leaned over the side of the bed and saw that there was a chamber pot underneath, but she wasn't sure about using it. How would she tell Mrs. Priest that it needed emptying? Or could she carry it down the steep stairs herself? But then Mrs. Priest's son, Ouredwin, might see her and make her feel really embarrassed.

She listened hard and thought she could hear someone moving about downstairs. Perhaps it would be alright to go down now and dash out to the lavvy – she'd have to do something because she couldn't hold on much longer.

Mrs. Priest was on her hands and knees, scrubbing the front doorstep, a large bucket with steam rising out of it by her side. She was talking loudly to someone else, using words that Amy didn't understand at all. Amy scuttled round the foot of the stairs, through the back room and out of the kitchen door as quietly as she could, almost groaning with relief as she reached the lavvy.

Mrs. Priest was emptying the bucket of water down the yard drain as Amy emerged.

"Oh! Indeed to goodness! There's a fright you gave me! What-ever are you doing out here in your nightdress?"

"I'm sorry, Mrs. Priest... but I needed to go..."

"*Preece* my name is, *Mrs. Preece,* no 'T' on the end, there isn't.

Well, it's just as well you're up and about, I was just coming to call you. Nine o'clock we've got to be down at the school, so in you go and get washed and dressed. We use the bowl in the sink. I've put your flannel for you on the side, and there's a towel on the back of the door – mind you don't go making a mess, though, I've just cleaned the floor. You've missed breakfast with Our Edwin, but I'll find you something when you're decent."

Amy wasn't sure which bits she was supposed to wash, so she quickly wiped the flannel over her face and soaped her hands, before hurrying back upstairs, while Mrs. Priest – *Preece* – banged some doormats against the coal house wall with surprising vigour for such a small woman.

Mrs. Preece was ladling porridge into a bowl when Amy came back downstairs. She put it on the table and motioned Amy to sit down. Suddenly Amy felt ravenous, but as she lifted a steaming spoonful to her mouth she was stayed by a cry.

"Grace! Grace first, girl! Indeed to goodness!"

Amy looked round quickly for the presence of another person, before realising, as Mrs. Preece sat down heavily on the chair opposite and piously put her hands together, what she was meant to do.

"I don't suppose the word of God is heard much where you come from," Mrs. Preece said with a sniff, "but very strong we are on it here. Now close your eyes."

She launched into a volley of words as indecipherable to Amy as those she'd heard on the front doorstep, but at least she recognised 'Amen', so knew when they were finished.

Mrs. Preece poured them both a cup of tea and cut a piece of bread and butter into small dainty squares for herself, all the while watching Amy eat her porridge and keeping up a stream of instructions and comments.

"Well, you're a bit tidier than some of them I saw yesterday, which is a blessing I suppose. Ashamed to send my child out like that, I would have been. And you're not scratching your head, which is another blessing – we'll find some hairgrips in a minute, though, to keep that fringe out of your eyes."

Her mouth caved in a bit in the middle, so that every muscle in her face seemed to be engaged busily in the chewing of each piece of bread.

"I wasn't going to take anyone at first – not at my time of life, and there's enough to do with Our Edwin. But Mr. Schofield, our Chapel Minister – thank goodness his limp stopped him from getting called up – said that we should all help as much as we could. So it's my Christian duty, see? And it'll be fine so long as you keep your bedroom tidy and don't get under my feet."

She paused to take a mouthful of tea, and then delicately ran her tongue over the back of her dentures to seek out any lingering morsels of food.

"What were the words you used – when you said grace?" Amy asked, watching the facial gymnastics with round-eyed fascination.

"Welsh, that was. The language of the gods, isn't it? Always spoken round here it was at one time, but not many bother so much now. Mr. Preece was very hot on it though – loved his Welsh bible, he did, before he departed. So we keep it up, we do, in this house, in his memory."

She pointed to a photograph on the wall of a fearsome-looking man with cold eyes and a large moustache.

"Still getting over my loss, I am. But at least I have Our Edwin – the image of his Dad, he is. Don't know where I'd be without him."

Amy had only seen Ouredwin briefly the night before – a tall, gawky boy who had stared at her with the same cold eyes as his father while she'd drunk her cup of cocoa. She gave a sigh of relief that Mr. Preece's departure was evidently a permanent one and she wouldn't be faced with his stare each evening as well.

She turned her attention back to Mrs. Preece, who was issuing a list of instructions in the rapid sing-song voice that Amy had to listen to very carefully in order to catch everything she said.

"You'll have to be up earlier than this from tomorrow, so that we all have breakfast together – I can't be doing with this palaver every day. Made allowances today I did, because you've only just arrived. Now, I don't know what you've been used to, but we keep everything tidy in this house – and we use the back way, mind, so that the front step stays clean, and no shoes in the house. You'll have to bring your daps home every day and keep them by the back door, seeing as your mother didn't see fit to send you with any slippers."

"I do have slippers – at home," Amy said quickly, to defend against Mrs. Preece's obvious criticism, "but we weren't told to bring those. And I don't know what my 'daps' are!"

She could feel tears pricking her eyes again. She didn't want to be here with this strange woman with her strange voice and funny face – which hadn't broken into a smile once since Amy arrived.

Mrs. Preece sighed. "Your shoes for games at school, that's what they are – daps! You can fetch them down here when you've washed up your breakfast things. Go and do that now – and no tears, mind. We could all sit and cry if we wanted to, but it won't change anything. I'm not giving my home to a cry-baby."

Which just made Amy want to cry even more, so she quickly took her breakfast things to the sink. When she returned from doing everything she'd been told, Mrs. Preece was holding a card.

"You have to send this to your mother, to say you've got here. I've already put our address on the top and it's got a stamp on it, so we can post it on the way to school. Here's a pencil."

The address was a jumble of unpronounceable words and took up a lot of the space. Amy would have liked to write about how scared she'd been last night and how different everything was here, and how much she was already missing her home, but Mrs. Preece stood over her and told her what to say:

"I have arrived safely and am being taken care of very well. I hope this finds you well also,
   Your loving daughter,
   Amy."

"Right," said Mrs. Preece when she'd put the pencil down. "Come along – we don't want to be the last ones in the school gate."

She took off her wrap-around apron as she spoke, replaced it with a cardigan and patted her hair as she checked herself in the mirror above the mantelpiece.

"We don't bother with those round here," she said, as Amy picked up the cardboard box containing her gas mask. "Might as well put your daps in there instead – they'll be a lot more use to you."

The gate in the high wall at the end of the back yard opened onto a rough stone lane, with the backs of another row of terraced houses opposite. Amy looked around. Again, not so different from home, except the back alley there was narrower and cobbled. But here, beyond the other terraces, rose a steep hillside, broken up into fields with one or two cottages dotted around on the lower slopes, and trees at the very top. That was nothing like home.

Further along the lane there was a break in the row of houses where they turned down towards the village and came to the main road which Amy recognised from last night. On the other side were more terraces and another steep hill. She had never seen so much green in her life.

Mrs. Preece walked swiftly, talking the whole time, with Amy almost skipping along beside her to keep up.

"I won't be doing this every morning," she said. "Only today so that you know where to go. Do this every morning and I'll never get everything done and be ready for Our Edwin coming in for his dinner. They're feeding you at school," she added, which made Amy think of the time her mother had taken her to London Zoo and they'd watched food being thrown to the animals.

There were some local children walking to school, and some other women taking evacuees. As far as Amy knew, it was only her class that had been left at this place, apart from one or two younger brothers and sisters, like Maisie's little brother. She kept a look-out for Maisie, as Mrs. Preece paused every now and then to pass the time of day with neighbours. All the talk seemed to be about the evacuees.

"How's yours been?"

"Not so bad. Not many clothes with them, though."

"Ever so hungry, mine was, poor little mite."

"Three great big lads I've ended up with – don't know why I've got so many."

"We'll all have to manage the best we can," she heard Mrs. Preece say, with a sigh, as if hers was the biggest burden of the lot.

The snatches of conversation continued over her head as they made their way past a few shops. One or two of the shopkeepers who were busy opening up smiled encouragingly as they went by, which lifted Amy's spirits a little.

She felt a lot better once Mrs. Preece had told her she could make her own way home and deposited her at the gates, and there in the playground was Maisie. Arfur turned up too, trying to pretend that he wasn't with a girl who was about the same age as them.

"What's your place like?" she asked Maisie straight away.

Maisie gave a familiar freckly grin. "They've got a daughter that's gone off and joined the Wrens, so we've got her bedroom. They've put a little bed in there for me brother as well. It's like a little palace, and they can't do enough for us. Never had a bed to meself before. I reckon me Mum'll be down here like a flash with the little 'uns when she hears about it! What about you?"

Amy thought of the stern face of Mrs. Preece, the cold eyes of her son and the fears she'd had during the night. But then she remembered her promise to her mother.

"'S alright, I s'pose."

Arfur had already gone in search of the other boys from their school but before the girls could follow him a teacher appeared on the school steps, clanging a large brass bell.

"That's our teacher, Miss Edwards," the girl who'd been with Arfur told them. "She's got a terrible temper if you don't line up quickly."

At the end of the day, though Arfur didn't like to admit it, he was relieved the girl, Rhian, was walking back to the farm with him. Coping with being at a different school, with kids who spoke in that funny, quick way, had been alright. His class was being taught by their own teacher from London, Mr Robinson, who was one of those sent out with the evacuees so as not to overload the village school staff. And because he was too old to join up, Arfur reckoned. They were in the Sunday school room behind the church which was next to the school, but at playtimes they'd joined the local kids and there'd soon been a game of football underway.

But the farm was something else. Arfur had been awake early in the morning, not because he was scared of the dark, but because of the quiet. There was always traffic going past the flat he and his Mum shared above the shoe shop. Cars, motorbikes, buses, and heavy lorries that made his window pane rattle when they went over an uneven piece of road just outside. But here there was nothing. Except for the screeching of some sort of animal every few minutes. It was a far more annoying noise than anything at home – he would have strangled the bugger by now if it had been his – even worse than the screeching and cackling that went on when his Mum came back with a crowd of friends after a night out. He never minded that, could even fall asleep during it, although sometimes he would wake up again because one of the men – Mum usually had more men friends than girl-friends – knocked a table or a lamp over and was making lots of noise trying to be quiet.

Sometimes there might be a friend staying over and next morning Arfur would bump into him in the scullery, dashing water on his face at the sink, braces dangling at the sides of his trousers and water splashing on his vest. It wasn't always the same friend, but they were all kind to Arfur and sometimes there'd be sixpence slid into his hand with a conspiratorial wink, although Arfur wasn't sure what he was supposed to have done to deserve the money or the camaraderie. After those nights his Mum wouldn't be up before he went to school, but when he got home they'd make toast in front of the fire together and Mum would make up stories about the people she knew, which would make him giggle.

So once her leg was better and she was out of hospital he'd go back – they were alright together, him and Mum. And he wasn't afraid of the bombs if they did come – he and Mum would survive, like they'd always done.

He'd had a good breakfast here, you had to give them that – except for the cup of very milky tea the woman had put in front of him. He was used to his tea strong and black, because there wasn't usually any milk in the flat in the mornings. Or much food, come to that.

"Time you were off," the woman had said when breakfast was over. "Rhian will walk with you, show you the path out of the farm."

He was about to say he didn't need a stupid girl to show him anything, but then he remembered what she'd said last night about cows and things. He wasn't too sure about them, so until he was he'd maybe follow Miss Soppy-socks around for a bit.

"Is your Dad away fighting?" she asked him as they crossed the yard.

"Haven't got a Dad."

She stopped in her tracks. "Everyone's got a Dad."

"Yeah, well, mine buggered off when I was little. Don't know where he is. But good riddance. Me Mum and me don't need him."

Rhian opened her mouth to say something but changed her mind.

"You shouldn't swear," she told him instead.

"Who says?"

"My Dad. He says that he'd still take his belt off to us, even though we're girls, if we swear in front of him. So he'll probably do the same to you if he hears you."

Her Dad immediately went up in Arfur's estimation. A quiet man like that was usually a bit soft in his experience, but perhaps this one was different.

They turned the corner of the yard to see a cockerel strutting towards them, a harem of hens gossiping and fussing about behind him. Rhian grinned as Arfur stood still.

"What's the matter? Not scared of old Lloyd George are you?"

"Lloyd George?"

The cockerel was advancing, lifting his legs up high with each strut.

"That's his name – our cockerel. Showing off he is, because his women are all about him – just like the real Lloyd George, my Dad says."

"Does he bite?"

"Bite?" There was scorn in her voice until she saw how uncomfortable he looked. "No," she said more kindly, "but he can give you a nasty peck sometimes, but you just do this – look!"

She shooed at the birds and flapped her hands so that the hens scuttled off, clucking indignantly to each other while Lloyd George retreated with his head held high, as if that had been his intention all along. Then he flew on to the fence and began to crow loudly.

"That was the noise that woke me up this morning!" Arfur exclaimed. "How do you put up with that bloody row all the time?"

"You get used to it, although he does start a bit early this time of year."

She ran off, so he had no choice but to follow, aware that the cockerel was watching him with an evil eye.

Now they'd walked back through what seemed like endless fields, the afternoon sun beating down on their backs, so that he'd taken his school jacket off and tied it round his waist. It seemed a much longer walk than at home when there would have been so much more to see. It would have been nicer to have been in the village with some of the others – they could probably have kicked a ball or something around the back lanes. Just his luck to be stuck in a house with two dopey girls. It could have been worse, he supposed. Some of the boys had come to school today with their hair almost shaved off, and one or two of the girls had had theirs cut suspiciously short and they all smelled of disinfectant. There were tales of them being poked and picked at like they were something the dog had brought in. But still – two girls!

He picked up a stone occasionally and threw it along the path. To his annoyance Rhian did the same and hers went just as far, which just made him scowl more.

"Where's your sister?" he asked Rhian eventually. "Didn't see her all day."

"She goes to the big school a few miles away, so she gets the bus before we go in the morning. She'll be back just after us, though, 'cos the bus drops her off at the end of the lane."

They reached the farmyard, and to his relief there was no sign of Lloyd George.

Rhian's mother was bustling about the kitchen as they entered, putting food on the table.

"Ah! There you are! Dad'll be here in a minute – we all have tea now, Arthur, so that Dad can do the afternoon milking later on. Then supper before bedtime. How was school?"

"Alright, I s'pose."

She gave him a swift smile. "Wash your hands quickly out the back, then. Show him, Rhian. Oh, good! Here's Bronwen."

"What's he been like?" Bronwen asked when Arfur was still out in the scullery.

"A bit moody," Rhian muttered. "What's the point of having a boy if he's so unfriendly?"

"Well, I think we're stuck with him now, so give him a chance," Bronwen said. "You'd probably be the same if you were dumped hundreds of miles from home. At least our Mam won't be pinching all your clothes to give him if she ends up feeling sorry for him – you know what she's like."

They began to giggle at the thought of Arfur in one of Rhian's flowery best dresses but stopped abruptly when he entered the room.

"Right," said Mam, ignoring the awkward atmosphere. "Dad's just coming so let's make a start. You alright sitting there, Arthur?"

She didn't wait for an answer as she started passing plates around. "We all help clear away when we've finished – you can help dry the dishes," she told him. "Oh, and you have to send a card to your mother."

"No need," he said, through a mouthful of food, "'cos I'll be going home in a few weeks – soon as she's better."

"I know," Mam said coolly, "but she'll want to know you're alright, I'm sure. If she worries about you she might take longer to get well."

Arfur shrugged, unwilling to concede the point.

Rhian's Dad came in then and they all started talking about their day and kept asking Arfur things so that he would join in. He didn't like it, though. There was something just too perfect about them all. Didn't they know there was a war on? Didn't they know that once the bombing started people in London might be happily going about their business one minute and be blown to smithereens the next? He thought of his Mum, then. What if the hospital she was in took a hit? The last time he'd seen her she had her leg stuck up in some sort of pulley contraption – she wouldn't be able to get out of that quickly if a bomb fell, would she? A feeling of panic began to well up in him. He should have stayed in London, kept a look-out for his Mum. If he'd been clever he could have got out of it somehow, stayed with one of the neighbours or something. Then he wouldn't be stuck here, playing bleedin' tea parties with people who had no idea what was really happening.

The panic made him start to choke on his food. As he coughed and spluttered the man gave him a hearty thump on the back of his chest. He got his breath then and at least he could pretend that the tears in his eyes were brought on by the coughing. He took a drink of water trying not to see the kindly eyes of the woman.

When they'd cleared away he was sent out to play with Rhian again, when he would much rather have had some time on his own. And it was the weekend now. He'd probably be sent to play with her all day tomorrow too. He didn't like playing with the girls at home – they always wanted to dress up in net curtains and get you to play weddings or something soppy like that.

Rhian didn't seem any more pleased than he was.

"Won't you come too?" she pleaded with her sister.

"Got homework to do. I want to get it done now so I don't have to do it over the weekend – I'll come and find you when I've finished," Bronwen promised.

Rhian looked at Arfur steadily for a moment and then sighed. "Come on, I'll show you my favourite tree."

They reached a gate into a field where cows grazed lazily in the corner. Rhian clambered over with practised ease.

"What about them?" Arfur nodded towards the animals.

"They're alright – just cows. You have *seen* a cow before haven't you?"

"'Course I have." He didn't say it was just on a wall chart in the butcher's shop with arrows all around it pointing to where the different types of meat came from. "But I thought it was bulls what had horns."

"So do cows – look, you can see their udders. Bulls aren't going to give you milk, are they?"

He supposed not, but decided not to press the point and highlight his ignorance further. Anyway, Rhian was already running across the field, towards a brook that gurgled around it. Two of the cows had caught her movement and were now ambling across the field in his direction. Several more looked up, chewed thoughtfully for a few seconds and then began to walk too. He quickened his pace towards Rhian, but it seemed that the cows quickened theirs, too. He began to trot, but now there were more of them trying to satisfy their curiosity. They were big, too. Bigger than they looked on that poster. Could trample you easily. That was it – he'd escaped the bombs only to be trampled to death by these buggers.

"Stand still!" Rhian was back beside him. "They're just nosey!

Look! As soon as you stand still, so do they. Now take a few steps towards them. Go on! Not scared, are you?"

"Why do you keep saying I'm scared?" Arfur snapped. "Just 'cos I'm not used to all these bloody animals like you are! You come up to London sometime, when everyone thinks all the time that the Jerries are coming over – then you'd bleedin' know about scared!"

But she was right. The cows had stopped moving as soon as he had. He took a step towards them, then another.

"Now put out your hand," said Rhian, "like this".

She held a hand out towards a cow, and moved closer still. The cow moved its head up and down a couple of times, then turned and ambled off. Arfur copied her and saw the cow nearest him do the same.

"They're timid, really," said Rhian, "but you wouldn't know that to look at them, would you? So, come on, race you to that tree."

She was right again. It was a good tree to climb, and she swung up into the branches like a monkey.

"You can see all of Penfawr from here," she said when they stopped about half way up.

He peered out from under a branch. Between the hills that surrounded them the jumble of streets that made up the village could be seen.

"Not very big, is it?"

"Maesteg's not far away. That's quite big. We go there on market days."

"Have they got a cinema? We usually go to the pictures every Saturday morning and then round the shops. Can we do that tomorrow?"

"Well, we can't go to Maesteg that often because there isn't enough petrol. There is a bus but it takes ages 'cos it goes all round the other villages. We can go in during the holidays, when my Dad has to go in for farming stuff."

"Doesn't matter anyway 'cos I won't be staying long. You can put up with anything for a few weeks."

Rhian didn't like to tell him that all the talk before he arrived had been of the evacuees staying until the war ended – and no-one knew how long that would be. And she had that feeling like she'd had last night, that, despite what he said, he was going to be with them for a very long time.

She remembered what Bronwen had said about being nice to him.

"We could go and find all your mates in the village tomorrow – see if they want to play with us? Sometimes my friends come over here and we build dams in the stream and things – your friends might like to do that too."

He shrugged. "Maybe."

He started to climb further up the tree, then stopped when they heard a shout from Bronwen, who was waving from the gate.

"Come on," Rhian said, a note of relief in her voice, "she'll play French cricket with us."

She began to scramble down the tree. Arfur would have liked to have stayed put, just to show her that he wasn't always going to do whatever she suggested, but there were still those cows to get past, and for some reason they had already started moving towards the gate, so the safest bet – just this once – was to go with Rhian.

"Dad says to fetch the cows in for milking," Bronwen told them, handing Rhian a twitchy-looking stick. Arfur watched as the two girls opened the gate wide for the cows, who trooped through as if they knew exactly where they were going. Any pushing and shoving and the girls kept them in line with a little poke of the stick and a few words, like they knew them all. He was reluctantly impressed. Rhian wasn't very big, but didn't seem a bit bothered that one of these great big animals might tread on her toes.

Later, he was sitting on his bed, looking out of the window, which was so low the sill was beneath the level of his bed. They'd played French cricket till supper time and for once he'd shown what he could do. There'd been plenty of crusty bread and cheese with beetroot when they came in, and then they'd sat round the wireless, listening to the news, while Rhian's mother had knitted with a furious clacking of the knitting needles, pausing every now and then with a frown when something on the wireless caught her attention. It was all too much for him again, so he'd come upstairs.

He was just about to get into his pyjamas when there was a tapping on his door.

"We always have a bath on Friday nights and wash our hair, and Mam says you've got to have your turn now," Rhian recited. "And she says... um... do you need her to come and give you a hand... and... um... do you want me to show you how the bath runs, because if you run the hot tap too quickly it comes out cold," she finished in a rush.

"I can manage," he said gruffly. "I've had a bath before, you know – and I don't need telling how to put the water in."

"Well, in case you don't know where the towels are, Mr. Clever Clogs, they're in the cupboard in the corner!" She pulled a face at him before turning on her heel.

He didn't care. He was getting a bit fed up of being bossed around by some stupid little girl – and the thought of her mother helping him made him so embarrassed that he made sure the door was tightly locked.

He ran the bath carefully all the same so that the water became quite deep. The bathroom was bigger than the one at home that they shared with the flat upstairs. His Mum usually commandeered that one before she was going out, but you had to put money in the meter and she never had much change so there was only about an inch of water. Sometimes he would jump in afterwards, but often he forgot and Mum would forget too if she was getting ready.

Rhian's mother came in when he was safely back in his bedroom and wearing his pyjamas.

"I've got you a toothbrush – I noticed that you forgot to bring yours," she said. "And... your clothes... I could see that you couldn't get much in your little suitcase..."

She picked up the clothes he'd been wearing, which he'd left folded on the chair.

"I usually take the girls' school clothes on a Friday night, for the wash, and they wear their play clothes at the weekend. Then, after they've bathed on Sunday night, they're ready with clean clothes for Monday..."

She frowned, clearly trying to think what to say next. Arfur stared at her. Two baths in three days! That was sometimes more than he had in a month!

"I ain't got no play clothes," he said, being sure to keep the note of defiance in his voice. He could see pity on her face, and he didn't like it. "And I don't need all them baths!"

"No, you probably don't in the town – but it's different here in the country. When you're out playing you can get really dirty and muddy on the farm – and you wouldn't want to go to school smelling of animals, would you?"

They always had an answer, these people.

He took the clothes from her and returned them to the chair.

"Well, that's all I've got with me," he said, "so I'll just have to keep away from the animals – which suits me fine. Bleedin' stupid, they are. I'm alright on me own."

His eyes challenged her to say something about his language, but she just bit her lip.

"Look, Arthur… I know you don't want to be here with us, and I can understand that you'd rather be back with your own mother. And I promise you I won't try to take her place or anything – that's why I've left you to find your way round with Rhian today. But I want your mother to feel that I've looked after you as well as I can while she's in hospital – she'd want that, I'm sure."

He continued to stare at her, trying not to blink because he didn't want her to see that mention of his Mum got to him.

"I'll tell you what," she said, "why don't you hang onto those clothes for now, and I'll have a think about getting you some more that you could wear around the farm. It wouldn't do to go back with your things all torn, would it?"

He nodded.

"Oh – there's just one other thing… Rhian's Dad and me… It's difficult if you keep calling us Mr. and Mrs. Llewellyn – it's a bit of a mouthful all the time, isn't it? We thought you could call us Auntie Edyth and Uncle Rhys… What do you think?"

This time he gave her something that was between a nod and a shrug.

"Right then." Her bright smile showed that she thought he'd agreed. "While the girls are having their baths, would you like to come downstairs and have some cocoa before bedtime?"

6.

Lydia's first sensation as she came round was of strong arms laying her on the bed, and cool hands brushing her hair from her face. It was only when the hands eased her shoes from her feet and she thought that they might then try to release her stockings from their suspenders that she fought through the fog that surrounded her, into consciousness.

"It's alright, it's alright. Lie still. You'll be fine."

Dr. Eliot's voice came to her as his face swam before her. "You fainted. You're in your room now and I want you to stay here."

"Grace?" It was about the only word she could manage.

"She's asleep downstairs, where you left her. You've only been out for a minute or two. There's nothing to worry about."

His voice was calm and caring so that she longed to lie back with her eyes closed and sink back into that delicious blackness. But there were other things to think about... the baby... her job... what if he asked for her to leave... where would they go?

She tried to sit up but the ache in her side stopped her.

"I said, just lie still." The voice was sterner now. "I told you to take things easy, but you women, you all seem to think you know better."

She looked up at him, to gauge his expression, which unfortunately looked almost as stern as the words.

"I can't stay in bed – I need to see to Grace!"

"I'll bring her to you when she needs feeding, but otherwise we can get on just fine. Either you stay in bed until I tell you to get up, or I'll be sending you into hospital! What if you'd fainted when you had the baby in your arms?"

She hadn't thought of that. She'd never fainted in her life.

"But there's cooking – and her nappies – and –"

"I'm going to give you a small dose of morphine to ease the pain and to relax you," he said, ignoring her words. "You'll still be able to feed the baby. Now stay there until I come back. I get the feeling that you're not very used to doing as you're told, but this time you really must."

He nodded at her and left the room. Everything was very still and quiet, and, try as she might, her straining ears could hear no sound from downstairs. She allowed her shoulders to relax a little but the underlying anxiety wouldn't go away.

"Why don't we see how we get on?" she'd said to him just this morning, and already she'd been found wanting.

He was soon back, carrying the still-sleeping baby in the wash basket, with medical bits and pieces tucked into the bottom.

"I thought you'd fret less if I brought her up here with you," he said, and then, without looking at her: "You should get undressed properly and into bed. Do you need any help?"

"No – thank you, I can manage. Perhaps you'd pass my night-dress, out of the top drawer?"

He stayed, looking out of the window, while she struggled out of her clothes, biting her lip at the pain in case he turned round. Then he listened to her chest again, before giving her an injection.

"I can see lunch is ready, I'll bring yours up. When did you last feed the baby?"

"Around midday."

He nodded. "Good. Then you should be able to get some sleep after you've eaten."

He brought her a tray with her food and a glass of milk.

"I'm sorry," she said, as he made to leave.

"What for? Being injured? It's not your fault."

"I promised I – we – wouldn't be a nuisance, and now you're having to look after us instead of the other way round. It wasn't part of the bargain."

"It's only for a couple of days. Let's reassess the situation after the weekend, shall we?"

He turned back again in the doorway. "I'm going to do some work in the garden, so I'll be able to hear the phone if it rings. I'll come back up later to see how you are."

And with a nod he was gone.

Lydia lay back when she'd finished her lunch, watching the breeze lifting the lace curtains where Dr. Eliot had raised the sash window a little. The pain in her side was easing and a voice in her head was telling her that this was all a fuss about nothing and she should get up and about, but the pillows were so comfortable, and she was overcome by a drowsiness so overwhelming that she could do nothing more but lie back and close her eyes.

Billy was in her dreams, smiling at her as he'd done when they first met, his periwinkle eyes and cropped blond hair making him look younger than his years. And more trustworthy. He was holding out his hand to her, saying, "*Come on, girl! Come with me! You'll be alright with Billy! Come on…*" But behind him, like two furies, their dark heads like thunderclouds, were the faces of her father and stepmother, contorted with contempt. "*Don't be foolish! Don't listen to him! You must stay! Stay! Stay!… Lydia… Lydia…*"

"Lydia… Lydia…" The voices had changed to one voice, softer, but insistent, and her arm was being gently shaken. She opened her eyes and there was Dr. Eliot, with a grizzling baby in his arms.

"She's ready to be fed. I took her out in the garden with me, but I couldn't pacify her any longer."

It took her a moment to recall where she was, to even remember that she had a baby. She shook her head to clear it of the voices and take in her surroundings. Dr. Eliot had his shirt-sleeves rolled up, displaying strong, tanned forearms which were wrapped around the baby, whom he was jiggling up and down in a surprisingly experienced way.

"Oh… right… sorry…" Lydia struggled to sit up, whereupon he put the baby down at the foot of the bed and quickly rearranged the pillows behind Lydia.

"Here," he said, lifting Grace up again, "if you put this last pillow on your lap, then put her on it just so, you won't have to lean forward to feed her, so there'll be less strain on your ribs and back."

"That's what she wanted," he said, as the baby began to guzzle greedily. He ran his hand through his hair in the same boyish gesture he had made the night before. "I came up to check on you and found she was awake, but you were flat out, so I took her outside with me. But I was a poor substitute for her mother."

"I hope she didn't interrupt your gardening too much."

"No – I was just about to stop for a cup of tea anyway. In fact, I've left the kettle singing away. I'll bring you a cup. How are you feeling now?"

"Better, thank you. The pain's much easier."

He gave his habitual grave nod. She could sense him slipping back into the formality he wore like a shroud. "Good. But I still want you to stay put for a day or two. Once you exert yourself you'd soon find it as painful again."

"Well!" Lydia spoke to the baby after he'd left the room. "I still don't think he's too impressed with me, but I think you're working your charm! He sounded almost human for a few minutes."

There was no doubting his good intentions, though. He brought her tea as promised and helped her to the bathroom.

"Have you been here – I'm sorry I can't even remember the name of this place – long?" she asked him, as he stayed to drink his tea, but didn't seem disposed to talk.

"It's called Penfawr. I've been here just over two years," he answered, but volunteered nothing more.

"There's something else," she said. Something she'd remembered while she'd been lying in bed. "The lady who brought me here – she said that you had a bad heart. But you carried me up here – maybe you shouldn't have... I'm sorry..."

'Sorry' seemed to be all she could say to this man when he gave so little back, but the thought of his heart condition had been bothering her.

"I had rheumatic fever when I was a child," he told her. "It left me with a murmur – it really doesn't affect me particularly, but I couldn't join up."

She would have liked to ask whether he minded not joining up, but he turned away from her again.

"Will you be alright?" he asked, when she'd just reached the point of wondering what was so interesting that he had to look out of the window the whole time. "I have to get ready for evening surgery."

"Of course," she replied. "We'll be fine."

He was back a couple of hours later, when she'd played a little with Grace on the bed, and then dozed with the baby tucked in beside her.

This time he was carrying a tray with ham, some broad beans and small, new potatoes on a plate. A newspaper lay by the side of the plate.

"First crop from the garden this year," he told her, a note of triumph in his voice. "I hope you like broad beans because I'm afraid it's going to be more of the same tomorrow."

"My favourite," she said firmly. "My fath– we used to have them a lot at home."

Grace began to squirm on the bed beside her.

"I'll take the baby downstairs and get her ready for bed, while you eat your supper," he said, picking Grace up as he spoke.

"But what about your food?" Lydia asked.

"I've already eaten," he told her. "I wanted to test the food before I inflicted it on you – like I said before, hopeless in the kitchen, but I can just about manage to boil potatoes, especially when they don't need to be peeled, and vegetables."

"And Grace? You don't mind?" Billy came into her head. Pacing up and down, his face mottled and petulant, demanding to know why it took so long to get ready to go anywhere, or why the baby was crying when there was nothing wrong with her.

She turned her attention back to Dr. Eliot, who was holding Grace very comfortably.

"I did paediatrics before I became a GP," he said, "and the ward was run by a dragon of a sister who insisted that we callow medics had to have hands-on experience of babies, otherwise we would never understand what women went through."

He smiled ruefully at the baby, his face transformed again as he relaxed. "A woman ahead of her time in many ways, which was strange for someone who had no children."

He looked back at Lydia. "Anyway, we'll be fine. Oh, and I've asked Rita – Mrs. Griffiths – to pop in briefly tomorrow, to deal with the nappies. My hospital experience didn't extend to the laundry, I'm afraid."

It was some time before he returned, with Grace swathed in a nightgown Lydia didn't recognise. He laid her in her makeshift cot before pulling a jar of ointment from his pocket.

"Arnica. I thought we should try it on your bruises."

Once again his cool hands were on her body, applying the ointment so gently that she didn't wince at his touch. She felt lulled, cocooned here in this room, and filled with a sense of well-being, despite her physical condition and the somewhat precarious nature of their existence in this man's house.

As he asked her to move forward more, she caught a glimpse

of his face in the dressing table mirror, his eyes lowered, intent on what he was doing. As if by telepathy he looked up and for a brief second their eyes held in the mirror, until they both looked away.

"You mentioned the Home Counties last night," he said as she was re-buttoning her nightie. "Do you not have any family there – who you could have gone to instead of being evacuated?"

She pressed her lips together hard before she replied. "No," was all she said eventually.

He waited for a few seconds in case she was going to elaborate. When she didn't he nodded slightly.

"I have some paperwork to do, then I'll bring you a hot drink and something more for the pain – providing I'm not called out."

"Dr. Eliot," she said as he was about to leave the room. He turned.

"I'm sorry – sorry that I can't explain more to you. My circumstances – they're very complicated. And I'm sorry again that we've landed on you like this – but thank you, for everything.

He inclined his head again. "It's not a problem."

When he'd gone she lay watching the late evening sunshine cast a glow on the hillside opposite. It was the sort of evening that brought back memories of drinking cocktails on manicured lawns, and feeling pretty in floaty dresses and wide-brimmed straw hats.

She was relieved when Grace began to remind her that she was the only one so far who had not had any supper.

7.

Amy was pleased when Monday morning arrived and it was time to go to school again. On Saturday she'd been sent unceremoniously out to play immediately after breakfast, with instructions to return at one o'clock sharp as Ouredwin would be home then for his dinner. "He has to work on Saturday mornings, too, now there's not so many men about, so he needs a good dinner when he comes in."

There hadn't been anyone about that early in the morning, so she'd wandered through the main street, looking in the uninspiring windows of the few shops, which were mainly for buying food, except for one that had old bits of furniture and odds and ends in it, a bit like the stuff the rag-and-bone man would have on his cart.

She tried to remember which street Maisie was staying in, but there were several that looked the same. The lady Maisie was staying with had fetched her from school yesterday, so they hadn't walked home together.

Eventually she found herself back at the school and with a sharp stone made a makeshift hopscotch game in the yard, until, with relief, she heard the chatter of other children's voices coming towards her.

It was Arfur, with the girl she'd seen him with the day before, and two of the other boys they seemed to have collected on their way.

"You alright?" Arfur said by way of greeting and then, when she nodded her head, went on without preamble: "We're going exploring, down by the river. You can come with us as long as you don't start squealing if you get wet."

But by this time Amy was beginning to worry that she wouldn't know when it was time to go back to Mrs. Preece.

"I'd better stay here, where I can see the church clock – unless you've got a watch," she said hopefully to the girl, knowing full well that her own friends didn't possess such a luxury.

The girl shook her head, but then said kindly, "Why don't I stay here and play with you, until you have to go?"

"Good idea," Arfur said at once. "The river's probably too dangerous for *girls*."

Rhian grinned at Amy as the boys ran off. "The river's only about an inch deep at this time of year – the brook round our field is deeper 'cos I dam it up! Stupid boys!"

"Arfur's alright," Amy said quickly. "He lives near me. Sometimes we all go down and play by the canal – Arfur likes messing about in the water, even when it's a bit smelly – and if there are bigger boys down there, Arfur always looks after me if they're nasty."

For the first time in her life, Rhian experienced a pang of jealousy. Her robust upbringing on the farm had never led her to want for anything more than the opportunity to be outdoors when the weather allowed and maybe occasionally to wish for more playmates when Bronwen refused to play with her. But now she wondered what it would be like to have Arthur stick up for her, to see something protective or sympathetic in those dark eyes which so far had only looked at her with scorn and hostility.

Not that she used those words in her head, to analyse how she felt. There was just something squirming in the pit of her stomach, and a realisation that Arthur wasn't always as scathing about girls as he made out. Well, she'd just have to persevere until she was his friend as well, not just someone he tolerated because he was in a strange place. There was lots of time – none of them were going anywhere.

"I've been playing hopscotch," Amy said now. "Do you want a go?"

"We play it differently here. Look – I'll show you."

Rhian took the stone from Amy, chattering away as she marked out different squares. By the time Amy realised it was past midday she'd learned a lot about life in Penfawr, even if sometimes Rhian spoke so quickly she couldn't always follow what she said.

"I have to go," Amy told her after another check of the church clock. "Don't you have to go home too?"

Rhian shrugged. "It's not our dinner time yet, but I suppose I'd better find the boys and tell them we should be making our way. I'll see if Arthur's friends want to come over to the farm this afternoon – you can come too if you want."

"I'll have to ask Mrs. Preece. She'll probably say I can – she didn't mind where I went this morning."

"Just say you're going to Llewellyn's Farm – it's on the road out the other side of the village."

But now Amy had to run to get back in time and couldn't remember the strange word. Not that it made any difference – Mrs. Preece had other plans for the afternoon.

After a dinner eaten in silence except for Grace, with Ouredwin's slightly moist eyes watching Amy throughout, Mrs. Preece announced, "There's clothes being given out for the evacuees in the chapel rooms this afternoon, two o'clock, so we're going there. Kit you out a bit more so I won't be washing all the time, and I don't want to miss the good stuff. There's plenty round here don't need the help as much as I do."

They were the first ones there, and Mrs. Preece quickly scanned the room in a practised way, before heading for a table of girls' clothes.

"Come and stand by here, nicely, so I can hold things up against you," she instructed Amy, who wondered how you could stand next to a table un-nicely. There were ladies, wearing overalls with badges on the front, standing behind the tables, some of them with tape measures round their necks. The one at Amy's table smiled at her.

"Petite, isn't she?" she said to Mrs. Preece. "There should be plenty here to fit her, specially as we seem to have got more girls' stuff than boys' – but then boys wear out their clothes so much faster, don't they?"

But Mrs. Preece wasn't listening. She was rummaging through the pile of clothes, her mouth sucked in so that her lips had almost disappeared, holding up garment after garment against Amy, and as quickly discarding all except the plainest and darkest.

The room began to fill up, some of the women with friends from Amy's class, but when she held up her hand to wave to them, Mrs. Preece pulled her arm back roughly and told her to stand still.

A pleasant woman with wavy fair hair and a wide mouth that looked as if it would smile even when she was sad – the opposite of Mrs. Preece – bounded up to the girls' table with a pile of dresses, jumpers and skirts.

"Can you take these?" she asked the woman behind the table. "I know we were supposed to sort some clothes out before the children arrived, but as usual I left it until the last minute. Then I found all of these – didn't realise how much I had stored away!"

She turned pleasantly to Mrs. Preece. "I've been given a boy, so these are no use to me at all. And Arthur's only got the clothes he stands up in, so I hope there are a few things left on the boys' table!"

She spied Amy hovering behind Mrs. Preece and immediately exclaimed, "Oh! I think these would be perfect for you – you're the same build as my Rhian, just a couple of inches shorter."

So this was Rhian's mother! How lovely it would have been to be placed with her. Arfur didn't know how lucky he was. And the dresses and skirts looked pretty. Amy gave Rhian's Mum a shy smile but before she could say that she'd met Rhian Mrs. Preece pitched in.

"Thank you, but I think I've got all we need for the moment. Mustn't be too greedy."

Edyth Llewellyn glanced at the drab stack of clothes already collected by Mrs. Preece and then the expectant face of Amy.

"Shame, because this little kilt skirt has hardly been worn – Rhian grew out of it too quickly. It would suit your little girl."

The kilt was in warm tones of red, with narrow straps to go over the shoulders. *Choose it, choose it,* Amy willed her foster mother, but Mrs. Preece thrust her bundle of garments towards the lady with the WVS badge, with a terse, "I'll be the judge of that, thank you very much," so that Rhian's mother had no choice but to retreat to the boys' table.

"Kilts, indeed to goodness!" Mrs Preece muttered as the WVS lady made up a parcel for her. "It'll be party frocks and fur coats next – for evacuees!"

By the time they left the hall, Amy had worked out a plan whereby she could tell Mrs. Preece that she'd been invited to the farm and then with a bit of manoeuvring manage to go there with Rhian's Mum. Never having been to one, she was sure that it would be like the toy farm she had when she was younger; where every type of domestic animal mingled around a small pond – chickens, ducks and ducklings, lambs, a cow, sheep, donkey, horse and pig, and a snoozing cat on a nearby wall. She would be able to stroke all the animals and cuddle the ducklings, and Rhian's mother would come out of the house with a tray of home-made lemonade and cakes so that the children could have a picnic under an apple tree.

But outside the hall Mrs. Preece fell into deep conversation with the plump woman who had been helping the man with the armband when they all arrived and, while Amy stood waiting for them to finish, Rhian's mother came out. She gave Amy another of her quick smiles before jamming her clothes parcel into a wicker basket on the front of a rickety old bike and cycling off.

The two women were soon joined by a third and they switched their conversation from Welsh to English, continuing to talk as if they would never stop. The plump woman seemed to be telling the other two something about the doctor and a baby, so Amy guessed there was a new baby somewhere which the doctor had brought in his bag, as they always did. Two girls from her class came out of the hall eventually, but just as they began to talk to Amy, Mrs. Preece's little group broke up and she grabbed Amy by the arm and hurried her away with a "Look at the time, now! The afternoon nearly gone and Our Edwin wants his tea early so he can go to the dance tonight at the Red Shed," as if it was Amy's fault that they had been delayed.

The weekend continued to get worse for Amy. After a tea-time spent quietly on her part whilst Mrs. Preece and Ouredwin conversed in their strange language, Ouredwin disappeared upstairs for a long time, whilst Amy carefully dried the dishes as instructed by Mrs. Preece. When Ouredwin reappeared he looked different. His hair was plastered down with some sort of greasy mixture, each side of a very wide, very straight parting, and he wore a sleeveless pullover over a striped shirt and tie, and wide-legged dark trousers, beneath which were quite startling brown and white brogue shoes.

"Off now, then, are you?" said his mother, who had looked him up and down with grim satisfaction and a nod of approbation. She helped him on with his jacket, smoothing and brushing the shoulders as she did so. "There's smart you look," she added as he picked up his hat and spent a few seconds looking in the mirror above the fireplace, getting the angle just right. "Any girl would be proud to dance with you." He seemed to take her admiration as his due, although Amy thought that his hair smoothed down so severely made his eyes look too close together.

When he opened the back door to leave, Amy could hear the sound of children playing in the lane.

"Can I go out to play?" she asked Mrs. Preece, who was still watching her son through the kitchen window, her eyes glowing with maternal pride.

"No, indeed you can't. Hair wash and bath night for you – so you'll be clean and tidy for the Sabbath."

Several jugs of tepid water were used to wash Amy's hair as she balanced on a small stool and leaned over the kitchen sink. Then Mrs. Preece filled a small zinc bath with a couple of inches of water which had been heating in a round gas boiler that ran off the same pipe connected to the gas cooker. The sides of the bath were cold and the water quickly turned cold too, so that Amy soon found herself shivering, despite the warmth of the summer evening outside, as she submitted to the indignity of an all-over scrub from Mrs. Preece. All the while she was aware that, should Ouredwin decide to come home early for any reason, he would walk into the kitchen and see her with no clothes on.

He must have been having a good time at the dance, though, because Amy didn't see him again until next morning. After another sleepless night fretting over the nameless terrifying creatures that were surely lurking in the darkest recesses of her bedroom, she was told to make herself clean and tidy – Mrs. Preece's favourite phrase after 'indeed to goodness' – because they were off to chapel straight after breakfast. Ouredwin was more soberly attired for this, with a darker tie than last night, and black shoes, but he still had the shiny flat hair.

There were one or two other evacuees in Ebenezer chapel but there was no chance to speak to them, and when she tried to turn round to catch their eye Mrs. Preece tapped her knee none too gently and hissed, "Sit up straight and behave yourself in the Lord's house."

The Lord's house had a lot of varnished wood in it. Row after row of highly polished pews with little doors to get into them. Pillars supported an upper level which went round the chapel in a horseshoe shape and held more rows of tiered seats. At the front of the chapel was an ornate rail, behind which was a carpeted area.

"There's a big pool under that floor, where they dunk you till you're almost drowned, when you get baptised. My turn next year," Ouredwin whispered when they first went in and he saw her looking around, but she didn't know whether to believe him.

Beyond the carpet rose the pulpit, with steps up either side. Mr. Schofield, the minister, walked up them stiffly, gripping the handrail, one step at a time because of his gammy leg, his face bravely noble. Behind the pulpit was the organ, its shiny pipes standing to attention majestically, in perfect symmetry, on each side. Amy could just see the back of the bald head of the organist as he energetically pulled out lots of buttons while he played, never once losing the tune.

She was wedged between Mrs. Preece and Ouredwin and became so hot that she wished she could take off her cardigan, but there was little room to manoeuvre. Ouredwin's thigh was pressed up against hers, making her leg feel even hotter, when she was sure he could have made more room if he'd moved the hymn books at the end of the pew, but she didn't dare ask him and risk receiving another hiss.

It was a relief when they stood up to sing the hymns, some of which she couldn't join in with because they were in Welsh. The minister spoke in English, in rich rolling tones, his voice thundering at times and at others as soft as wind shushing through trees, but Amy could follow little of what he said. She occupied herself by reading the inscriptions of the memorial tablets dotted around the walls as far she could see without having to turn round, but they still seemed to sit there for what felt like hours, so that when they finally emerged the sun made her blink so rapidly she had tears in her eyes.

Dinner was left-overs from Saturday, the potatoes a little black around the edges from where they'd stood overnight in the larder. "No cooking on the Lord's Day," Mrs. Preece said.

There didn't seem much of anything on the Lord's Day, Amy decided. Just when she'd plucked up the courage to ask if she could go out to play in the afternoon, she was whisked off to the chapel again for Sunday School. Mrs. Preece was one of the helpers at Sunday School, which meant she sat at the back of the room with some other women and gossiped until it was time to break up into groups for the stories. At least Maisie and her little brother Sam were there, and Amy could sit with them so that she and Maisie were able to whisper furiously to each other when there was a lull in the proceedings.

After tea, Mrs. Preece announced that she was off to chapel again for evening service. "Always have the choir of an evening, singing up in the balcony," she told Amy. "Lovely sound they make."

Amy's heart sank at the thought of sitting through another service, but then Mrs. Preece told her that children didn't go to the evening service. Apparently young men didn't have to either, so Amy could stay at home with Ouredwin, which, Amy felt, was an even worse prospect.

Mrs. Preece rammed a hatpin into the boat-shaped hat she'd worn in the morning, making Amy wince because it looked as if the pin was going right into her head.

"I'm stopping for a deacons' meeting afterwards, so I want you in bed before I get back, and you mind and be a good girl," she said, as if Amy was going to run completely wild without the warning. *And doing what?* she wondered mutinously, as everything she had asked to do today had been forbidden because it was Sunday.

But for the first time since her arrival, Ouredwin smiled at her and said, "Don't worry, we'll be fine," and Amy decided that they probably would.

"You mustn't mind our Mam," he told her conspiratorially as soon as the front door slammed – Mrs. Preece using it on the Sabbath because she was wearing her best clothes. "She goes to chapel all the more since our Dad died. I think she wants to make sure she'll be with him in the afterlife."

He gave a laugh at this, which had a hint of girlish giggle to it. Amy didn't know what to reply, so they sat in silence for a few minutes, his moist eyes as watchful over her as before.

"Do you like reading?" he asked eventually. "Only I've got some old books and things from when I was little up in my bedroom – would you like to see?"

It was the first bit of relief from this day of unremitting

boredom for Amy, and one of the things she had disliked most about this evacuation business was not being able to bring her favourite books with her, so she eagerly agreed.

Ouredwin's room, next to Amy's, was only a little larger than hers and seemed pretty cheerless, despite being bathed in a glow from the setting sun. He rummaged about under the bed until he pulled out a cardboard box which held a couple of books of Bible stories and a pile of old copies of *Sunny Stories*.

Amy fell on the children's magazines with a cry of delight. "My mother used to buy me these every week and I'd read them before bedtime!" she exclaimed, having the sense not to add "when I was a lot younger," in case he thought she wasn't grateful for his kindness. Besides, reading them again, no matter how babyish they seemed, would make her own home seem that little bit nearer.

"Take one to look at now, if you like," he said, "and I'll tell you what – borrow one whenever you want, as long as you put each one back after you've finished with it. You can come into my bedroom at any time, as long as I'm not asleep!"

Amy would have liked to ask him why he'd kept such childish things when he was clearly almost a grown-up but she thought that might embarrass him, so she simply said, "Thank you," picked up the top copy and made her way back downstairs.

She sat for some time at the table, leafing through the magazine, expecting Ouredwin to find something else to do, but he sat opposite her, just watching.

"How old are you?" he asked after a few minutes.

"Nine," she told him, and then, out of politeness asked how old he was.

"Seventeen," he said, but offered nothing else.

Then, just as she was engrossed in a story, he said, "What do you like best at school?"

"Writing," she said, "and reading," indicating the magazine. "But I don't like sums so much. Did you like school?"

"Not really," he said. "I like it better now I'm out at work. A man's job I do now, see. At the sawmills. Staying put too, if I can, so I don't get called up later on."

Eventually the sun went down behind the mountain at the back of the house, so the light from the one narrow window in the room was too poor to read by properly and she had just about finished this edition.

"I'd better go to bed, now, before Mrs. Preece comes home," she told Ouredwin, getting up reluctantly from the table because she knew her bedroom would be even more gloomy. "Thank you for this – I'll put it back in your box."

She was hoping he might offer her a cup of cocoa, to delay the moment when she would have to climb the stairs, but he just said, "Alright, then." But his eyes weren't as cold as they had been before, and he gave her a small, almost secretive smile before she left the room.

She made a quick dash out to the lavvy first, which, when the door was shut in the evening, was almost as scary as her bedroom, save for a sliver of light that peeped through the gap between the bottom of the door and the floor. When she returned to the kitchen she washed her hands and face and cleaned her teeth at the sink, before passing through the living room where she'd been sitting with Ouredwin, to reach the hall. There was no sign of the lad downstairs, unless he was in the narrow front room that was evidently kept "for best', so she picked up the copy of *Sunny Stories* and made her way upstairs.

"Oh!" Her hand flew to her mouth in surprise, letting the magazine fall to the floor, as she opened the bedroom door and found Ouredwin sitting on his bed, his shape dark against the fading light from the window behind him. "Ouredwin! I thought you were still downstairs! You made me jump! Sorry!" She scrabbled on the floor to pick up the magazine and put it tidy. "I was just returning this, like I said I would."

"I'm not *your* Edwin, you know," he said as she put the copy back in the box. "You only say 'our' when it's your family – like 'our Mam', 'our Dad'."

"Oh!" she exclaimed again, but this time in embarrassment. She'd heard so many strange names since she'd got here that she thought Ouredwin was just another.

"I can hear you through the wall, you know," he told her as she straightened up. "Why do you cry in the night?"

Amy felt her face reddening. "I miss my mother," she said at last, "and… and… well, I don't like the dark. It frightens me. Even though it's summer – with the blackout curtains it's very dark. And it's even darker here than it is at home."

"You shouldn't be scared. Besides, I'm just next door – always look out for you, I will."

He seemed an unlikely hero, with his funny hair and strange eyes, and long, thin body. "Like a piece of streaky bacon," Amy's Gran would have said, but Amy was grateful nevertheless. His were the first really caring words she'd heard since she arrived.

"Thank you," she said, and then, when he said no more: "Good night."

She was tucked up in bed when she heard the door knob turn.

"It's alright – it's only me, it is." Edwin was this time silhouetted in the ray of light from the landing. "Just wanted you to see that I was keeping my promise."

He moved into the room and sat on the end of the bed.

"Not scared any more, are you?"

She shook her head.

"That's good," he said, stroking her hand where it lay on top of the bedcover. "Don't want any frightened little girls in this house. Friends, we are, see? You and me, we'll be friends."

He carried on talking, steadily, in a quiet monotone, until Amy felt herself lulled into that delicious sense of well-being before sleep finally takes over. It was funny how things turned out. The weekend hadn't been up to much, one way and another, but, here, most unexpectedly, was a new ally.

Her last thought before she succumbed was that she must remember his name was *Edwin*.

8.

It was nearly a week later before Lydia ventured into the village. She stayed in bed for another two days until a mixture of guilt, restlessness and decreased pain made her impatient to be up and about. Over the weekend Dr. Eliot had continued to care for her and the baby with an imperturbability which seemed at odds with his rather hostile reaction to her initial arrival. She put it down to the good behaviour of the baby during this time and perhaps his realisation that at least a housekeeper who would be well enough to work in a short while was better than having no housekeeper at all.

He left her twice on the Sunday; in the morning to visit two patients he was worried about and just after lunch to attend to an emergency, but on both occasions returned to her room to check that she was alright.

"I'm sufficiently better to feel bored," she told him at the end of the afternoon. "I haven't spent so long in bed since Grace was born."

He scrutinised her face and then gave his habitual nod. "You look better for it. You've lost that haggard look and the dark circles round your eyes have gone. It's amazing what even a short rest can do for the body."

"Haggard and sunken-eyed, eh! You really know how to charm a girl!" The words were out with a smile before she realised how flirtatious they sounded. And he was her employer, with whom she had to share this house without his thinking that she was some loose, scheming woman. And she was supposed to be a grieving widow!

"It's been very difficult to rest in London since Dunkirk," she told him in a rush, almost choking on her words in her confusion. "Worrying about what's going to happen next seems to have made it all noisier and busier. Everything here seems so serene by comparison."

"Would you like to sit by the window for a while? The fresh

air would do you good."

He helped her out of bed into the rocking chair, with no indication of what he thought of her ill-judged comment, and then placed the baby, in her drawer-bed, on the marble-topped table, where she kicked and coo'ed as she watched the movement of the lace curtains in the breeze.

"Thank you, that's wonderful," Lydia said. "I could simply drink in this view for hours."

She could see the road through the village running parallel to the ribbon of river, where the sunlight playing on the water was the only movement. On the edge of the village were small low-roofed cottages, some of them just single storey, but further along the houses were more densely packed. Each side of the road were short runs of stone-fronted terraces, most of them opening directly onto the street. Not the prettiest houses in the world, but somehow they looked right in this place, as if, shoulder to shoulder, they stood solid and resolute against the might of the hillside which rose either side of the valley floor.

There were more terraces on the far side of the river bank, although she couldn't see from this angle where there was any connecting bridge. These houses, already coping with the rise of the hillside, looked more prosperous, with steps going up to the front door and small front gardens bounded by iron railings. At the back their steep gardens melted into the fields and trees beyond.

The trees themselves, heavy-boughed with summer finery in all shades of green, formed thick bands above the fields, sometimes hiding the tops of the hills from sight, sometimes exposing them like a bald pate.

On this particular afternoon the birds in the trees around the house and the distant baa-ing of sheep on the far hillside were the only sounds. Everything dozed in the heat: it could only be a Sunday. Not as mellow as the landscape from her youth, but Lydia hadn't felt such tranquillity since –

"Yes, it is lovely," Dr. Eliot's voice breaking into her thoughts sounded as if he had only just realised this as he too gazed through the window. "You're seeing it at its best, too. The valley gets a lot of rain throughout the year and it's pretty cold in the winter."

Lydia watched as a huddle of people came into view, tiny dots on the landscape. It looked like a family taking a stroll along the riverbank. A family. Something she and Billy had never properly achieved. Perhaps, though, the people only looked happy from this distance. Perhaps their lives, too, were punctured by arguments and disharmony and they were bickering with each other at this very moment. After all, no-one else, least of all her family, had any inkling that her marriage had been less than happy. Except, perhaps, for the people next door, who must have heard Billy's drunken rages, but in that neighbourhood such noise wasn't unusual.

A movement beside her made her realise that Dr. Eliot was still there. In her reverie she'd forgotten his presence.

"I'll leave you, then – you should be alright sitting here for a while."

She wished she were brave enough to ask him to stay with her, so that she wasn't left alone with the wistful thoughts that kept intruding during her enforced idleness. For a second she thought she saw something in his face that showed he would like to stay, but it was so brief she could have been mistaken, and then, before she could even thank him once more, he was going down the stairs.

On Monday it was Rita who brought her up a lunch tray, assuring her in cheerful tones that the doctor was managing fine. "I've brought a few left-overs from yesterday's dinner for you both," she said. "I'd been doing some meals for the poor man, anyway, while he was on his own, seeing as he can't cook, so no harm for another day or two."

Lydia decided not to tell her that the 'poor man' had done quite well over the weekend; she simply thanked Rita for her kindness. But Rita was already playing with the baby.

"Why don't I just take this little one out for a stroll in the fresh air, seeing as how you've got that pram for her? Missed having a baby, I have, now mine are older. I'll bring her back when she wants her tea."

"Shown her off good and proper around the village," she told Lydia on their return. "And a real little love she was, too – smiled at everyone, she did."

So Lydia wasn't surprised, when eventually she was allowed to push the pram down the steep path through Amos's field, that so many strangers stopped to speak to her and ask if she was feeling better. She strolled carefully along the main street, taking note of the goods displayed in the small shops dotted here and there amongst the rows of houses, many of them seeming to be nothing more than the front room of a house, simply with a bigger window. It was only in the largest shop in the middle of the village, which appeared to be the post office on one side, a general grocery store in the middle, and a hardware shop on the other side, that she encountered a less friendly atmosphere. Mrs. Owain Owen was standing at the post office counter, with a small, shrewish woman of indeterminate age whose mouth caved inwards as if she had no teeth.

"I was sorry to hear about your poor husband," the woman said when Mrs. Owain Owen introduced Lydia as the doctor's new housekeeper. She eyed Lydia's dainty little cream straw hat before continuing, "I don't suppose there was time to find proper mourning stuff before you came away."

Lydia bit her lip. Her announcement when she arrived that she was a widow had been so spontaneous she hadn't really thought it through. "It's not something I believe in – displaying my grief openly – I prefer to keep it to myself. Wearing black won't change anything," she prevaricated then cursed herself as she realised the woman was dressed head to toe in black and therefore doubtless a grieving widow herself. The insulted expression on the woman's face confirmed this.

"Still! You're up and about now!" Mrs. Owain Owen declared. "Heard you weren't well. I didn't realise that there was anything wrong when we left you at Dr. Eliot's." She sounded aggrieved, as if she and her husband had been misled over the quality of the goods they were offering to the people of the village.

Despite her best efforts, Lydia could feel herself taking on a haughty manner. "Well, we all try to overcome our problems when we're reliant on the goodwill of others, don't we? But as you said, I'm up and about now, and fully able to undertake my duties."

She felt quite gratified that the women looked slightly abashed at her response, but it was spoilt somehow when everything she asked for from the kindly looking woman behind the counter was unavailable. "We had some this morning, but they went straight away," was the answer, or, "If you'd been in yesterday, we still had some of those."

In the end she had to ask the woman what foodstuffs she did have that would make her coupons stretch a little bit further.

"Need to be an early bird in these parts," the woman with the squashed-in mouth commented, with satisfaction rather than sympathy, breaking off from her conversation in Welsh with Mrs. Owain Owen as they left the shop. Mrs. Owain Owen did have the grace to turn back, however, with a small piece of advice. "Seeing as you've got the baby to see to and you're looking after the doctor, Mrs. Thomas here would keep a few things by for you, if you tell her what you want."

Lydia recounted this to Rita next time they snatched a cup of tea together because the surgery was quiet.

"Ah! That will have been Mrs. Preece," Rita explained from Lydia's description. "Mr. Preece was Mrs. Owen's brother, so they're very close – even more so since he died. And they were both very friendly with Miss Williams." She gave a chuckle. "You have to be careful in these parts if you dare to speak ill of anyone, in case they're related to the person you're talking to. Not many people move away, see – I think we've got relatives in every street in the village. Nice, it is, to have your family round you – to help you out when you've got problems."

She glanced speculatively at Lydia, but when she could see that Lydia wasn't going to take the bait she gave another chuckle. "Mind you, it stops you getting up to any mischief, either, because someone is bound to find you out, and then it's round the village before you can say 'Jack Robinson'."

As she grew stronger, Lydia gradually put the house to rights, moving from room to room with the baby either in her wash-basket carrycot, or outside in her pram when the weather was fine. Before long there was a polished lustre to the furniture of which even Mrs. Owain Owen would have been proud. Lydia couldn't make the sitting room look any less formidable, though, even when she filled a vase with some straggling roses from the garden and placed it on a table in the window.

"It's all so *brown*," she told Grace, who gurgled back at her in complete agreement. "It could do with a colourful rug in front of the fire, and some decent pictures on the walls, and different curtains and –" she gave a hollow laugh, "listen to me – anyone would think the place was ours. When we both know," she tickled the baby's tummy to lighten her words and the feeling of desolation that was creeping over her, "we *all* know that I'm the housekeeper and you're a poor orphan and we're only here until this war ends and then we'll be going... home..."

When she had the baby with her, Lydia talked or sang to her constantly, which occupied her own mind against too many of these thoughts. But when she was on her own, undertaking some tedious job such as rinsing nappies or mopping floors, it was difficult keeping all the nagging doubts and worries at bay. What had happened to Billy? Had he survived the explosion? She was in no doubt that if he had survived but injuries were stopping him from being sent overseas, then he would be looking for her as soon as he was fit enough. There was little love left between them, but as far as he was concerned she and Grace were his, and he wasn't going to let go of either of them easily. It was the thought that another man might get his hands on his attractive wife which had often tipped him over into one of his rages.

If she and Grace could stay here, they were probably alright. It would be very difficult to trace two surplus-to-requirement bodies added to a whole trainload of evacuees. But it was another reason, amongst many, why she couldn't go back to her family in Sevenoaks. Not until she knew for certain. It would be the first place Billy would look.

It had been so different when they met early in 1939. War was still only being talked about, but there was already an urgency in London, an air of suppressed excitement that permeated even the dull book shop in the Edgware Road where she was assistant manageress. It had made her declare to her family that if there were to be a war, she was going to 'do her bit'. And later, when she announced that she was pregnant, this led her father to declare angrily that he hadn't realised 'doing her bit' would be lying flat on her back for some Tommy.

"Billy's not some raw squaddie, he's a trained guardsman," she'd flashed back, but her father wasn't listening.

The excitement had been there amongst the young, before they savoured the reality of war. Billy was already an infantry-man in the Irish Guards, based at Wellington barracks, with a daredevil look in those periwinkle eyes. He'd insisted on taking her to a Lyons corner house for a cup of tea after she had tripped on the pavement and literally fallen at his feet in Birdcage Walk.

He'd made her laugh then with his tales of guard duty outside Buckingham Palace and the next day had turned up at the book shop, urging her to come to the cinema with him because he didn't know how much longer he was going to be in London.

"Probably going up to Windsor, for more training until them at the top make up their minds when we're going to put a stop to Hitler and his thugs," he told her. "So this might be the only chance I have to make you fall in love with me!"

He was different from the earnest young men she had dated so far, who came from backgrounds similar to hers and spoke seriously about the rise of Fascism and Mr. Churchill's doom-mongering. Billy had a jingoistic confidence in his ability to "sort out the Krauts" almost single-handedly, and an infectious liveliness that made her want to act recklessly for the first time in her life.

She had been ripe for the picking, she realised now. Bored with her decorous middle-class upbringing and the sedate dances and dinners after which her escort would diffidently ask permission to kiss her – when all the time she had wanted to be swept off her feet, presented with an ardour to which she could, she knew, respond with passion.

Billy had swept her away with his unabashed desire for her, and his energy which was definitely sexual rather than nervous. She had never before met a man with such cheerful confidence in his ability to charm, regardless of any difference in their backgrounds.

"You're a classy lady," he told her, "but I can make you happier than any of those stuffed shirts you normally mix with."

And he was right. Their short romance left her breathless and dizzy as he whirled her around London, showing her places and sights she'd never encountered on her sedate railway journeys from Kent to the book shop. Within a few weeks she felt that she'd known him for years, and he treated her like a princess.

"I might not have had the education, but I know how to treat a lady – *my* lady," he said.

She tried to explain to her family how she was falling in love with this rough diamond, although it was impossible to tell them of the thrill of his fit lithe body against hers when he held her in his arms. Or of the persuasive nature of his argument that they should grab whatever life could offer them because their future was so uncertain.

By the time she found out that she was pregnant, Lydia knew that she loved Billy, and his enthusiasm had managed to make light work of their predicament.

"Well, we were always going to get married, weren't we, girl? 'Cos no-one'll ever love you more than me. And what an 'andsome pair we'll make – you looking so beautiful and me in me best uniform!"

The simple ceremony at the register office was bereft of family on both sides. Hers because they refused to have anything more to do with her unless she came to her senses and returned home, and his because he said that he simply didn't have any. Lydia didn't care, though. The love and longing shining out of Billy's eyes were enough and when she took her vows she was sure that they would make each other happy, no matter what. So fellow soldiers from his barracks were the witnesses, and a larger group joined them in the evening to celebrate.

Billy wasn't violent then, even though he was drunk. When they finally returned to the little house in Bermondsey that he'd managed to acquire ("The landlord's a friend of a friend – owes me a favour," he'd told her, tapping his nose), the drink simply made him maudlin.

"I can't believe I've got a girl like you, Lydia," he told her over and over again in the darkness of their sparsely furnished bedroom. "I'm the luckiest bloke in England, and now I've got you I'm never going to let you go!"

The violence came a few weeks later, when he was back from the predicted stay in Windsor and the drink convinced him that she'd been seeing another man. The back of his hand across her face was so sudden that she staggered back, horrified, before sinking down onto the sofa, her hands folded over her body to protect her baby. He continued with a verbal assault, insisting that as she'd been so free and easy with her favours to him, how could he believe that she wouldn't be the same with other men when he wasn't there?

In complete disbelief that this could be the same man who had so recently declared that he would love and protect her forever, she had sat, immobile, with as much dignity as she could muster, refusing to respond to his taunts.

Next morning his remorse was overwhelming. "Forgive me," he pleaded. "I'll never touch you again, I swear!"

"It's like you were another person," she told him coldly. "No-one has ever laid a finger on me before, not even my parents when I was a child. And *you* are supposed to love me more than anyone else in the world."

"*I do! I do!*" he insisted. "It's just that when I get a drink inside me it's like I can't believe I've really got you. I get so afraid I'll lose you to someone else."

"You'll only lose me if you ever treat me like that again."

"I won't, I swear it."

"Then you'd better stop drinking, to prove it."

Which he did, for a few weeks, while her pregnancy was in the early stages where they could still enjoy going out together. They were the best weeks, she decided, looking back. Billy was doing his utmost to convince her that he would never treat her badly again, and she was happily proving that she could make a home for them in the mean little street, and that it mattered not a jot to her that it was so different from her upbringing.

But when war was declared, Billy was anxious to see some proper action and became irritated that he was still at home in the holding battalion. He took to spending his off-duty time with his fellow guardsmen, and invariably came home the worse for wear. His whole appearance changed at these times; his eyes becoming menacing slits and his lips puffy and slack, so that he was no longer the good-looking Jack-the-lad she'd fallen for.

Sometimes he would be maudlin, like on their wedding night. "I'm so lucky – I've got the most beautiful wife in London, and you're going to have my baby. What more could a man want, eh, girl?" he would repeat, clutching her to him, and she would quell the nagging doubts that beset her most of the day. At other times he would be in a fearful rage, telling her that he knew she would leave him one day because he would never be good enough for her, and he would be impervious to her reassurances that it was not so.

As the phoney war continued Lydia, too, began to wish that Billy would be sent abroad. By this time she had come to realise that the Billy who had wooed and won her was only one facet of the man, whose myriad problems really stemmed from enormous insecurity that made his moods mercurial. When sober he would often sneer at the changes to her body and her looks, altered by tiredness and worry over how they could manage if he continued to drink away so much of his pay.

"Not many men would look at you now!" he'd tell her. "In fact, *you're* lucky that *you've* got *me.*"

But when she tried to make herself presentable with tidy hair and fresh make-up and a smile on her face to welcome his return from duty, in the hope that he would spend some time at home with her, he would accuse her of trying to attract other men and insist that she told him who had been to the house.

"You've got it all wrong!" she would cry in exasperation. "And who on earth do you think is going to look at a seven months' pregnant woman?"

If she told him that she was worried about their life together he told her not to nag. When she tried to explain that it was difficult to make ends meet he told her that she'd have to try a bit harder to be an East End housewife.

"My old Mum always managed with whatever me Dad tipped up for her when I was a nipper," he said, and Lydia had to bite back the retort that it was probably the reason why the poor woman died a pitifully early death.

Only once did he try to hit her again while she was pregnant, but this time, ever wary that it could happen, she was too quick for him and moved away from the threatening arm, her anger every bit as great as his.

"Just you dare!" she hissed at him from the other side of the kitchen table. "One blow and I'll be out of here before you know it – and then you'll never see me again, or this baby for that matter!"

It was the old ebullient Billy who visited the hospital after Grace was born, handsome and smiling in his uniform, making the other mothers envious of the pretty girl who still had her husband at home when theirs were goodness knows where.

"The most beautiful baby in the world!" he declared as he

held Grace in his arms, "And I'm the proudest Dad! I'm going to be so good to you!" he told the sleeping baby.

And Lydia knew that at that moment he meant every word he said, and listened with new hope in her heart as he outlined all the things the three of them were going to do together.

But the reality of life with a small baby, and their different expectations, soon brought both of them down to earth with a bang. Lydia's dewy new-mother looks and the quick return of her figure, as she had actually gained little weight during her pregnancy, re-awakened Billy's longing for her.

"We can't yet – it's too soon," she told him, pushing away his advances soon after he'd brought her home from hospital. "We're supposed to wait six weeks – so that I'm properly back to normal."

"You look fine to me! Aw, come on, girl! I could be sent away any day now – six weeks will be no bleedin' good then, will it?"

The baby had stirred then, so Lydia picked her up and began feeding her. Billy watched for a few moments, his face contorted with a strange sort of jealousy before he stormed out of the house.

She'd hoped that the baby would bring them closer, and had held romantically rosy pictures of the two of them sitting in front of a cosy fire, cooing over the new arrival. But Billy's picture was completely different. He didn't see that a baby should make any difference to the life they led before.

Christmas had come and gone quietly because Lydia had been heavily pregnant, but now Billy wanted her to go out with him in the evenings, as they had done so many months ago, to "make up for lost time."

"We can find a babysitter to leave her with," he said when Lydia asked what she was supposed to do with the baby, "and she can have a bottle – same as other babies do!"

"I don't want to leave her with a stranger – she's far too young!" Lydia protested.

"Then let's take her with us! We needn't be long."

"Billy! It's still only March! My baby's not being left out in the cold night air while her mother is inside a pub drinking! It's not –"

Billy had grabbed her and pushed her against the kitchen wall before she could finish. His breath told her that he'd already had a few on his way home. "*Not what?* Not what they do where you come from? What would you do there, then? Have some nanny for her, while you sat at a posh dinner party? Well, it's not like that in Bermondsey!"

"You're being ridiculous!" Lydia cried, trying to push him away. "I was going to say *it's not good for babies* to be left in the cold air – she's only a few weeks old! And I'd want to be the one to look after her, wherever we lived! Let go of me, Billy – you're hurting me!"

But there were brandy fumes clogging his brain and fire in his belly now, as he held her tightly. "Let's stay at home instead then," he said thickly, "and you can practise being a wife again as well as a mother."

His body weight had her pinned against the wall as he kissed her neck hotly and his hand kneaded her tender breast.

"Billy! Please! Not like this!"

But the more she protested the more excited he became. She twisted and turned in his grasp until eventually they both toppled to the floor, her arm and shoulder receiving a glancing blow from the side of the table.

And there, on the cold kitchen floor, their marital relationship was resumed.

Billy had gone off to the pub when his apologies for his behaviour were met by her silent disdain. Tears had trickled from her closed eyes, tickling her ears and soaking her dishevelled hair. She'd lain where he left her until the front door slammed, and then made her way upstairs.

She didn't see him again until he arrived home the next evening, when she placed his meal on the kitchen table.

"Is this it, now then? The silent treatment?" he demanded when no words were spoken.

Lydia pulled down the neck of her blouse, exposing her purplish-blue shoulder.

"Perhaps you'd like to talk about this?"

His face took on a bullish expression. "I didn't mean to hurt you – that was an accident. You just got me so wound up, I couldn't control myself!"

"Oh! So that makes it alright then! We used to *make love* – last night was bodily assault! What's got into you, Billy – apart from the booze?"

The baby woke up then, before he could answer. Billy picked her up, but not before he'd seen the involuntary movement from Lydia to stop him, even though it was hastily retracted.

"What's the matter?" he shouted, rocking the baby in his arms. "You don't think I would hurt her, do you? She's my little girl!"

"And I was supposed to be your princess! I don't know what to think any more."

The baby's wails made further talk impossible. Billy silently handed her to her mother and left the house again.

It was a relief when two days later he was posted abroad with his unit. Later, when news came of the evacuation of Dunkirk, Lydia tried desperately to quell the tiny thought that he might be one of those who didn't make it back.

While he was away she spent futile hours wheeling the pram through the streets, searching in vain for somewhere else she could live with the baby, although she had little idea of what they would live on once her savings were gone. She reflected now that there must have been a reason, deep down, why she had never mentioned her Post Office savings when she and Billy were setting up home.

During one of her walks she crossed Tower Bridge, desperate for a break from the dingy streets behind her. As she studied the adverts in a small post office window, the door opened and a young man came out. He stopped when he saw her.

"Lydia! How are you? Haven't seen you for ages!"

"Hello, Reggie."

Reggie had been a junior member of her father's law firm, an old tennis partner of hers, and one of those who had bored her with his careful, diffident politeness. Now, in his smart uniform, he seemed to have grown in stature and confidence.

"So! What brings you to this neck of the woods?" he asked. She could almost see the perplexed thoughts flitting across his brain as she stepped back and he took in the pram and the baby.

"I live in London, now," she told him. "As you can see – married, baby, the lot!"

"So this little one is yours?" He was having difficulty keeping the surprise out of his voice and didn't seem quite so assured after all.

"Yes. Didn't you know?"

"Oh! No – your family didn't… um… I mean we'd heard that you had… um… well, that's terrific! Wonderful!"

Wonderful could hardly have described the state of her marriage, but, as Reggie floundered in all the confusion of his class because, too late, he recalled that he *had* heard something, Lydia lifted her head. Her parents had clearly been too ashamed to mention that they had a grandchild, even to someone she'd known as well as Reggie.

"Yes. I married a guardsman and we're living over the river in Bermondsey – the Rotherhithe end. Do you know it?"

"Um… can't say that I do. Don't get much further than this part, I'm afraid – I'm organising things in the Tower at the moment." He nodded at the sprawling monument behind them. " Getting it ready for P.O.Ws, that sort of thing. Difficult times for everyone, aren't they?"

She nodded. "Especially for the poor lads who were stuck at Dunkirk. My husband's one of them, you know."

"Oh, gosh! How dreadful! Has he… I mean, is he… ?"

"He's fine as far as I know. I understand those caught up in it are being allowed some leave. He should be home any day now."

For the first time her heart didn't sink at this thought. There was still a remnant of pride that Billy had gone unflinchingly to serve his country without the cushion of a commission or friends in the right places. The Reggies of this world would probably stay in a safe desk job for however long this war lasted and then use their wartime titles afterwards to give them status. Just like her father had done following the last war.

"That's good! Excellent!" He began to rub his hands together in a hearty manner, *just* as Lydia had seen her father do when speaking to someone he considered his inferior but he wanted to seem jolly.

The place where they were standing was busy, and several times they were jostled by people who stepped past the pram.

"Well, I'd better cut along – right in the middle of something at the moment, I'm afraid," Reggie said.

Lydia decided to be more provocative. She rested her hand on his arm and gave him her most winning smile. "Oh! What a shame! I was hoping we could have a cup of tea together, catch up on everything."

"Love to, some other time. We'll probably bump into one another again – or… I say…" a frown creased his brow as the thought occurred to him, "shouldn't you be somewhere else? They believe the places along the river are going to take an awful hammering, you know, now Hitler's got the whole of France under his belt."

Lydia's smile grew steelier. "And where do you suggest, Reggie – Sevenoaks?"

"Well… um… not a bad idea, you know… I'm sure… well, I'd better be going. It's been good to see you, Lydia."

"And you."

He gave a half salute and began to walk away, then turned and took a few steps back.

"I'm sure… if you were really stuck… my people would help out…"

Lydia was equally sure that his people, close friends of her parents, would do nothing of the sort, but she appreciated the gesture.

"Thank you, Reggie," she said gravely. "Good-bye." And this time she began to walk away, pushing the pram resolutely as if she knew exactly where she was planning to go.

She wondered whether Reggie would even tell 'his people' about their encounter, but she thought a lot about it later. Declaring to him that she was a wife and mother made her question whether she was giving up too easily and she decided that she would try her hardest to make their marriage work when Billy came home. Perhaps once he'd rid himself of the frustration of not feeling part of the war, he would be calmer and more loving again.

The first night of his return was all that she could have hoped for. He exclaimed over how Grace had grown, and held Lydia close and told her how much he had missed her. "Showed your picture to all the men, whenever I got the chance. They were jealous of me – *me*! Ordinary Billy Dawson married to the most beautiful girl in the world!"

Their lovemaking had all the tenderness and excitement of their first months together and afterwards she took the opportunity to talk to him about making their marriage work, of how they could be truly happy together if they trusted and believed in one another.

It was a short-lived idyll. The next evening he met a few mates for a drink. A couple of hours later he pushed past the baby sleeping in her pram in the hallway and burst into the living room where Lydia was sitting by the fire listening to the wireless. In three strides he was across the room and dragging her from her chair.

"*Trust one another!*" he shouted, "*Believe in one another*! Is that the sort of bullshit you fill every man up with?"

Before she could get her balance he'd pushed her onto the floor and was undoing his belt.

"Billy! No! *Please!* What are you on about?"

"A man can't even go out for a drink with his mates without hearing his wife's been playing up to some other bloke the minute his back's turned!"

Before she could say anything more the belt was lashed across her body, making her scream in pain.

"It's not true! I swear! I don't even know what you're talking about!"

But Billy wasn't listening. The belt was raised again, his face twisted in anger.

"Bob Webster saw you! Walked past you on Tower Hill when you were offering to take some poncy officer to tea!"

The belt came down. "You're *my wife!*" And again. "Do you hear me? *My* wife!"

When it was over Billy sat in the chair, his head in his hands.

Slowly Lydia pulled herself up. She caught sight of herself in the mirror above the fireplace. Looking back at her was a bewildered person she didn't recognise. Her normally burnished chestnut hair was a tangled mess, her eyes large in a face pale from shock. A thick red weal was beginning to show where the edge of the belt had caught her across her neck.

"The only time I've walked to Tower Hill I bumped into an old friend who used to work with my father. I was telling him about you and our baby." Her voice was barely audible, but ended with a mocking note: "I was hoping he'd go back and tell my family how *proud* I was of you!"

She walked stiffly through to the kitchen where she poured

warm water into the sink, from the kettle standing on the hob, and slowly took off her clothes. Carefully she bathed and dried the stripes across her body before dressing again and, with all the dignity she could muster, walked back through the living room.

"You make me do it," Billy said, as she opened the door into the hall. His voice held a sob. "Lydia –"

She didn't stay to hear any more. She went into the hall, picked up the baby who was just beginning to stir, and carried her upstairs.

Next day, when she went out, Lydia wrapped a chiffon scarf around the mark on her neck. She was still in a daze. How could this be love? How could the man who had vowed to care for her for the rest of his life, and who was capable of such passion, turn on her like this?

The local greengrocer, who had teased about her eating up her greens when she was pregnant, served her as usual. "Thank you, Mrs. Dawson. Mind how you go."

A plump middle-aged woman, who had just been served by the young assistant, looked across. "Dawson? You the girl I've been hearing about who's married young Billy?"

"Yes. Yes, I am." Instinctively Lydia pulled the chiffon scarf closer round her neck, but not before the woman had seen what she was trying to conceal.

"Home on leave, is he?" she said with a grim smile.

Lydia followed her out of the shop. "What did you mean – about Billy being home on leave?" she asked.

This time the woman's smile held more pity. "I've seen you about before, just didn't know who you were. Used to look a bit proud, I always thought – but not now. And this is a bit of a give-away," she touched the ends of the scarf. "Not your usual style on a warm day, is it?"

She peered into the pram. "Pretty little thing – like her mother. Look, love, all the Dawson men lay about their women when they've had a few. Billy's Dad was the same – reckon it's the Irish in their blood. You won't change a Dawson."

The woman's words echoed in Lydia's brain as she pushed the pram home, slowly, because the tops of her legs ached. "*You won't change a Dawson.*"

Passing a telephone box she felt for some pennies in her pocket and retraced her steps. Her hand hovered over the receiver for a few seconds before she lifted it and put the pennies in the slot. It was some time before it was answered, minutes in which she nearly changed her mind. Then she heard the curt, familiar voice.

"Captain Grant."

She pressed the button and waited for the pennies to clang down through the call box.

"Ha-hallo, Father," she faltered. "It's me. Lydia."

There was silence for a moment before she heard a deep exhalation of breath. Then the line went dead.

She wasn't sure where she walked next, only that it took some time before she was back at the little house that no longer felt like home when it had Billy in it.

So that was that. She really was on her own now – except for Grace. Without Grace she could have just walked away without another thought. But where could she go with a young baby? She felt as trapped as she'd ever been in the cold, humourless home of her childhood.

The question whirled round and round her head for the next few days. She wasn't sure how long Billy's leave would last but each day her nerves were more and more tightly drawn. When he was in the house he tried to make light conversation as if nothing had happened, until her monosyllabic answers drove him into a sulky silence. When he went out in the evening she made sure she was in bed before he came home, but still she was fearful of the mood he might be in.

When she heard of the new wave of evacuation plans she made enquiries of how to register. In the end there was no chance. Billy's arrival home earlier than usual one night, and his discovery of the bag she had packed in readiness, led to the final assault on her body. This time he used his boots. Only the explosion stopped it.

9.

They were waiting for him, as he knew they would be, outside the boys' entrance. The girls' entrance was at the front of the school, but the boys had to go round the back. A convenient place to pick on someone because usually the teacher on duty was round the front, seeing all the children off the premises. The entrance to the boys' toilet was opposite, where a pungent smell of old urine constantly hovered, wafting into the cloakroom area when the wind was coming off the mountain.

He wished Kennie was with him, but Kennie was getting into too much trouble with the people he was billeted with because of torn shirts and dirty trousers, so Arfur had purposely not walked out of the classroom with him today. He sighed as the three Welsh boys surrounded him. Looking straight ahead, he did his best to push past them as the taunts began. If he could get as far as the corner of the building, where there was more chance of being seen, there might not be a fight today.

The familiar name-calling began. He tried to block it out, but they were each side of him, shouting in his ears. Some of the words were lost on him, spoken in thick Welsh accents, and so fast. *Little cockney bastard* came across loud and clear, though. That was from Cledwyn, the biggest of the lads and the clear ringleader.

Out of the corner of his eye he could see more lads waiting to see today's entertainment. Some of them were from his class, but they wouldn't come to his defence. Too lily-livered. They were the real bastards, he decided. And it was them who'd told these Welsh country bumpkins what some of the words they now enjoyed using actually meant. Well, none of them were going to get any sport this afternoon, not while these idiots just called him names. He could ignore that.

They were making it difficult to get past, circling round and jostling him with their thick shoulders. Sturdy little sods, these Welsh boys.

"*Got no Dad – never had – 'cos his Mam was really bad.*" Arfur's fists bunched as the chant picked up all round him, but he managed to keep his arms by his side. They were getting on dangerous ground now. They could say what they liked about him, but he couldn't let them bring his Mum into it.

"*Kissed the men – dropped her drawers – like the other London whores.*"

Right. That was it. Arfur's left arm shot out and cuffed Cledwyn across the side of his head.

"You leave me Mum alone – she's better than all your stupid Welsh mares!"

It was the signal for the three Welsh boys to jump on him and try to drag him to the ground. Not without difficulty though, as Arfur became a whirling dervish, throwing punches and kicking indiscriminately. He managed to see off the two smaller boys by pushing one into the other, catching them both off balance, so that it was just him and Cledwyn rolling around on the school yard, as was usually the case. He felt a button pop off his shirt as Cledwyn grabbed it in his meaty hand, but managed a satisfying elbow under the other boy's chin in return.

With a howl Cledwyn rolled over, flattening Arfur beneath him, his arm raised to hit him. But his hand was suddenly grabbed from above and twisted with some expertise as a female voice shouted at him:

"Get off him, Cledwyn Jones, you great oaf! Stop picking on him the whole time – he's done nothing to you, he hasn't!"

Surprise made the boy hesitate, allowing Arfur to push him away and scramble to his feet. Cledwyn made to grab him again, but only succeeded in pulling Rhian to the ground as she grimly held onto his hand.

"Teacher coming!" one of the other boys shouted, at which they all melted away. With a look of scorn and fury, Cledwyn followed them.

"Haven't finished with you!" he told Arfur as he moved away.

"Yeah –and I haven't finished with you, neither!" Arfur shouted after him, before rounding on Rhian. "And next time you keep out of it! I don't need some stupid girl to help me sort him out!"

"*Sort him out?* He was pulverising you! Anyway, I was fed

up with waiting for you round the other side." She picked up his school cap and tried not to wince at the graze on her knee from where she had fallen. "And our Mam's going to be furious when she sees the state you're in – again. Come on, let's get going or they'll be waiting for us further up the street."

They'd got as far as the little alleyway that separated the end of Victoria Terrace from Albert Terrace when Cledwyn appeared again – this time with just one mate, Meredith.

"Still got your nursemaid with you then?" Cledwyn jeered. "Walking you home, is she, in case you hurt yourself?"

Rhian opened her mouth to retaliate but was stopped by the look of fury on Arfur's face.

"You see?" he hissed. "This is why I told you to leave me alone."

He took a step towards the other boy. "Say that again Cledwyn, you clodhopper!"

R hys Llewellyn took the cup his wife had ready for him and eased himself down in the chair with a tired sigh.

"Sorry I was late for tea," he told her. "This good weather is making everything ready at once. The tractor and cutter are coming tomorrow, so I wanted to get all the other jobs done today. Where are the children?"

"I sent them out to play." Edyth sat down opposite him and surveyed her husband. His strong arms beneath his rolled-up shirtsleeves were tanned already, but his face looked grey with exhaustion and there were furrows on his face that she was sure weren't there last year. "Are they sending anyone to help you?"

He helped himself to a scone and thought how nice they used to be when they had currants in them.

"Nobody free," he said. "I've been lucky to get the equipment – everyone wants it while the weather is so good, and it might be thundering by next week. But there are no spare hands to be had – already allocated to another farm, or else they've gone and joined up."

He ran his hand over his face. "There's talk of getting more Land Army Girls by conscription, so that may help in the future. In the meantime, my lovely," he patted Edyth's knee, "we'd better pray that it doesn't rain for the next three days."

His wife bit her lip. "There's also another little problem, which I don't really want to bother you with, but you should know about it."

She picked up a grubby grey garment from the kitchen table, which turned out to be a torn shirt of Arthur's.

"Apparently he's been fighting a lot with the local boys – either in the school playground or on the way home. I think our Rhian pitched in as well to-day, the state she was in when they got back here."

"Have you talked to them about it?"

"I've tried. Arthur won't say anything at all and Rhian doesn't know what started it, but that Arthur and a couple of the local lads don't get on. And to cap it all, she and Arthur then started squabbling because he told her that he didn't need a girl to fight his battles for him!"

Rhys had always been happy to leave the girls' day-to-day upbringing to his wife, but they'd never had any trouble with the children before. Then again, he reflected, they'd never had a boy before.

"Do you want me to speak to him?"

Edyth nodded. "He clearly resents me taking the place of his mother, so I don't get much more out of him than rough politeness. But he might confide in you."

"Alright. But not tonight – I need to get back outside." He stood up and stretched his aching back. "If you can round up the children, you can send them to pick some strawberries – that should keep them quiet till suppertime."

Arfur had only tasted strawberries once. He'd never seen them in such quantities as this. When he was picking them with Rhian and Bronwen they competed to see who could find the largest one. Some of the ripest ones they ate as they went along, as they'd only be squashed in the basket, according to the girls. He felt happier than he had all day, and managed to push the thought of school out of his head for a couple of hours.

The feeling of dread was back next morning, though. Yesterday's scrap had been stopped when the mother of one of the other boys had waded in, pushing them apart and making some tart comments about the uncouth evacuees who had landed amongst them. He wanted to shout at her that it was her son who'd started it, but then he would have to have told her what her son had said, and he didn't want to do that.

But he knew that today the taunts would start again and he also knew that he wouldn't be able to stop himself from lashing out. He lagged behind Rhian until she told him irritably to get a move on or they'd both get a late mark.

"I don't feel very well," he said. "Got a belly ache. I think it was all those strawberries last night."

Rhian stopped and scrutinised his face. Her Mam always used the word "peaky" and perhaps that was how he was looking now. He certainly didn't seem himself.

"You'd better go back then and see our Mam. She'll give you some stuff. I'll tell them at school."

But he didn't return to the farmhouse. He wasn't sure how convincing an act he could put on under Auntie Edyth's concerned gaze, and she might want to tuck him up in bed, when it was far too nice a day for that.

He skulked around the perimeter of the farm and eventually settled himself under a low, wide tree by the side of the brook. There were no animals in this field, so he wasn't going to be disturbed. He could stay here all day – or at least until he was hungry – and no-one to bother him. He'd been telling them since he got here that he just wanted to be left alone. Mind you, he'd still rather have been on his own in London, or somewhere with a bit more to do than this place. Even in the village there wasn't much to do and if he went along the main street today someone was bound to poke their nose in and ask him why he wasn't at school.

At least being by the brook was a bit like being down by the canal at home where they all liked to play. Except there weren't such interesting things to be fished out of the brook.

A wave of homesickness swept over him. For the noise and the bustle; for bus conductors who made cheery remarks to old ladies huffing and puffing to get up onto the platform; for delivery boys who could ride their bikes along the street without holding the handlebars, while they whistled the latest popular songs; for the games of street football he played with his mates until the ball hit someone's window and then the woman in the house would come out and chase them away with her broom. And for the sight of his Mum, sitting on the end of the bed, getting ready to go out, hair in curlers and her mouth a wide slash of crimson which left a ring of colour on the fag hanging out of one side. Her face would be screwed up to avoid the smoke getting in her eyes as she ran a pair of silk stockings through her hands to check that they weren't damaged.

His own eyes felt as if they had smoke in them. He dashed his hands across them impatiently. No good sitting here feeling sorry for himself. What he needed was a plan. There must be a way to get back to London. If a train could get him here, then a train must be able to get him back. They'd laid on special buses to bring them from the station, so he wasn't sure where it was but he could find out. They hadn't been on the buses for long, so it couldn't be very far.

The water in the brook was rippling over smooth brown stones. Maybe later he'd have a little paddle. For now, he'd just lie back and make his plans in the early morning sunshine... at least that was better than sitting moping or being at school and facing the taunts for another day...

Bugger! No sooner had he settled himself down than he heard a great rumbling from the other side of the field. He rolled over onto his front but kept low amongst the tall grass so that he couldn't be seen. Uncle Rhys was manoeuvring a huge tractor through the gate, with a big piece of machinery tied to the back of it. Bringing up the rear was Auntie Edyth, dressed in breeches and carrying a large basket.

Arfur quickly shinned up the tree so that he could see without being seen. After a few moments the tractor began to rumble down the side of the field towards his tree, the machinery churning up the grassy stuff which Auntie Edyth gathered into bundles and stood them leaning drunkenly against each other.

To his dismay the tractor stopped when it reached his corner of the field and Uncle Rhys gazed up into the tree. Hell's bells and bloody Nora! He'd been seen! Now he'd be for it.

But Uncle Rhys simply called up, "Instead of skulking up there, you could come down and give us a hand – we've got all this field to do by dinnertime," as if it was the most natural thing in the world to find him up a tree instead of at school.

By the time Auntie Edyth reached them, Uncle Rhys had

explained what he wanted Arfur to do.

"I've found the extra pair of hands we needed," Uncle Rhys told her.

She shaded her eyes with her hand and stood looking at them both for a moment. "Do you think he's strong enough – to do it properly?"

"'Course I am!" Arfur declared. "Strong as a bloody ox!"

She frowned slightly at the language, but just nodded at her husband. "Alright then, we'll see what he can do."

Arfur joined her behind the machines, copying her until he could gather and stack the bundles in a rhythm that made it easier and less back-breaking. He couldn't understand these people! If he'd skived off school at home, his Mum would have given him a sharp clip round the ear. Put a lot of store by an education, his Mum did. "East End kids like you'll only get on in this world if you do proper learning," she'd told him. But this lot, who sounded a lot better educated than him or his Mum, let him skive off without saying a word!

They stopped by the gate half-way through the morning for a drink of cold tea from Auntie Edyth's basket, and again at dinner-time when she handed round chunks of bread and cheese and some strong pickled onions that made Arfur cough when the vinegar hit the back of his throat. Afterwards, Uncle Rhys said to his wife, "I think the lad and I can manage the next field on our own this afternoon – give you a chance to catch up on things in the house. What do you think, Arthur?"

Arfur nodded through his last mouthful of bread, so Auntie Edyth packed up the remnants of their picnic and headed back to the farmhouse.

"We need to cut the field the other side of the farm now," Uncle Rhys told him. "You'd better climb up here beside me – it'll be quicker than walking."

The tractor was too noisy for any conversation, but when they reached the next field and Arfur had jumped down to open and shut the gate to let the tractor through, Uncle Rhys switched the engine off and jumped down beside him. Leaning against the side of the tractor he took a packet of cigarettes from his pocket.

"Might as well have a few minutes before we start," he said. "Then we can get this field done in one go if you work as well as you did this morning."

He inhaled deeply on his cigarette and gazed around him. "Lived here all my life, I have. And I still think it's the best place in the world. My father had the farm before me and all I wanted to do was keep it going when he died."

He took another drag before turning to face Arfur, his eyes narrowed against the smoke, just as Arfur's Mum did when she had something important to say to him.

"It's not the same for you, though, is it?" he said. "I can see that. Must be like the back of beyond, coming here. We went to London once – for our honeymoon. Exciting sort of a place, isn't it? Must be hard, coming to the country like this."

Arfur had his head down, hands in pockets, his foot kicking ineffectually at the enormous tractor tyre. After a moment Uncle Rhys spoke again.

"Your Auntie tells me there's been some trouble at school. Want to tell me about it – sort of man-to-man? Because you can't stay home every day, you know. You'll have to go back there."

Arfur gave a few more kicks at the tyre, while Uncle Rhys waited, his face fixed on the horizon again.

"Some of the boys," Arfur said at last. "They've been saying things – about me not having a Dad. They've been calling me Mum names – worse swearing than me! – so every time they do that I fight them. They shouldn't say it – not about me Mum, 'specially when it makes all the other kids laugh."

Uncle Rhys nodded thoughtfully. "You know they'll keep saying it every time you let them see you getting angry, don't you? Every time they see they're getting a rise out of you?"

"But I can't let them get away with it – it's me Mum! It's not fair!" Arfur shouted.

"I know, I know. But it's you that'll be getting into trouble for fighting, not them, and that's not fair either. And if you get into trouble at school for it, they'll expect me to sort you out when you get home, so you'll get it in the neck twice."

"So what am I supposed to do?" He kicked moodily at the tyre again.

"Well… let me think. I reckon there's a couple of ways you could play this. You could decide who's the biggest, or the worst of them, and sort him out once and for all. Not scrapping in the playground, like a pack of dogs, but a proper fight, one to one – somewhere away from school. Only you'd have to be sure that you'd win, and –" he winked at Arfur "– you'd have to promise not to tell your Auntie that it was me who suggested it! Or… you divide and conquer."

"What's that supposed to mean?"

"Well, again, you decide who the ringleader is, the one who always starts it. Then you make friends with the others who always follow his lead. For instance, you could invite them back here after school or on a Saturday – there's not a lad I know who doesn't like messing about on a farm and in the water. Then Auntie Edyth'll give them a slap-up tea, and they'll never bully you again, 'cos they'll want to keep coming back. And the one who's the ringleader will soon want to be your friend too, when all the others tell him what a great time they've had. It'll be up to you, then, if you decide to let him join in."

He let these ideas sink in for a minute or two. Then went on, "Of course, the manly thing to do would be to let him join in, because it makes you the better person. Harbouring a grudge never gets you anywhere."

"And Auntie Edyth wouldn't mind? Giving everyone some food?"

Uncle Rhys shrugged. "Well, I don't suppose you'll be bringing the whole class with you – and anyway, that would still be easier than her having to find more clothes for you all the time because your shirts are in shreds!"

Arfur frowned. In London they hardly ever went into each other's houses. Most of the mothers just wanted you out from under their feet, not bringing mess into the house, and he hardly ever took anyone back to the flat because… well, if he was truthful, there wasn't much to take them back to. It didn't matter for him and his Mum 'cos they understood each other, but there had never seemed any point in taking any of his friends home, where maybe they'd meet one of his strange assortment of 'uncles', or his Mum might be wandering about in her underwear.

"Come on," Uncle Rhys broke into his thoughts. "We'd better get a move on or this field won't be finished. You can think about what I've said while we work."

He stubbed out his cigarette on the wheel hub before swinging back up onto the tractor. Arfur squinted up at him. "Would I be able to bring some of my friends from home here, as well? The ones who are staying in the village. Show them what it's like to live on a farm?"

"Of course you can," Uncle Rhys said, deciding that he'd worry about squaring it with Edyth later on. "Ready, lad?"

Arfur nodded and set to, walking behind the tractor. It was harder without Auntie Edyth to help him but Uncle Rhys made no comment about their slower progress when they stopped for a drink. By the time they finished the field, Rhian was back from school and walking across the field towards them.

"I thought you said you were ill!" she said crossly to Arfur.

"I started feeling better after a bit, and yer Dad needed a hand."

"Well Mam says tea's ready, so you'd better hurry up and get into the kitchen," she told them both, before turning on her heel.

"Don't you want a lift on the tractor?" her father called after her.

"No thank you, I'm fine," she said with another flounce.

Uncle Rhys and Arfur shared a look which said, "Women!" before climbing onto the tractor in companionable silence.

What did you say it was called?" Arfur asked as they were washing their hands in the scullery. "Something about conkers?"

"Conquer. Divide and conquer. It means overcome your enemy."

"That's it. Well, I reckon I'll give it a try – it might work."

Uncle Rhys nodded. "Psychology, see? You can outwit them much better by using your brain and a bit of psychology – works on the animals on the farm, too." He leaned a bit nearer to Arfur and there was a chuckle in his voice. "And it works on women – especially when you're surrounded by them like we are in this house!"

"Yeah, well I'll try it this once," Arfur said. And then, to Uncle Rhys's back as he made his way into the kitchen, "but if it doesn't work, Cledwyn Jones'll get a good bloody thump!"

Rhian glowered at him all through tea and spoke only to make barbed comments about what he'd missed at school. But Arfur didn't care. There was something very satisfying about tucking into his tea after a hard day's work, and hearing Uncle Rhys say "we" every time he mentioned anything about the day.

"I think I'm going to need a hand again tomorrow, so the lad here'll have to stay off again," Uncle Rhys said as he got up from the table to start the milking. "Just for one day, mind, then it's back to school."

"Oh! That's not fair! I could –" Rhian started to say, but stopped as she got a hefty kick under the table from Bronwen and a 'look' from her mother.

She was still glowering at him when they were sent out to play. "There's nothing clever about helping with the grass-cutting, you know – I've done it lots of times."

Arfur was about to make a simmering retort when he remembered Uncle Rhys's words. What did he call it? Psychology? And it was supposed to work on women. Looking at Rhian's angry little face he decided that he didn't want to sort out the lads at school only to make an enemy of her instead, even if she was just a girl.

"Yeah, well, I'm just learning aren't I? And today wasn't a treat, you know – more of a punishment if you ask me, 'cos they found me skiving off school. And I still can't do stuff like milking those cows, can I?... P'rhaps you could show me some time."

It worked! It actually bloody worked! Rhian's face started to clear and there was even a hint of a smile. "Huh! You'll have to stop being scared of them first... but I could show you if you like."

At the end of the next day, Uncle Rhys gave a nod of satisfaction. "You've done well, lad. And seeing as you've done the work of a man about the place, I reckon I need to pay you. A shilling a day I'll give you, and there'll be more later on when we're harvesting."

Arfur's face glowed. Two shillings! He'd never had that much in one go. He could put it away ready for his fare back to London!

"There's just one thing, though," Uncle Rhys went on. "When I'm employing men on my farm, I expect them to mind their language, especially when there's women and girls around. So the pay will be docked – tuppence a time – if I hear any swearing." He paused. "Is that a deal?"

He held out his hand to Arfur, to show there was no undue harshness in his words. After a second Arfur took it. It would be blo… It would be hard, but he reckoned he could do it.

"Deal," he said.

10.

Occasionally Lydia would wonder what Billy would think if he could see her now, busy running this quite large house with very little regard to her appearance. During her marriage she had kept her hair in loose bouncing waves around her shoulders, because that was how Billy liked it, but now, going about the daily chores, it was more often than not tied up in an old scarf, whilst round her slender body was wrapped an overall belonging to Miss Williams. Who must, Lydia thought each morning when she tied the apron strings twice round her waist, be a lady of considerable dimensions.

Once the pain in her ribs had eased it hadn't taken her long to fall into a firm routine during the week, dominated by surgery hours and Dr. Eliot's comings and goings. Rising early, she would have a line of washing out on a fine day, before pushing the baby down to the village shops almost as soon as they were opened.

Preparing meals for the doctor was also no hardship as he didn't seem to mind what she put in front of him. Luckily, domestic science had figured largely at school, which Lydia had enjoyed in a detached, scientific sort of way. And once she'd had time to root around in Miss Williams' domain, she'd found a cupboard at the back of the larder which was brimful of tinned food, and quite a few packets of sugar and tea. Miss Williams had clearly been an inveterate hoarder, even before the war, as some of the aged tins testified, but Lydia silently thanked the woman for her presence of mind. The contents of the cupboard might have to last a long time, but she would enjoy the challenge of eking them out as much as she could.

The daily walk to the village was a delight and Grace didn't seem to mind the bumpiness of the path through Amos's field, where the sun glinted through the trees and bounced off the whitewashed walls of the cottages at the far end. When they first arrived there had been drifts of golden buttercups amongst the tall russet-tipped grasses, and snatches of purple clover, with dense clumps of dock leaves dotted around like miniature trees. Around the edge could be seen bright red poppies amongst the white heads of cow parsley peeping out from under unruly hawthorn hedges where blackbirds darted in and out, whilst in the taller oak trees song thrushes sang their hearts out. Sometimes Lydia would catch sight of a rabbit disappearing over the far rise, and along the shadier parts of the path the air would be sharp and tangy, before the sun had warmed it, with an elusive scent from some of the trees that made Lydia pause to try to identify it before the sensation was lost.

Other mothers and women with whom she passed the time of day in the shops warned her that this warm weather wouldn't last. "We never get the fine weather for this long in the valley. It'll be nothing but rain once the school has broken up for the summer," they prophesied. But for the moment Lydia drank in every scent, colour and sound. Years later, when she looked back on this part of her life, she would see it in bands of colour; red and orange for the months when Billy had swept her off her feet, grey and drab for the months of her marriage and life in Bermondsey, green and golden for her time in Penfawr, no matter that the winter months turned out to be as depressing as any elsewhere.

Returning to the house she would don the headscarf and voluminous apron and set to whilst Dr. Eliot was in his surgery. Often he would come through for his elevenses to find her balanced precariously on tiptoe on a kitchen chair, running a duster over the top of the kitchen dresser, or cleaning a window with old newspaper. Sometimes she would turn and find that he had been standing there for she knew not how long, a smile twitching at the corners of his mouth at the spectacle of his housekeeper singing nonsense songs, slightly off-key, to the baby gurgling in her basket. At others he would appear pre-occupied and hurried, and not a little irritated if his tea wasn't ready to be swallowed quickly so that he could set off on his house calls.

But Lydia soon learned from Rita that his irritability usually stemmed from frustration when a difficult case refused to respond to treatment, or when he had to refer a patient for tests at the hospital in Swansea because he suspected a serious ailment.

"Almost takes it personally, he does, when he sees someone who doesn't respond to his magic touch," Rita told Lydia one morning when the doctor had rushed off with barely a word to her. "He got a call during surgery that someone out at one of the farms has been taken poorly, and he's been trying to get this man to see a specialist for months. Then, of course, when he was itching to get out there, it seemed that every patient in the surgery decided to take an age telling him what was the matter."

"I know the signs now," she went on, picking up the baby for a quick cuddle before she went on her way. "He'll come and ask me to make up a bottle of pepto-bismuth or whatever, with his voice ever so courteous, but I can see by the look in his eyes that something else is bothering him and he's desperate to get away."

Lydia remembered the bleakness of his face that first morning when he told her that the patient he'd been called out to in the night had died, and she wondered if being a doctor was something you could do for the whole of your life if you took it that much to heart.

Sometimes on a fine evening, with Grace now settling early and sleeping right through till early morning, Lydia joined the doctor out in the garden after surgery, helping him to weed the vegetable plot or water the runner beans which were growing healthily. Very often they worked in companionable silence, but then would stop for a drink, sitting on the ramshackle bench in the corner of the garden from where there was the same view of the valley as from the bedrooms. If they stayed until dusk was falling they would catch sight of bats swooping noiselessly and so swiftly that it was difficult to follow their progress.

"This is the first time I've tried my hand at gardening," he told her during one such pause in their labours. "I had no idea it could be so rewarding."

"You seem to know what you're doing – did you have to look it up in a book?"

He gave a little chuckle, which cleared the intense look from his eyes and made him look younger. "Better than that. I just let it be known to some of my patients that I wanted to start 'digging for victory'. Then there were plenty of people ready to give me advice – apparently the subject of the 'doctor's garden' has been the cause of some debate in the Prince of Wales. I invited a few old-timers to come along and tell me what I should be doing, but I had to stop that because they nearly came to blows as to which variety of cabbage I should try, or what I should do if I got carrot fly!"

"So presumably you took the best bits of advice from everyone, thanked them all profusely, and then got on with it yourself," she suggested, smiling with him.

"That's about it, yes."

She nodded her approval as she surveyed his handiwork. "Not all advice is good advice. That's what I would have done too. Listened and then done it my way."

"I can imagine you would," he said.

She turned her head back quickly at the dryness of his tone.

"What do you mean by that?" she asked with asperity.

"Oh, it wasn't a criticism," he assured her under the ferocity of her gaze. "It's just that you have an air of self-assurance, which didn't desert you when the Owain Owens turned up with you that evening, and – well – you've already made the job your own.

"And," he went on, "most young women who lose their husbands and their homes would return to their families."

"I've told you already – it's complicated," she said, her voice rising defensively, then she relaxed her shoulders and sighed. She owed him some sort of explanation.

"My father objected to my marriage. He was a Captain in the last war, and is very keen on 'keeping up standards', so a working class son-in-law from the East End was not what he had in mind for his only daughter."

"But what about now – when you're on your own. Wouldn't he…?"

"I called – when… before I came here. He put the phone down when he heard my voice. And I found out from someone else that he hadn't acknowledged to anyone that he has a grandchild."

"And your mother?"

"She died when I was ten – my father married again a couple of years later, and although she's not the wicked stepmother of fairy stories, we haven't been close and she's completely under my father's thumb."

"I see."

They were quiet for a few seconds then both began to talk at once.

"I'm sorry –"

"So you're stuck –"

Lydia gave a tight smile. "You first."

"I was going to say I'm sorry, I shouldn't have pried – but you must admit your arrival here was somewhat shrouded in mystery."

"And I was going to say that you're stuck with me, I'm afraid – unless you're finding it all too much, and I'll ask Mr. Owain Owen to place me somewhere else."

Her voice held the formal quality that she had detected so often in his – it must be catching, she thought wryly.

"I'm very pleased with your work here. You're very welcome to stay until it's safe for you to return," he said almost as formally, inclining his head.

She wondered if she should tell him more. To offload the exact circumstances of her marriage and her arrival here would be a certain relief. But she hesitated. What if he told her she should try to find out if Billy was alive? Or sacked her for telling lies in the first place? Or told the authorities and they would tell Billy where she was? She couldn't risk it, for herself or Grace.

"It might be nice to try to get the rest of the garden into better shape," she said instead, looking around again and deliberately making her voice light. So many conversations with this man began easily and then became edgy.

"That would be a good idea – if you could tell me which are weeds and which are flowers," he answered in similar vein.

She thought of the lush lawns and neat flower beds at home, maintained with almost military precision by her father and the gardener who had once been his batman. And of the flower arranging she had learned at the genteel girls' school, together, thankfully, with household management which at least had stood her in good stead for her present situation.

"Now that's where I can definitely teach you a thing or two," she told him with a laugh to banish the memories of interminable dinner table conversation which had centred on the state of the roses or the delphiniums or whatever. "Did you learn nothing else as you grew up except how to be doctor?"

"Guilty as charged," he confessed with a smile, as relieved as she to have moved onto safer territory. "I grew up in London, did my training in Edinburgh, and then returned to London to set up a practice, so this is the first time I have lived anywhere that has a garden. I'd be very pleased for you to supervise the sorting out of the flower beds."

Although there were moments of restraint, it was easier to talk in the garden than in the house. There, the distinction between employer and housekeeper was more marked and Lydia found it harder to cross the divide, especially once she was well again and the intimacy of the doctor/patient relationship ended.

She usually prepared a late supper, as there was only time for a small afternoon tea before evening surgery. Sometimes Dr. Eliot sat in the kitchen to have his supper with her, shunning her offer of setting his meal in the dining room, and at others he would invite her to join him in the sitting room, with trays on their knees, so that they could listen to the latest news of the war on the wireless.

"I'm sorry there's no wireless for you to listen to in the kitchen," he said. "Miss Williams would never have it – she claimed it stopped one working hard if turned on during the day, and during mealtimes it interrupted one's digestion." He gave a small smile, "I don't think that's been medically proven, but I always found it didn't do to contradict. She didn't read the news-papers either. I think she preferred to hear snippets of news in the village, which gave her an interesting but slightly skewed version of world events!"

Often he would ask her whether she would like to listen to a play or a music programme, but Lydia usually made her excuses and returned to the kitchen.

It took her a while to realise why she felt uncomfortable in the sitting room that she was trying so hard to make more homely. One evening, after a companionable supper when they had listened to the wireless and debated the state of the war and Mr. Churchill's leadership, it dawned on her that this is what she had envisaged marriage should be like. Their talk had been a lively exchange of views and he had listened to what she had to say.

Perhaps, for once, she would have to concede that her father had been right. Her marriage to Billy would never have been this stimulating intellectually. Oh, Billy knew exactly what was going on in the war and had definite views about it, but these had always been presented more in the style of a rant for which he wanted her support, than a mutual airing of opinions. In that way he hadn't been so very different from her father, though each would have been horrified at the thought. Lydia's father liked to think himself a liberal, but in fact he still expected the women in his household to agree with his staunchly held views on everything from the government of the day to the state of the Empire.

Now, watching Dr. Eliot, still in his shirtsleeves, picking up the newspaper and scanning its contents, and politely thanking her for the cup of abominable coffee made with chicory essence, was too much for her. She escaped to the kitchen and made herself busy so that she needn't think of what the future held for her and Grace or berate herself for the foolishness that had brought her to this situation.

I've got Grace, she told herself fiercely, *and she's the most wonderful thing in my life, so I shouldn't have any regrets.*

She spread some old blankets and a sheet over the kitchen table, plugged the small iron into the light fitting overhead, because that was the only way it would reach, and took out her feelings on the ironing. She had to sprinkle it with water first, because it had become stiff as a board in the sunshine, and then use all her weight on the iron to make an impression, but she welcomed the effort involved. She wanted to feel exhausted when she finally flopped into bed so that she wouldn't have to think about Billy, or what her life had become, or the man sitting reading quietly in the room across the hall...

During the afternoon she often took Grace for a walk along the country lanes beyond the village. One day, about a month after her arrival, she came across a woman perched on a wooden stepladder, energetically clipping a hedge each side of a farm entrance.

"Ah!" the woman exclaimed as Lydia came towards her, "so the pram did come in useful after all. It had been in one of our outhouses for so long, I wasn't sure if it would be any good."

"The pram was yours? Oh, I'm so glad I've met you so that I can thank you for it – it's been a godsend."

"It was just lucky, really, that I happened to be in the village when Dr. Eliot was asking around." She climbed down the ladder. "So – let's have a look at this baby I've been hearing so much about. Oh! She's beautiful!"

"She's doing very well," Lydia said. "I think all this country air agrees with her." Not to mention a mother who is less anxious, she thought.

"That's good." The woman gave her a keen look. "It can't have been easy for either of you – given the circumstances... I heard about it in the village."

Most of the time Lydia was very guarded with people who referred to her widowhood and offered sympathy. Usually she gave a non-committal reply which she hoped conveyed that she would rather not talk about it. But there was something straight-forward about this woman that made her wish she could be more honest.

"We weren't together very long before war broke out, so, frankly, if it wasn't for Grace it would sometimes be hard to think that I ever was married," she said after a pause – which, in essence, was more or less the truth.

"Poor you. Look, I'm just about finished here," the woman was saying now. "The lorry drivers from the War-Ag were complain-ing that they couldn't see the entrance to the farm easily enough – you'd think they'd have other things to worry about, wouldn't you? Anyway, a nice cup of tea is next on the list before the chil-dren arrive home from school. Would you like to join me?"

She rubbed her hands down the sides of her breeches before offering one to Lydia. "I'm Edyth Llewellyn, by the way. A bit of a mouthful, so please call me Edyth."

"I'm Lydia and yes, I'd love a cup of tea."

When she first arrived, Lydia had sworn to keep herself to herself so that she wouldn't have to field questions about her past. But, except for her brief exchanges with Rita as she bustled in and out, there were many hours in the day when she only had the baby for company. Too many hours for thoughts she didn't want to crowd her head. And when she saw the friendliness and camaraderie of the women in the village it was very hard to keep herself aloof.

Edyth led her down a long narrow drive which opened out to a circular area in front of the farmhouse.

"Let's wheel the pram around to the back, then we can sit and have a cuppa in my favourite place," she told Lydia.

Edyth's favourite place turned out to be a rose garden, set

back through a little wicket gate to the rear of the house. Two rickety garden chairs and a battered wrought iron table were set in front of an arch of rambling roses.

"This is the one place the children aren't allowed to roam," she explained as Lydia gazed around her in admiration. "And as my husband Rhys is usually too busy to sit for very long, it's become my own little haven.

"Mind you," she laughed, "I'm usually not here for many minutes before I have to pick up a pair of secateurs and start some dead-heading. But at least roses don't need too much fuss and will just get on with it. I'm really too impatient to be a farmer's wife!"

"How many children do you have?" Lydia asked as they sipped their tea.

"Two girls – Bronwen who's going on fourteen and Rhian who's nine. And we have an evacuee staying with us – Arthur, who's a year older than Rhian."

"I've seen some very harassed mothers in the village trying to cope with the sudden influx," Lydia said with a smile. "How are you managing with Arthur?"

Edyth grimaced. "Some days better than others. He's had a rough time of it, poor lad. His mother's in hospital, broke her leg in the black-out by all accounts, and he doesn't seem to have anyone else. He absolutely hated being here at first, but I think he's starting to get used to us. How about you and our enigmatic Dr. Eliot?"

"Well, I think he absolutely hated us being here at first, but I think he's starting to get used to us!" Both women laughed.

"Why enigmatic?" Lydia asked.

"Oh, you know, he's such a good doctor, very kind and considerate to his patients and all that, but he never gives much away. Up in that house with a gloomy old housekeeper – oh! I mean the last one, not you! – it doesn't seem right for a young man. Never see him out and about socialising."

Lydia nodded. "I know what you mean, but I think he's just the quiet type. He seems very happy with his own company, reads a lot, that sort of thing. Grace thinks he's wonderful, though – she literally drools every time he speaks to her!"

Edyth put her head on one side. "And what about you?"

"No," said Lydia, "I definitely don't drool when he speaks to me!"

Edyth laughed again. "I meant, are you happy with your own company?"

Lydia considered for a moment. "On the whole, yes, I think I am. To be honest, I've been so busy proving that I can be an efficient housekeeper and a good mother that I've not had much time to feel lonely. It is nice to have a chat with someone else, though."

"Well, now you know where we are, you must come again – I usually try to have a bit of time to myself in the afternoon."

"I'd like that," Lydia said, as a clock began to strike somewhere deep inside the house. "But I'd better be going now – the doctor has a quick, early tea because of evening surgery."

Walking home with a box of eggs and a small crock of cream that Edyth had insisted she took, Lydia's spirits soared. She hadn't known, when she boarded the train, that she would end up surrounded by such good-hearted people – apart from some of Mrs. Owain Owen's friends, but then there were people like that everywhere. The hardships of war-time London and her life with Billy seemed a million miles away. Goodness knows what would happen to them both when the war ended, but that didn't seem to be going to happen soon, and the outcome might still be grim, but here one could almost pretend it wasn't really happening. Just like one could pretend that one had never been married.

Maybe they could stay here anyway, war or no war. Maybe if Miss Williams suddenly wanted to come back, Dr. Eliot wouldn't let her because Lydia was doing such a good job.

It would be a lovely place for Grace to grow up. And as for herself, she was happy simply to be Grace's mother. So even if she never knew what happened to Billy it wouldn't matter. It would only be important if she wanted to marry again, and she had already vowed that her short time with Billy had been all the marriage she ever wanted to experience.

"I think we're going to be alright, just the two of us," she told the sleeping baby. "I think it will all turn out for the best."

11.

Bedrooms today, it is – before you go tearing off to play,"
Mrs. Preece announced the minute Amy was in through
the back door.

"But we changed the beds on Monday," she answered. Before
school, which meant she'd had to get up extra early, so that Mrs.
Preece could 'get cracking' before breakfast. Which also meant
that Monday morning breakfast had been a slice of bread with a
scrape of marge.

"So we did. Monday washing, Tuesday ironing, and Wednesday I turn out the bedrooms. You've been here long enough now
– might as well earn your keep. Come with me."

Amy followed her up the stairs into Mrs. Preece's bedroom,
where she had never been before. The room was almost taken up
by a high, iron bedstead which sagged deeply in the middle. It
looked as if you needed to take a run from the landing to propel
yourself into it. Mrs. Preece wasn't an awful lot taller than Amy –
how on earth did she manage?

Above the bed was a large picture of a man, set in a heavy
wooden frame. He looked almost as terrible as Mr. Preece, except
it wasn't him. Perhaps it was God, Amy thought, although he
looked far more forbidding than in her Bible story book at home.

She realised Mrs. Preece was talking to her and waving a short
brush in the air.

"I want you to clean under the beds for me. Takes my breath
it does, to get down there, so you can do it while you're staying.
Here you are."

She thrust the brush into Amy's hands and gave her a little
push. "Come on, I haven't got all day."

Amy got down on the floor and half slithered under the bed.
The lino was cold on her bare legs, and it was very dark. The
bed sagged so much that there was barely room for her to slide
underneath.

"I can't see very well," she called, fighting the urge to slide back into the room as the dark, confined space threatened to overwhelm her. Mrs. Preece would only shout at her and make her do it again, so it was better to get it over with.

"Just move the brush in steady strokes from the top to the bottom," Mrs. Preece's muffled voice floated down to her. She quickly did as she was told, not looking at the balls of fluff she collected in case they contained spiders. What if they didn't, because the spiders had escaped, but might be just about to crawl over her legs… or her back… or her face… !

She could bear it no longer. There was dust in her mouth and in her nose. It was choking her. She shot out backwards from under the bed, catching Mrs. Preece on the ankle with the brush.

"Mind what you're doing, you silly girl!" Mrs. Preece hissed at her. She grabbed the brush from Amy and swept up the debris into a metal dustpan.

"I couldn't get my breath," Amy gasped, sitting up against the side of the bed. "It was very squashed under there."

"Nonsense – and you just a slip of a little girl. Come along, there's Our Edwin's and yours to do yet."

Amy followed her into the two other bedrooms, neither of which was so bad because the beds were smaller.

"There now," Mrs. Preece said when they'd finished, satisfaction with a job done giving a hint of kindness to her tone. "Not been touched for a while those floors haven't. Couldn't get down there myself with my back. But they won't be so bad next week."

So cleaning under the beds became Amy's Wednesday job, just as Monday morning was stripping the beds, Monday evening was helping to fold the sheets ready for ironing and Tuesday evening was helping to put all the linen away. Thursday was shoe-cleaning, Friday was sweeping the back yard and Saturday was doing whatever odd jobs Mrs. Preece asked of her so that they could all rest on Sunday.

Amy didn't really mind the odd jobs because she then would be sent out to play, away from Mrs. Preece's pinched gaze. She knew that some of the evacuee children had a much harder life in the smaller cottages beyond the village, where there still wasn't an inside tap, so water had to be fetched in buckets. And after the first week, when she was sent upstairs on her own, she didn't crawl right under Mrs. Preece's enormous bed, but lay down at each side and swept as far as she could reach.

But the main difference to her life was the ally she now had in Edwin. She still found his stare unnerving but at least when she looked up and met his eyes there was a hint of warmth in them that hadn't been there at first.

He had persuaded his mother to let Amy have a night light, over-riding her huffing and puffing that it shouldn't be necessary for a girl the age she was.

"We're not having the electric light on all night just because she has some silly notion about the dark – she should get used to it like everyone else!" she declared.

So Edwin set up a small, floating candle in a saucer of water, with a special shade around it so that it gave just enough glow, from the floor by her bed, for her to feel safe and not scared.

"I'll fix it up every evening and blow it out once she's asleep," he told his mother.

"There now!" Mrs. Preece said to Amy. "Aren't you a lucky girl to have Ouredwin to look after you like this? Kindness itself, that boy is!"

Which meant that Edwin came into her room every night once she was in bed, and, on the nights his mother was out at the chapel, he would stay and talk to her, until she felt so drowsy she was ready for sleep.

"There's nothing to be afraid of," he would tell her. "I'm going to look after you and we're going to be special friends, just you and me. And all night I'm just next door, so I'm listening out for you all the time."

His voice, monotonous and slightly adenoidal by day, took on a hypnotic quality at night, so that Amy felt safe and reassured that he would take care of her. When she wrote her weekly letter to her mother she told her that she was getting on much better, and, although she was missing her and Gran very much, she had plenty of friends, including Edwin.

Her promised visit to Rhian's farm eventually materialised. It seemed that Rhian's parents didn't mind how many children swarmed across the fields or played in the brook as long as they didn't hurt the animals and always closed the gates. Saturdays were the best days, when, after a morning of chores and dinner as soon as Edwin came in from work, she would be allowed to make her way to the farm and stay there until bedtime if she wanted, as long as she didn't expect any tea when she got back to the house.

They quickly formed a little gang – her, Rhian, Arfur, Kennie (who was from Bermondsey too), and Cledwyn and Meredith who lived in the village. Cledwyn and Arfur had done nothing but fight at first, scrapping almost every day in the school playground and getting into awful trouble for it, but they seemed to be good friends now. They still argued sometimes, and that would often lead to a wrestling match, but all in all it seemed good-natured.

Maisie joined them occasionally, but she didn't really like the rough and tumble of their play or the way everything they did seemed to involve getting in a mess. So Amy was very pleased that Rhian had become her friend and that Arfur was kind to her.

"Don't let on, but I was scared of some of the animals as well, when I first came here," he confided when she was reluctant to walk past the cows. "But there's nothing to be frightened of, honest – just stay with me and Rhian." He didn't mention that the cockerel still gave him the evil eye.

Rhian's Mam was nice, in a brisk, energetic sort of way. She was quite bossy when they all piled into the farmhouse, making them wash their hands in the scullery and take their dirty shoes off, but that was fair enough. She would also ask them what they had been up to, in an interested way, just like Amy's Mum would have done, and smiled her wide smile and made sure Amy and Kennie were fairly clean and tidy before they went back to their billets. Amy thought Arfur was very lucky to have landed where he had. She could imagine Rhian's Mam tucking her up in bed at night, perhaps with a goodnight kiss, rather than the "Time you were going up – make sure you put your clothes tidy before you get into bed," which was all she got from Mrs. Preece.

There always seemed to be home-baked bread on the go at the farm, and something strange called 'laver bread', which Rhian swore was made with seaweed, but Amy and Arfur weren't sure she was telling the truth. It tasted alright, though, and filled them up so it didn't matter if Amy missed her tea.

On fine days they ate sitting on a bench outside the back door. Rhian told them that her Mam used to make great lemonade but couldn't now because of the sugar ration, so they made do with cups of water.

But even that tasted different, Amy thought, and couldn't decide whether it was because they were sitting in the sunshine, or because it came from something called a 'boring hole' on the farm. Sometimes, she decided, it was possible to be happy even when you were a long way from home and you hadn't seen your family for ages.

One Sunday night Edwin sat by her bed as usual but this time he held her hand and began stroking the back of it.

"Talking to a butty of mine, I was yesterday," he told her. "He was telling me all about his little sister. And I was thinking how much I'd like a little sister.

"You could be my little sister," he went on. "I'd like that. Would you like that, Amy? Would you like me to be your big brother?"

Amy nodded, thinking that really she would like to go to sleep. But Edwin was very kind to sit with her, and she wouldn't want to disappoint him. "I've always wanted a brother or sister."

"There you are then," he said. "We can pretend we're brother and sister. And my butty, he was telling me that he keeps lots of secrets with his little sister. So we'll keep secrets together, is it? Just the two of us?"

"Mmm," Amy murmured. "I'm tired, Edwin."

"Well you go to sleep then, and I'll watch over you." He leaned forward and kissed her on the forehead. His kiss was as moist as his eyes always looked. "Goodnight little sister."

The weather broke as the women in the village had predicted, just before the children were due to break up from school. The day had been hot and heavy, with barely a touch of breeze, and as the afternoon stretched into evening, the sky grew dark.

Dr. Eliot sat in his surgery, even though there were no more patients. There was a restlessness in him which he was doing his best to quell. It had nothing to do with the impending storm, he knew that.

For the love of Mike! He threw down his pen, causing it to splatter ink on the blotter that sat squarely in the middle of his desk. He had been attempting to write to his parents, which he did erratically, usually filling two sheets of paper with banalities and generalities because they were not a family who ever spoke of what was in their hearts.

He knew what he would have liked to write, had his parents been the types who invited confidences.

I have a new housekeeper, he would have put, *a young woman who is an intriguing mix of stubborn independence and artless vulnerability. I don't really know where she comes from or what her true story is, and I've only known her for a few weeks, but she fills my waking hours and snatches my sleep from me. She's not beautiful, but she has the most compelling eyes I have ever seen, which fill with such warmth when she looks at her baby – did I mention that there is the added complication of a baby? – that I long for her to look at me in the same way, but I can't handle it if there's any chance that she's going to.*

He put his head in his hands and tried to imagine his parents' reaction if he sent them a letter like that. They weren't bad parents, quite the opposite in fact. Had wanted the best for their son and their daughter and had striven to provide it. Their daughter had married well and gone to live in South Africa, and their son – well, their son had always felt the weight of their expectations upon him because he had turned out to be naturally bright. Their approval when he did well at school had been quiet but he hadn't been immune to the pride in their voices when they assured each other that he was 'going to make the best of himself' and there-fore the sacrifices they made in their everyday life were worth it.

Neither parent wore their heart on their sleeve, but simply 'got on with it', and, whilst they knew that their son was delving into the mysteries of the human body during his medical studies, neither cared to consider too deeply what that entailed. Advice to their children on the intimate side of life had consisted of his mother telling her daughter to always 'keep herself nice' until she was married, and his father gruffly warning him to 'keep himself clean' and treat women respectfully. Emotions were never discussed, and he had never seen his mother weep or his father lose his temper.

They had retired to his mother's native Scotland, where she took quiet satisfaction in referring to 'my son, the doctor'. She'd liked it even more when she had been able to say, "My son, the *London* doctor," and they had been rather mystified over his sudden retreat to a backwater in Wales. But then, he reflected, they hadn't known Jessica.

Jessica had burst into his life when he was just making the transition from hospital life to being a family doctor. He'd been lucky enough to acquire a practice following the death of the incumbent doctor, using money which his prudent parents had invested wisely on his behalf for just such an opportunity.

Brimming with excitement and enthusiasm, and a determination to be the best doctor in London, meeting Jess seemed to be a rightful part of the jigsaw.

"Oh, I haven't got anything wrong with me," she told him when she presented herself at his evening surgery. "It's just that I heard there was a dashing young doctor who has taken over here, so I wanted to come and see for myself." She held out her hand as she slid into the patient's chair. "Jessica Golding.

"I'm hoping," she went on in confidential tones, leaning forward so that her perfume wafted across the desk, "that you're going to be tall enough so that I can wear high heels when I'm out with you, but of course, unless you stand up I'm not going to find out, am I?"

It was impossible not to smile back at her engaging, pixie-shaped face, even while he was trying to think of some witty reply, because somehow he already knew that she would expect it.

On this occasion she saved him the bother, though, by continuing to talk without pause. "I'm five feet nine, you see, which means I have deliciously long legs but also means that with a hat and heels I need an escort who is at least six feet tall, especially if I wear one of those Wallis Simpson style hats which add a good couple of inches. And a man really does need to be the taller, doesn't he? The Prince barely manages it with Wallis, have you noticed? Although at least his eyes compensate, and he is very sophisticated. Shame they're not around any more, really, they always provided such good gossip.

"Oh dear! You're looking at me very sternly! You're going to turn out to be one of those earnest types, aren't you, which is a pity when you're so attractive. And you're just about to tell me that I'm wasting your time. I tell you what, perhaps you'd better have a look at me anyway. I've been feeling pretty run down lately – perhaps I need a tonic or something."

He had to get up and move around the desk then, and he saw the look of triumph on her face when he literally measured up to her expectations. She had the very pale skin of a natural redhead, carefully made up to conceal the smattering of freckles on her cheeks. Her rich auburn hair was pulled tightly back from her face, making her green eyes look slightly slanted, but the harshness was relieved by the froth of curls on the top of her head.

"Hmm, I think you could be a little anaemic," Andrew told her, after she'd shown him her tongue and he'd looked at her fingernails and eyelids. "I'll give you some iron."

"There you are! I knew it was a good idea to come and see you! I'm sure I'll feel marvellous very soon now that I've got you looking after me. And you'll make me feel even better if you say you'll come to a little soiree of mine on Friday – I only live around the corner – and I can introduce you to all sorts of exciting people. Help you to feel at home."

Andrew wasn't sure how he'd cope with exciting people. Most of his friends in recent years had been fellow medical students, who had been working as hard as he to get on, making them the earnest types she had just denigrated. One or two had been a bit dashing in a reckless sort of way, which often gave them a certain success with women of which Andrew had felt envious but had been unable to emulate.

He was aware that this highly attractive young woman was waiting for his answer. Looking at her bright flirtatious face, he decided that it was time he threw off the shackles of dependability which, he knew, gave him a stolid air. He had come this far, achieved what he had set out to achieve, and lived up to all of his parents' expectations. Perhaps now it was time to live for himself a little.

All of this he decided in a few moments.

"I'd be delighted to come along," he said, with his rare smile, to which she gave a little squeal of delight.

"Excellent! 23 Westbury Gardens, eight o'clock. Don't be late because there'll be loads of people wanting to meet you."

Which almost made him change his mind, but before he could say anything more she swept out of the surgery with a formal "Thank you, Dr. Eliot" for the benefit of two other patients in the waiting room, and a handshake that contained the smallest of squeezes.

He needn't have worried about the exciting people because by the time he arrived at Jessica's house – a little late because his surgery ran over – she had already elevated him to the status of a celebrity.

Introducing him as "my Doctor Eliot" to the group of well-dressed young people sipping cocktails in her drawing room, she followed this up with, "You see? Like I promised – immensely clever *and* very handsome."

The women, all, like Jessica, as smart as paint, seemed willing to laugh at his slightest witticism which, along with the strength of the gin in the martinis, gave him the courage to be bolder than ever before in mixed company. With girlish coyness several of them asked for medical advice and, when he jokingly said that he couldn't possibly make a diagnosis without a full examination, he was surprised at how many of them arrived at his surgery in the ensuing days and weeks to sign on as patients. Impressed by his careful consideration of their problems, however minor, they were soon recommending him to friends and family and his practice quickly blossomed.

"I knew they'd all love you!" Jessica exclaimed. "Aren't you thrilled I found you?"

The men either worked in some obscure way in the city or in the 'service', which he soon learned was the civil service, not one of the armed forces. They used their surnames when addressing each other, or nicknames, which made them sound as if they were still at school, but their manners were impeccable, as was their attention to the ladies present.

Andrew also soon learned that they were all well off, including the women, several of whom, like Jessica, had allowances from wealthy fathers which enabled them to live lives of unashamed luxury. He had never been in close contact with people like them and was overwhelmed by these exotic butterflies who flitted from one social engagement to another, filling their days with purposeless determination, the mainstay of which seemed only to see and to be seen. They were almost a parody of the 'bright young things' who had emerged after the Great War, to the delight of the gossip columnists who fed off their outrageous, profligate antics.

And Jessica intrigued him the most. Her intoxicating perfume, the silks and cashmeres with which she clothed her slender body, the imperious tilt of her immaculately coiffed head, her Mona Lisa smile which could be at once seductive, promising much, or hold a slightly contemptuous sneer, and her self-assuredness – all held an allure that quickly captivated him.

She was undoubtedly the leader of the pack. Heads turned and faces lit up when she entered a room and the men were always quick to offer her a drink, or to light her cigarette, which made Andrew wonder why she had chosen him as her preferred escort.

"Bertie Newman and all the others are such *boys,*" she told him when he fished for a reason. "Whereas you…" She scrutinised him through a cloud of exhaled smoke, considering. "You have that little air of reserve around you – leaving a girl feeling not quite so certain. The strong, silent type – you must know what that does for a woman.

"Besides," she went on, a playful smile on her carmine lips, "you're a doctor. You know a woman's body better than anyone else – what more could I want?"

She made no bones about her willingness to share his bed – or, more often, for him to share hers. "Those dreary little rooms you have above the surgery can hardly be described as a love nest, can they darling? Far better that you spend the night here."

Andrew's more provincial background led him to feel uncomfortable the first few times he encountered members of her staff as he was letting himself out of the front door early in the morning. But with a grave "Good morning, sir," they appeared not to turn a hair. And then he would forget about it as he hurried home to make himself presentable and prepare for morning surgery. Sometimes, if it had been a late night with lots of champagne flowing, that also necessitated taking a cold shower and some aspirin to ensure he was bright enough to give his patients the attention they deserved.

It was almost, he realised much, much later, as if he became two people.

There was the accomplished doctor in his surgery or visiting patients at home, who listened attentively to their complaints, his face a study of concentration, made careful examinations and felt a quiet glow of satisfaction when a difficult diagnosis proved to be right, or a very sick patient began to respond to his care, or a complicated delivery resulted in a healthy baby and happy parents.

And then there was the dashing young doctor, often wearing his admittedly slightly worn dinner jacket, who accompanied Jessica to the theatre or to dinner in some of the most fashionable restaurants in London, and who impressed her with his ability to dance when they visited a club.

It was unsurprising, therefore, when quite often these two lives clashed.

The first eruption was when Andrew felt unable to accompany Jessica to a white tie charity gala.

"I don't possess a pair of tails and I have little inclination to acquire any," he said, somewhat curtly when she pressed him over the matter.

"But you must come, darling – no-one else dances as divinely as you, and I'll have no-one else to partner me. And it will be such fun. Everyone will be there. I'll *buy* you the suit."

"I don't need you to buy anything for me, Jessica. I already sponge off your hospitality enough as it is. And it will be an absurdly late night, when I have surgery next morning – I'm sorry, but I'm going to miss this one. If everyone is going to be there, then you'll hardly be short of company."

Jessica remonstrated and pouted as prettily as she could, which made his body yearn for her, but he held fast to his decision. So she resorted to a tantrum which included the accusations that he didn't really care about her, but stopped short of 'after all I've done for you', although the unspoken resentment hung in the air between them.

They didn't see each other for a while after that, during which time Andrew worked hard at catching up on his paperwork and putting his surgery in order. He told himself that if such a minor episode resulted in the ending of their relationship, then it clearly wasn't a relationship worth pursuing. Jessica was a spoilt young woman who, like many of her breeding, expected the world to revolve around her wishes and desires.

But when, after a few days, Jessica telephoned him with, "Darling, we haven't seen each other for ages – when are you going to take me to dinner again?" – he had to relent. His rooms above the surgery were lonely and oppressive and the thought of seeing her bright chattering face again and the possibility of later exploring her lithe body which she offered up so willingly were too much to resist. And, having caught up on some much needed sleep, he was sufficiently invigorated to tell himself that he could cope once more on the merry-go-round of Jessica's life.

But gradually there emerged a pattern of spats when his work intruded on the social life that was so important to her, followed by periods of silence, followed by making up, which he began to find extremely wearing. Jessica, on the other hand, seemed to thrive on this turbulence, her green eyes glittering like emeralds during an argument, and deepening to darkest jade when they made up passionately. She saw nothing untoward in the peaks and troughs of their relationship and urged him to find a locum so that they could go away on holiday together – or, even better, an assistant so that Andrew could be freer in the evenings.

His initial concerns over what this degree of high living would do to his bank balance was soon dissipated by his swelling patient numbers. But dealing with the problems of young women which were often due either to neuroses or over-indulgence hadn't been his reason for entering general practice. He soon began to feel a level of dissatisfaction when his waiting room was full each morning of people who had nothing more wrong with them than too much time on their hands and too little else to think about.

At the same time he came to realise that being "too serious" was a misdemeanour in Jessica's social circle. Occasionally he would have liked to have a discussion about the state of the country, about the dire warnings being issued by Mr. Churchill, about the situation in Spain, or about the vast differences he saw in the lives of those he socialised with and those who lived in the poorer streets around his surgery. But even the men with quite senior civil service posts, which one would have hoped they had gained by brain power and not simply string-pulling or nepotism, were reluctant to hold such a conversation.

"We keep that sort of stuff for the club, you know," one of them advised. "Not the sort of thing the ladies want to hear about."

Deep down he knew it wasn't really the life for him, but no matter how much he convinced himself that he should move away from it, there was always Jessica, with her witty tongue, able to make him laugh even if the subject matter was banal. And, when they were alone, there was Jessica, holding him in thrall to her beautiful face and demanding body which oozed sex appeal.

One morning, after a particularly long surgery, she came into his room and, after kissing him perfunctorily on the cheek, flung herself down in the patient's chair. Andrew was already packing his visiting bag, his mind on what else he could use on the varicose ulcers of an elderly lady on his list.

"It's lovely to see you," he told Jessica as he took out his handkerchief to wipe her lipstick from his face. "But I'm in a terrible rush today – I don't suppose you could go through and see if Miss Chambers would see her way to making me a cup of coffee before I go out?"

Miss Chambers was a recent addition to the practice; a sensible lady of indeterminate age with iron grey curls attached like cladding to her very round head. She had already taken it upon herself to organise the patients as they waited their turn, rather than let them work it out for themselves. As soon as she heard a patient leave through the surgery door she would break off from what she was doing to bellow through the dispensary hatch, "Mr. Wilkins – into the doctor, *now,* if you please' – often making anyone waiting for their medicine jump in alarm, and leaving Andrew little time to write his notes in between seeing people.

Like his patients, he was a little in awe of her and hadn't yet got round to requesting that she prepare him a drink at the end of surgery before they went their separate ways.

It didn't look as if he was going to get a cup on this particular morning either.

"I haven't got time for that if you're on your way out," Jessica told him. "I need to speak to you."

She sat up straighter in her chair. "It's Celia," she told him, "Celia Bingham – she needs to come to see you."

Pondering absently on the fact that nearly all Jessica's female friends had names ending in "a" as he continued to check his bag, he almost didn't hear her next words.

"She's in the club, poor thing, and of course there's no way she wants the scandal, so I told her you'd sort it out for her."

"You did what?" He looked up sharply and suddenly became very still.

"Celia's pregnant. In a terrible state over it, so I explained how understanding you were, and –"

"Understanding about what? Are you talking about an abortion?"

"Of course, darling. Like I said, she can't possibly have it, so naturally I told her you'd help."

"Naturally?"

"Oh, don't look so outraged! You must have known that one of the women flocking to your door would present you with this little problem sooner or later."

"I think you'd better go straight back and tell her you made a mistake." There was a coldness in his voice that even Jessica couldn't miss.

"But she can't have a child! Think of the scandal! Her family would cut her off without a penny!"

"Then I suggest she finds somewhere to sit out the next few months and then goes to a good adoption agency."

Jessica stood up to face him across his desk, her normally pale face darkening with her own anger. "You're serious? You're not prepared to help?"

"Deadly serious! Apart from anything else abortion is illegal, in case you've forgotten – and it's not what I came into medicine to do."

"Of course I know it's illegal! But, come on darling, there's no need to sound so naïve. We both know there are doctors in London who help girls out when they're in this sort of bother. And you can charge a hefty fee."

Andrew's lips set in a grim line as he leaned across the desk towards her. "Then Celia should find one of them. Now I need to go, I've got patients to see."

"But Andrew, I promised Celia! And you're really not in the position to be so high-handed you know."

He was already heading for the door. Now he stopped and turned back.

"What's that supposed to mean?"

"Well, why do you think so many women have become your patients? They've seen how accommodating you can be, how terribly *kind* you are over the tiniest problem – and they know that you are my lover. So naturally they assumed that you would also be completely understanding if they encountered a problem of a delicate nature. They don't come to see Dr. Eliot, you know. They come to see *Jessica's doctor."*

He stood transfixed as the awful truth of her words hit him. How had this crept up on him? How had he been so foolish as to allow the ideals with which he had entered general practice to become so tarnished in such a short time? He was probably talked about in the same way as they talked about their latest dress designer. *"I've found this awfully good little man, you know. He'll do anything for me and he's very discreet. Jessica Golding put me onto him."*

He was filled with a terrible rage against himself and against the woman in front of him. For the first time he saw cruelty in the set of her beautiful mouth, and arrogance in the set of her shoulders and the tilt of her head.

He spoke with dangerous calm, his voice at odds with the fiery anger in his brain. "Perhaps you would be kind enough, in that case, to tell them that I am no longer Jessica's doctor, that I don't care if I am no longer their doctor, and I certainly am no longer Jessica's lover. Now, if you'll excuse me, like I said – I have sick patients to see."

He marched through the door, leaving her standing in the surgery.

"You're being ridiculous, you know!" she cried as she followed him into the hall. But the only response was the slamming of the front door.

Hearing the noise, Miss Chambers emerged from the waiting room. "Is anything the matter?"

"Oh, go to hell!" said Jessica, before also slamming out into the street.

It would have been fine if it had ended there. But a few evenings later, when Andrew had been experiencing nothing but relief that he had stopped a bad situation from becoming worse, there was a phone call from Jessica.

"Darling, I know we both said some unforgivable things the other day, but I just wanted to tell you that Celia is all sorted out now and to ask if you would like to come to the ballet with me tomorrow? I've got tickets for the new young dancer, Fonteyn, who everyone is raving about, in *Giselle."*

Although unsure of his unforgivable part in the argument,

there was little point in being anything other than magnanimous.

"Jessica, it's very good indeed of you to call like this, but I really think things are better left as they are, don't you? Our lives are too different for things ever to have worked in the long run, so this is, I'm sure, the best way to part."

Within minutes she was hammering on the door at the side of the building which led to Andrew's flat above the surgery. As soon as he opened the door she pushed past him up the stairs, talking over her shoulder as she went.

"We have to talk about this, Andrew. We can't part over a little misunderstanding which is all cleared up now – turns out Celia wasn't actually up the duff after all, silly girl! A panic over nothing in the end!"

She turned to him in the small darkly-lit hallway.

"Darling, let's just go back to how we were, don't you think? Forget about the whole silly incident?"

She had her hands on his chest, imploringly, a quizzical smile on her face, like a little girl who knows she's done wrong but wants to be forgiven.

Gently Andrew took her hands and led her into the sitting room.

"I'm sorry Jess, but if it hadn't been this occasion, there would have been another like it very soon. We're not properly suited in any way if you think about it, and I can't afford to have my professional life compromised by people getting the wrong idea about my ethics."

He tried to make her sit down, but she refused.

"Don't do this Andrew – we're good together. These silly little arguments mean nothing."

"They mean a lot to me. And, like I said, in the end we're just too different. You deserve someone who can make a much better fist of wining and dining you and taking you to all these wonderful places than I can."

She became quite shrill in the end, no matter how carefully Andrew tried to put his point of view.

"You need me!" she cried, the green eyes narrowing to slits in a face contorted with fury. "A doctor from the sticks trying to set up in London. Without someone like me to give you some cachet you won't get anywhere!"

"I'll just have to do my best and go it alone," he answered, falling back on the stiff reserved tone that always masked inner turmoil.

"No-one has ever done this to me before," she told him, "and I'm not going to let you get away with it. Telling me you love me one minute and then rejecting me like this! You're clearly totally untrustworthy and I'll make sure everyone knows it."

"I haven't ever told you that I love you," Andrew said, thankful that his diffidence had always stopped him uttering those words, although he had come very close to feeling that way about her at times.

"Oh, I think you did. And in the end, whose version is anyone going to believe?"

"I shouldn't think in the long run anyone will actually care," he said wearily.

"We'll see," she said before sweeping out of the flat.

There were lots of phone calls after that and visits from Jessica, regardless of whether he was in the middle of taking surgery. Eventually Miss Chambers, tired of having this woman interrupt proceedings on an almost daily basis and being extremely rude, gave in her notice.

"I'm sorry Doctor Eliot," Miss Chambers told him, "I've worked for a number of doctors in my time, but I've not encountered anything like this. And if you take my advice, you'll be careful who you get involved with in the future."

As the days passed, with the visible dwindling of affluent members of the community seeking his care, Jessica became more and more hysterical, her calls ranging from wild declarations of love to sudden bursts of weeping about how he'd broken her heart. Finally, as Andrew held firm, even more convinced in the face of her unbalance that he was doing the right thing, she threatened to ruin him.

"I'll have you struck off!" she cried. "I've got plenty of friends in high places who will speak on my behalf to the Medical Council."

"You can't have a doctor struck off because of a love affair," Andrew said.

"You can if he has an affair with a patient!" There was a note of triumph in her voice.

"But I haven't been treating you for anything," he protested. He had only been 'Jessica's doctor' in the possessive sense.

"You prescribed iron for me on my first visit to your surgery," she reminded him. "So technically I'm your patient – and there were people in the waiting room when I left to prove it."

"But that was before we became involved! I didn't treat you at all while we were seeing each other! No medical council will be interested in that."

"Maybe not – but mud sticks, especially the way I throw it. You'll be ruined, darling Doctor Eliot, whichever way you turn!"

By this time it hardly mattered that Miss Chambers was no longer there, as his patient list shrank further. The local people who had got to know him valued his skill and his bedside manner, and had no knowledge of the gossip surrounding him in other quarters, but that didn't help to pay the rent or further the practice. Jessica was ominously quiet at this point, making Andrew dread the next post arriving on the mat or the next telephone call in case it was a summons to explain himself to the medical board.

In the end a chance meeting with an old acquaintance from medical college saved the day. Dr. Michael Parsons was one of the self-assured ladies' men with whom Andrew had trained and often envied, and he now had his eye on becoming a successful London practitioner. Without hesitation Andrew offered his practice for sale.

"It's a mixed population," he told him when he showed him round. "Salt of the earth people in the smaller terraces around the practice, but just a few streets away, once you get to York Square, you'll find a completely different clientele."

The glint in Dr. Parson's eye at the prospect of moneyed patients convinced Andrew that he was doing the right thing in offering him the practice. Within what was probably the most miserable few weeks of Andrew's life, as he was shunned by any of those 'friends' he chanced to meet as he went on his rounds, the deal was done. During that time he had also found a little practice in a Welsh backwater called Penfawr.

Thankfully, feeling ten years older, and many years wiser, he left London, vowing that from now on he would fulfil his promise to himself to become a top class general practitioner and he would never allow a woman to get in the way again.

Now, taking up his pen once more, Dr. Eliot finished the letter to his parents with a few comments about the weather. The lowering sky glimpsed through the surgery window made the evening feel later than it was. Pushing his chair away from the desk he decided he should check on things in the garden before the storm broke. His head full of memories of what he still saw as his disgrace made him reluctant to go through to the house and see the woman who was churning his emotions into more confusion than Jessica had ever achieved.

Lydia sat in the rocking chair in her room, giving Grace her last feed, which usually made her drop off. Tonight, though, the humid air was making her fractious, her little body just becoming hotter as she snuggled against her mother. The window was wide open, but it made little difference and Lydia was aware of her dress clinging to her damply.

"I think you'll be far better in your bed," Lydia told her, moving across the room and settling her in her drawer-cot. The baby made no sound, content to lie on the cool sheet.

"Goodnight, little one," Lydia said, as the first rumble of thunder could be heard in the distance. Moving back to close the window she saw where, way down in the valley, the ribbon of river finally disappeared between two rounded hill-tops, forked lightning seemingly bouncing off the sides of the hills. Then she saw the rain advancing, like a swarm of militant bees, moving up the river bed towards the village, its progress marked by huge claps of thunder and more lightning.

She heard the doctor come upstairs to close his bedroom window, and went out onto the landing.

"Have you looked out of your window?" she asked. "It's the most amazing sight – down in the valley – you can see it from my room. Come and look!"

He followed her into the room.

"See! Down there!" She leaned over and pointed. "Look how the storm is approaching!"

Together they stood and exclaimed over the relentless march of the rain. As it grew nearer the sky all around the village darkened further, illuminated intermittently by the lightning.

"You're not scared of storms?" he asked as an enormous clap

of thunder seemed to break overhead and the first raindrops splattered on the window-sill.

"Not at bit," she replied. She glanced over her shoulder to the sleeping baby. "And, by the look of her, neither is my daughter."

As she turned back their eyes met, and she became aware of how close together they were standing. Suddenly it felt as if the electricity of the storm had entered the room. It sparked and crackled between them. Despite the lack of light, it seemed to Lydia that everything about him was highlighted. She felt acutely conscious of the strength of him, of the dark hairs on his wrists against the white of his shirt cuffs, of the slight sheen on his skin across his cheekbones from the humid evening, and of the depth of colour in the brown eyes that were boring into hers. A sharp memory of his cool fingers on her body when she was ill filled her with a different heat.

"I've never seen a storm approach like that, but it probably happens a lot here. You must think me silly for getting excited." She tried to keep her voice light but it sounded unnatural to her own ears.

"Not at all. I've not seen it sweep up the valley all the time I've been here. But then I've not had anyone to point it out to me before. And you may have noticed I tend to go about with my head down when I'm working."

For a few seconds there seemed nothing more to say but still they stood as the storm raged.

"*Lydia…*" His voice was the faintest whisper above the lashing of the rain, but she could hear the want in it.

It made her keen towards him, her lips parted as she turned her face up to his.

The shrill ring of the telephone in the hall broke the spell. He turned and left the room.

Lydia stayed where she was for a few minutes, looking down the valley but this time not seeing the rain.

When she went downstairs he was pulling on his mackintosh.

"I have to go down to the village – a baby arriving early. I've written the address on the pad in case there are any more calls."

His voice sounded the same as ever, with that curt edge which signified that his mind was already on the patient he was going to see. And then he was gone.

Lydia went back upstairs to sit in the rocking chair. The thunder was now a distant rumble, but the rain continued relentlessly. *Had he whispered her name?* She tried to tell herself that she had imagined it, but deep down she knew this wasn't so. She could still hear the ache in the word. *Would he have kissed her if they had stayed there a few moments longer?* She twisted her wedding ring round her finger as she sat deep in thought. She was still a married woman. A married woman who had already made one huge mistake. She couldn't afford to make another.

Confusion about her own feelings and those of the doctor fogged her brain, so that when Grace stirred she lifted her out, more for her own comfort than that of the child.

Andrew arrived home much later, to a house in darkness downstairs. The delivery had been a difficult one, to a hitherto childless couple who were speechless with joy over the safe arrival of a small but perfectly formed son. He would have liked to have shared the exhilaration with Lydia – he always thought of her as Lydia – sitting together in the kitchen, which seemed so much more homely than when Miss Williams had been there.

He made his way upstairs, still hoping that she would be about, and hoping, too, that the dropping of his guard earlier that evening could be forgotten about and they could continue as they were.

Her bedroom door was wide open, the room lit only by the gentle arc of a bedside lamp. Lydia was asleep in the rocking chair, her head resting on the back. Her long, dark lashes made a crescent of shadow on her cheeks. The baby was on her lap, a tiny arm flung outwards in complete abandonment to slumber. A small blue vein stood out at the base of Lydia's neck, where the skin was still pale despite the summer sun. He wanted to press his lips to it, to feel the softness of her skin and inhale the perfume of her. The vulnerability of sleep stripped her of her self-sufficient air, increasing his longing to hold her in his arms, to feel her body against his, and to whisper words of tenderness and love.

He watched them for several minutes, until his desire for her threatened to overwhelm him. With a deep sigh he tiptoed back downstairs to lock up.

A my was relieved to hear Edwin's voice as the thunderstorm raged on the other side of the black-out curtain.

"Are you alright, little sister?"

He called her that all the time when he came into her bedroom, but never in front of his mother. In fact, downstairs he spoke little more to her than when she first arrived, but if she caught his eye he would give her a small, secret half-smile that seemed to remind her that he was her protector.

"I don't like the thunder," she admitted to him now, in a whisper in case Mrs. Preece should hear, although it was doubtful with the noise going on outside. Edwin didn't usually stay in her room when Mrs. Preece was downstairs, so it was as well to be careful. He'd told her that if his mother found out that he kept her company at bedtime, instead of simply preparing her night light, there'd be an unholy row.

"She'd say what a baby you are, and that you don't need watching by anyone but the Lord," he'd said, "and she'd probably take the night light away to teach you a lesson, so best we don't say anything at all."

"The thunder won't hurt you," he said now, tiptoeing to her bedside. "Look, I'll lie down beside you, then our Mam won't hear me moving about – ears like a fox she's got."

"What does she think you've come upstairs for?" Amy asked.

Mrs. Preece took no interest in what Amy did when she sent her out to play, or at school, but whoever was in the house had to constantly report to her their intentions.

"Told her I was coming up to my room to sort out some children's books for you that are in the bottom of my cupboard."

"Too good to that child, you are," his mother had said. "You make sure she doesn't damage anything you give her."

A long, low rumble of thunder stole over the roof-tops as Edwin lay down beside Amy, putting his arm around her protectively. She nestled into his shoulder, hoping that the storm would finish soon.

"I'm glad you're with me," she whispered. "I'm not scared now."

He held her closer, caressing her arm on top of the bedclothes.

"And I'm glad you want me to be with you." He kissed her forehead and then, without warning, he kissed her on the lips, which Amy didn't think was really right, and not just because his lips were soft and wet. Not even her Mam or Dad kissed her on the lips. But then, there were lots of things they did differently in this place, perhaps this was one of them. She didn't like it, though.

"You're my beautiful little sister," Edwin told her, "and our secret this is, wanting to be together."

After a few minutes the thunder seemed less. Amy kept very still and quiet so that Edwin wouldn't want to kiss her goodnight again. She could hear his breathing getting stronger and she would have thought he was asleep first if his hand hadn't been stroking her arm. By the time the storm was over, she was asleep herself.

12.

"Anyone at home?"

Lydia heard Edyth's cheery tones from along the garden as she was hanging out the washing.

"We're round here!" she called, dropping a sheet back into the basket and hurrying to unlatch the side gate.

"Oh! I'm so glad I've caught you – I was keeping a look-out as I came through the village in case you were shopping. Gosh!" She stood still and looked round admiringly. "Someone's been working hard here! This was a mess the last time I saw it."

Lydia laughed. "Dr. Eliot was going great guns with the vegetable patch, but he challenged me to do something about the flower borders. Then, as soon as they were a bit tidier, I told him the garden still wouldn't look any good without the grass being cut regularly. So he went down to the second-hand shop in the village and came back with an ancient lawn mower."

"Second-hand shop? Oh – you mean Morgan Grinder!"

"*Morgan Grinder?*" Lydia spluttered.

Edyth's eyes twinkled. "I know. Awful habit we have in Wales of giving people nicknames. But he does the knife-grinding for everyone, you see, as a little sideline. He's been there since Adam was a lad, and he'd be very pleased to hear his old junk shop being given such a polite title!"

"Well, I must confess the lawn mower did seem to be held together with rust, but Dr. Eliot spent ages taking it apart and cleaning it all up. I think it would have been quicker to have cut the grass with a pair of shears! It's nice for Grace, though, because she's started rolling over now, and doesn't always stay on a blanket when I put her on the ground."

Edyth went over to admire the baby who was having her morning nap in her pram whilst Lydia finished hanging out the washing.

"Would you like a cup of tea?" she offered as she snapped the last peg into place.

"If I'm not holding you up from anything else. I've come to ask you a favour."

Once they were seated at the kitchen table, Edyth explained.

"Now that the school holidays have started, some of the families with evacuee children are finding things a bit difficult – most of them are old enough to be grandparents, as they're the ones with more room in their houses. Anyway, it's a bit of a strain for them – especially when the weather's bad like it was all last week – so I'm trying to start up some activities for the children and I wondered if you'd like to help?"

"Me? What could I do?"

"I've arranged for us to use the Red Shed for indoor activities, so you could help with those – playing games, sing-songs, that sort of thing. And I thought we could get them involved in the war effort, teach the girls to knit and so on. What do you think?"

"Well, I suppose so…"

"Oh, do say you'll give it a try," Edyth urged, holding her cup out for a refill. "You can bring Grace with you, which would delight some of the little girls. You could even teach them about how you look after her."

"I wouldn't be able to do it every day…"

"Oh, you wouldn't have to," Edyth assured her with a winning smile, sensing victory.

"Just a couple of mornings or afternoons a week. To tell you the truth –" she lowered her voice as if she could be overheard, "– the likes of Mrs. Owain Owen have volunteered to help, and, worthy women though they are, the children would just feel they are back in school. I'd be so grateful for some younger blood."

"Alright, I'll give it a try. As long as you tell me exactly what you want me to do each time. When are you going to start?"

"Next Monday, I hope. It would be wonderful if you could be there for the first morning, to help me get it off on the right footing. Of course, on fine days I'll get them all hiking or playing games on the old rugby field – make sure the little perishers are worn out before we send them home! I'm going to rope in some of the older men for that. Mr. Robinson, their teacher, is going to help but he can't do active things because he's got a gammy leg from the last lot."

They were interrupted by Dr. Eliot in search of his elevenses.

"Oh! I'm sorry!" Lydia said, jumping up. "I didn't realise what the time was."

"Don't worry," he said as she re-filled the teapot, "I'm not in a hurry today."

"I've come to take your housekeeper away from you, I'm afraid," Edyth told him as he lowered himself onto one of the kitchen chairs.

"What?" His head shot up. *Really alarmed, he looked,* she told her husband later.

"Oh, it's alright, I don't mean permanently," she assured him. "I just want her to come and help me keep the evacuee children occupied a couple of times a week."

She noticed his shoulders relax as Lydia placed a cup of tea and a slice of carrot cake in front of him.

"We can't exclude the village children, of course," she went on, "which means there's quite a number to consider, so I'll be grateful for all the help I can get."

"I think it's a splendid idea," he said. "Mrs. Dawson spends far too much time stuck in the house." He looked at Lydia with a small twist to his lips. "My fault probably, for implying that I didn't think you were up to the job when you first arrived."

"Well, I wasn't the best of candidates," she conceded, smiling back.

It was such a small exchange, and they didn't even look each other in the eye, but for a brief moment Edyth felt as if she shouldn't be there. The impression was such a fleeting one that she couldn't be sure afterwards of why she felt it, and they continued to talk about the evacuees generally until the doctor swallowed his last mouthful of tea, left his visiting list with Lydia and went on his way.

It wasn't anything I could put my finger on, and I'm sure there's no funny business between them," Edyth said that evening when she and Rhys were alone in the sitting room, "but there was something…"

"Not match-making, are you Edyth?" Rhys raised a quizzical eyebrow and regarded her with an amused expression.

"Of course not!" she said immediately. "The poor girl has only recently lost her husband. All the same… they would make such a nice little family, though, the three of them… in time of course…"

"*Definitely* match-making," her husband grinned. "Poor Doctor Eliot, perfectly happy as the local bachelor with the women-folk falling over themselves to be agreeable. Then the minute someone comes along who hasn't got a face like a chewed dap like Miss Williams, there's a rush for the confetti and –"

His words were muffled as his wife good-naturedly threw a cushion at him. "Only speculating, I was!" she said. "Makes a change from talking about the milk yield – and the only bit of romance I seem to get these days is discussing someone else!"

Rhys stood up, the twinkle in his eye finding a response in his wife's vivacious face.

"Soon remedy that," he said, pulling her to her feet.

"Well, I only hope the Owain Owens don't have the same thought I had when they visit, or Mrs. O. will have Lydia out of there before she can turn round," Edyth murmured as she allowed her husband to lead her up the stairs.

Lydia had already had one visit from the Owain Owens. She'd kept them in the kitchen and made them both a cup of tea, which, she had come to realise by now, the Welsh seemed to drink by the gallon.

"We just wanted to make sure your health is fully restored, having heard that you were laid up," Mr. Owain Owen told her.

"Luckily, living in a doctor's house, any sign of ill-health can be remedied quite quickly, can't it?" she answered, smiling at him to take the sting out of her words.

"Heard from Miss Williams, we have. Terrible state her sister's in. *Cancer, it is, down below,*" his wife said, the last few words mouthed confidentially to Lydia with a grimace. "So it looks like Dr. Eliot will be needing help for quite some time."

She surveyed her surroundings, her critical eye missing nothing.

"Would you like to see round the rest of the house?" Lydia asked.

"Oh, goodness me, no, indeed!" Mrs. Owen shook her head. "It wouldn't be proper, going round the doctor's house. We just wanted to see that everything is alright for you – that is Mr. Owain Owen's job as Billeting Officer, after all."

"Well, as you can see, Grace and I are very cosy in this room here, and Miss Williams' old bedroom is quite comfortable, so I certainly have no complaints. As to whether I'm doing a good job – you'd have to ask Dr. Eliot about that."

Lydia picked the baby up then and, fearful that there might be a repetition of their first encounter, Mr. Owen stood up.

"I'm sure we don't need to bother you any more," he said, edging his way towards the door. "You're obviously settling in well, which is our main concern."

"And I'm very grateful to you for taking the trouble to find a home for Grace and me," she told him with a smile. Whilst she found his wife immensely irritating, she had to admit that Mr. Owen was a well-meaning little man.

"You know she'll be reporting back to Miss Williams and the rest of her friends, don't you?" Rita told her after their visit. "But don't worry, there'll be nothing bad she can say, so she'll be announcing you as one of her success stories! Just don't cross her, that's all – you'll find she's got a long memory and a quick tongue if she thinks she's been slighted."

Lydia was pleased that Edyth had asked her to help with the children. Although she was on nodding acquaintance with other mothers when she was out pushing the pram, she hadn't made any other friends and, after the solitary life she'd also led in Bermondsey, she felt in need of some female company.

The first morning saw a motley collection of local children and evacuees turn up, but luckily the sun was shining, so they were able to be entertained outdoors in the field next to the hall. The Red Shed was simply a large corrugated iron building with a rudimentary kitchen at one end, and an even more antiquated toilet at the back. It had been built for the local rugby team and had hosted many a post-match tea, but there was little use for it now that so many of the men had been called up. It had recently been painted camouflage green, rather haphazardly in places so that bits of red still showed through, like a tree just starting to show its autumn hues, but to the villagers it would always be the Red Shed.

As Edyth had predicted, several of the little girls were fascinated by the baby, who was on her best behaviour and beamed at them every time they spoke to her.

"Can we push the pram round the field?" one of them asked

when they had been caught out in a game of rounders and subsequently lost interest.

She turned out to be Edyth's younger daughter, Rhian, who already seemed to be firm friends with the smaller London child by her side, who nodded vigorously when Rhian went on, "Amy and me'll look after her really well."

They set off round the field, one pushing the pram while the other pranced alongside, pulling faces to make the baby laugh, and then solemnly changing places at each corner. Round and round they went, until a large skipping rope was brought out which caught their attention.

"I've never played with a baby before," Amy confided breathlessly to Lydia when they handed the pram back. It wasn't strictly true, because Maisie's mum had one baby after another and Maisie often appeared with one on her hip, but they were babies who grizzled and whose faces were always smeared with food or dried-up snot that looked like a map of tiny scars, so that Amy had never found them appealing.

"Well, you've been very good nursemaids," Lydia smiled at the pale child. "You've even got her off to sleep for me. Come on, let's see what your skipping is like."

"Where's the little lad who's staying with you?" Lydia asked Edyth when they grabbed a break.

"Ah – sore point," Edyth replied. "It seems I can do all sorts of things with these children here today, but I don't seem to be making much headway with Arthur."

She sighed and for once a furrow appeared on her usually smooth brow. "The trouble is, he's been determined that he's not going to stay here since the moment he arrived, and every time we think we're getting him to settle down, something else crops up. Fighting in school it was, the first time, because the boys were saying things about his mother. Now, it's because he hasn't heard from her – I feel so sorry for him."

She and Rhys had both thought there'd been a big breakthrough when Arthur had been allowed to help with the mowing and had developed a working relationship with Rhys. But a short time later he had again become truculent and resistant to all their attempts to draw him into their family life.

Rhian had finally divined what was wrong.

"Why doesn't the farm gate have a number on it, like everyone else?" he'd asked her one morning on the way to school.

"'Cos we haven't got a number," she answered him. "We're just Llewellyn's Farm."

"Yeah, but how does anyone know that, if you haven't got it on the gate?"

"But everyone knows it, so why should we need to put it on the gate?"

"Huh! Reckon you're famous, do you?" he sneered. "Not everyone in the world knows about your precious farm and your bleedin' family, you know."

"Well, everyone we *want* to know about it knows where it is, so there!" she retorted hotly, "and if they're not sure, they've only got to ask in the village, 'cos everyone there can tell them exactly where our farm is, 'cos my Dad gives them all milk."

They were glaring at each other now, all progress along the path to school halted.

"Alright then," Arfur shouted, "so what if there was a new postman and he was doing his rounds really early so no-one in the village was up – then he wouldn't be able to find the farm. would he? So he'd probably chuck all the letters in the river or something instead, so you'd never get them then, would you?"

"That's just stupid," Rhian said. "Idris Lewis has been bringing our post for donkeys' years, my Mam says."

"Yeah, well, so he might be too old and die one of these days, and then the new postman won't know where to come, will he? And I hope that's on your birthday, so you don't get any cards – then you'll know what it feels like!"

He stormed off ahead of her then, so that they didn't speak again all day. But in the playground Kennie told Rhian that he'd had a letter from his Mam and when she checked, so had lots of the other evacuees, some of them every week.

"I know what it is that's upsetting you!" she told Arfur on the way home that afternoon. "It's 'cos you haven't had a letter from your Mam, isn't it?"

She was a bit breathless because she'd had to run to catch up with him as he doggedly made his own way back to the farm, so she was pleased that he stopped when he heard her words. She drew back, though, at the fury in his eyes.

"It's none of your bloody business!" he shouted. "And if you say anything about me Mum, I'll flatten you, even if you are a girl!"

Deciding now was not the time to remind him that her Dad would dock his pocket money if he knew he'd sworn, Rhian nevertheless stood her ground.

"I'm not going to say anything about your Mam. But if you're worried because you haven't heard from her, why don't you just say so, so that someone can do something about it?"

"'Cos I'm fed up with everyone interfering and feeling sorry for me. We were alright, me and me Mum, until everyone started poking their noses in, and we'll be alright again, soon as I get back to London."

He turned back to the path, but not before Rhian saw him dash his hand across his eyes. He was right, she did feel sorry for him. How awful to be so far away from the only parent he had, and not to have heard from her.

She decided she had to persevere, even if he did decide to thump her.

"Have you written to her?" she said to his back.

There was silence for a moment, then, "'Course I have. Mr. Robinson makes us send a letter home every week. Mine's gone off to the hospital where me Mum is."

"Well, perhaps she hasn't received them." Rhian was suddenly inspired. "Perhaps there's a new postman in the hospital – like you were saying – and he hasn't given your letters to the right person!"

"They go to the ward, stupid, then the Sister gives them out – I saw them do it when I had to go to hospital with the quinsies – and the Sister's gonna know who me Mum is."

"Why don't you ask my Mam and Dad about it – they'd help."

"'Cos I don't want to. Just leave me alone."

He stomped off along the path, his shoulders hunched. He was fed up with all the talking this family did. Whatever they were thinking or feeling, or doing, they thought it was alright to say it out loud. Mealtimes were the worst. Probably because there were too many bloody females in the house. Bronwen would be full of what was happening at her school and Rhian would be trying to match her with something that had gone on in her class, while Auntie Edyth would be telling Uncle Rhys word for word a conversation she'd had with someone in the village. And in between there'd be comments like, "I've got so-o-o much home-work to do," or "I'm really hot," or "Mmm this mashed potato is nice." Why did you need to comment on the mashed potato, or any food for that matter? Food was food and you just shovelled it in, you didn't need to talk about it.

Sometimes in the flat above the shoe shop his Mum wouldn't be so jolly when he got in from school and there'd be no making toast and giggling together. Some days she'd be sitting curled up in the chair just smoking one cigarette after another, in front of a fire that was barely lit, and wouldn't want to speak at all. But he didn't mind. He'd make some tea for them both and try to build the fire up if there was anything to hand that he could use, and he'd sit there with her, just keeping her company. It was always alright again in a few days, when she was seeing her friends once more and going out. Then she might be humming as she got ready, a cigarette in the corner of her mouth, already tinged with the deep red lipstick she wore. But they didn't need to *talk* about it – they both just accepted the good days and bad days.

Deep down there was a very small part of him that knew he and Mum didn't live like other people, but he didn't like to acknowledge it. Because to do so would imply some criticism of his Mum, and the haphazard way she provided for them both. There was also the question, which had occurred to him once or twice, of *how* she provided for them. Most of the other kids he knew had a Dad who went out to work and brought money home, even if a lot of it was spent first at the pub and their Mum had to go in and find him so she could make sure of getting what was left. He didn't know how his Mum got hold of the money that seemed to come in irregular lumps, so that sometimes they had to sit very quietly and pretend to be out when the rent man was knocking on the door, but other times they'd splash out on a fish and chip supper and a bottle of Vimto. He knew it didn't come from the father who'd cleared off before he was even born. But, somehow, he also knew it was better not to ask.

Occasionally, when they were all sitting around the tea table in the farmhouse, it would be brought home to him how comfort-able it all was, with regular good food, even if it was only bread and cheese and endless beetroot or over-ripe tomatoes. Or sometimes he would catch himself having such fun when a gang of them were playing by the brook or in the fields, that it would feel like the best times he had ever had. Then a black wave of guilt would wash towards him, hitting him first in the pit of his stomach and then rising as if to engulf him so that he could hardly breathe. How could he be so disloyal to his Mum who was lying in hospital, undoubtedly feeling as miserable as the days in the flat when she didn't see her friends?

He would have to flee the scene of his distress then – a spilt teacup releasing him from the tea table, or a surly word breaking up the game, which he knew was unfair of him.

On this particular day he reached the farmhouse way ahead of Rhian, who seemed to have given up following him. Scowling, he flung his cap on a hook by the scullery door and dashed up to his room, pushing past Auntie Edyth in the kitchen and staying there until she called him for tea. He would have liked to have refused to come down, but his treacherous stomach was already complaining that it was empty, breaking down his willpower.

Besides, he told himself as he slowly made his way across the landing, *if I don't go down, she'll only come up here and ask me what's wrong, and that would be far, far worse.*

His refusal to join in any of the conversation was ignored until Rhian, looking steadily at him across the table, said, "Arthur's upset because he hasn't heard from his Mam."

"Am not! And I told you, mind your own business!" He'd just managed to stop himself inserting a swearword under Uncle Rhys's watchful gaze. If he was sitting nearer he would have kicked her shin under the table.

There was silence for a moment, during which Arfur decided that if any of them said just one word – *one word* – that even hinted that his Mum wasn't being as good as the other mothers who'd already written to their children, then he'd be off and they'd never see him again, never mind that he didn't have enough money yet to get back home.

But Uncle Rhys just said, "Well, perhaps that's something Arthur and I can sort out after tea. Now eat up, please, I've got work to do."

After tea, though, Uncle Rhys went back to work without

another word to Arfur. But later, when Arfur was skulking about near the orchard because he was too cross with Rhian to play with her, Uncle Rhys asked him to help put the chickens in the hen house for the night.

"Tomorrow," Uncle Rhys said, as he shot the last bolt across, "I'll make some enquiries. Find the number and phone the hospital. It may be that your mother's been moved to a different hospital because she's getting better. I've heard they're doing that – moving patients around –" He hesitated to say why, so stopped abruptly.

"Anyway, I'll find out – tomorrow," he said.

"But the trouble was," Edyth said as she relayed what had happened to Lydia, "Rhys didn't get very far. He managed to phone the hospital, and apparently she's still there and doing fine, so there's no easy answer as to why she hasn't bothered to write.

"You should have seen Arthur's poor little face," she went on. "Full of hope but trying not to show it when he came in from school, and then just going all sort of closed up when Rhys told him."

"I bet you'll hear from her any day now, then," Edyth had said, to which he'd answered tersely: "'Course I will. Know that, don't I? You don't have to tell me," and her arms had ached with the desire to hold him very tightly and somehow take away the misery.

"So he didn't want to come here today," she said to Lydia, as she drained her tea cup and stared at the leaves left in the bottom as if they could give her an answer to Arfur's problems. "He's stayed with Rhys, who at least will find him plenty to do which might stop him brooding too much."

She settled the cup back on the saucer. "Have you heard from your family?" she asked, as they stood up.

"I don't have any family," Lydia replied, moving off to settle a dispute which had erupted over possession of a football.

"Arthur was alright with me today," Rhys reported to Edyth later that evening. "A bit quiet, but seemed happy enough once he'd earned sixpence. I said he could come into Maesteg with me next time I go, so he could spend some of his money, but he said he's saving it up to buy something nice for his Mam. That was the only time she was mentioned."

"I just hope he hears from her soon, then," Edyth said. "Breaks my heart, it does, to think of him with no-one. Mind you, Lydia seems to be in the same boat. Told me she had no family – and she looked just like Arthur does when she said it. Made me feel bad for asking. Imagine having no family at all! I mean, even if she hasn't got parents, you'd think there'd be in-laws who'd want to keep in touch, especially with the baby and no father and everything."

She thought about her own family, who seemed to make up half the village of Bryntwyn, where she'd lived until her marriage. There, if you had a new baby, you'd have grannies and aunties and goodness knows who else calling in all day, with plates of food and knitted baby clothes and lots of advice which, if it wasn't always welcome, would at least be well-meaning. Her own mother had come on the bus three times a week when Edyth had each of her babies, tackling many of the household chores with her strong, capable arms.

"I'd stay over, but your father would never manage on his own. Helpless, he is," she would say, shaking her head and disregarding the fact that she had colluded in his helplessness by pandering to his every whim throughout their married life.

Sometimes she had Auntie Ginnie in tow, who didn't do as much but would happily sit and sing in a thin reedy voice to each baby until it fell asleep. She always kept her hat on because she was visiting, and sometimes she'd fall asleep before the baby, with her hat tilted forward drunkenly over one eye.

"I wonder how Lydia managed when she had the baby? Don't know what I would have done without my Mam when I was lying-in." Edyth was blinking rapidly at the memory. "Or through those first weeks, especially when –"

"Well, if your hopes and ambitions in that direction come true, Lydia will soon have Dr. Eliot looking after her!" Rhys diverted the flow, knowing where this kind of reminiscence often led, and feeling too tired this evening to cope with the emotion of it.

"Ooh! I never said anything of the sort!" she insisted, though he was pleased to see there was now a glimmer of a grin on her face. "And don't you go repeating anything like that to anyone, or they'll think I'm a right busybody, when I was only surmising!"

"Me? I don't have time to gossip like you womenfolk when you're out doing the shopping!"

"Don't give me that!" His wife was smiling broadly now. "I've seen you jawing away with old Delwyn Parry when he's called over – and don't tell me you've spent all that time talking about silage! Gossip just as much as the women, you men do, only you like to say it's business!"

13.

The Llewellyns would both have been surprised if they could have known what was going through Andrew Eliot's head at that moment. He had just finished hoeing between wigwam poles of runner beans, and was sitting on the rickety garden bench while Lydia fetched some glasses of water.

He was lost in thought, but this time he was not berating himself over the loss of a patient or worrying about a difficult diagnosis. Instead, he was calling himself all sorts of a fool for allowing this situation to have arisen. He should have been firmer with that Owen pair when they had turned up on his doorstep with Lydia. He hadn't been near a woman in over two years, how did he ever think he could share a house with a vibrant, attractive girl and not feel stirred in some way? He should have turned the whole idea down from the start.

But he had sensed her vulnerability on that first evening, in the same way as he could divine that a patient's pallor wasn't going to be a simple case of iron deficiency or that a cough was going to need more than a bottle of linctus, even before he'd carried out any tests. Sometimes it was as if he could see right through the clothes and skin of his patients to what was going on underneath, to where the organs and mechanisms of the previously well-oiled machines that were their bodies were breaking down. In the same way he had seen through the bravado of Lydia's performance when she first arrived, the nervousness and desperation behind the self-contained, cool acceptance of her situation. And he had known that the injuries he tended in those first few days were not the result of an accident as she described it.

But *even then*, even knowing that there was something about this girl's past that didn't ring true, he didn't stop himself. He could have kept his distance. Could have insisted on taking his meals in the dining room, for example. He didn't have to invite her into the sitting room in the evening to listen to the wireless, or, as was becoming more frequent, to spend time together in the garden before enjoying a final hot drink in the cosy kitchen. He wasn't bound to seek out her opinion on whether our boys could overcome the Luftwaffe, or whether London was actually going to be reduced to a pile of rubble.

He had tried, he told himself. Sometimes, after eating a meal in brooding silence, he had taken himself into his surgery and tried to attend to paperwork, but all the time he had been waiting for a knock on the door and her kind offer of a cup of coffee or some help.

At other times, on his afternoon and evening off, old Dr. Crouch – who was really retired now – sat in his surgery, taking an inordinately long time with each patient because he was a bit deaf, so conversations became circuitous and confused. Then Andrew would take himself off walking on the hillside, his stride long and purposeful. Occasionally it worked, so that he came back refreshed and relaxed and slept well without thinking of Lydia being just the other end of the landing.

And yet at other times, like when he surprised a pheasant who scuttled crazily along the path in front of him before gathering the impetus to fly away, or when he saw three buzzards circling the hilltop before one swooped to pounce on its unseen prey, he simply found himself wishing that she was there to share it with him.

Even when he put a firm check on the thoughts whirring round his head, he somehow couldn't stop his spirits lifting every time he returned to the house, which felt so much more of a home than when Miss Williams had been housekeeper. Lydia hadn't made any sweeping changes, it was simply knowing that she was there, within the stone clad walls that had always seemed cold and severe. Now, when he walked up the drive to where the house sat proudly surveying the valley, there was even a benignity about the deep bay windows that had previously looked blank and unfriendly.

Fanciful thoughts, he knew, for one who had always leaned towards the scientific, but he couldn't rid himself of the sense that Lydia, and her baby, belonged there, with him.

Yet it wasn't as if Lydia imposed her personality on him or the house in any forceful way. It was rather that her very self-sufficiency and reserve added an extra attractiveness to her physical features, so that to be the recipient of a confidence or to have the complete attention of her smoky-lashed eyes, followed by a smile of understanding or complicity, felt like an immense reward...

"Here we are!" Suddenly she was in front of him, proffering a glass which he took with brief thanks. She was wearing a faded skirt and blouse, topped with a voluminous apron of Miss Williams, which he'd seen her wear to do the messier jobs indoors. It emphasised her slender waist, although there was a slight post-pregnancy swell still to her tummy which, for him, simply reinforced her femininity. As she sat beside him on the bench she wiped her hand across her brow, tucking in a strand of hair behind her ear, in an action that was becoming so endearing to him that he had to concentrate hard on taking a long draught of his drink.

"Shall I water the tomatoes for you before we finish?" she asked, apparently oblivious of the effect she was having on him. "The weather forecast says it's going to stay dry for a while."

"Yes. Thank you," he answered, cursing the curtness he could hear in his own voice.

There had been a day or two of awkwardness between them after the evening of the storm when he had whispered her name so longingly. He'd been in agonies over whether he should say something, and in even greater agony that Lydia might, but in the end they had fallen back into the routine of their days that had now become established, and covered the awkwardness with mundane exchanges until it faded away. She gave no clue as to whether she had even heard him, for which he was grateful, although part of his mind tortured him with pictures of what might have passed between them had the telephone not broken the spell. Or what their chances would have been if they had met when she hadn't been recently widowed. Or if they weren't bound by the decorum necessary when sharing a house under the watchful gaze of a village full of people whose humdrum lives made them lock onto any whisper of scandal and blow it up to the size of the barrage balloons now hovering over British cities and ports. He'd had his fill of gossips in his previous practice. He couldn't allow that to happen again.

I wish she'd never come here, he told himself as he rose to finish his gardening. He watched her take the can to the water butt at the side of the garden shed… *because I won't be able to face the day when she will leave…*

Mrs. Preece was off to Band of Hope.

"Can I come with you?" Amy had asked, as Mrs. Preece patted her hat into place in front of the living room mirror.

"Indeed to goodness, no," she replied. "For grown-ups, it is, who've *signed The Pledge*. You don't do that till you're older and you can forswear the Demon Drink for ever," which left Amy with no idea as to what she was talking about.

"You stay here and be good for Our Edwin." Mrs. Preece said with a final pat and a sucking in of her mouth.

Edwin came in through the kitchen door. "We'll be fine – always good for me, she is," he said, with a smile at Amy.

She gave a little smile back and returned to the book Rhian had lent her. She was pleased they'd formed a gang with the boys and went about together so much, although the others never came here, except sometimes to the back door to call for her. Usually they met at the river, or at Rhian's farm, or at the playing fields.

Amy liked the games and activities that had been organised for the children, but liked it especially on the days Rhian's Mam and Mrs. Dawson were there. She liked feeling important helping to look after little Grace, and usually they all walked back through the village together, and sometimes Rhian's Mam would invite her back for tea. Other times, she and Rhian would find excuses to help Mrs. Dawson push the pram all the way up to the doctor's big house on the hill, and once they'd even been invited into the kitchen for a drink.

She still missed her own Mum of course, and would have given anything to see her, but the long summer days weren't nearly as bad as when she first arrived.

She didn't like going back to Mrs. Preece's house, though. Mrs Preece always seemed to find something wrong that somehow ended up with Amy feeling it was her fault, even when she'd been out all day playing. Edwin usually stuck up for her if he was there when his mother was sounding very cross, which Amy was grateful for.

But it also made it difficult for her to tell Edwin that she didn't really need him to sit by her bed any more. With the little night light on, and now she had got used to her surroundings, she was no longer scared, and, with being outside all the time, she was usually tired enough to go off to sleep almost as soon as her head hit the pillow.

But each night she would hear the slight creak of the door and then Edwin's soft footfall across the lino. If his mother was in the house he didn't stay long, just time enough to give her a cuddle and a kiss goodnight. She'd asked Maisie whether she kissed her brothers on the lips and Maisie had shrieked with laughter and said, "He wants to be your boyfriend!" Which was ridiculous of course, when Edwin was more or less grown up. Perhaps, as he hadn't had a sister before, he didn't know it wasn't right. But then he had insisted, when she asked him, that it was what his friend did with his little sister, so perhaps everyone was different.

When Mrs. Preece was going out in the evening she wouldn't let Amy stay out playing late: "Not to cause Our Edwin any trouble," she said, as if Amy was going to go on some sort of rampage the minute Mrs. Preece's back was turned.

Which meant that Amy would barely have time to put her nightie on before Edwin was in her room, so eager to keep her company that she almost felt sorry for him.

Tonight was no exception. She was just climbing into bed, tucking her bare legs in under the sheet, as he came through the door.

He lit the nightlight as he always did, but tonight it seemed to accentuate the brightness of his eyes as he turned towards the bed.

"There's cosy you look, little sister," he said, in the quiet, soothing voice he always used in her bedroom. "A bit warm tonight, though, isn't it?" he went on, easing himself onto the side of the bed and leaning forward to stroke the hair across her forehead. "You feel very hot."

"No – I'm fine," she told him. "Just ready to go to sleep."

"Well you'll never get to sleep tonight with all these heavy blankets on you. Let's take them off and cool you down a bit."

The bedclothes were whisked off before she had time to grab at the sheet. She knew he was trying to be kind, but there was something deep down inside telling her that she should keep herself covered.

But it was too late.

"Turning a lovely brown, your legs are, with all this playing in the fresh air," he said, his hand stroking her thigh.

"Please Edwin, I'm really tired. I'd like to go to sleep now," she whispered, but he wasn't listening. His hand had travelled to the top of her leg.

"What's this?" he said, sounding almost excited. "Your knickers on in bed? No wonder you're hot, little sister – be better if you took them off."

"No, Edwin! I can't do that!" She knew this was definitely wrong. You didn't take your knickers off for anyone – or your vest for that matter. Not even her father ever saw her undressed.

But Edwin didn't seem to be listening, he just kept on tugging at her knickers. The sudden need for the protective love of her father, who was goodness-knew-where at the moment, made her choke on a sob.

"It's alright, little sister," Edwin's voice was next to her ear now. Somehow he was lying down next to her, but his hand was still working down below. Waves of shame spread over her, so that now she did indeed feel hot. Hotter than she'd ever been in her life.

His breath was hot too, she could feel it on her cheek.

"Edwin, please! Leave me alone!"

But still he wasn't listening. He wasn't the kind big brother any more. He was a monster, worse than any she had imagined coming to get her in the dark.

"Lie still!" His voice was harsh, threatening. She closed her eyes as tightly as she could, aware of her heart beating so rapidly she could feel it pounding in her ears. She tried to think of her mother, of home, of anything that would blot out what was happening.

She didn't know how much later it was that Edwin's voice came to her again. He'd shifted his weight away from her and he sounded normal again.

"A lovely little sister, you are," he said. "And now we have another secret to share."

He was sitting on the side of the bed again, tucking the bedclothes around her just like he did on other nights.

"I don't want to have that secret, Edwin." She was barely able to get even a whisper out.

"But you told me you'd always wanted a big brother," he said, his face looming closer to her. "Glad I was with you, you said, when it was thundering."

Somehow, while he was talking, his foot shot out and tipped the night light over, so that the candle fell into the water and went out. Amy gasped at the sudden blackness surrounding her.

"Oops!" Edwin's voice held a little giggle. "Awful dark, isn't it, without the light?"

As her eyes adjusted, she could make out his gangly frame bending over to right the saucer with a clatter, and search for the matches. He talked as he did so.

"Lucky I got this for you, wasn't it? All because I wanted to look after you, see. Now, our Mam, she would take it away, given half the chance – if she thought you didn't deserve it. Doesn't understand what it feels like to be scared of the dark, does she? Especially in an old house like this that's full of spiders and good-ness knows what sort of other nasty stuff."

Amy didn't answer. She hadn't thought about the dark for ages. She wanted to be brave enough to tell him that she didn't care, that she'd rather the dark and be left alone. But what if that did happen – what if she was alone in the night… and all the strange shapes that rested quite happily in the recesses of the room during the day reared up into terrible creatures that threat-ened to choke the life out of her… what would she do then… ?

Edwin was still talking as he straightened up from lighting the candle. "She'd be jealous of our little secrets, too. Probably take it out on you, she would."

Amy pictured Mrs. Preece, with her mouth set in a grim line, looking crosser than she'd ever looked before as Amy tried to tell her what her son had done. She knew that Edwin's words held a warning. There was a strange squirming feeling in her stomach that she was pretty sure was never going to go away. How could she tell anyone, anyway, about the things Edwin had just done, without shrivelling up with shame?

"So tell me we'll keep our little secrets, and then I can go on looking after you," he said.

She nodded, miserably. He leaned over to kiss her but she

turned her head quickly enough for the kiss to land on her cheek.

"There we are, then. Off to sleep now, little sister, I'll see you in the morning."

But his voice held no comfort, like it had before. Now it seemed to hold a warning.

14.

Mair Parry was cleaning the grate when she heard somebody at the door. She gave a little smile of satisfaction at the thud-thud of the heavy brass knocker because she had cleaned it vigorously just two hours earlier, as she always did twice a week, buffing it with a piece of soft flannel from her husband's worn out underwear. The person now using it with such authority would be able to see their face in the lustrous metal, distorted by its curves into a parody of their usual self, if they stood close enough to try to peer through the small diamond pane of glass just above it.

She gave the little grunt of late middle age when forcing once-agile knees to straighten up to standing, and put out a hand to the back of a chair to help her get to her feet. She swiftly undid the apron she wore for doing the dirty jobs, wiped her hands in it and left it at the side of the fireplace before hurrying through the hall to the front door, where the knocker had just fallen again – a short, impatient rap this time.

Mair's shocked little "Oh!" as she opened the door wasn't one of surprise at the wiry little man on the other side. She'd known Emrys Hughes for most of her life. She'd seen him come back from the Great War, partially deafened by the explosion in a bunker that had left him the only one alive and, some said, slightly weaker in the head.

Her shocked little "Oh!" was because of the envelope Emrys was mutely holding out to her. An irrational picture of the young telegram boys in the films her husband Delwyn sometimes took her to see popped into her head. Usually American, the telegram boys wore uniforms with shiny brass buttons to match her door knocker, and little hats set at a jaunty angle, and they whistled cheerily as they cycled along wide, tree-lined streets of clapboard houses.

Emrys didn't look like that at all. His old postman's uniform, that looked as if it had belonged to someone else, was as sombre as his expressionless face, and she'd never heard him whistle like the boys in the films. The envelope looked exactly the same, though.

She swallowed the "Oh" back into a throat that was suddenly so parched that no other sound would come out.

"Telegram for you, Mrs. Parry," Emrys mumbled, fixing his eyes on her hands, which she was rubbing down the sides of her clothes – not because they were dirty this time, but because they felt clammy and the ends of her fingers were tingling slightly.

She didn't want to take it. If she didn't take it she wouldn't have to face what it might contain. But he was holding it out to her, with no more words that may have given her a choice in the matter.

"Thank you," she managed, in a voice so small that Emrys would have had to lip read, before closing the door without noticing the ray of sunshine that bounced off the gleaming knocker.

She sat for some time at the kitchen table, staring at the innocuous brown envelope which she knew would contain the words that would change her life for ever. Or finish it completely.

She wondered if Emrys knew the message inside. The proper postman, Idris, always seemed to know what was in the letters he delivered. If you were outside whitening the step or wiping down the window ledges when he arrived, he would tell you.

"Letter from your old Mam," he'd say. "Not so good these days, is she?" or, "Only a bill it is, today, for the electric." And he'd know whether it was a red one inside because he'd remember when he'd brought you the earlier one.

But you didn't see Emrys so often. He usually did the odd jobs around the back of Thomas's shop that doubled as the post office, or brought the parcels, balancing them on the basket of his ramshackle bicycle. Or, now, delivered the telegrams.

Mair continued to sit on the kitchen chair until she heard the clock in the front room striking the hour. *Delwyn will be home for his dinner, soon.* The thought seemed to bring her back to the day. She stood up and retrieved her apron from where she had hastily flung it she didn't know how many minutes ago. When it was firmly tied around her comfortable waist she picked up the envelope and slid it into her apron pocket. For a little while longer she could keep her boy with her, and she could carry on making plans for his next leave and could picture the front door slamming so that the knocker bounced of its own accord, and his exuberant step along the hallway, kitbag over one shoulder and his Pilot Officer's hat on the back of his head. She continued her chores, so familiar to her that her hands worked automatically without engaging her mind.

She had been going to wait until Delwyn had eaten his dinner, but one look at his dear, bluff face made her resolve crumble. At that moment his world still contained the gnawing anxiety that made them both turn away from newspaper reports, and take a long time to get to sleep at nights, but it also contained the tiny flame of hope which had sustained them thus far; that 'no news is good news'; that God would take care of their Lloyd.

Delwyn was still holding his cap as she proffered the buff envelope. She saw the tiny flame extinguished.

"It came... this morning. I couldn't..." she managed, as he threw his cap aside and turned the envelope over in his strong, work-a-day hands.

She kept her eyes on his face as he tore it open and she saw his features change into those of an old man as he scanned the message.

"He's gone, love," he told her, raising his eyes to hers and seeing his own agony reflected there. "*Killed in action,* it says."

"But he's our only one, Del," she whispered, nothing but her lips moving. "Why take him? Why take all we've got?"

She sank down into the same chair where she had sat for so long this morning, when she had still been able to pretend. As her head came down to rest on her arms, her husband moved around the table and put one hand on her shoulder, the telegram crushed in the other.

Lydia took the call just as the doctor was parking his bicycle at the front door after completing a string of visits following morning surgery.

"It's Delwyn Parry here, it is – can the doctor come?" the voice said. "Had a bit of shock, we have. Our son –" Lydia could hear his voice wobble here; "our son," he went on after a pause. "He's been killed... killed in action... and the wife's taking it pretty bad. I don't know what to do with her – just sitting there, she is, can't get her to move. I think she's in shock – can the doctor come?"

"He's just got back from his calls now – I'll tell him straight away," Lydia promised.

"Tell him Delwyn Parry," the man repeated. "He knows where we live."

"I will," she said, "and – and I'm sorry –" But the line went dead before she could be certain that the man had heard her.

Dr. Eliot looked enquiringly at her as he came through into the hall.

"I'll go now," he said, picking up his bag again when Lydia told him. "He was an only child, they'll be devastated."

"Mr. Parry sounded very worried about his wife," Lydia said.

Dr. Eliot nodded, taking long strides towards the front door. He was worried about both of them. Delwyn Parry already had angina and a shock like this could do terrible things to a man.

Lydia went back to the kitchen, covered the doctor's dinner with a plate and put it back in the oven to keep warm. After a moment she did the same with hers. Somehow it didn't seem right to sit calmly and eat a meal when just a short distance away two people's lives had been shattered. Behind her, Grace was rolling over on some cushions on the floor, alternately chewing and babbling at her little toy rabbit. Lydia smiled at her and gave thanks that she had had a daughter.

It was over an hour before the doctor returned. Lydia could see from the set of his face that it was better to simply place his dinner in front of him rather than say anything. But after a polite "Thank you" and a few mouthfuls, he pushed the plate away.

"Would you like to come for a walk this afternoon?" he asked. "I feel the need to get out for a while but, to tell you the truth, I could also do with the company."

"Yes – yes, of course," Lydia said, "but where would you like to go? The pram won't manage the paths up the hillsides."

"If we go out past Llewellyn's farm there's an old track on the left, which eventually winds in between the hills – I think the pram would be alright on that, and if it's not we can leave it on the side and I'll carry Grace. Unless – unless you had other plans?"

"No, none." She shook her head, grateful that this afternoon wasn't her turn at the Red Shed. He'd had several late night call-outs recently and the strain could be seen around his eyes.

As they walked through the village it was obvious that news of the Parrys' loss had already been made known to most people. There were one or two people about, talking in hushed voices, who turned to look and nod as Lydia and Dr. Eliot went by, but there were no children running around. At times like these they were taken indoors and told to play quietly.

Lydia didn't need to ask where the Parrys lived. Just before the streets gave way to countryside was a small lane with a terrace of five houses set along one side, with front gardens enclosed by dark brown wooden fencing. All five had their sitting room curtains closed as a mark of respect. The front door of the second house opened as they passed, disgorging a small, barrel-shaped man and the woman with the squashed-in mouth whom Lydia had met a couple of times. The man gave them a quiet, "Good afternoon," but the woman simply stared.

"The Baptist minister and his right-hand woman," Dr. Eliot muttered when they'd walked on a bit further.

"Will there be a funeral?" Lydia asked cautiously.

The doctor shook his head. "I doubt there will be a body to bring back. And they won't know yet anyway – they'll have to get in touch with Lloyd's unit. Those two were just visiting to bring some comfort I think – although they wouldn't be my personal choice in these circumstances – but then I'm not from round here."

There was a flatness to his voice that she hadn't heard before. She waited until they had turned off onto the track before she spoke again.

"It must be difficult to find any words of comfort when people have lost their only child," she said. Then, after a second's pause, "Even for a doctor who's more used to dealing with loss."

The track, whilst smooth enough for the pram, began to steepen and with a "Here, let me," he took over the pushing as if he hadn't heard what Lydia had said.

After a few moments, though, when he had seemed intent on looking at the prettiness of their surroundings, he turned his head towards her.

"It's the sheer waste I can't understand. When someone has reached the natural end of their lives, there's something about the rhythm of events that helps to make it seem alright. We're born, we live out our lives, and then we die. And very often you can see in the eyes of an elderly person that they are tired and ready for the end."

He gave a despairing shake of the head. "But when it's someone young, someone whose adult life has barely begun… it's hard. Lloyd Parry was only twenty. And the stupidity of it is that there will be other women, all over Europe, whichever side they're on, breaking their hearts like Mrs. Parry, for their fine young men. And this devastation has been caused by the mega-lomaniac ambitions of one man, and the evil of those who have chosen to listen to him."

His hold had tightened on the pram handle and his lips were set in a thin line. He was looking ahead again, but Lydia wasn't sure if he was seeing their surroundings.

"I'm always reminded of a poem by Yeats, written during the last lot," he said. "*An Irish Airman Foresees his Death*…"

"*I know that I shall meet my fate, somewhere amongst the clouds above,*" Lydia recited softly. He turned his head to her again, sharply.

"You know it!" He stopped walking.

"It's one of my favourites."

He looked at her for a little longer, then carried on pushing the pram. "It's the lines, *No likely end could bring them loss, Or leave them happier than before,* that I always think about. There are going to be so many young men who will make that ultimate sacrifice before – *if* – we manage to defeat Hitler, and that's looking by no means certain at the moment, is it? And they'll be remembered with all the glory of parades and services – another generation wiped out like the last time.

"And just like last time," he went on, almost unaware of Lydia's presence now as he poured out his feelings, "they're all too young to have made their mark on life, aren't they? They'll be remembered collectively, but their individual passing won't have an effect on anything else – no children left behind to continue the family line, no great contribution to society or the world, except by their death. All that's left is people like those two I've seen today, who will just become old before their time. Sometimes it all seems so pointless."

Lydia didn't know what to say. Her thoughts were with

another young man, whose fate she still was unsure of. What if Billy was dead? Would there be anyone at all who would mourn his passing? Or would give a thought about the child he had left behind – *his* only evident contribution to the world – sleeping peacefully at this moment in a pram being pushed by another man? She herself had no feelings left for Billy, except profound regret that the happy life she had envisaged with him had turned to dust.

Dr. Eliot's sense of desolation at the waste of young lives was catching, wrapping itself around her like a shroud. Billy's life, if he was still living it, was a waste if it continued to be dominated by drink. Their marriage had been a waste, the only good thing salvaged from it being little Grace. Lydia wondered what she would tell her daughter about her father as she grew up. Should she pretend he was one of the valiant fallen, so that Grace could be proud of him? Perhaps, if he was still in the army, that would actually become his fate anyway.

She tried to push her thoughts away and find some words of comfort for the decent man walking beside her, but they failed to come and a glance at his profile showed that the fresh air was doing little to lift his mood.

Further along she saw two large boulders at the side of the track which looked as if they had been placed there deliberately as an invitation to rest.

"Shall we sit for a few moments?" she suggested, indicating the stones.

The track had taken them up and round the side of a hill so that the view was now one of a wide valley floor where the river meandered in deep curves, its banks gouged from winter swell, and both sides flanked by a patchwork of fields. On the further side, more hills rose in varying degrees of steepness, some heavily wooded. No sign of the war which today had touched the village so forcibly. A little piece of heaven, Lydia thought.

She contented herself with staring at the view, searching for a comment to make which would lighten the mood, whilst aware of the doctor's gaze upon her.

"I'm sorry," he said at last.

"What for?" she asked, realising as she turned towards him that they were sitting very close together. "Feeling sad at the senseless loss of someone you knew? That's nothing to apologise for."

"Yes there is. I had overlooked the fact that you had suffered a similar loss – I didn't mean to bring it all back for you. I'm sorry."

Lydia dipped her head onto her chest, unable to meet his gaze. She said nothing for a moment or two. When she raised her head again he was still looking at her, and she felt once more the same awareness between them that there had been on the night of the storm.

She met his eyes and began to speak, slowly and deliberately. "My marriage was one of those things I think people would refer to as a 'whirlwind romance'," she said. "We hadn't known each other for very long before we married, and – well, the marriage was nothing like I thought it would be. Apart from having Grace, there was nothing else to hold it together. I – I was in mourning for my marriage long before we came here. And now it's ended, it feels like it never happened – or happened in some other life that has nothing to do with my life now, and precious little to do with me having a child."

She gave a little shake of her head when he didn't speak straight away. "The only way this news about Lloyd Parry has affected me is as a mother – I had no idea motherhood would heighten the emotions to the extent that it has. And I can't imagine how I would cope if anything were to happen to Grace – so how that poor woman must be feeling, to have lost her only child…"

As she spoke she felt tears well up. Sitting in the sunshine overlooking a view that surely must be close to paradise, she felt sorry for them all. Inexplicably sorry for a couple whom she'd never met, but she could still hear Mr. Parry's voice as he tried to tell her what was wrong over the telephone. She felt sorry for her own child, who would grow up without a father's love, and she felt sorry, not for herself exactly, but for the situation she was in. She realised now what a child she herself had been when she was swept off her feet by Billy, with an idealistic view of love and marriage that, she had been convinced, could cast aside obstacles of class and background. And perhaps it would have done if they had both been a little wiser, and if Billy's jealousies hadn't made him so violent.

She felt sorry that she'd had deeper, more meaningful conversations with the man sat beside her than she'd ever had with her husband. Perhaps that, too, would have changed if their relationship had had a chance to mature. But it made her realise that here, in this little corner of South Wales, which she still didn't know very well, she had met a man who, had they met in other circumstances, she would have wanted to get to know much, much better.

Her sorrow encompassed him as well. He was a good man. She knew that very often he didn't charge his patients for his visits, or charged a small amount that didn't cover the number of times he went to a house or saw someone in his surgery. She'd seen how often he had appeared burdened with anxiety or over-work, but had never heard him complain that being the only doctor in the village and all the outlying farms was too much for him.

It wasn't fair. He deserved an equally good woman by his side, to break through the reserve and aura of loneliness that at times seemed to swamp him. And, with sudden clarity, which only deepened her pain, she realised that if such a woman were to come along whilst she, Lydia, was still his housekeeper, she would be searingly jealous.

All this emotion swirled around her head in a matter of seconds. Dashing away her tears with the heel of her hand she attempted to give a watery smile, while avoiding his eyes.

"I thought I was coming along on this walk to try to cheer you up – and now look at me! I hardly ever cry! It's just sitting here – it's all so beautiful… but there are so many sad, bad things happening all around us…"

"*Lydia.*"

It was her name on a puff of wind again, a caress. With one hand under her chin, he gently turned her face to his. He held a large white handkerchief in his other hand, with which he slowly wiped away her tears, his touch gossamer light, belying the burning intensity of his eyes as they solemnly held hers. A simple action, taking only a few moments, during which she felt he could see into her very soul. Nothing Billy had done, even in their most passionate moments together, had ever made her feel as wanted, or as cared for, as this.

"*Lydia.*"

His head moved forward until their lips met. Slowly, almost

languorously, he teased her into responding, until she could bear it no longer and broke away with a cry. She buried her head in his shoulder, her body heaving with silent sobs, as he held her, one hand caressing her hair.

She didn't know how many minutes they sat there, but as her sobs subsided, she heard him say with a wry note, "Well, I've only known a few women in my time, but I've never managed to reduce them to such distress quite so quickly."

She raised her head with a weak smile, taking the handkerchief that was proffered once more. Her sorrow threatened to overcome her again when she saw the smile he gave her in return. She knew that she had the power to make this man happy, but instead she was more likely to break his heart. She would have to tell him the truth and risk the consequences. It was this awful knowledge, as soon as she felt herself answer his kiss, that had made her cry with such desperation.

"Andrew…" It sounded strange to use his name aloud for the first time. She realised that she had never heard anyone else use it. He was forever defined by his title, 'the Doctor', on whom everyone else could depend, make demands, seek reassurance, ask for the impossible when reality was more than they could bear – yet no-one knew him intimately enough to call him by his given name.

Before she could go any further he put his fingers to her lips.

"Sssh!… It's all right. You don't have to say anything. I know it's very soon, and I'm sorry – but I've been wanting to do that for quite some time!"

His fingers traced the outline of her mouth, making her gasp. How could this complex, reserved man be so sensual? Her head moved towards him again, almost against her will, as he took his hand away, but she stopped herself. She could go no further until he knew and had judged her.

"No… it's not that –" Her jagged breathing made her voice sound different, less confident. She strove to be more assertive. "I have to explain… tell you more about myself… it's not easy…"

She had to steal herself to go on, knowing that she risked losing everything she was on the verge of discovering. She swallowed hard and was about to say the most difficult words she had ever had to utter in her life, when Grace, who had been stirring for some time unnoticed, chose to let out an imperious wail that Lydia knew would not stop until she was attended to.

The baby's cry seemed to break the spell that surrounded them. Lydia lifted her out of the pram and settled down to feed her. For the first time she felt embarrassed to be exposing her breast in front of the doctor, and she sensed he felt the same. In unconscious imitation of poor Mr. Owain Owen, he stood up and scanned the horizon, pointing out the landmarks in conversational tones as if the previous interlude had never happened.

By the time the baby was settled back in her pram a strong breeze was blowing.

"This is coming from the coast – I think it might bring some rain with it," Andrew said. "Perhaps we should head for home."

Home. Lydia almost choked at the sound of the word. The cosy kitchen which owed nothing to fashion and everything to comfort had become her home in such a short time, especially when the doctor, *Andrew,* was sitting the other side of the hearth from her. She hadn't made much impact on the rest of the house but she had made bright new cushion covers for the two kitchen armchairs.

Andrew had even commented on how cheerful they looked.

"We've been teaching the little girls how to use Edyth's old sewing machine," she'd told him. "And Edyth had some remnants, so I thought new covers would be a good idea – especially as they're washable for when Grace dribbles on them. I hope you don't mind?"

He'd looked about him then, as if for the first time. "Not at all," he'd said with a small smile. "This place is a bit drab, isn't it? Please feel free to make it your own."

So she had, as much as restrictions would allow. There'd been just enough material left to make a pair of curtains, but she hadn't put those up yet. She'd promised Rhian and Amy that they could help her, as they had done most of the machine sewing so that the hems zig-zagged a little in places, but she'd told them it was excellent.

She would talk to Andrew when they reached home, she decided. The bleak thought arose that it would then probably be her home for very little longer. It made her shiver.

"Are you cold? Would you like my jacket round your shoulders?" Andrew asked.

"No. No I'm fine, thank you." She managed a strained smile whilst wishing that they could have stayed together longer on the boulders so that she could have savoured the feel of his arms around her for a few minutes more.

As if by mutual consent they talked about inconsequential things on the way back. Reaching the edge of the village, Lydia said, "I think I should take the pram from here, don't you?"

He raised his eyebrows in surprise.

"Well... people might think... you know..." She floundered under his quizzical gaze. "It looks so proprietorial, if you see what I mean."

"Ah! You mean they might think there was something between us if they see me pushing the pram like a proud father?" There was a smile twitching at the sides of his mouth.

"Yes... well... it could look quite..." She hesitated to use the word 'intimate', because she was dreadfully aware, as he looked at her, of the spark, now more of a flame, between them once more.

He relinquished the pram handle without forcing her to go on, but the smile grew.

"Perhaps they have a point."

Lydia only just made out his murmured words, before he changed the subject again and made his voice more circumspect. She needn't have worried, though, as there were only one or two people about in the village.

Thankfully there was plenty to do with preparing their evening meal and settling Grace for the night before she had to think once more about her confession. Andrew made himself busy in the garden, tying in bean and pea tendrils and checking tomato trusses before the storm that was threatening took hold, so there was no mention of what had passed between them during the afternoon.

After they had listened to the evening news, which just seemed to be getting gloomier by the day, no matter how carefully the BBC tried to dress it up, she asked if she could switch the wireless off.

"Like I said this afternoon, I need to talk to you," she said, aware that the thumping of her heart was at odds with the careful calmness of her words. She sat on the corner of the sofa where she had perched on that first evening. Somehow it was better to face him in the more austere atmosphere of the sitting room.

He sat back in his armchair, his eyes trying to meet hers, but her head was cast down, as if concentrating on her interlaced fingers in her lap.

"All right," he said equably.

Lydia raised her eyes to his. "I'm not really a widow – at least I don't think I am – I'm not sure. I wasn't, when I got here, as far as I know, and I may not be now."

Aware that she was making no sense, and that he wasn't going to say anything at this stage, she took another deep breath.

"My marriage turned out to be an unhappy and violent one. Just before the gas explosion, Billy – my husband – had found out that I intended leaving him and attacked me. After the explosion I took Grace and fled. I left Billy on the floor, just alive, I think, because there was a faint pulse, and I went to the station and joined the evacuees coming here. That's why Mr. Owain Owen didn't know where to place me – I wasn't on any of the lists."

"Lydia –"

"No, don't interrupt me, please –" Damn the man! Why did the very way he said her name make her insides flip, when she needed to be strong to get through this?

"I'm sorry that I lied to you," she went on, "but at the time I was scared and confused. I just wanted to get away as far as possible and this seemed the perfect haven where I could sit out the war and wait to see what happened. I hadn't really thought things through, so when I was asked where my husband was I said he'd been killed. And once I'd said that, I couldn't go back on it. And it would have been all right." She was finding it hard to get the words out through the sobs which threatened to choke her. "It would have been all right, it wouldn't have mattered, if I hadn't – if you – if we hadn't…"

She bit hard on her lip before continuing. "So I think it would be best if I left here. I'll see Mr. Owain Owen tomorrow."

He gave no response. The only visible movement was the rise and fall of his chest and the slight twitch of a muscle in his cheek.

Lydia stood up slowly and walked out to the kitchen. The bright red chair cushions seemed to mock her with their cheerfulness. She wouldn't even hang the new curtains now. Little Amy would be disappointed.

She felt numb. Automatically she reached for the kettle and turned to the sink.

Andrew was standing in the doorway.

"I knew," he said.

"Wh-a-at?"

"Not properly, but I knew you were hiding something. Your injuries when you came here – there were boot marks on your skin, for goodness' sake. And you never get any post – army widow's bumpf and things."

He moved into the room until they were facing one another.

"Don't go." His voice was low and hoarse, his eyes pleading.

"I'll end up hurting you."

"I'll be hurt if you leave."

"But how can I stay… now that we've… now that there are feelings… and I'm not free… and…"

His arms came round her so quickly that the kettle in her hand clattered to the floor. This time his kiss was passionate, intense, as if its very force could make her change her mind. It was impossible not to respond to his urgency, to the feel of his body against hers.

"We can sort things out…" he murmured breathlessly when they eventually pulled apart. "Find out what's happened to your… husband. You can file for divorce if necessary."

"No!" Her vehemence made him let go of her arms.

"It's not as simple as that," she went on, shaking her head.

Taking a deep breath she sank onto one of the chairs at the table and waited until he did the same.

"I can't risk Billy finding out where I am – and if I file for divorce, he'd contest it, I know he would. I left him after all."

"But your injuries – I'd be witness to those –"

She gave a little smile at his naivety. "What? The man I've been sharing a house with? What do you think his side would make of that? My father's a solicitor – I've heard round the dinner table how they can make mincemeat of people if they choose to. Believe me, it would be all about a wife playing fast and loose while her brave husband was doing his duty defending his country.

"And there's something else," she went on, while he thought

about what she had already said. "He'd want Grace, that's definite – and if I was portrayed as some sort of scarlet woman he'd
probably get her."

They sat for a few moments longer, one of her hands in both
of his, their heads bent but not quite touching. Almost absent-
mindedly his finger traced the outline of the veins on the back of
her hand.

"So you see," she said gently, forcing the words out when no
part of her being wanted to utter them; "so you see, it would be
better if I left. If we let this… infatuation… die its death…"

"*Infatuation!*" His head shot up, his expression more pained
than at any time when he had returned from a difficult visit. "Is
that how you see this?"

"I don't know! Maybe… perhaps we've been thrown
together…" She wanted to pull her hand away so that she could
turn aside from his pain and attempt to deal with her own. But
his grip was too tight. The force of his gaze compelled her to
return it.

"Do you remember the night when you arrived?" he asked.

She nodded.

"Well, seeing as this is owning-up time…" Now it was his
turn to take a deep breath. "When you turned up on my doorstep
that evening… I was overwhelmed… from that first sight of you,
standing there so slight with a baby in your arms, and looking so
defiant but scared at the same time… I think I fell for you right at
that moment."

She couldn't help but smile. "You had a funny way of showing
it – you could hardly speak to me!"

"I know – but then I never have been one for charming the
birds off the trees."

"You've become a hit with everyone in the village, though."

He gave a wry smile in return. "It's easier when I'm 'the doctor'
and I know what I'm talking about. It's much harder when I'm
being plain old Andrew Eliot."

She wanted to say that she liked plain old Andrew Eliot much
better, but he was talking again.

"When I first came here, a couple of years ago, it was my way
of hiding from the outside world as well. I'd been very hurt…
a love affair had fizzled out, on my part anyway, but when I

tried to end it she made all sorts of claims against me... called my professional integrity into question, that sort of thing... it all turned very nasty..."

He paused, as if even now the memories were too difficult.

"You don't have to tell me this – you don't owe me any explanations," Lydia said.

"Yes – I do!" He collected himself. "What I'm trying to say is that you bowled me over, when I'd vowed to steer clear of women, and yet you obviously had a troubled past. Even if what you said had been true, at the very least that made you a grieving widow with a baby to care for – so I was determined not to let my feelings get the better of me."

He smiled properly for the first time that evening. "Failed miserably, I'm afraid!"

Then he became serious again. "So here I am, falling in love with a woman who I've only known for a couple of months, and who isn't sure whether she's married or not."

Falling in love. He'd said he was falling in love with her! The words sent prickles of heat down her spine whilst at the same time she knew that she couldn't, wouldn't, be the one to hurt him again.

"What would you have done if this afternoon hadn't happened?" she asked, as evenly as she could.

He shrugged. "Gone on hoping that I could contain my feelings for you, until you felt able to tell me more about yourself. I was sure that you would, one day – although the more time I've spent with you the harder it's been."

"That's just it!" she cried. "It's going to be harder and harder, isn't it? Now that we know... now that we both..."

He raised an eyebrow quizzically, saying nothing, willing her to continue. She knew that he was waiting for her to declare herself. She looked steadily at him.

"Now that we both feel the same about each other."

There. She'd said it. Any last shred of independence she held in reserve was demolished by her admittance.

"If I left, *now*, there's a chance we could both –"

"There's a chance we could both regret it for the rest of our lives," he interrupted. "We've each made mistakes – surely we should try to get this one right, not just give up on it because it's going to be difficult?"

"I could tell Mr. Owain Owen that I'm not happy here – that it's too quiet, or that we're not getting on." Her words were coming out in a rush, so that he couldn't interrupt. "He could arrange for me to go somewhere else – it can be done – then there's a chance we'd forget…"

She could hear her voice changing as she tried to choke back the tears that threatened. "I'll just bring you trouble – it's too hard… and if you've been through it all before, how can you contemplate it happening again?"

"Because I've done a lot of thinking during the past few weeks. And I've realised that hiding away, trying to pretend one is happy when it's patently not the case, is no way to live. I know, just know, that you would never willingly hurt me, and I'll protect you until my dying day, so surely together we can deal with this."

"You say that now, but what if –"

She was stopped by his hands reaching out to hold each side of her face.

"Do you want to leave?" he asked gently.

A kaleidoscope of pictures whirled through her brain. Andrew coming into the house with his rapid step, absorbed in whatever situation he'd just returned from; looking across at her with a smile as they worked in the garden; his earnest face when they discussed the progress of the war; his tenderness when he played with the baby; his quick laugh when she mimicked some of the people in the village; the need in his voice when he whispered "*Lydia*"…

"Do you want to leave?" he asked again.

"No."

15.

The doctor's house looked a bit grand close up, but Arfur wasn't going to be put off. Rhian and Amy had been here, with Mrs. Dawson, so he could come here too, couldn't he? Besides, he was here for a proper reason, not just to pull soppy faces at Mrs. Dawson's baby. He needed to see the doctor.

He hesitated on the gravel drive in front of the house. Should he go into the door at the side marked 'Surgery'? Or should he go round the back instead of knocking on the front door? The woman who lived in the biggest house near them in London always shouted at delivery boys who went to the front door, refusing to have anything to do with them until they went round the back.

He could see from the glass that there was no-one else in the room, but then he noticed a bell to the side of the surgery door. Probably Mrs. Dawson would answer it anyway, and she was nice, so it wouldn't matter too much. He pressed it quickly before he could change his mind.

It wasn't Mrs. Dawson who came to the door but a woman in a gleaming white overall. He thought he'd seen her in the village with her children, although she didn't look as efficient without the white coat. She had a concerned smile on her face as she opened the door, though, so he took a deep breath.

"Is he in? The doctor?" he asked.

"Yes, he's just finished surgery. Have you got a message for him? Is somebody poorly?"

"I need to see him," Arfur said.

The fixed expression on his face gave nothing away.

"Children usually have to be seen with their parents – or a grown-up who's in charge of them," Rita said, recognising him at once. Her own boys had mentioned Arfur on numerous occasions, with the sort of hero worship reserved for lads who constantly got into trouble but didn't seem to care.

"I just want to talk to him – ask him something. Don't need no

171

grown-ups for that," Arfur said, one foot already over the step so that she couldn't close the door on him.

"Sit down by there," Rita told him, indicating a bench, "and I'll just find out if he can see you."

She was back in a moment, her overall rustling as she came in the door. "You're in luck, just going out on his calls he was, but he'll see you now. Don't you keep him long, mind," her voice held a warning note, "because he's a very busy man. So no messing."

She showed him into a room that held a heavy wooden desk with lots of forms and important-looking pieces of paper on it, a brass lamp, a large blotter, and an inkwell. A tall glass-fronted bookcase stood against one wall, and on another was an eye chart.

Arfur moved to the end of the room, closed one eye tightly, and began to read down the chart when a door on the opposite side of the room opened and in walked the doctor.

"You wanted to see me?" he asked, pointing to a chair for Arfur to sit down, as he moved behind the desk. Blinking rapidly because he now couldn't see very well out of his left eye, Arfur decided to stay standing.

"I just wanted to ask you," he said, "about how long it takes for a broken leg to get better."

The doctor frowned. "Who has a broken leg?"

"Me Mum – but she's not here, she's still in London. That's why I'm here – 'cos she bust her leg. But I want to know when it's likely to be mended."

"I see. Well, it depends on which bit of her leg she broke, and how bad it was."

"She broke the top bit," Arfur said, pointing to his thigh. "They put all these ropes and things on it."

"And when did she do it?"

"June – just before all the 'vaccees came down here."

"Hmm – let's add the weeks up, then." Dr. Eliot strode over to a calendar on the wall, muttering as he flicked through it.

"If I remember rightly, you all arrived in the early part of June, and if your mother broke her leg just before… and it's nearly the end of August now, then by my reckoning her accident will have been nearly twelve weeks ago…" he turned back to Arthur, "so she should be well on the mend now."

"So will she be coming out of hospital soon?"

"It's really difficult for me to say because I haven't seen your mother, so I don't know what sort of fracture – break – she had. But it's possible she's walking a little bit with crutches now, and she may be allowed home shortly."

Arfur's face shone. "She'll be home in no time, she will. A proper fighter, me Mum – and she won't have liked being stuck in hospital."

The doctor smiled. "That's just the sort of patient I like – someone who is determined to get better quickly. It really helps – especially when you have to get walking again. And that can take a bit of time, you know. It can be painful after you've been stuck in bed for weeks on traction – that's what they call the ropes."

But Arfur's optimism refused to be dimmed. "She'll do it in no time. I know her. She won't mind a bit of pain if it gets her out of there."

"Then she sounds a very brave lady. Now – is there anything else I can help you with? Because I really should be getting along to see my other patients."

"No, that's it. Thanks, doc. See ya."

Arfur wheeled round and left the room the way he'd come. He sauntered down the drive, whistling, leaving Andrew wishing all his patients were so easily satisfied.

Arfur mentally re-jigged his plans as he made his way back to the farm. The doctor had told him all he wanted to know. His Mum would be on crutches by now and, knowing her, she would have made sure she was out of hospital as soon as she could get about on them.

"Nasty places them 'ospitals, full of sick people," he could hear her saying when she fetched him home from having his quinsies done.

He hadn't gone to the children's club in the village this week because all the talk was of the other evacuees' mothers coming to see them. A special train was being put on, and there had been great excitement, and a lot of boasting, as each child confirmed that their parent was definitely coming. But now he could join them, 'cos now he was certain that his Mum would be there as well.

He knew his Mum. She'd spring it on him as a surprise. That's why she hadn't written. She'd turn up on her crutches, having made sure they'd got her the best seat on the train and the bus, and lots of people to help her, 'cos that was what she was like. She could turn on her charm and give people her cheeky smile, and they'd all do their best for her.

And once she was down here, he'd be able to persuade her to take him back to London. That bit would be easy, 'cos she wouldn't want to be parted from him either, and he could tell her about the bit of money he'd saved up that he now wouldn't need for his train fare. Run to a good few trips to the pictures and a fish supper afterwards, that would.

He was pleased he'd plucked up courage to go to see the doctor. He'd only seen him in the distance before, and he'd looked a bit scary, like all doctors did. But he'd been nice. Didn't go on about why didn't Arfur know how his Mum was from her letters, like lots of other people would. And he'd said Mum was brave and wished she was his patient. He was all right, that doctor.

I think I've just seen one of your young protégés," Andrew told Lydia when he went through into the house. "Rita said his name was Arthur."

"Yes, he's the lad staying with the Llewellyns," Lydia replied. "Is he all right? Only I know Edyth is worried about him."

"He wanted to know when his mother's broken leg would heal. Luckily I remembered just in time not to ask whether he'd heard from her. Isn't he the child who hasn't had any word since he's been here?"

"That's him. Mr. Llewellyn phoned the hospital a while ago and they said she was doing well – but there was no reason why she couldn't contact Arthur. He's a sad boy – full of bravado on the surface, but worrying his little heart out underneath."

Andrew raised an eyebrow. "Not unlike someone else I could mention," but finished with a smile so that Lydia could smile back at him.

"Has Rita left?" he went on.

"A few minutes ago – while you were still in the surgery."

"Good – then I can do this." He leaned forward and kissed her resoundingly on the lips. "See you later."

He picked up his bag and was gone before the imprint of his mouth on hers had left Lydia's lips. She stood for a while, savouring the moment, before she shook her head with a slight smile and returned to her chores.

It had taken a long time, that emotional evening, to thrash out what they were going to do. Lydia had been convinced that to develop any sort of relationship, no matter how much they both wanted it, would be madness, but Andrew had urged her to change her mind.

"The way things are going at the moment, we don't know what the future will be for any of us," he'd said. "Even if the RAF keep Hitler at bay in the skies, he's not going to give up. He'll send all he can to destroy us – I think we're still at the beginning."

"At least just say you'll stay, for the time being. See how we go on," he'd insisted eventually, when the continued nearness of his body, and the earnestness of his voice – this, from the same man who could barely say two sentences to her when she first arrived – were beginning to wear her down so that all she wanted to do was fold herself into the security of his arms and stay there.

"Tomorrow," she'd said at last, too weary almost to see, let alone think straight. "Let's decide tomorrow."

She hadn't been able to sleep, though. Hadn't really expected to, despite feeling bone tired. As soon as her head touched the pillow her brain seemed to wake up, swirling thoughts around her head like leaves in the autumn wind. She was buffeted by indecision. Every time she convinced herself that staying here would only lead to trouble, three words of Andrew's repeated in her head: "*Falling in love… falling in love…*"

She tortured herself with tantalizing pictures of how good it would be to let this first awakening of feelings blossom into something stronger. But then her whirring mind would take her back to the fact that she was still a married woman, and was currently living a lie.

And her marriage had been the result of a whirlwind courtship. Was she in danger again of letting her feelings overrun and take her into a worse mess than she was in already?

It didn't help that the baby, cutting her first tooth, was fractious and woke up several times, so many hours were spent sitting in the rocking chair.

By five o'clock Grace was finally sleeping, but Lydia was wide awake. She'd had enough, and decided to go downstairs to make some tea.

Standing by the back door, cup in hand, she'd watched the day wake up. The dawn chorus was still in full pelt and there was a fresh expectancy carried on the slight breeze that rounded the corner of the house. A new day, which, deep in her heart, she wanted to be just like the day before, and the one before that.

Soon there were stirrings down in the village. She heard the rumble of the bus taking the colliers to the morning shift, and the chug of the first train to Maesteg and beyond. She wondered how many of the miners resented being hundreds of feet underground when they'd had a glimpse of this beautiful day.

It wouldn't be beautiful for some, though. The Parrys would be waking up to the renewed knowledge that their days would never be bright again. It would be a day to be got through somehow, like all the days ahead, until, maybe, time might stretch a little healing patina across their hurt, enough for them to live with it.

Her own problems seemed insignificant by comparison, but nevertheless had to be addressed.

She was setting the table for breakfast when Andrew came into the kitchen. It wasn't until she saw his face, the hope and fervour in his eyes, that she knew what her answer would be.

"Well?" he'd said, without preamble.

"I'll stay," she'd replied, equally briefly because she could feel his tension. "For now. But there are conditions. You said last night we should see how we get on, so we stay exactly as we are – doctor and housekeeper, so there's no speculation in the village."

He'd nodded. "Of course."

"And that means –" This was difficult. She wasn't sure which words to use. "I think we should take things slowly… not rush… we still hardly know each other, so just because we're in the same house, doesn't mean we should… you know…" She was hurrying her words and could feel her colour rising.

He'd nodded again seriously, but she could see the corner of his mouth twitching as it did when he was trying not to smile. "You mean you don't want me to take advantage of the fact that your bedroom is just along the hallway?"

"Yes – I mean, not that I thought you would, but it's best to say, isn't it? To be honest about these things now, before they get too complicated –"

"Don't worry," he'd interrupted. "Your honour is safe – especially if you keep wrapping yourself up in Miss Williams' old aprons!"

"Good," she said firmly, "because then I shall be able to look those old women in the village straight in the eye if there is ever any hint of gossip about us."

That was several days ago. No difference, they had pledged to each other. Everything would carry on just the same. Except, of course, it didn't. Everything about their relationship shifted imperceptibly. There were the kisses, like just now, sweet and stolen when they were on their own. There was a lightness in Andrew's step, in his voice when he called her name as he came into the house, in the frequency of his smile. She was surprised that Rita failed to notice anything different when the electricity seemed to zing between them whenever they were in the same room.

For her own part, Lydia felt more secure than she had at any time since before Grace was born. She wasn't swept along by the reckless desires that had marked the beginning of her relationship with Billy. Here was something solid, she recognised, something borne of truly caring for another person.

Not that there wasn't the same urge to possess each other physically, though. The celibacy that Lydia insisted on added to the tantalizing need for one another and at times she was close to capitulating. But it wasn't only Andrew's reputation she was concerned about – having long ago ceased to care about her own – she continued to be aware that her own emotional state could not cope with another badly judged relationship.

The intimacy of their lives together made it hard come night time, though, to hang on to that resolve. They made sure that they climbed the stairs separately, after a lingering goodnight in the kitchen or the sitting room. Lydia usually went up first, listening for the creak of his footstep on the stairs as she lay chastely in her bed, torturing herself with what it would be like if he turned left instead of right on the landing, aware that the same thoughts would be going through his mind.

But she knew it was the right thing to do. Once she had made the decision to stay, she wanted to take time to savour the delights of getting to know this man properly, to peel away the layers of his masculine reserve and explore the complexities within.

A my hated the night time. She hated it now even more than when she was afraid of the blackout and had no night-light. She hated it especially on the evenings that Mrs. Preece went out.

She tried to stay out of the house as much as possible, and on the evenings Mrs. Preece went to meetings, she would have liked to stay out of the house all night. But, of course, those were the very times when Mrs. Preece would call her in early, "so that I know where you are before I leave."

Amy would try to delay things indoors. Find things to do, little jobs around the house that she could busy herself with and say that Mrs. Preece had asked her to do them, so that she could stay up later. But, inevitably, Edwin would fix her with those strange eyes and say, "Time for bed, little sister."

She never thought of him as "Our Edwin" any more. Every bit of her mind concentrated on disconnecting itself with the things that he did. Removing the "Our" from his name, even in her head, helped to reinforce the disconnection.

One night, when she was reassured because Mrs. Preece was downstairs, so Edwin would only spend a little time in her room, "tucking her in" as he called it, he came in and lay down beside her. Amy immediately tensed. This was what he usually did when his mother was out. It was the precursor to his hands fumbling under her nightie, and the weight of his body eventually on hers, so heavy that she thought she might suffocate, while he whispered in her ear, the whisperings gradually giving way to strange grunts and moans.

"Our Mam's fallen fast asleep over her knitting, she has." His voice held the hint of a girlish giggle. "Those poor Army boys will never get those socks she's making at this rate. So I thought I could say a proper goodnight to you tonight – been nearly a week since Mam's left us alone together."

"What if she wakes up and wonders why you're upstairs with me? Perhaps you'd better not stay here tonight, Edwin." She tried not to make her voice sound too pleading. She had already learned that that seemed to make Edwin more excited.

"I'll just have to tell her that you begged me to come into your room – that you wanted me to get into the bed with you and play our little games," he whispered, no sign of a giggle in his voice any more. "Dirty little girl, she'll think you are, then, won't she?"

Amy lay still, trying to take her mind to another place while Edwin wriggled and writhed on top of her. She made herself think of the following week when her mother would be coming to visit her. If she could just hold on that long, then everything would be all right. Her mother would understand and take her home again. She hadn't been able to tell her mother what was happening to her in her weekly letters home in case any of the teachers saw what she had written, and if she tried to write from this house, Mrs. Preece would read it. But once Mum was here, with her dear, sweet smile…

Edwin seemed to take longer than ever, until the tears that Amy usually shed when he'd finished began to seep from her tightly closed eyes, running down into her hair and onto the pillow.

Suddenly he stopped as the landing light was switched on. "That's our Mam," he whispered, scrambling off the bed and scrabbling at the buttons on his trousers.

"Stay there," he warned her. "I'll see to her."

Amy froze. What was he going to say to Mrs. Preece? She heard their muttered voices on the stairs. What if he was telling her that Amy asked him to do all those things? Mrs. Preece would come barging into her bedroom any minute now and do goodness knows what to her.

She needed the lavvy. She often did after Edwin's visits. But she was too scared to even get out and use the chamber pot under the bed. Mrs. Preece might hear her and demand to know why she was still awake, and she'd see that Amy had been crying and…

Her distress and her need started the tears up again. As they soaked into her pillow, she could hold on no longer. A corresponding wetness began to seep around her body, comforting at first in its warmth.

The voices died away on the stairs. But it was too late. Her shame complete, Amy curled herself into a tight little ball and prayed harder than she had ever prayed in Mrs. Preece's chapel that her mother would come soon and take her away from all of this.

The bed wasn't too wet next morning, although it smelled a bit. Amy made it extra carefully, so Mrs. Preece wouldn't be tempted to come in and tut and pull at the bedclothes as she sometimes did. Amy stripped and made her bed up herself on Monday mornings, so if she could get the sheets downstairs next Monday and into the pile beside the gas boiler in the kitchen, Mrs. Preece need be none the wiser.

Everything seemed normal when she went down for breakfast but she couldn't stop her heart thudding fast when Mrs. Preece exclaimed, "Ah! There you are!" But it was alright. She only went on to say, "Taking your time this morning, young lady, and here we are, waiting to say Grace."

Edwin ignored her completely but Amy could barely swallow a mouthful of porridge. "I'm sorry Mrs. Preece, but I'm not hungry," she said when the woman told her to eat up.

"It'll be there for you again tomorrow, then," Mrs. Preece said, her mouth working busily in disapproval. "And don't you come in here later on telling me you're hungry when you've turned away from good food."

Amy had no intention of returning to the house for the rest of the day. After completing her chores she made her escape as quickly as possible, joining her friends on the field next to the Red Shed where she would have her dinner. But even though Mrs. Dawson was there with baby Grace, which would normally have made it one of her favourite days, she found it hard to concentrate and take part in the games the others were playing.

It had happened quite a lot lately. One minute she'd be playing with the rest of them, the next she would be in this sort of frozen state, where she wasn't thinking about anything in particular. It was like her mind just went blank. The others often got impatient with her, especially if they were in the middle of a game of rounders or something, when they'd start shouting, "Come on Amy! Wake up! You could have got him out then!" She was usually one of the last picked for a team now, but she didn't really care too much about that. The times when she was 'somewhere else' were quite nice. For a few moments there was no nagging worry at the back of her mind, no dread about what might happen to her that night in Mrs. Preece's spotless spare bedroom.

Once or twice Mrs. Dawson had asked her if she was all right, and she had wished so badly that she could tell her. But last night wasn't the first time that Edwin had said that she was a 'dirty little girl'. How could she tell Mrs. Dawson about that? She probably wouldn't let her touch baby Grace ever again. And what would Edwin do if he found out she'd told on him? More than likely he'd tell everyone it was all her doing, and then she'd die of shame.

So she usually smiled and told Mrs. Dawson, "I'm fine, thank you." And Mrs. Dawson's concerned smile in return would make her turn away in case she cried because Mrs. Dawson reminded her of her mother.

The day began to get better. There was lots of talk of the parents' visit next week, which even Arfur joined in with, because apparently his Ma was coming too, with a pair of crutches. Then Mrs. Dawson found her and asked if she and Rhian wanted to come back after dinner and help put up the kitchen curtains they'd made.

"I can't," Rhian said, pulling a face. "Me and Bronwen got to help Mam this afternoon, we have. But you go," she told Amy when she saw her downcast expression, "'cos I'll be going out to play with Arthur afterwards, but if you go home after dinner you won't have anyone else to play with."

So Amy found herself pushing the pram importantly through the village on her own, until they reached Amos's field where Lydia had to help her up the steep slope.

"I'll just have to get some food ready for Dr. Eliot before we see to the curtains," Lydia told her once they were in the house. "Would you like to keep an eye on Grace for me, while I do that?"

Grace stayed in her pram in the hall with Amy bobbing up and down playing 'peep-bo' which made the baby chuckle and dribble. Soon the front door opened.

"Lyd – Oh!" Doctor Eliot, whom Amy had only seen briefly in the past, strode into the hall. "Giving Mrs. Dawson some help, are you?" he asked. Amy nodded shyly because he seemed to be frowning, which meant he probably didn't want her to be there. She was getting used to that feeling recently. But then he smiled at her, transforming his severe face.

"That's good," he said. "Mrs. Dawson has told me what an excellent assistant you are."

Amy beamed and carefully wiped the baby's chin with a muslin cloth, to prove the doctor's point as he walked past her into the kitchen.

"I didn't realise you had another of your waifs and strays here," he said, wrapping his arms around Lydia and kissing her cheek as she spooned something delicious onto a plate.

"Her name's Amy – she's one of the little girls who helped me make the curtains," she said, tapping his hand away. "I've told her we can put them up when you've finished your lunch – we've had ours."

"In that case, I'll take a tray into the surgery and catch up with some paperwork, and leave you both to it."

"She's a sad little scrap," Lydia told Andrew later, when Amy had reluctantly set off for the house she simply couldn't think of as home. "I'm sure she's lost weight since she's been here, and she's very listless at times."

"Probably homesick," Andrew said. "It must be a terrible upheaval for some of these children."

"And she's staying with that woman we saw coming out of the Parrys' house the other day – the one who looks like a bulldog chewing on a wasp – so it can't be much fun."

"Ah!" Andrew recognised the description. "Our devout Mrs. Preece. The poor kid probably gets a sermon dished up with every meal."

"I was trying to get Amy to open up a bit this afternoon, but the most I could get out of her was that she wished she could stay on the farm with Arthur – you know, the lad who came to see you. I can't seem to get her pinched little face out of my head this evening."

Andrew smiled at her. "You're becoming quite the mother hen, aren't you?"

"And no-one's more surprised that me!" she answered. "I really do want to take them all under my wing!"

"It's what love does for you," he said quietly, the ardent expression on his face making her redden slightly and bend over her mending basket.

He was right, she knew he was. Already the relationship between them was colouring everything, so that she woke every morning in a state of delicious anticipation for the day ahead.

Her heightened emotions made her quick to smile and laugh, so that she had to be careful in the village that she didn't appear as a 'merry widow'. But she was also quick to be moved by the pain in Amy's eyes, or the distress of any of the rag-taggle bunch of children who turned up at the Red Shed each day. And all of this mainly because of her growing feelings for Andrew, made all the more tantalizing by their self-imposed celibacy. But when he looked at her as he was doing now, or said her name in the seductive way he had that turned her insides over, it was harder and harder not to simply throw all caution to the wind.

"We could try to help," he was saying now, "if you're really worried about Amy. The little bedroom at the back of the house is still empty, if you're happy to go on having Grace sleep in your room."

"You wouldn't mind?"

"Of course not – like Mr. Owain Owen said when you first arrived, if Miss Williams had still been here we would had to have taken some children. And," he gave a slight grin, "I have a very competent housekeeper who provides me with everything I need, so if she thinks she can manage, then that's fine with me. There's only one condition, though – I'm not going to be the one to approach Mrs. Preece."

"Coward! But I think that's a super idea, and Amy loves helping to look after Grace – it could be the very thing she needs. I'll sound her out about it first, before I tackle the battleaxe."

"Good. Now put that darning down, woman, and come over here and show your appreciation of my generosity!"

16.

The day had gone so much better than Amy had hoped. Her afternoon at the doctor's house had done a lot to help her push all those horrible feelings away, and Mrs. Preece was dishing up her tea when she got in and didn't shout at her, so she couldn't have discovered Amy's guilty secret upstairs. And when Edwin arrived home and announced that he was going out for the evening, her spirits rose even more. There were only five days to go until her mother's visit – she was sure she could hold out until then. For the first time in many weeks she went to bed without the dragging apprehension that had become her usual companion.

So she was doubly dismayed to find, when she woke, a large wet patch in the bed. Not again! How could she have done this without even waking up! Mortification swept over her – perhaps she really was a "dirty little girl" like Edwin had whispered.

She could do no more than the day before. Having made her bed as carefully as she could, she lowered the sash window to get rid of the fishy smell before going downstairs. She somehow swallowed her porridge (even though she was pretty sure it was the same helping that had been dished up the day before, as Mrs. Preece had threatened), then did her chores to the best of her ability before heading for the Red Shed. With a bit of luck her bed would be dry by tonight, as it had been last night, when the smell had almost disappeared.

Today, though, nothing managed to lift her spirits. By mid-morning a soft rain was falling and there were only two WVS women supervising activities in the Shed, who left the children pretty much to their own devices as long as they behaved. Amy had settled down in a corner with a book, to try to distract herself from her feelings of impending doom, when the door of the Shed was flung open.

"I've come for Amy Smith," Mrs. Preece's voice boomed through the room. "Need her at home, I do, this minute.

"Come along, miss," she said as soon as Amy emerged from the book corner. "No good skulking over there."

Amy fled through the door in case Mrs. Preece should announce to the world the reason for fetching her. Once outside Mrs. Preece grabbed her hand and marched her back to the house so quickly that Amy had to trot to keep up with her.

"Up those stairs and strip that bed," she ordered as soon as they entered the kitchen. Amy, red-faced from embarrassment, took off her shoes and hurried up the staircase, with Mrs. Preece close behind her, determined to have her say while the child did her bidding.

"Never known the like of it," she scolded. "With a pot under the bed, and you too lazy to get out and use it. Could smell it, I could, as soon as I came in the room to close the window."

"I-I-I couldn't h-help it!" Amy stuttered, close to tears as she pulled back the covers and tugged the bottom sheet free.

"Top sheet as well, if you please," Mrs. Preece barked. "It's soaking as well, seeing as how it was tucked in over the other one. And then you can bring a bowl back up here and scrub the rubber sheet – stinking, my house will be, at this rate!

"And – couldn't help it, indeed!" she went on, making no effort to help Amy as she bundled the sheets on the floor. "Chamber pot under the bed, a night light because you're such a baby, and just like a baby you go and wet yourself! Be putting you in nappies next, we will."

The mental picture which that threat conjured up sent Amy scurrying past the little woman, with the wet sheets in her arms.

"Scrubbing brush and disinfectant under the sink!" Mrs. Preece's voice followed her. "Oh, I'd better fetch it, or you'll be slopping it on the staircase and then there'll be more work for me to do."

She carried on grumbling as she filled an enamel bowl with hot water from the kettle and added enough disinfectant to make Amy's eyes smart. The words 'charity' and 'my time of life', interspersed with unintelligible Welsh words, filtered through to Amy as she scrubbed the rubber sheet.

But it was when they were back downstairs and Mrs. Preece was still going on, this time with reference to her mother's parenting skills and the dirty little girl she'd produced, that Amy snapped. Her mother had taken a pride in her being the cleanest child in her class.

"*I'm not dirty*! I told you I couldn't help it! And don't you say those things about my Mum! When she gets down here next week she'll take me back to London with her, so then you needn't be bothered with me any more!"

"That's enough from you, madam!" Mrs. Preece shouted back shrilly. "Offered you a good Christian home, I did, and this is how you repay me!"

But Amy's eyes were sore from the disinfectant, her hands were sore from the almost scalding hot water and her heart was so sore and full that she thought it would burst from her chest. Tears streamed down her face.

"I didn't ask to come here and I wish I never had! I hate you, and I hate Edwin, and I hate this place!"

Suddenly all the swearwords she had ever heard Arfur use came into her head, and no sooner had they done so than they were pouring out of her mouth in a torrent. She didn't know if she was using them in the right way, didn't know what half of them meant, but it was enough to turn Mrs. Preece's face white with fury.

"Now you're showing your true colours – told me I was lucky to have a dainty little girl, they did, but you're no better than the other dirty ragamuffins spoiling our village! Never been spoken to in my life like that, I haven't. And there's only one place for a disgusting little animal like you – in the coal house! See if that doesn't make you change your ways!"

As she spoke she grabbed the child's arm and began to pull her out through the back door. Now it was Amy's turn to blanche. The coal house was a small lean-to brick shed opposite the back door, filled, as its name suggested, with coal and kindling. And it was also windowless – the darkest hole Amy had ever seen. Someone at school had said that they had rats in their coal house. And rats were black, so she wouldn't know they were there until she felt them running up her legs, ready to gnaw at her face…

She began to pull back, screaming with fear, while Mrs. Preece continued to shout at her and slap her across the back of the legs as if she were urging a reluctant donkey to move.

Their macabre prancing was suddenly halted when a voice said,

"What are you doing, Mam? I could hear you down the street."

Edwin, home from the early turn at the sawmills, had come in through the back gate.

"She's a dirty little *mochyn*!" his mother cried. "Wet the bed she has, then comes out with nothing but filth! Mouth like a sewer! So she can go in the coal house where the rest of the dirt is, she's not fit to be in a God-fearing house!"

Almost hysterical now, Amy continued to scream until Edwin put his hand on her shoulder. "It's alright," he told her. "We'll sort it out."

Across the top of her head, he said, "Not a lot of point in that, Mam, no matter what she's done. She'll only get her clothes dirty, then there'll be another lot of washing and cleaning for you to do."

He waited for a moment and then added, "I wouldn't like to see you with even more to do, not when you have all this extra work as it is."

His Mam folded her mouth in on itself so that her lips all but disappeared while she considered what her son said. Amy pulled her arm free of Mrs. Preece's grip and now all that could be heard were the child's dry, hiccupping sobs as she gradually calmed down.

"Well, I can't abide to set my eyes on her," Mrs. Preece said at last. "I want her out of my sight!"

"Then send her up to her room for the rest of the day, and she can go without her tea," Edwin suggested. "Give her time to think about how she's behaved."

Being confined to her bedroom was fine with Amy. She wanted to get away from both of them. She made up the bed with the clean sheets Mrs. Preece had thrust in her arms before pushing her roughly in the direction of the bottom step of the stairs. Through the banister Amy had seen Edwin leaning against the kitchen door frame. For an instant their eyes had met and he gave the briefest of smiles. Despite her distress, Amy had known that it wasn't a smile of compassion. It wasn't even a smile of pity or understanding. It was a smile of triumph.

For those few minutes in the back yard he had been her hero – he had saved her from a terrible punishment, just like he'd saved her from going to bed in the dark. And if that was the Edwin she always saw, then he would be her hero for evermore.

But what about the Edwin who came whispering and fumbling in the night? Who did those awful things to her which big brothers, according to him, were supposed to do to little sisters who adored them? She still hated that Edwin. And she knew that somehow he would find his way upstairs this evening and want to giggle in her ear about how he had saved her from her Mam. And he'd also want his reward...

She lay curled up on her bed, feeling shivery even though the room was warm. Her mind was in such turmoil that she wished she could go to sleep and never wake up again. What would Mrs. Preece do if she wet the bed again tonight? How could she stop herself from doing it when it happened in her sleep? She would have to stay awake all night, that was the answer. She knew how difficult that was from happier days when she had tried to stay awake to see Father Christmas bring her presents. Perhaps she would have to walk up and down her bedroom floor all night. But then Edwin might hear her and come in again...

Five days. She only had to last five days and then her Mum would be here. If she could get through tonight then it would only be four days. And when she explained everything to her Mum – well, maybe not everything 'cos she couldn't imagine telling even Mum about the things Edwin was doing to her – when she explained how unhappy she was her mother would tell her that she'd been very brave to stick it out. Then the feeling that she was the most unworthy, unpleasant child in the whole world would be banished.

It was some time later that her door opened and Edwin appeared.

"Mam says you've got to go downstairs and go out the back, so you don't make any more mess," he said in a loud voice. 'Going out the back' was their way of saying 'going to the lavvy'.

Amy stood up and put her daps on. As she moved past Edwin he whispered, "Here's some bread and marge – eat it while you're outside. I couldn't get any cheese to go with it or our Mam would have noticed. Put it inside your cardigan."

Amy would have liked not to take it, but she was feeling hungry, and there was a strong smell of their evening meal wafting up the stairs, which made her tummy growl. And Edwin *was* being kind. She took the little package with a mumbled "Thank you," and would have continued to think better of him if he hadn't rubbed his hand down the side of her body as she went through the doorway and whispered, "I'll see you later." As it was, the four words went round and round her head, so that the bread and marge, eaten hurriedly with her back against the lavatory door, might as well have been cotton wool.

She hadn't been offered anything to drink, but she managed to slurp some water into her mouth when she washed her hands in the kitchen. Mrs. Preece was sitting in the living room, through which Amy had to go to get to the hallway, but the woman ignored her completely as she slunk past.

She wished she had something to read. A book would have taken her mind off the night ahead. She changed into her nightdress as the twilight grew, but she didn't dare get into bed in case she fell asleep.

Edwin arrived some time later, as he had promised, as she had known he would. He made her lie down with him, and at first she had to force herself not to draw comfort from the warmth of his body beside hers. How nice it would have been if he had simply cuddled her.

But he was far too excited for that. "Lucky I came into the yard when I did, wasn't it, little sister?" he whispered urgently. "Don't know what our Mam would have done otherwise. Shut in that coal house you would have been, for goodness knows how long."

His hands were already working on her body. Then, in one sudden movement, he was causing her so much agony that she opened her mouth to cry out.

"*Sssh!*" His hand went over her mouth while his body moved up and down urgently, faster and faster, until the pain was excruciating. Jagged strips of light darted up and down inside her tightly closed eyes, in time with the stabbing in her belly.

Finally he rolled away from her, panting heavily, but the pain was still there. As his breathing subsided he began whispering again. Something about the coal house and what his Mam would do if she ever found out that Amy had encouraged him to 'comfort' her in this way. She didn't hear all the words. She didn't need to. She knew that he was all that stood between her and the terrible little woman downstairs, but part of her mind was numb with bewilderment. What had she ever done wrong to deserve being treated by either of them in this way?

When Edwin left, she had an overwhelming desire to use the lavvy. Slowly, her whole body aching, she eased her way out of the bed and fumbled underneath for the chamber pot. Relief that she had not messed up the bed was blotted out by the exquisite pain she now experienced as she tried to 'go'. And, within seconds, she was desperate to go again.

I'll just sit here all night, she decided, *then I'll be all right.* She dragged the top cover off her bed and wrapped it around her shoulders. Beyond tears, she gave a little moan of utter despair as she leaned her head on the side of the bed.

H ell-o-o-o!"
Lydia heard Edyth's familiar call as she was cleaning out the range next morning. Then Edyth's smiling face appeared around the kitchen doorway.

"Can we come in? We come bearing gifts!"

"Of course you can," Lydia smiled back as she stood up and began to unwind Miss Williams' apron. "You've timed it really well, actually – I'm just about finished with this."

Edyth's face disappeared again, but her voice could be heard outside the back door. "Right, you lot. In there quietly – I can't see the baby, so she's probably having her morning nap, so don't make a noise."

A quartet of children trooped in, each one carrying a section of a playpen.

"I thought it was time you could do with this for Grace," Edyth said, bringing up the rear. "It's not in the best of condition, I'm afraid – I've used it quite a lot when we've had to bring lambs into the house – but I've given it a good scrub."

"Oh, that's wonderful!" Lydia exclaimed. "I've been worried that she's going to hurt herself rolling around this stone floor. You've been so good to me, Edyth – what would I have done without you?"

Edyth had already supplied a cot for the baby once she had grown too big for the drawer, and a high chair which now resided in the corner of the kitchen.

Edyth laughed. "Well, it's stopped Rhys nagging me about

hoarding stuff. I kept telling him that we would find a use for it all again one of these days."

She supervised the stacking of the pieces against the wall and then sent the younger children out into the garden, with a stern warning that they weren't to go near Grace's pram until the baby woke up of her own accord. Bronwen she instructed to do some shopping in the village.

"And what do you think of the new curtains?" Lydia asked her as the children were leaving. "We put them up together the other day, didn't we, Amy?"

The child nodded listlessly, seeming not to notice Edyth's admiring remarks, before following the other children through the door. Her face looked paler than ever, making the few freckles on her cheeks stand out as if they'd been painted on. Her eyes were red-rimmed, with dark smudges under them. Lydia watched her go with concern.

"Unhappy little thing, isn't she?" Edyth said, following her gaze. "Rhian seems to think she's very homesick."

"I think she's looking a lot worse than when she first came here, and I almost couldn't get her to go back to her billet the other day," Lydia said. "In fact, I've been talking about her to Dr. Eliot and he's suggested that we ask her if she'd like to come here to stay. There's a little back bedroom that's not used."

"Mmm. That would be a good idea. I shouldn't think she gets much warmth from Mrs. Preece, that's for sure. She was on my doorstep first thing this morning, because there's no children's club at the Shed today – they're getting it ready for a bring-and-buy this afternoon. She's hardly said a word all morning, though, except that she's looking forward to seeing her Mum on Saturday. Perhaps one of us could try to have a word with her mother – she could give her permission for Amy to come here."

Lydia nodded. "And Arthur seems in better spirits – how have you managed that?"

Edyth smiled. "Not me. Dr. Eliot's good words. Apparently he's told Arthur that his mother should be up and about on crutches by now, so the lad's convinced that she's going to turn up here with the other parents, to surprise him. Not that he's said anything to us, but Rhian told us why he's suddenly turned all sunny." She bit her lip. "I just hope he's not disappointed. He'll be putting such store by it – if only for the other kids to see that his mother is as good as theirs."

The children were back indoors a few minutes later. "We'd like to go up the mountain to play – can we?" Rhian asked. "On our own? "

"I don't see why not," Edyth said. "You all seem to have masses of energy today – it would use some of it up."

"Then why don't I give you a bit of a picnic to take with you, and you can go from here, rather than go all the way back to the farm," said Lydia, moving towards the pantry. "I've just done some hard-boiled eggs for lunch – you can have those and I'll do some more for us."

"And if Mrs. Dawson can find you some old tins you can pick some winberries for her, in return for your lunch," said Edyth.

"Winberries? What are they?" Lydia asked.

"They're a sort of cross between a blackcurrant and a bilberry, I suppose," Edyth explained. "Grow up the mountain, they do, low on the ground, in amongst the heather tussocks. Winberry tart can't be beaten, if you like things a little bit sharp."

"Are you going to go too, Amy?" Lydia asked, as she rooted around in a cupboard for some containers.

Amy had been winberry picking with the others the week before. Her tin had been almost full when she'd slipped and slid down a little hilly slope – a "tump" the children called it – scattering the lot. She wouldn't have minded that so much, but at the bottom of the tump was a reedy patch, with a small pool of water in the middle. In the pool was a lamb, long dead.

As Amy scrambled back up the slope, visions of the lamb struggling to survive, and of its mother wandering the hillside, wondering where its baby had got to, filled her head, so that her eyes filled with tears. The others had thought she was crying because she'd lost all her winberries, and she could tell they felt she was being tiresome, even though Arfur kindly offered her half the amount he'd picked.

She shook her head now, in answer to Lydia's question.

The women's eyes met over her head.

"Would you like to stay here with me, instead?" Lydia asked her, to which the child nodded, with just a fraction more enthusiasm than she'd shown so far.

Rhian tried to persuade Amy to go with them, but gave up after a few minutes with a guilty feeling of relief. Amy had been a bit of a nuisance lately, always miserable and very quiet – just when Arfur had cheered up and started to be good fun again.

"Amy can go with you next time," Edyth said as Bronwen returned and declared that she wanted to go up the mountain as well.

When they had all left Amy helped Lydia to construct the playpen in a corner of the kitchen, and spread a blanket and some cushions on its base. When Grace awoke Amy helped to spoon puree, which was a horrid shade of green but smelled good, into her mouth, and managed a giggle when the baby gurgled at her and more food seemed to come out of her mouth than had gone in. But otherwise she was quieter than Lydia had ever known her and shrank even more into her shell through lunch with the doctor.

After lunch they tried Grace in the playpen, propped up on cushions as her new-found ability to sit up still sometimes deserted her so that she keeled over. The baby wasn't too keen until Amy climbed in too, and began to play with her.

"It's lucky you're so slight, or you wouldn't fit, which would be a shame as you're so good with her," Lydia said, and was rewarded with a faint flush of pleasure on Amy's cheeks. She left them together while she went through to clean the surgery and when she returned it was Amy who was curled up on the cushions fast asleep, with the baby playing contentedly beside her.

Later, when Amy had woken and was sitting at the kitchen table with a glass of milk in front of her, Lydia broached the subject of her moving into the doctor's house.

"Are you happy staying with Mrs. Preece?" she asked.

There was a moment's pause before Amy answered in a small voice, "Yes, thank you."

"Only we've been talking – Dr. Eliot and me – about how you don't have anyone your own age at Mrs. Preece's and you seem... well, we think you're not as happy as you were at first. We thought perhaps you might like to stay here, as you enjoy being with Grace so much, and all your friends come here a lot anyway," Lydia said. "What do you think?"

The child's eyes lit up at first but then clouded over as her head dropped down on her chest. Slowly she shook her head.

"I could come to the house and ask Mrs. Preece to let you come here, so that you wouldn't have to say anything," Lydia suggested, having seen the initial flicker of response.

Pictures of Mrs. Preece standing over her and shouting, and Edwin, staring at her with those strange eyes, daring her to speak out of turn, crowded into Amy's head. She could hear their voices, telling her what a dirty little girl she was. Mrs. Preece's tone high-pitched and rasping, while Edwin's voice whispered in her ear, as insistently as his hands did those terrible things to her body, reminding her what his Mam, and anyone else for that matter, would think if they knew what she let him do. They seemed to loom larger and larger over her, and behind them on the wall was the photograph of dead Mr. Preece, stern and god-like, as if he, too, were sitting in judgment on her.

"Amy?... Amy?" Lydia's voice forced its way through those in her head, pushing them aside. She blinked as if suddenly exposed to a strong light.

"Amy... are you alright? Did you hear what I asked you – about coming here?"

Amy fought to ignore the warm concern in Lydia's voice. "Yes. Thank you," she said at last. Then, after a moment, "But can I tell you a secret?"

Lydia leaned forward and smiled encouragingly. There was clearly something bothering Amy and, whatever it was, she obviously needed to talk about it.

"My mother's coming here in four days' time," Amy confided, "and I'm going to ask her to take me home with her, so I won't need to come here to stay. But thank you very much for asking me," she finished, in imitation of the way she had heard her mother speak when she didn't want to hurt someone's feelings.

Lydia frowned. She didn't want to worry Amy by talking about what was going on in London, but she thought it unlikely that any mother would want to take her child back there at the moment.

"I think it's a good idea to talk things over with your mother, and I'm sure she'll do whatever's best," she said carefully. "Is there anything that I can help with before she gets here?"

Oh, how good it would be if Mrs. Dawson would just put her

arms around her the way she did around the baby, and hold her, rocking slightly, while Amy poured out all the dreadful things that had happened to her! The desire to rush around the table and throw herself into the young woman's arms was overwhelming. But what could she tell her? That she wet the bed like baby Grace? That she had secrets with Edwin that she felt too ashamed of to even think about herself, let alone put into words? Even kind, lovely Mrs. Dawson would push her away then and want nothing more to do with her.

By some superhuman effort Amy stayed where she was.

"I just want my mother to get here," she said. "And I'd better go now – it's nearly my tea-time."

She slid from the chair and headed for the back door. "Thank you for my dinner and letting me play with the baby and everything."

"You're very welcome, any time, you know that," Lydia replied equally gravely as she saw her out through the back door and watched as the small figure made her way sedately round the side of the house. Amy was about the age she had been when her own mother died. She could still recall the sense of desolation when she realised she would never see her again, and the futile longing for everything to change back to how it had been. She decided she would find a way to talk to Amy's mother when the visitors arrived on Saturday.

F*our days, four days.* The words repeated themselves in Amy's head in time to her feet pounding along the path through Amos's field. If she could get through another night it would only be three days. Three days were nothing. She could hang on for three days. When Edwin came to her room tonight she would shut her eyes very tightly and pretend to be fast asleep, even if he tried to shake her awake. And he wouldn't try too hard tonight because his mother didn't go out on Tuesday nights, so she might hear him. Then, when Amy awoke tomorrow morning it would only be *three days.*

She tried to push away the gnawing anxiety of what would happen if she wet the bed again tonight. Apart from the glass of milk Mrs. Dawson insisted on her drinking she had had hardly any other liquid all day, so surely she could hold on tonight.

Four days today and three days tomorrow. She repeated the phrase in her head and made it fit in time to her steps right up until she opened the gate into the back yard, when her courage seemed to desert her, to be replaced with a black dread that settled on her shoulders, pushing down on her so that it felt hard to breathe.

There was no-one in the kitchen, so she decided she would creep through and go up to her room. With a bit of luck there was no-one in the house at all.

But Mrs. Preece was in the living room, folding the ironing from yesterday's washing into neat piles.

"Ah! There you are!" The first words she'd spoken to Amy since last night. She put the clothes down and lifted an envelope from the table.

"There's been a letter from your mother." Amy's mother addressed the letters to Amy, but Mrs. Preece always opened them and then told Amy the contents before she had the pleasure of reading the words to herself so that she could hear them in her mother's voice.

"She can't come down on Saturday after all!" There was a note of triumph in Mrs. Preece's voice, although Amy was too shattered at her words to even register it. "Your Gran is very ill – your mother can't leave her. She'll have to come another time. Although I don't know when that'll be. They can't keep putting on trains and wasting fuel just to cart mothers around the country to see their children. There's better things – oh!"

Mrs. Preece stopped short as Amy snatched the letter from her hand and ran back through the kitchen and out of the back door.

"Just a minute, young lady! You come back here!" Mrs. Preece's shrill tones followed her down the yard and she knew she would be in terrible trouble again later but she didn't care. She ran along the back lane, towards the road that would take her to Amos's field. She had to see Mrs. Dawson again. She had to tell her.

Breathless and sobbing, she hammered on the back door of the doctor's house. Lydia appeared, the baby in her arms, but with a "Oh, Amy, whatever's the matter?" she ushered Amy through the door and in one swift movement plopped the surprised baby in the playpen.

"M-m-y m-m-mother," Amy managed. "Sh-sh-she's... she's...

not coming..."

"Not coming? On Saturday? But why not?"

Amy held out the single sheet of paper, grubby and tear-stained. Lydia scanned the contents quickly.

"Oh, I'm so sorry – I know you wanted to see her so badly."

Lydia scooped the forlorn child into her arms, where Amy clung as if she never wanted to let go. Automatically Lydia stroked her hair and murmured the nonsense words with which she soothed Grace when she was fractious.

"Your mother says she'll try to come down as soon as she can," she said when Amy's sobs had subsided a little. "It might only be a couple of weeks – you'll see, it'll go really quickly."

Her words seemed of little comfort to the child, who continued to shake with emotion.

"Tell you what," Lydia said after a few more moments of crooning, "why don't I come down to Mrs. Preece's with you and ask if you can stay here, if only for a little while – maybe until your mother is able to visit, and then we can talk to her about it. What do you think?"

Amy moved away from Lydia's arms, her face red and blotchy from crying and strands of hair slicked wetly across her cheeks, with other pieces sticking out in tufts from her head. She didn't answer the question, just nodded, as if speech was now beyond her.

Lydia ran a cloth under the cold tap and gently wiped and dried Amy's face, before smoothing her hair down with her hands and adjusting the bow with which Mrs. Preece insisted on lifting Amy's fringe away from her face, but which did nothing to enhance the child's pinched features.

Lydia wondered if she should go through to the surgery and speak to Andrew about the little girl, but he would already be seeing patients, and what could he do? He couldn't examine Amy without her foster mother being there and what would he be looking for, anyway? Besides, if she was able to bring Amy back here, to stay, they could both spend time trying to get to the bottom of why she had become so unhappy and withdrawn.

With the baby in the pram they set off once more down the hill, Lydia trying to make light conversation, but giving up after a couple of minutes as Amy resolutely held the side of the pram handle and kept her eyes on the ground. So Lydia rehearsed a little speech to give to Mrs. Preece instead, knowing that the woman's gimlet eyes could be intimidating.

But it was the gawky-looking son, Edwin, who answered the front door, to whom Lydia had never spoken before.

"Hallo," she began, "I'm Lydia Dawson, Dr. Eliot's housekeeper. I was wondering if I could have a word with Mrs. Preece – about Amy."

"Busy in the kitchen at the moment, she is," the boy said, leaning up against the door jamb, obviously with no intention of letting Lydia into the house.

His strange light-coloured eyes roamed over Amy's subdued figure.

"What's the matter, Amy?" he asked. "Not been in any sort of trouble, have you?"

Amy shook her head, without lifting her eyes.

"She's upset because her mother can't come to visit on Saturday, with the other evacuee parents, so I was wondering if she could stay with us – me – at the doctor's house for a little while. You see –"

"You don't want to leave us, do you, Amy?" the boy cut in, addressing her exclusively. "What would I do without you in our house? Lonely I'd be after all these weeks – like a little sister she is to me, Mrs. Dawson."

His voice was soft, with a caressing sound within its Welsh lilt. "Timid little thing she was when she first came, but I helped her, didn't I Amy? Make sure there's nothing to scare her, watch over her I do."

"Yes, I'm sure you do," Lydia said, "but Amy's been very quiet lately, and I think she's lost some weight – I think she's been more homesick than at first, so I thought maybe I could help take her mind off things…"

"Nothing bothering you, is there, Amy?" Edwin asked. "You don't want to leave me, do you, when we've been getting on so well. *Do* you?"

Amy raised her eyes to Edwin's. "No, Edwin," she said softly.

But Lydia had seen the child's grip tighten on the pram handle as she spoke. Things weren't right here, she could sense, but felt uncertain how to proceed if Amy wasn't going to say that she wanted to leave.

At that moment there was a bustle behind Edwin as Mrs. Preece appeared, pulling the front door open wider so that she could stand alongside her son.

"Something the matter, is there?" she asked, her eyes moving up and down Lydia's figure, her expression already bathed in disapproval.

"No – not as such," Lydia faltered. Then she remembered Amy's small body clinging so frantically to hers, the wracking sobs that seemed to stem from much more than disappointment. Lydia drew herself up straighter. She could be more than a match for the Mrs. Preece's of this world if she set her mind to it.

"It's just that Amy has clearly been becoming more and more homesick as time has gone on, and now, as you'll know, her mother not visiting on Saturday has been a tremendous blow. So I was merely offering for her to come and stay at the doctor's house for a little while – Dr. Eliot agrees it might help to take her mind off things. She likes playing with the baby and helping to take care of her, so I thought –"

"You thought you could get a little nursemaid for nothing!" Mrs. Preece interrupted. "Too much for you now, is it? Having to get your hands dirty running a big house and care for a baby? Not enough time to run around playing Lady Bountiful!"

"That's not the case at all!" Lydia responded angrily. "I've no desire to play Lady Bountiful. I just help out at the Red Shed when I can – 'doing one's bit', I believe it's called! I've got to know Amy and the other children and I don't like to see any of them unhappy! Perhaps we could talk to the Billeting Officer –"

Too late she remembered that this dreadful woman was related to the Owain Owens.

"There'll be no need for that, indeed to goodness!" Mrs. Preece's voice was becoming more shrill. "I don't know what tales the child has been filling you up with, but Mr. Owain Owen already knows that I keep a clean, respectable, God-fearing house here! Better than anything these London children will have been used to, so I'll thank you to keep your nose out of our business!"

Edwin leaned across and unfurled Amy's fingers from the pram handle.

"She doesn't even want to go, anyway," he said. "Come on,

Amy, let's get you inside."

And with that he led the child into the hallway.

"Knew her place, Miss Williams did," his mother told Lydia, leaning forward over the front step. "No hoity-toity ways, trying to tell other people what to do – and she wasn't a charity case, playing on the doctor's goodwill, or whatever else you've had to do to stay there."

"How dare you!" Lydia began, but before she could say any more the door was firmly closed in her face.

She stood for a few seconds, her mind seething with the woman's snide remarks and chagrin at her inability to help Amy, before she turned and made her way back along the terrace.

There was something not right about the encounter, quite aside from Mrs. Preece's insults, and when she had collected herself a little, Lydia tried to work out what it was. For all the woman's nastiness, the son had seemed to be quite pleasant to Amy, caring even. So was the child simply unhappy because Mrs. Preece ran a tight regime that didn't allow for much kindness? If so, she would be one amongst several of those who had taken evacuees in but treated them with a distant firmness rather than wholeheartedly as one of the family. Even a child slightly less robust, as Amy seemed to be, shouldn't wilt so much under those conditions, especially when there was every opportunity to meet and play with friends and so on during the day.

And if Mrs. Preece was short on affection, then the son didn't seem to be, so Amy wouldn't be completely starved of a kind word.

She began to push the pram up the steep slope of the field, Mrs. Preece's nastiness taking second place to the conundrum of what was upsetting Amy. A niggle of disquiet that she couldn't pinpoint had settled in the back of her brain, and she couldn't dislodge it. Then it suddenly struck her so forcefully that she stood still, putting her weight against the pram to stop it rolling back down the hill.

Edwin had kept his eyes on Amy the whole time. In the same way that Billy had focused on her, Lydia, when in the grip of some irrational jealousy. He would fix his piercing blue eyes on her face with concentrated intensity whilst asking, in a very reasonable voice, "Where did you go today?" or "Did you meet anyone to talk to this afternoon?" To an outsider he would have appeared to be the epitome of a caring husband. Only Lydia would be aware of the undercurrent of menace in his careful tone, of the desire to control, and ultimately the need to punish if he thought that she had betrayed him in any way.

And that was how Edwin had looked at Amy. How he had spoken to her. His eyes, pale globular imitations of Billy's, nonetheless had held the same focus, and his soft, almost girlish voice had elicited the same acquiescence that Billy had always sought from Lydia.

That was it! The boy had some sort of hold over Amy! What had he said? *"Watch over her, I do"…"like a little sister, she is".* He probably threatened her with all sorts of retribution if she were to show disloyalty by telling anyone that she was unhappy. Did he hit her? Lydia tried hard to think if she had seen any marks or bruises on Amy's skinny little body other than the normal bumps and grazes from childhood escapades. But then, if Edwin truly was like Billy, any marks he made would be well hidden from casual observers.

Lydia's first instinct was to go back down the hill yet again and hammer on the door until one of them answered and then demand that she be allowed to check Amy over. She had almost turned the pram round before she stopped once more. What right had she to demand anything? She wasn't related to the child, and, if she antagonised that pair even more, Amy could well be the recipient of their joint anger.

It would be better to talk the whole thing over with Andrew. Perhaps he could intervene in some way, find an excuse to examine Amy and talk to her – maybe she would tell a doctor if anything was troubling her.

Amy's haunted eyes plagued her as she trudged on through the field, intertwined with memories of her own treatment by Billy. She might have got it wrong, of course. Her interpretation of life in that little terraced house might be coloured by her own experiences. But then she recalled Edwin's intent gaze and felt again that there was something amiss.

It was good to arrive back at the house and busy herself with preparing the evening meal. This evening, more than ever, she wanted the reassuring feel of Andrew's arms around her.

17.

I f they peered very carefully through the grimy window at the side of Morgan Grinder's shop, the children could just make out a pile of tangled fishing nets peeking out from under some orange boxes full of something unrecognisable.

Morgan Grinder's shop was really more of a shed, crammed with a wide assortment of old furniture, tools – mostly broken – and other clutter, which spilled out onto the tiny forecourt. At the rear the clutter stacked up so high that it was impossible to see what was there. Just inside the door was the equipment from which Morgan acquired his nickname and which gave him most of his meagre income.

Not that he was ever seen to spend very much. He lived in an ancient caravan on an overgrown plot behind the shed. Over the years a narrow path from the shed to the caravan had been trodden through the tangle of nettles and weeds, with a second one leading to a rickety lean-to at the side of the caravan which housed a primitive toilet, comprising a piece of wood with a hole in the middle, under which was a foul-smelling bucket. The land adjoined the river, from where he obtained his water supply.

As well as not having been seen to spend much money, Morgan had also never been seen looking clean and tidy. His clothes, all an indeterminate shade of dirt, remained the same throughout the year – a pair of corduroy trousers held up with string, and a shirt which had probably once been a red and black plaid. Over this was a ribbed pullover which had a large hole in the front, with strands of wool, dropped stitches and a hint of his prodigious stomach, where a button had been lost on his shirt, poking through it. A greasy flat cap sat on his head, and his feet were encased in a pair of crusty boots.

Many a well-meaning lady of the village had given him neatly pressed clothes their husbands no longer needed, to which he always said, "Thank you, Missus. They'll do me nicely of a Sunday," after which the clothes were never seen again. Morgan never appeared on a Sunday, so it wasn't known whether he ever changed into the fresh clothes on that one day of the week.

Some people in the village disapproved of Morgan's disreputable appearance and his occasional wanderings through the main street late at night, drunkenly singing to the moon. They tended to be the ones who didn't offer him bundles of clean clothes. For the most part, though, he was tolerated as a 'character', because everyone knew how handy he was with a soldering iron when something needed repairing. And often, after much ferreting about in the dark recesses of his 'shop', with lots of muttering, Morgan could produce the very thing one was looking for, as in the case of the doctor's lawn mower. And now, the children had their eyes on the fishing nets.

"You go and ask him," Rhian said to Bronwen; "you're the oldest."

"Yes, but I won't be able to persuade him to give them us for nothing – you know I'll end up promising to pay for them." This was true, Bronwen's heart generally being much softer than her sister's.

"Oh, I'll go," Arfur said impatiently. "We'll never get the bloomin' things otherwise, will we?"

In the end the two girls followed behind him and nodded when he explained to Morgan what they were after. "Trouble is," Arfur explained, "we ain't got no money to pay for them," blithely forgetting the pile of sixpences and threepenny bits mounting up at the back of his bedside drawer. That wasn't spending money, anyway – it was emergency train fare.

"Well…" Morgan pushed his cap back a little, so that a bit of a tide mark could be seen on his forehead; "don't suppose I'll be finding much use for them. Given them by an ol' fisherman in Swansea Bay, I was."

They had to wait while he told them a perplexing tale about the fisherman which none of them understood. He only had a few teeth, so that his speech was gummy and slurred, which along with his heavy Welsh accent made him almost unintelligible to Arfur's English ears. It was worth it, though, to get the fishing nets for nothing, and at least they could while away the time marvelling at the depth of ingrained dirt on Morgan's face, hands and neck, and nudge each other if they saw something move in his filthy, tangled beard.

They were planning to make a rope-bridge between two of the trees each side of the brook after Arfur had told them all about the *Tarzan* film he'd seen at the cinema in London. They'd had to beg pieces of old rope from a reluctant Rhys, because he was sure there would soon be a shortage, but the fishing nets would make a big difference to their plans.

No sooner had they returned to the farm, though, to sort through their treasures in the yard, when Edyth could be heard calling.

"Rhian! I need your help in the garden for a minute, please!"

Edyth's voice held the tone which brooked no argument. Sighing, Rhian dropped the length of rope she'd been trying to untangle and with an "I'll be back, so don't start without me," she followed her mother around the back of the farmhouse. Her mother was such a practical woman, on the whole, except for her garden, where she spent lots of time fussing around her plants and flowers – and for what? You couldn't eat them, and, having spent all of spring and summer nurturing them, Edyth spent most of the autumn clearing them away or cutting them back.

Now the other two would be getting on with the job while Rhian helped her mother. She had a slightly mutinous look on her face as she went into the garden. It had better not take long. She wanted to show Arfur how good she was at tying knots, but now he might see Bronwen do it instead. Bronwen had shown them to Rhian after she'd learned them at the Girl Guides, and could still do them the best, but Rhian hated it if Arfur expressed admiration for anyone else.

"I need to tell you about something," her mother said as soon as she'd gone through the little gate, "and I didn't want Arthur to overhear. Your father is bringing a puppy over from Harris's farm later on. We want Arthur to have it, to look after, like you've got Rags."

"But Rags isn't a puppy any more – she's quite old," Rhian pointed out.

Edyth saw her daughter's face darken as she tussled with jealousy at Arthur's luck in having a puppy to care for against needing to be kind and generous to someone she thought a lot of.

"We felt you should give it to him," she told her. "He's so

amazed at the things you can do with Rags – I'm sure he'll want your help."

Rhian's face cleared. Rags was really one of the farm dogs who lived outside. But when she wasn't needed by Rhys, she became Rhian's dog, following her about when bidden and developing a great knack for games of hide and seek. Arthur had been very impressed the first time they had played this game, and with the way Rags could play dead on request. Rags usually performed for Bronwen, too, but to his chagrin had consistently refused to follow any of Arthur's instructions.

"It's probably 'cos your voice sounds so different," Rhian told him. "Perhaps you need to learn to speak with a Welsh accent first."

"Does Bronwen know about the puppy?" she asked her mother now, while she mulled over the fact that it was to belong to Arthur.

Edyth nodded. "She also knows why we're doing this – it's your father's idea really. You know Arthur is convinced his mother is coming down here this weekend? Well, we're not so sure that she is – we've had no word and neither has Mr. Owen or any of your teachers. So Arthur may be very disappointed, and we thought having a new puppy to care for might possibly help to take his mind off things."

"But what about when the war ends and he goes back to London?" Rhian asked, "I don't think it's a very good place to keep a dog."

"It's not a sheepdog, it's one of the Harris's Jack Russell's – they're small enough to cope with in a city as long as they get exercise," her mother said, deciding not to add that the way things were going this war was not going to be over quickly and it would no longer be a frisky puppy by then.

The more she thought about it, the more Rhian liked the plan. She was still as convinced as she'd been when Arfur first arrived that he was going to figure in her life forever, but she hadn't told anyone else this. Now, if he had a dog of his own, there would always be a link between them, even if he went back to London after the war.

Their rope bridge was more complicated to build than they'd imagined, Arfur having convinced them that the way it looked on the film it would be easy, but they had fun trying, and came into the farmhouse for tea in a state of easy bickering about what they could do tomorrow.

After tea, Rhys fetched in a small shopping bag which he handed to Rhian.

"This is for you," Rhian said, walking round the table to Arfur. At that moment there was a scuffling from inside the bag and the tiniest brown and white head popped up.

"It's a wire-haired Jack Russell," Rhian told him. "We thought you might like to have him to train, like we've trained Rags."

She lifted the puppy out and held him towards Arfur. "Here. You take him."

Arfur took the puppy, looking at it gravely as it wriggled in his arms and licked his hand.

"Runt of the litter, he was," Uncle Rhys said. "That's why Mr. Harris didn't mind us having him – needed a good home for him to go to."

Arfur was touched. Apart from the random sixpences doled out occasionally by his Mum's men friends, there had been few times in his life when he had been given a present. But after a few moments he held the puppy back out to Rhian.

"He's lovely – but I can't take him, can I?"

"Why not?" Rhian frowned. Much as she liked Arfur, he had this annoying habit of not responding according to plan.

Arfur sighed as he looked round their expectant faces. "I'm not stopping – I told you that from the start. I was only here till me Mum's leg got better. So when she comes here on Saturday I'll be able to go back with her – and I won't be able to take a puppy 'cos it'll need training, won't it, to do its business, and we won't be able to do that living in a flat."

Rhys and Edyth exchanged anxious glances while Arfur spent a moment imagining his Mum's reaction to a puppy that made a mess all the time. Not that she was houseproud, far from it, but she wouldn't have the patience to care for a small animal.

It was a lovely little puppy, though. For a moment he had a glimpse of the hours of fun he would have had training it, and how proud he would have felt when it came to him when he called. But his Mum needed him, he knew she did, and London was where he belonged. When he went back with her after the weekend, they'd slip straight back into their life together and all this would become like a dream. Of course, not many of his friends would be there – they'd all be here still, playing on the mountainside, and down by the river, and coming over to the farm to maybe finish the rope bridge... He swallowed hard before shaking his head as if to rid himself of the pictures that were flashing through his mind.

"There'd be a right old barney if I told me Mum we were taking a puppy back with us," he said, as much to convince himself as everyone else.

"Barney!" Bronwen exclaimed. "That's a great name for a dog! That's what you should call him!"

She took him from Rhian, holding him up in the air. "Barney." The puppy squirmed, his little paws scrabbling as he was held aloft. "See! I think he likes it too. Why don't you just look after him for the next few days, Arthur – missing his mother, he'll be, so he'll need special attention. Then we can take care of him after that."

She received a grateful look from her mother for her diplomacy, but Arfur was having none of it. He headed for the door.

"No point is there, if I'm not stopping!"

They could see him through the window, stomping across the yard, hands in his pockets and his shoulders hunched.

Edyth sank into her fireside chair. "Well, that's been a waste of time! Did you know he thought he was going back to London, Rhian?"

Rhian shook her head. "He's just been saying about his Mam coming down, that's all. Never talked about going back with her – but I suppose he said it so much when he first came here that he thought we'd all got the message."

"So what do we do with this little bundle?" Bronwen asked, still holding the puppy who was now nestled in her arms.

"We keep him," Rhys said. "We'll introduce him to Rags, see if she'll mother him for a little while, get him used to not being with his own litter. And I don't want you two girls fussing with him too much for the next few days." His voice was firm as he gazed out of the window, through which Arfur could no longer be seen. "He's Arthur's puppy."

Rhian followed her father's gaze. "Shall I go after him?"

Rhys shook his head. "Leave him for now. He'll probably prefer to be on his own for a while. You and Bronwen sort out the puppy, see if he'll settle with Rags. Your mother will find some food for him. But remember – he's Arthur's."

Rhian sneaked a few cuddles with the puppy during the evening, under the pretext of helping Rags to get used to him. The older dog was quite disdainful for a while to have a tiny puppy scrabbling about all over her, getting up and moving away whenever he approached. But after she had nudged him about a bit, sometimes none too gently, she gradually allowed him to share her bed.

"You've got to be kind to Barney," Rhian whispered as she stroked Rags's soft head, "like we've got to be kind to Arfur. 'Cos, no matter what he says, I think both of them are stopping."

Arfur stayed outside until late. When he joined Rhian in the kitchen for their bedtime glass of milk the puppy was curled up against Rags in a basket in the corner – a rare treat for the farm dog, who was usually kept outside.

No mention was made of Barney by either of them. Instead, Rhian asked if Arfur wanted to do the rope bridge again tomorrow, as they'd originally planned.

"'Course," said Arfur. "I said we'd finish it, didn't I?"

Saturday morning, Arfur was the first one downstairs, apart from Uncle Rhys who was already out seeing to the cows. As soon as he opened the kitchen door, the puppy came skittering across the stone floor to greet him. Arfur allowed himself the luxury of picking him up, whereupon the puppy nuzzled into his neck and tried to lick him.

"Scruffy little thing, aren't you?" Arfur said to him. Bright eyes, partly obscured by tufts of wiry fur, peered back at him. "Could have been a bit of a pair, you and me, if I'd been staying, 'cos I'm a bit scruffy too. But I gotta go home, see? And you've gotta stay here on this farm, where they'll look after you very well, 'cos they're alright, really."

The puppy began to squirm, so Arfur took him out by the back door and watched him until he squatted down on the path.

"Good boy," Arfur said, as he took him back into the kitchen.

"Bright little beggar, aren't you?"

Aunt Edyth was soon downstairs, but showed no surprise that Arfur was already up and dressed, despite the fact that he had retained the townie's dislike of early mornings and often had to be cajoled into coming down in time for breakfast.

"Ah! Good! No mess on the floor this morning," she said, looking round the kitchen carefully.

"That's 'cos I've let him out – but Uncle Rhys was down before me, so he might have cleaned some up."

Edyth just nodded and concentrated on stoking the range into action and filling the kettle.

"Perhaps you'd help me lay the table for breakfast," she said as she carried cups and saucers from the dresser. She smiled at him. "Not usually down here in time to give a hand in the mornings, are you?"

Edyth watched him for a moment as he set the cutlery out, chewing on the side of her lip. The tension in his slight body was almost palpable, so that she had to force herself not to put her arms round those bony shoulders and hold him close.

"Arthur," she said after a while, "please sit down for a moment, I need to talk to you."

Arfur slid into the nearest chair, and looked across at her, his dark eyes willing her not to say anything. But she took a deep breath and persevered.

"Have you thought – well, I'm sure you have, because you're a bright lad – that perhaps your mother isn't well enough yet to travel down here today? It's just that we've had no word, and neither has anyone else, so it could be that her leg isn't quite healed yet. It's a difficult journey to make..." Her voice tailed off under the unwavering ferocity of his gaze.

"Dr. Eliot said she should be getting better by now." His eyes didn't leave Edyth's, as if, by sheer power of his will, he could ensure that his belief that his mother was coming was correct. "I know me Mum – once she's up and about there'll be no stopping her, and she's a great one for surprises."

"I'm sure she is," Edyth said evenly, "and I'm also sure from what you've told us that she wouldn't miss seeing you for the world. But Dr. Eliot was only making a clever guess. There could be lots of reasons why she might not be well enough to travel yet... I – we – just don't want to see you get your hopes up too far and then be disappointed."

"She'll be here."

The bus bringing the parents from the station at Maesteg wasn't due until late afternoon. By dinner time Arfur had fallen out with Rhian, told Bronwen that he was glad she wouldn't be bossing him around after this weekend, and had tuppence docked from his money because Uncle Rhys heard him swear.

Too sick with excitement, mixed with an anxiety he was determined to quell, Arfur's robust appetite deserted him, so that he merely pushed the food around on his plate. After dinner Uncle Rhys said, "If you come and help me outside for an hour, I'll have the time to drive you into the village for when the bus gets here."

Arfur wanted to meet his Mum on his own, so that he could tell her things in the sort of way they always spoke to each other – and so that he could warn her to mind her language before she got to the farm.

"It's not far to walk – I'll be all right," he said.

"Yes, but your mother won't, if she's on crutches," Uncle Rhys reminded him, and there was no way he could answer that.

Uncle Rhys seemed to take an age over the chores he'd decided they must tackle for the afternoon. As the time neared for the bus to arrive, Arfur was hopping from foot to foot with impatience, but Uncle Rhys continued to clear away his tools in his usual methodical fashion.

"Right," he said at last. "Time we were going. Into the house and wash your hands and face and comb your hair. We don't want your mother to think we haven't been looking after you properly."

There was quite a throng of adults and children waiting at the bus stop near the school. Many of the children were looking tidier than Arfur had ever seen them, making him wonder if their mothers would actually recognise them. Most of the foster mothers were smartly turned out as well, some of them having donned their Sunday hats to make a good impression on their visitors. Arfur couldn't help chuckling to himself.

"Do you want to go and stand with the others?" Uncle Rhys asked.

Arfur could see his friend Kennie in the queue, and Maisie with her little brother, but some sense of self-preservation made him hesitate.

"I'm fine here," he said.

The bus arrived about half an hour late, by which time several of the children were looking more like their normal dishevelled state, and some of the smaller ones had become quite fractious. As the bus pulled up, Mrs. Owain Owen, resplendent in a straining tailored two-piece that had probably fitted her better across the chest some years before, made them all move back along the pavement, while her husband stood ready by the bus doors, clipboard in hand.

Mothers carrying small cases for their brief stay began to emerge, with some also struggling with smaller children who had not been evacuated. Arfur saw Kennie claim his mother, then, a few minutes later, Maisie's mother appeared, a small child clutching her skirt hem and an even smaller one in her arms. His own Mum was probably waiting until some of the fuss died down – it would be difficult enough manoeuvring her crutches down the narrow aisle of the bus without all the other mothers getting in the way.

The crowd began to disperse quite quickly, with foster mothers shepherding their visitors away, some of whom looked quite dazed as they were besieged by their garrulous Welsh hosts on one side and their excited offspring on the other.

The last few mothers stepped down. Arfur saw a familiar dark head with waves bouncing on her shoulders. He leaned forward and was just about to cry out, "There she is!" when a little girl on the pavement pulled away from the hand that had been holding hers and ran into the woman's outstretched arms.

Arfur and Uncle Rhys sat in silence as Mr. Owain Owen had a few words with the driver before the engine rumbled into action and the bus slowly moved away.

After a few seconds, Uncle Rhys said, "I'm sorry, lad."

Arfur turned his head to look out of the side window without replying.

"Best be getting back, then, I suppose," Uncle Rhys said, starting up the car. "Aunt Edyth'll be getting tea ready."

When they pulled up in the drive Rhian was waiting on the

porch steps in unconscious imitation of the evening when Arfur had arrived. This time, though, he didn't wait for Uncle Rhys to tell him where to go. He jumped out of the car almost before it had stopped and, pushing past Rhian, rushed up to the little bedroom at the back of the house.

He wasn't going to cry, he wasn't going to cry. Rubbing his eyes with his knuckles, he curled up on the deep window ledge, staring unseeing across the view of the village, to the hillside beyond. In the village there would be excited children telling their mothers what they'd been getting up to in this place that was so different from home. There might be some sneaking the chance to complain about things, but he knew there wouldn't be many of those. Except perhaps for one or two who were staying in isolated little cottages where there was no running water and they still used oil lamps and candles. But all of them, moaning or otherwise, would be having the best weekend since they'd got here.

Well, he didn't care. He'd only wanted his Mum to come down so he could show everyone how smart she was when she did herself up, and how lively and funny she was. She probably wouldn't have liked it here any more than he did when he first came. They could have had a giggle together, though, about the funny way everyone spoke and about how their idea of fun was a dance in the Red Shed. They could have...

He wasn't going to cry. He'd just go back to his first plan. The coins were mounting up. He'd soon have enough to get back to London on his own. 'cos he wasn't staying, that was for sure.

He was still on the window seat when there was a brief knock on his door, and Rhian came in, her tongue between her teeth as she concentrated on not spilling the contents of the tray she was carrying.

She put the tray on the bed. "You've missed tea, so Mam told me to bring you some up."

Arfur continued to stare out of the window as if he hadn't heard.

Rhian stood uncertainly by the bed. "Mam'll be upset if you let it go cold."

After a few moments she moved towards the door. Her hand on the doorknob, she turned back. "If it was me – if my Mam hadn't come, I'd be bawling my head off. Really brave, I think you are."

Still no sign that Arfur had even heard her. "And," she swallowed hard, "if it was me I'd hate it if everyone went on about it. So we won't – any of us – not unless you want to talk about it – that's why they sent me up with the tea instead of a grown-up."

She pulled the door open wider but still didn't leave. "I wasn't supposed to say anything – anything at all. But I thought you might like to know that we can go round together still and I won't say about it. 'Cos we're butties – mates – and butties always understand."

She left then, closing the door carefully behind her. On the landing she took a deep breath, because she felt all shaky. She'd wanted to tell Arfur that she loved him – like people did in the stories in *People's Friend* that her Mam liked to read, and sometimes she and Bronwen giggled over. But you couldn't tell a boy things like that when you weren't quite ten. Even though she knew she loved Arfur more fiercely than any of the women reckoned they loved the men in those soppy stories.

Back downstairs they were still talking about Arfur's disappointment in subdued tones. Eventually Rhys said, "Well, I'd better be getting back outside – I've still got things to do." He cast his eyes around the kitchen until they alighted on Rags and the puppy. "And tonight I want Rags back outside – the puppy'll need to learn to be on its own sometime, and Rags will get spoilt if she's in here all the time."

He looked back at his family. "And I don't want any of you down here making a fuss of the pup if he's noisy in the night. You're to let him be."

Rhian wanted to protest that Barney was far too little to be left all by himself if he got lonely, but she knew that tone in her father's voice. He didn't use it very often, because he was generally very gentle and easy-going. But when you heard that firmness creep in, then you knew that he meant what he said, and any argument would lead to him sounding very cross indeed.

It was well into the night when Arfur heard the sounds. He'd only slept fitfully, drifting off and then waking again, distress and deep disappointment stifling him, so that he had to sit up in bed and take some deep breaths.

He must have woken like that at least three times before he heard it. There were no other noises coming from downstairs, so it was late enough for everyone to be in bed, but it wasn't early enough in the morning for that blessed cockerel to start his row.

He turned over and tried to go back to sleep, but there it was again, high-pitched and just a bit creepy. He got out of bed and lifted down the black-out curtain, which was suspended across his little window from a bamboo pole.

The moon was so bright that it was almost as light as day outside. But nothing was moving in the area around the house as far as he could see. He listened again. The noise was coming from the kitchen, immediately below his room. Then it dawned on him what it was – it was the puppy, crying.

He climbed back into bed. If that was all it was, then someone else would see to it. It wasn't his problem. It wasn't his puppy.

He lay for some minutes longer, but each time he thought the pup had settled down and gone to sleep it started up again. Now he was properly awake and knew he wouldn't drift back off easily. He'd just lie here, with that knot of dismay churning in his stomach, wondering how he'd get through tomorrow when everyone knew his Mum hadn't turned up, after all his bragging.

The puppy's crying was becoming a full-scale howl. How could anything that small make such a huge noise? He would have thought the older dog would have sorted it out by now – he would have done if he'd had to share a bed with it.

Eventually he padded out of bed again and peered out onto the landing. There was no sign of movement anywhere else and all the bedroom doors were firmly closed. Were they all deaf in this house? They seemed to hear alright when he swore, even when he did it under his breath.

He made his way downstairs where the cries seemed to be coming directly from the other side of the kitchen door. He opened it slowly in case he hurt the puppy on the other side. Immediately the puppy scrambled through the gap, its cries reduced to whimpering as it fussed around his feet.

"Oy!" he said, picking him up. "What's this entire bleedin' row about? Noisy little perisher!"

He stroked him as he carried him back to his bed, to settle him down with Rags, but the sheepdog wasn't there.

"Ah! Been left on your own, have you? That's why you're making such a rumpus. Well, I know how that feels, but I'm not making a hue and cry about it, am I?"

The puppy licked the hand that was stroking it, and nestled into Arfur's chest. Arfur knelt down by the side of the basket, which was lined with an old blanket. He lay the puppy down and wrapped the blanket round him like a cocoon, but immediately the puppy began to whimper again.

"Look, you're all warm and cosy – there's nothing to make a fuss about!"

But the puppy wasn't listening, and tried to scrabble back out of the basket. Arfur gently pushed him back. "Not much fun when you're missing your Mum, is it?" He sat back on his heels as another thought struck him. "Blimey! You're never gonna see yours again, are you? You poor little sod! At least mine'll be there when I get back to Bermondsey."

He stopped trying to make Barney settle down again. Instead he lifted him so that the puppy's scruffy little face was level with his. "Reckon we should stick together, then, don't you? Come on!"

He took him outside the back door and murmured encouragement until the puppy obliged with a little puddle. Scooping him up again, Arfur whispered, "Good boy. Now you've got to be really quiet until we get upstairs. Got it? Otherwise you're on your own again."

Once in his bedroom, Arfur set Barney down on the pillow beside him. After a bit of sniffing about, the puppy gave a sigh of contentment and curled up in a snug ball, Arfur's hand reassuringly patting his back. "That's it," he said. "You stay there so I don't roll on you, then we both might get a bit of sleep before that bleedin' cockerel starts up again – makes a worse row than you, he does."

Aunt Edyth and Uncle Rhys were already in the kitchen when he went down next morning, so he couldn't sneak Barney back on his bed like he'd hoped.

"He was making a terrible racket in the night – I had to come down and stop him," he said, a note of defiance in his voice in case he was going to get told off.

"We were told we weren't to get up to him if he cried!" Rhian declared, coming into the kitchen behind Arfur.

"Yeah – well I wasn't down here when you were told that was I? So I didn't know – and someone had to do something, anyway, 'cos he was kicking up a right old shindig."

"I hope he didn't do any puddles in your room," Aunt Edyth said.

"I took him outside first, didn't I?"

"Well, let him out again now, and then he'll be ready for some food, I expect – and then you can get your breakfast when you've given him his."

"I don't know what he has," Arfur said.

Uncle Rhys stood up. "I'll show you. Come on."

When they were finally sat round the breakfast table, Uncle Rhys said, "He'll probably cry again tonight, you know. He'll do it every night until he's a bit older and has settled down more."

"Can't Rags come back in?" Arfur asked.

Uncle Rhys shook his head. "She's a farm dog, a working dog. She'll get too soft in the house all the time."

He turned to Aunt Edyth. "Maybe it was a bit of a mistake, getting another animal – it's not as if he's likely to amount to much around the farm."

"He's just lonely – he'll be fine in a while," Arfur said quickly, Uncle Rhys's tone making him fearful of what he was going to say next. "And if he makes a fuss tonight, then I'll see to him."

Uncle Rhys grimaced. "You'll be making a rod for your own back if you do – he'll get to rely on you and then you'll have to see to him all the time. I thought you didn't want to do that."

Arfur shrugged and tried to scowl at the same time. "Got nothing else to do at the moment, have I?"

Rhian was about to ask whether Arfur was going to be allowed to take Barney up to his room again, because *she'd* never been allowed to do that when Rags was a puppy, so it wouldn't be fair – *again*. But as she opened her mouth to speak she caught the glimmer of a wink pass from her father to her mother, and a frown aimed at her from Bronwen, so, understanding finally dawning, she yawned instead.

Usually Arfur was made to go to chapel with the two girls and their mother on Sunday mornings, but today Aunt Edyth said he didn't have to go. "You look tired from Barney keeping you awake half the night. You'd better stay here. Don't want you snoring halfway through the sermon," she said with her wide smile.

So he found himself in the house on his own for once, with nothing particular to do. The clear night had turned into a wet early morning, but now the clouds were drifting away. He could find Uncle Rhys and help him do some mucking out, but then Uncle Rhys might want to talk about Mum while it was just the two of them, and Arfur wasn't ready for that. He was aware that they were trying to be really kind – all that stuff about him being too tired to go to church hadn't fooled him at all – but he couldn't decide whether that made it all easier to bear, or harder. Sometimes doing stuff like picking an argument with Rhian was better because then he could shout and stamp his feet and kick things.

He sat scuffing his foot against the foot of the table until the puppy came scampering across the floor and began to jump up against his leg, sharp little paws scratching at his skin.

Arfur sighed. "Stuck with you again, am I?" The puppy jumped up and down, then gave a short, high pitched bark, which surprised him as much as Arfur.

"S'pose we could go for a bit of a walk, couldn't we? Tire you out a bit. Come on then – I'll take you round the farm. We're not going near them cows, though – not till you're a bit bigger and can keep out of their way..."

He carried on talking as he left the house, the puppy at his heels.

18.

Two days after the mothers' visit, the children of Penfawr went back to school, to sighs of relief from many of the foster mothers, and in some cases from the children themselves.

The new term couldn't have come quickly enough for Amy. Absorbing herself in school activities gave her a sense of security and escape from the oppressive atmosphere of the Preece household and the hours of finding something to do and foisting herself on other people when she was turned out of the house to play. But at the end of the week, during Sunday School she sat through the singing of the songs, her lips barely moving. *Jesus loves me, this I know,* which they seemed to sing every week, gave her no comfort. Jesus couldn't possibly love her, because if He did He would stop what was happening to her. But perhaps by now she was too bad a little girl even for Jesus to care about. Maisie would still sit beside her, as she did at school, but Amy was tired of hearing of the wonderful life Maisie was enjoying with her foster family. She preferred to be with Rhian and Arfur and the others, when at least she could benefit from the kindness of Rhian's mother and Mrs. Dawson.

She had been terrified of what would happen after Mrs. Dawson's attempt to help. But for a few days it had actually made a bit of a difference. Mrs. Preece spent many hours proclaiming loud and long on the shortcomings and effrontery of 'that piece' who had dared to take over the role previously played by Miss Williams, who was now elevated almost to sainthood. Her own role, to anyone who would listen at chapel or in the village, was one of martyrdom, having undertaken to do her best for this – largely ungrateful – urchin from London, only to have it thrown in her face by a bit of a girl who "says she's a widow, but doesn't look like she's done much grieving to me. I'd be interested in seeing her marriage lines."

Nevertheless, for a short while her invective was directed

away from Amy and she was also aware that some of the visiting mothers were friends with Amy's and would doubtless be reporting back, so at least for that weekend she had been less harsh towards her.

Edwin's reaction had been Amy's main concern. The first night after Mrs. Dawson's visit she had lain in bed trembling as she waited for his inevitable visit. He wasn't too concerned with physical things when he did arrive, but cross-questioned her in rapid hissing whispers as to what she had told Mrs. Dawson.

"No-nothing," she had stammered back, "except that I'm missing my mother... and I didn't mean to get you into trouble, Edwin."

Eventually he seemed satisfied that their secrets were still safe, and left her alone, a faint bruise on her arm where he gripped her being the only sign of his visit.

By the end of the first week back at school, though, he had returned to his old habits. Amy had given up protesting by now. Neither did she listen to his whispered words of affection. He couldn't possibly mean them, she knew, when he went on to do such terrible things to her body which were so painful. She concentrated instead on blanking it out, all of it, so that she could almost rise above the bed and look down on the body that was being assaulted and believe that it had nothing to do with her. And afterwards, if she was so sore that she ended up wetting the bed, then she distanced herself from that as well. She stripped the bedclothes off, washed the rubber sheet and re-made the bed, all the while barely registering the telling off she was getting from Mrs. Preece. It didn't matter any more. Nothing mattered until she could see her mother again and be safely back at home. When she got there, everything would be like it used to be and this would be another life, happening to a different person.

She still saw Mrs. Dawson almost every day, as she would walk through the village with Arfur and Rhian until they reached Amos's field, when she would make her way up to the doctor's house.

Mrs. Dawson, when they were on their own, asked her if Edwin ever hurt her. "Sometimes older boys might be thinking they're having fun – you know, with some rough and tumble – and not realise that the other person is a lot smaller," she'd suggested. But

Amy had just said, "No, Edwin doesn't do that," and then turned her attention to Grace and refused to say any more.

Sometimes the others would come to the doctor's house too, and Mrs. Dawson would give them a drink and something to eat if she'd been baking.

One afternoon she greeted them with flour all over her hands and quite a lot on her face from where she'd brushed her hair back. "Ah! I'm glad you're all here!" she'd exclaimed. "You can be my guinea pigs. I've just made my first batch of bread – your mother has been giving me lessons, Rhian. So would you all like to try it and tell me what you think?"

They hadn't needed any more encouragement and had sat round the kitchen table eating chunks of the bread with the faintest glimmer of butter spread over it, whilst the baby sat in her high chair, sucking on a crust and chortling. Doctor Eliot had come in then, and was persuaded to try some too. He'd teased Mrs. Dawson that she looked like a ghost with all that flour on her, and he made them all laugh as he pretended to choke on the bread, until Mrs. Dawson had pretended to hit him. Even Amy had giggled, until she was reminded of the similar way her parents had carried on when they were a happy little family together, and she'd felt such huge sobs threatening to overwhelm her that she had got the hiccups.

After such afternoons Amy would make her way slowly back to Mrs. Preece's house. Mrs. Preece never bothered that she didn't go straight home, only too pleased for her to be out of the house until tea-time, but Amy already knew she would have to go straight back there once the days grew shorter and it would be dark soon after the school day finished.

Mrs. Preece had tried to stop her going to the doctor's house. "I don't want you going up there and telling all sorts of stories to that woman," she'd said, before adding that she hadn't realised she would have a liar living in her house, on top of the other trials and tribulations Amy had brought with her.

But Amy decided that as she was so good at keeping Edwin's secrets, then she could keep this one too. On the rare occasion when Mrs. Preece asked her where she'd been, she simply said, "Out playing with my friends," and, if pressed further, "on the Red Shed field."

Arfur hadn't wanted to go back to school. He hadn't wanted to face the taunts of the other children. But on the first morning, when someone had jeered, "So did your Mum come to see you, then?" Rhian had stepped in so fiercely with, "She's still poorly in hospital, and my Da says that if anyone's got anything to say about that, they'll have him to deal with!" that nobody else dared mention it.

"I don't need you to stick up for me!" Arfur had hissed as the bell rang for them to go their separate ways.

"Didn't say you did," Rhian replied, still fierce enough for her glare to match Arfur's, "but I never have liked that Tommy Stokes. Thinks he's clever, he does, even though he can't get past his six times tables."

Edyth called to see Lydia at the end of the first week of term.

"Just about got the house straight from them going back to school, and now I'm missing them being around the place," she said.

"And I'm going to miss my sessions down at the Red Shed," said Lydia. "They've been a lot of fun."

"Oh, I've still got plans to keep you occupied, my girl," Edyth reassured her. "There are still Saturdays to be taken care of. I'm going to try to get a film show going in the Shed on Saturday mornings – so many of the evacuees talk about 'going to the pictures', I thought it would help them to feel more at home.

"And I've been talking to the teachers at the school," she went on. "They would like to do more P.E. and games with the children, but old Mr. Robinson can't do them because of his limp, poor thing. The lady teachers do some games with them in the yard, but to be honest the boys can run rings round them."

Edyth had been talking so earnestly she hadn't heard Andrew come into the room.

"Sounds like the boys could do with a bit of rugby training," he said, as Lydia poured him a cup of tea.

"Oh! Dr. Eliot! Sorry – I'm monopolising Lydia again – am I holding you up?"

"Not at all. I've not too many house calls this morning, so I'm not in a rush."

"Well, you're right about the boys needing a bit of rugby training. Mad about it we are in the valleys, of course, but I reckon the evacuee boys would enjoy it too. The problem is, the only men fit enough to practise with them are the colliers, and most of them are working flat out now."

"I could do it with them," Andrew said, making both women look up quickly.

"I didn't know you played," Lydia said, then added hastily, "Not that there would be any reason why I should, of course."

"I went to a minor public school," Andrew said, glossing over Lydia's slight discomfort, "and then I carried on playing at university. Can't say I was one of the best, but at least I know all the rules. The children here are quite young, of course, but no harm in starting them off on the basics."

"That would be wonderful," Edyth enthused. "But when could you fit it in?"

"Well, if it's alright with the school, I could manage an afternoon, if it was straight after lunch – as long as they realise I might be called away some days."

"Oh, I'm sure they'll be happy with that. I'll speak to them later today."

When Andrew had gone on his rounds Edyth, who could have sworn she heard him whistling as he went through to his surgery to collect his bag, turned to Lydia.

"What a turn up! He's been invited to nearly everything that's been going on in the village since he's been here, and not joined in once – and now, to have volunteered! Have you been waving some sort of magic wand?"

She stopped when she saw the closed look on Lydia's face and decided it would be wise to change the subject.

"If only all the problems with the evacuees were so easy to solve," she said with a sigh.

"Arthur again?" Lydia asked, latching on with relief to a different topic.

"Yes, Arthur again. Rhys had already phoned the hospital when Arthur seemed so convinced that his mother would be coming down here. The sister said she was discharged early last week, to her home address apparently, so we were hoping against hope that Arthur's intuition was right. But of course she didn't turn up, and there's been no word. So we've spoken to Mr. Owen, and he's going to get in touch with the authorities up there who deal with evacuation to see if they can get hold of her."

"Oh, poor Arthur. How's he taking it all?"

"We haven't told him any of this so far – we've let him think that his mother is still in hospital because her leg isn't better. We'll wait to see what Mr. Owen unearths before we say anything to him. But I don't know, Lydia…"

Edyth's shoulders slumped and her usual energy seemed to seep out of her. "He's such a sad little boy at times – all the more so because he's so determined that he can cope with everything and that it would be soppy to show that he cares. I long to put my arms around him like I would if he was mine, but he holds off against any show of physical affection."

"You're doing all you can," Lydia said, re-filling her friend's cup, "and he seems happy when he's on the farm and with the other children."

Edyth nodded. "Rhys is very good with him – talks to him man-to-man, which Arthur responds to. It was Rhys's idea to get the puppy, you know – although it almost backfired when Arthur wanted nothing to do with it, but he shows it a lot of affection now."

She took a long drink of tea and then sat looking at the empty cup for a few moments.

"I always wanted a boy, you know – for Rhys, of course, with the farm to pass on – but for me as well. Not that I don't love my girls to pieces, mind you. But lost one, I did – a miscarriage – between the two girls. I don't know really what it was – the midwife wrapped it up in newspaper, I remember, and took it away. But I've always fancied it would have been a boy."

Her mobile mouth began to wobble. "And sometimes, when I look at Arthur… well, he's so dark, could almost be Welsh, and it makes me think… it's how it would have been, you know, if that pregnancy had…

"Well! Listen to me!" she suddenly cried, her ready smile firmly back in place. "Going on to you about things that happened ten years or more ago. Not going to help, is it?"

Lydia put her hand over Edyth's and gave it a squeeze. "Well, whatever happens with Arthur's mother, I think you're going to hang on to him for quite a while yet. The war news isn't looking too good, is it?"

As the month of September wore on, it became even worse. There had been some euphoria in the country when the RAF appeared to be overcoming the Luftwaffe and Churchill's tribute to 'the few' had made the people of Penfawr think again about young Lloyd Parry. But this had been followed by Churchill's dire warnings about worse to come, and early in September his words rang true when Hitler changed his tactics. Whilst he had so far concentrated on trying to wipe out RAF bases, he now turned his attention to bombing London and other major cities, and there was real fear of invasion.

The children were told to carry their Mickey Mouse masks again, and there were weekly drills in the school for what to do in an air raid and how to put your gas mask on. Even though the people of Penfawr and other small villages dotted through-out the valley knew that they would not be directly targeted, there were already stories circulating of bombs intended for big cities like Liverpool missing their objective and landing on areas outside the city. Many of the women and young girls throughout the valley worked at the munitions arsenal in Bridgend, which, although it was well camouflaged under a roof covering of grass, everyone knew was going to be a target for German bombers. As would the docks in Swansea and Port Talbot.

The designated street wardens and auxiliary firemen in Penfawr became more vigilant, as did the members of the Home Guard, who practised rigorously twice a week and now looked more the part with proper equipment and guns instead of broom handles.

But London was the first, the main, target, and during the first weekend of September there were nearly one thousand deaths in the capital. Listening to the news, Lydia was reminded of the conversation she'd had with young Reggie that day on Tower Bridge. Her part of London was going to get a dreadful hammer-ing, he'd said, and she wondered, now that his words were coming true, if any of the houses in that area of the capital were still standing.

At the farm, Edyth and Rhys waited for the late evening news at 9 o'clock when the chores were finished and, more importantly, the children all in bed. With still no news of Arthur's mother, they didn't want him to be even more upset by fears of what may be happening in the bombing.

Lydia found herself drawn more into the war effort in the village now that the children's club no longer took up her time. The WVS organised a 'Make Do and Mend' afternoon once a week in the Red Shed, where Lydia's sewing skills, honed in the genteel girls' school she had attended, were soon in demand. Door to door collections resulted in mounds of flannelette sheets, worn in the middle, threadbare blankets, and old jumpers being donated. The flannelette sheets were transformed into any number of babies' and children's nightclothes, the blankets were patched together to make new ones or, occasionally, to make an unusual but serviceable jacket, and the jumpers were unravelled for the wool to be re-used.

Often, in the evenings, she sat by the fireside – a welcome place now that the nights were drawing in and showing a definite chill – putting the finishing touches by hand to a garment she had sewn earlier on Miss Williams' old machine. Andrew would be in the other chair, listening to the wireless or reading the paper. Sometimes she would look up and find his eyes on her.

"Did you know you have a habit of running your tongue around your lower lip when you're concentrating?" he'd said one evening.

"No, I didn't," she'd smiled back at him.

"It's very… *endearing*," he'd said, and she'd seen the look of naked want in his eyes and had had to bend her head again and concentrate on her work. Otherwise she would have cast it to one side and flung herself into his arms, and to hell with propriety and reputation.

One morning, over breakfast, at the tail end of the month, Andrew looked up from a letter that had arrived in the morning post.

"How do you fancy a day out in Swansea?" he asked. "Just the two of us? I've got to go for an interview at the hospital there."

Lydia's eyes widened in alarm. "You're leaving Penfawr?"

He laughed, "Don't be silly! It's just that I want to do a bit more for this war than sit it out here safe and sound. I can't join up, and I can't do things like firewatching as I'd have to be on call as well. So I've persuaded old Crouch to do an extra day a week and I've applied to help out in the Casualty department in

Swansea. They need more doctors with minor op skills. I trained as a surgeon before I went into general practice, so it would be good to sharpen up my scalpel again."

Lydia let her breath out in a sigh of relief. "In that case, it's an excellent idea, and I think it would be very good for you."

"And I think it would be very good for you to have a day away from this place," Andrew said, taking hold of her hand. "You've not been out of the village since you got here – I'm surprised you haven't had cabin fever by now. I've got enough petrol put by to use the car, so I thought we could make a day of it. And I'm sure Edyth Llewellyn would take care of Grace just this once, so you could have a proper break. I know Rita would love to have her, but she'll have her work cut out holding the fort with old Crouch. What do you say?"

"I'd love it."

"Good. Then perhaps you could ask Edyth when you see her? It's next Tuesday. I have to be there for half past ten, but the interview shouldn't take long, and then we'd have the rest of the day to ourselves."

Edyth agreed willingly, in exchange for giving Lydia a list of things to look out for in the shops, just in case. "And you might have time for a walk along the sea-front," she said. "That'll put some colour in your cheeks."

Although, she thought later, Lydia was looking so well, and had coloured up so prettily when she told Edyth the reason for the favour, that there was little help needed from the elements.

19.

The *Admiral* was busier than she'd ever seen it before she went away. A wall of noise hit her as she pushed through the inner door from the blacked-out entranceway. The room was only lit by wall lamps so that dim pools of light, through which blue cigarette smoke curled, contrasted with shadier areas where young men preferred to sit with girls who 'might' so that they could murmur wicked suggestions in their ears and make them shriek with laughter.

Eileen Atkinson looked around her. Some of the faces were familiar, but many were servicemen who spoke with a variety of accents, few of them local. Over in the corner old Jock thumped away at the piano, a pint glass set among the ring marks on the top of the instrument, slopping weak-looking beer over its sides when he hit the lower notes which made the piano rock slightly on uneven feet. *He still sounds as if he's wearing boxing gloves,* Eileen thought, *even though it's the same tunes he's been knocking out for years.*

A couple of young men were singing along, making the best of the duff notes, aware that they looked good in their uniforms and hoping the young women listening to them thought so too.

Eileen was pleased she'd made the effort, even though her leg was killing her in these heels. Wartime rations were making some of these girls look very attractive, paring down their puppy fat to reveal good cheekbones and sleek legs. Eileen knew she was still a match for them, but also knew that she couldn't let herself go in any way. That was why she'd waited a few days before coming out. She'd needed to get a Eugene perm, even though it had cost her twenty-five shillings. At least being in hospital had cost her nothing, and Max had left her a few bob "just in case you need something" on the rare occasions he'd visited, which she'd not used.

She walked over to the bar.

"Hello, Bob," she said to the barman.

"Hello, stranger," Bob said, with an appraising smile. "Not seen you in here for a bit."

"I've been away. *No* – not that sort of away," she said, in response to Bob's raised eyebrow. "Fell over in the bleedin' blackout, didn't I, and broke me leg. Been in the Infirmary ever since. Has Max been in?"

"No, not yet – expecting 'im any minute, though. You want a drink?"

"Only if you've got a gin," she said, lighting a cigarette and looking round the room again through narrowed eyes.

Bob grinned. "I'll see what I can do. As a bit of a welcome home, like."

She'd settled herself in one of the dimmer corners when Max arrived. His eyes lit up gratifyingly when he spied her.

"Hello, doll! Back in the land of the living at last – and lookin' good!"

She gave him her most winning smile as he settled down beside her. "Hopin' you're gonna give me a good night out, after what I've been through. And –" she gave a playful little pout, "you haven't come to see me for ages."

"You know them 'ospitals give me the creeps," Max said. "Besides, been busy, haven't I? Got a lot of deals going on at the moment. People need stuff, you know, when there's a war on, and I'm the man they need to get it for them."

He winked as he moved closer to her, putting his hand lightly on her leg. "Anyway, you want a good night out, doll, I'll see what I can do. How about goin' up West?"

"As long as I don't have to walk too far, Max – this leg still gives me a bit of gyp at times. I could do with a decent meal, though, after what I've eaten these past few weeks."

"*Café Royal* here we come, then."

"*Café Royal?*" Eileen was impressed. "You have been doin' well for yourself. I might even forgive you for not visitin' me too often."

Max chuckled and opened his overcoat to reveal the top of a flask sticking out of an inside pocket. "And a little drop of something for later – back at my place if you like, 'cos you've not got your kid with you no more, have you?"

Eileen shook her head. "No, all yours tonight, Max!"

"Then I'll just have a quick one to wet me whistle and we'll be off."

Her eyes followed him to the bar, but her mind was on the problem of Arfur, which kept niggling away at the back of her head no matter how much she tried to push it away.

She'd meant to write to him when she was in hospital, she really had. She'd had a visit one day from a posh-sounding woman in a white coat who said she was the lady Almoner.

"Is there anything I can do for you, my dear? Letter writing or anything like that?"

Eileen had taken offence at the condescending voice, and the implication that she couldn't put pen to paper herself. Alright, she wasn't very good with her letters, admittedly, not had much education to speak of – but she didn't need some woman with a plum in her mouth to remind her.

"It's me leg I've broken, not me bleedin' arms," Eileen had growled at her, and refused to say anything else, so the woman had gone to pester the patient in the next bed.

Just to show the woman, Eileen had got as far as buying some paper and a pencil from the trolley that the League of Friends brought round a couple of times a week. She'd even managed to write, *Dear Son, Thank you for your letters. Be a good boy,* but she hadn't known what to put after that. Then she'd realised that she hadn't bought any envelopes and the next time the trolley came round they didn't have any, due to shortages.

Somehow, after that, she kept putting it off and putting it off. Arfur wrote to her every week, from his school by all accounts. She knew he was living on a farm, and she could tell he was getting on alright.

Tomorrow. She would sort it out tomorrow, she promised herself as Max came back with the drinks. Write him a proper long letter and she could even find out about going to see him. One of his recent letters had said something about mothers being able to go down to Wales to visit their kids. Virtuous from her good intentions, she beamed at Max as he returned with the drinks and set about enjoying herself.

They took a taxi to the restaurant, where the food was good enough to forget that rationing existed. It felt wonderful to be out and about again. Eileen could feel all the old sparkle coming back as she leaned forward opposite Max so that he got a good glimpse of her cleavage to remind him of what he'd been missing all these weeks.

His flat was only a couple of streets away from her little place over the shoe shop, but it was so much better set up, with decent furniture and good carpets.

"Make yourself at home, while I pour us a nightcap," Max was saying, pulling the flask of whisky out from his coat pocket, when the air raid siren went.

"Oh hell's bells!" he exclaimed. "That's typical bloody timin', isn't it?"

"What shall we do?" Eileen asked.

"Better get down to the shelter in Albert Street. It's not safe to ignore it." He helped her ease her arms back into her coat, then put his on. "We'll take this with us, though," he said, tucking the flask away again. "Gord knows how long we'll be down there, and we'll need something to keep us warm."

The shelter was already filling up when they got there, so Eileen produced an exaggerated limp. "Need a proper seat for this young lady," Max announced, pushing their way through. "Just been in hospital with a broken leg." He made deft use of his broad shoulders until they had a seat together against the shelter wall, ignoring the dirty looks and caustic comments from women who eyed Eileen's high heels. The shelter didn't smell too good, and soon dull thuds, some of them loud enough and near enough to make the shelter shake, intruded into the business of everyone settling down together. But snuggled up against Max, her belly warmed by good food and nips of whisky, Eileen really didn't mind spending the night there – she'd had a lot worse. The few nights since she'd been out of hospital she'd spent in the little basement room at the back of the shop that the owner let the tenants use when the sirens went off. But this felt safer.

It was several hours later when the all-clear sounded. Staggering out, their eyes adjusting to the early morning light, their bodies stiff and minds fuddled from lack of real sleep, they found a dramatically changed landscape.

Most of Albert Street, where the shelter was, still stood, but many of the buildings had their windows blown out. Round the corner, George Street and Max's flat had escaped much of the devastation. But in the other direction from the shelter, towards the street where Eileen lived, there was little that was recognisable. Rescue workers, cigarettes clamped between grimly-set lips, were already clambering over mounds of rubble and round the edges of large craters. Here and there firemen were calling to each other and extinguishing small fires. Eileen looked about her in disbelief, not even sure in which direction her street now lay.

"Looks like my gaff's alright," Max said, having already run round the corner to check. "Why don't we go back there and grab some breakfast? Then we can go and see what's happened to your place."

Eileen shook her head. "I gotta go round there now, Max. I won't rest easy till I see if there's anythin' left."

But when they got there only part of the front and one side of the shoe shop was still standing. The rooms at the back had disappeared, along with the flats above it. If Eileen had been in the basement storeroom she would have been buried underneath all the masonry. Perhaps some of her neighbours were – it was difficult to know.

"All gone," she said, her voice hoarse with shock. "Everything I had – and God knows it wasn't much – all gone."

She picked her way across to two rescue workers carrying an empty stretcher.

"There was a basement under this building – you got down there from the back, underneath all this rubble – there might be people there."

The two men exchanged glances. "Used to live here, did you, love?"

Eileen nodded.

"Then you've had a lucky escape. We'll do our best to find anyone else, but don't go doing too much clambering about yourself – we're not sure that side wall is safe," said one of the men. "If you go round to the old infant school in Sycamore Street, they'll take your details and help you out. Give you a cuppa as well."

Max had been poking about in the remains at the front of the shop. He joined Eileen as the men moved away. "Come on, doll. No point hangin' round here any more. Let's go to the café down the other end of my street. You don't wanna go to that school – I've heard they're using it as a morgue as well."

"You can stay at my place, now you're on your own," he went on as he led her away, "and I'll get you kitted out with some things. Hang on a sec –"

He looked round to make sure none of the rescue workers were about, then took his coat off, bent down and wrapped something in it.

"Found a few pairs of shoes that match and don't look too battered," he said with a wink. "No good leavin' 'em there, is there? Somebody might be needing 'em."

Eileen felt a bit better when they'd had some breakfast and she'd had a cigarette or two and a drop of Max's whisky in her tea to calm her nerves.

Max, though, seemed as chipper as ever. Back in his flat he said, "There's nothin' to worry about, love, honest. I can take care of you – look!"

He opened a drawer and pulled out a handful of clothing coupons. "Surplus to requirements, you might say, and there's more where they came from. And think about it – the authorities will think you've gone under all that dust and rubble. So they won't be callin' you up for war work – you can stay with me, and I've got plenty for the two of us."

Eileen was doubtful. Max had never seemed the settling down type to her. "Are you sure, Max – that you want me around all the time? 'Cos I'll have nowhere else to go if you get tired of me and chuck me out."

He put his arms around her. "Now how could I ever get tired of a girl like you, eh? Besides, I've got lots on the go to keep you busy as well if you get bored with just lookin' beautiful. And with your little lad away, we can be cosy as anything, just the two of us."

Arfur! She was going to write to him today! Now she didn't even have his address any more – his letters were lost in the destruction of their home. She took another slug of the whisky-laced tea and looked about her. Max's comfortable flat could be hers – and if they got bombed out of this one, then Max would look after her again, as long as she played ball.

Arfur's obviously in a good billet, she told herself. All that country air's just right for a growing lad, and he'll be safe from all the mayhem going on round here. Max wouldn't be so interested in her if Arfur was around, she knew that from experience and from the couple of times he'd mentioned it already. But she could dig herself in here with him for a while, maybe gather a little nest egg for her and Arfur for when the war was over – after all, she knew almost as many tricks as Max did. And Arfur was a good lad – he was like her, he was good at looking out for himself. He'd turn up when everything was back to normal.

She pushed away the flash of memory of her and Arfur in the flat together when times were hard, huddled over the little gas fire, with him doing all he could to cheer her up. Thinking thoughts like that never did anyone any good. Just gave you pangs in your chest like heartburn.

She put on her brightest smile for Max. To show him that nothing got the better of Eileen Atkinson.

"I think you need to take me shoppin'," she said.

L ydia spent the rest of the week looking forward to her day out in Swansea. She was going to try to get hold of some material to make clothes for herself for the winter, but had nothing special to wear for the day out itself. The summer clothes she had arrived with were already proving too insubstantial for the sharp winds that sometimes blew in from the coast, heralding the start of autumn. Both Edyth and Rita came to her rescue, the one with clothes that were too small for her, and the other with items that she swore weren't her colour or somesuch.

"You've got your figure back lovely," Edyth said, as Lydia paraded in front of her in a dress which, whilst too small for Edyth, would still need some judicious darts added to be the right size for Lydia.

Edyth sighed. "No matter that I'm on the go from morning till night, I still seem to have got bigger across the beam these last few years." She grinned. "I keep threatening Rhys that I'm going to wear trousers, or one of those siren suits that I've seen them wearing on the newsreels when we've gone to the pictures. You should see the look on Rhys's face! I've told him that Mr. Churchill wears one, but he just said, "Well, and he smokes big fat cigars too, and I don't want to see you doing that either!"

Edyth turned up on the Tuesday morning bright and early, having decided it would be easier to care for Grace in her own home. Lydia knew that Rita would come through for a cup of tea and a gossip with Edyth when Dr. Crouch finished morning surgery, and between the two of them they would spoil Grace rotten, which helped to quell her butterflies at leaving her baby for the first time.

"And Rhian's coming here from school, and will probably have Amy in tow, so there's no need for you to come rushing back, so have a nice time, the pair of you," Edyth said, waving them off with the baby in her arms.

Once in the car, Lydia pulled out a little hat covered with net to match the jacket – donated by Rita – which she was wearing. "I wouldn't dare put this hat on in the village, it's far too gay," she explained. "Rita apologised for giving it to me, but said she didn't have anything that was a more sombre colour. But today I can just be me – not a mother, or a wife, or a widow – just me."

She adjusted the hat until she was satisfied. "And that feels good," she said with a little nod.

The drive, through a series of valleys and hillsides until they reached Bridgend and the road to Swansea, was stunning, the trees already showing shades of russet, crimson and gold. Traces of early morning mist were still clinging to some of the deeper valleys, giving the little towns and villages, when viewed from a high mountain road, an ethereal quality, hiding the grim reality of many of them. Here and there they came across pithead wheels and coal tips, with freight trains chugging busily across narrow hillside railtracks.

As they drove they talked of Andrew's first attempts to teach the boys rugby and of the weekly film shows Edyth had started.

"Apparently, lots of young couples – some of them only a few years older than Edyth's Bronwen – filled up the back row," Lydia said with a chuckle. "So Mr. Owain Owen paraded up and down with a torch, and any couples who were canoodling had the torch shone on them with a cry of *I'll tell your Mam!*"

"Perhaps we should go one week," Andrew said.

"What – and canoodle on the back row? Mr. Owain Owen wouldn't know where to shine his torch!"

Once they'd arrived in the middle of Swansea, Andrew dropped Lydia outside a tea room where they arranged to meet later, then drove on to the hospital.

"Good luck," Lydia said as she closed the passenger door, before taking a deep breath as she looked around her. The air was tangy with the smell of the sea, and seagulls swirled and screeched overhead. Although she loved her new home in the country, it felt good to be amongst the hustle and bustle of busy streets again. They weren't as large as the streets in London, of course, nor the buildings as imposing, and she clearly wasn't seeing the town at its best, with sandbags everywhere and windows criss-crossed with tape. But there was a general air of purpose as people went to and fro, and some of the ladies going past were very stylishly dressed, making her pleased she'd added the hat to her outfit.

She made her way along the pavement, pausing to look in the window of a ladies' dress shop to get some idea of the fashions for autumn and winter. Further along was an indoor market, its stone front as imposing as a town hall. Inside there were fresh food stalls, mainly selling vegetables which were piled high.

Further into the market she discovered some stalls selling material, so she whiled away a happy time deciding what to buy. Eventually she settled on some serviceable tweed, which would make up a couple of skirts, and found her clothing coupons would stretch to a length of dark blue material with a small flower print, which would be just about enough for a dress.

Purchases made, she strolled back to the tea room where she was just tackling a dry-looking bun when Andrew arrived. He didn't see her at first, so he stood looking around, his hat in his hand. Lydia had seen him, but waited a moment to raise her hand in greeting, to look at him as if he were a stranger. She liked what she saw, she decided, taking in his lean frame, immaculate this morning in his dark grey suit and white shirt. There were only other women in the tea room, and several looked up admiringly as, spying Lydia, he skirted round tables to reach her.

"Have you been waiting long?" he asked, planting a kiss on her cheek as he sat down.

"Only a few minutes – I asked for two cups, and this won't be stewed," she answered, pouring some tea for him. "How did the interview go?"

"Almost a mere formality. Not because I'm so impressive, more because they're pretty desperate. I'm going to do all day each Wednesday – I think I could cancel my morning surgery if

Dr. Crouch is unwilling, and he could just do my house calls and the evening stint. They want me to start next week."

"It seems quite a journey – it'll be a long day, especially in bad weather," Lydia said.

"I'll probably just drive to Bridgend and then get the train – they run till quite late." He leaned forward so that he could speak more quietly. "It'll be good to feel I'm doing my bit – and to be honest, I think they're preparing for a bit of an onslaught. That's why they want doctors who can deal with a bit of surgery – they know it's only a matter of time before Cardiff and Swansea get hit."

"Anyway," he went on, taking her hand, "don't let's think about those things now – let's enjoy the rest of our day out. Where shall we go for lunch?"

"Well, I suppose we could have something here later on," Lydia said dubiously, eyeing the remains of the dried up bun she'd been unable to finish.

"Oh, I think we should aim for something a bit grander – who knows when we'll get the chance again? Tell you what, I saw a nice looking hotel as I made my way over here. Why don't we stroll in that direction, have lunch there, and then we could drive out to the Mumbles and get a bit of sea air. How does that sound?"

"Marvellous," Lydia said, gathering up her things as they prepared to leave.

Outside, he took her elbow to steer her to the pavement edge. "We need to go this way," he said, then tucked her arm into his as they crossed the road. They strolled down the street opposite, heads together as they paused to look in shop windows.

The hotel was indeed a grand affair, with brass lamps aloft stone balustrades on each side of the steps leading up to the entrance.

"Don't worry – they'll still be offering the British Menu," Andrew said with a smile at Lydia's surprised expression.

"I'm joining in your pretence," he told her, when they'd been ushered to a table. "Today we are a couple who are footloose and fancy free." He looked at her with such steadfastness that her heart began to thud. "The only true part is how I feel about you."

20.

Peggy Hopkins usually enjoyed visiting her sister Elsie in Penfawr. She didn't do it very often, on account of her Jimmy being so bad with his rheumatism, so when she did it was an Occasion. This necessitated the donning, in summer, of her green gabardine double-breasted coat and her black straw hat with the wide brim turned up a little on one side, which she fancied made it look like the ones the Queen wore. Even though she'd had hers long before the King and Queen came to the throne.

Late September was a difficult time, however. Sometimes a little too cold for the summer coat, but still too warm for the winter one of dark brown wool with the fur collar. So she compromised by adding a scarf neatly tucked into the neck of the green gabardine, and black gloves rather than her lighter summer pair.

It was often a good month to get a bit of sunshine, though, especially away from the biting wind that had already begun to blow at times through Swansea. Bracing sea air was all very well for day trippers in the summer who inhaled deeply and enjoyed the smell of ozone as they strolled along the front. It was different when you lived there all the time and the chilly wind heralded the wet and stormy months ahead.

But Penfawr was often sheltered from the worst of the wind at this time of year. It might rain at times like stair-rods, but it didn't lash at you quite so much. And anyway, as Peggy invariably remarked to her Elsie when they were sat down together in the best front room – Elsie liked it to be an Occasion as well – and Peggy was easing her feet out of her shiny black shoes a little because they always made her ankles swell so, *it made a change*.

This visit, however, she wasn't enjoying as much as usual. The meat in the stew Elsie had prepared for dinner had been tough, lodging itself in Peggy's stomach and giving her indigestion, which she tried to overcome by sucking a peppermint and burping discreetly behind her hand as she listened to Elsie's talk of the village.

Usually the talk, all in Welsh, went from topic to topic as Elsie gave her the round-up of the latest gossip, some of it of people Peggy knew from when she'd been a girl in the village, before she'd married Jimmy and been whisked away to Swansea. Other snippets might be of newcomers since her time, but over the years she felt she knew them as well as Elsie did, their habits and their business having been told to her in such detail. It usually made up for the regular interspersion of eulogies to Elsie's son, Edwin.

Today they had started with a satisfactory shaking of their heads at the loss of poor Lloyd Parry and running through an inventory of his family tree, always a necessary part of discussing any death, and the list of mourners. There were one or two of his family whom they could have dwelt on at length but Elsie seemed intent on pouring out nothing more than a diatribe against the unfairness of having had an evacuee foisted upon her – and clearly the most troublesome one in the whole village.

Peggy switched off after a while and concentrated on using her tongue to remove a piece of beef that had become lodged behind a back tooth. Once it had been satisfactorily dispatched she turned her attention to her sister again and tried to catch up.

"And what about the young doctor?" she asked when Elsie paused for breath and Peggy felt she couldn't stand another minute of evacuees.

Dr. Eliot had been the subject of several previous surmisings due to his single status and enigmatic personality, with quite a lot of information about him being fed to them by the much lamented Miss Williams.

"Huh!" Elsie said now. "He's been duped like the rest of us. Our Betty and Owain did their best, finding a young woman to take Myrna Williams's place. But she's a right madam – full of London ways, and with a baby to see to as well. A widow she is, or *says* she is, but I wouldn't be surprised if that baby was born out of wedlock. I feel sorry for poor Dr. Eliot – she must be leading him a pretty dance."

"Just as well he's got himself a lady friend, then, isn't it?" Peggy said, before Elsie could go on about evacuees again. She sat back in satisfaction as her words brought Elsie to a halt.

"Lady friend? He hasn't got a lady friend!"

"Saw them myself, I did, in Swansea," Peggy said. "In *Nell's Tea Room*. Must be a Swansea girl, because she was there waiting for him to arrive."

"Are you sure it was him?"

"Of course I'm sure. You introduced us the last time I was here, remember? When we were waiting for my bus. Anyway, in the tea room he passed me as close as I'm sitting to you here now, he did. Didn't see me, though. Only had eyes for the young woman in the corner. Kissed her on the cheek when he sat down.

"And when they'd finished their tea," she went on, Elsie's nonplussed expression making her enjoy herself for the first time that day, "they went off arm-in-arm across the street. Looking at the shop displays, they were – I could see them because I was at the table by the window. *Jeweller's shop*, they were looking in." She wasn't completely sure about this, but it was a good embellishment.

Elsie's mouth worked furiously in time with the speed of her thoughts. How could Dr. Eliot have got to know a young woman in Swansea? He hardly ever left the village. She'd have to get to the bottom of this one – what a lot she'd have to tell them at chapel once she did!

"What did she look like?" she asked.

"Quite a pretty little thing. Not tiny in height, you know, but slender. Dark hair and eyes. Smart jacket and hat she was wearing."

It couldn't be – no, it couldn't be… "Did you hear her speak – you know, was she Welsh?" Elsie asked.

"I was too far away to hear," Peggy said, "and they were talking very close together. Very close in all sorts of ways, I'd have said."

They continued to mull things over throughout their last cup of tea before Peggy had to get her bus back to the station. Elsie Preece waved her off, then turned to walk down the main road, thoughts buzzing. If Dr. Eliot did have a young lady tucked away in Swansea, then that would be one in the eye for that minx of a housekeeper, who clearly thought she'd got her feet nicely under the table. Or… if Mrs. Preece's wilder suspicions proved to be correct, then there must be goings-on up at that house that Betty and Owain would have to put a stop to. Either way that piece would be out of there eventually, and serve her right.

She made her way to Thomas's shop, not because she particularly wanted anything, but so that she could look out for anyone who might shed further light on her sister's assertions. She was disappointed, though, because there was only one old man in there, taking a long time to buy two stamps from the post office counter.

But she gave a quick prayer of thanks to the God she considered her own personal property when, as she turned the corner near her terrace, she met Rita coming towards her.

"Just been seeing my sister off – back to Swansea," she told her as they came abreast. "Good for her to get out, it is – terrible time she has looking after her husband."

"Oh! Well, I hope you've had a nice day together, then," Rita said, trying to hide the surprise in her voice at Mrs. Preece's friendliness. The woman had hardly spoken to her since Miss Williams left.

"I don't think her eyesight's as good as it used to be, though," Elsie Preece went on. "Tried to tell me she'd seen Dr. Eliot in Swansea the other day, but I said no, it couldn't have been, indeed to goodness. Too busy Dr. Eliot is, to go off to Swansea for the day, I said."

"No – your sister was right." Rita felt pleased to score over the old busybody. "Dr. Eliot had to go to a meeting at the hospital last week."

"Oh – it wasn't at the hospital she saw him. In the town she said he was, having a cup of tea with someone, so she must have been mistaken after all."

"Well, he gave Mrs. Dawson a lift in, so she could do some shopping. Your sister probably saw him collecting her for the journey back," Rita said, wondering why she was wasting minutes talking to this woman. "I'd have gone myself but I had to help Dr. Crouch. Mrs. Dawson brought us all some lovely fresh fish back, though. So kind of her. Better go now – the children will be out of school soon. Not fetching your little girl today, then?"

Rita knew how much the child was left to her own devices and how much time she spent with Lydia. But there was something about this woman's prying that made her want to give a dig back.

Mrs. Preece pursed her lips. "She's old enough to find her own way back," she snapped.

She went on her way, thoughts of Amy immediately pushed from her mind. Far too many other things to think about. *Living over the brush*, that's what they were clearly doing, the two of them! How disgusting! And her supposedly with a husband who'd given his life for King and Country, and hardly cold! Of course, she'd looked like trouble from the start, that one. Feeding her baby in front of people!

Righteous indignation filled her breast. Thoughts of what the doctor was getting up to with that brazen hussy filled her head, making her body flush with heat. That was probably why the madam had wanted Amy to go and live there – to provide a smokescreen for their goings-on. Just as well she'd put a stop to that idea – saved the child from being thoroughly corrupted, she had!

It started as a whisper. Just a word or two here and there about the doctor having been seen out cavorting in Swansea with his housekeeper. Words dropped into conversation like the first snowflakes falling, randomly and hardly noticed and melting away at first, until they fell more furiously so they began to stick. With each whisper, suggestions became definite, hints became facts and such scant facts as there were became exaggerated as Mrs. Preece's malicious tongue wagged stronger and stronger.

There was no need for any degree of circumspection with her sister-in-law, Betty Owen, of course. Over cups of tea in Betty's kitchen, Mrs. Preece's eyes held the gleam of a zealot.

"I've had my suspicions all along," she said, folding her mouth even further into her face. "Saw them a while back, I did, walking through the village – it was the day when the Parrys heard about poor Lloyd. I could see there was something between them then. Probably off to some out-of-the-way place so that they could carry on together – and everyone else in the village grieving for that lad and his parents!"

"But now," she went on, finishing a morsel of Welsh cake and dabbing a handkerchief at the side of her mouth, "kissing and cuddling in public, they were, in full view of everyone, according to our Peggy, when they thought no-one they knew would see them. Goodness knows what they get up to in that house together when they're alone. Living in sin! Ungodly, that's what it is!"

In just over a week, Mrs. Preece's knowledge of what the two of them were apparently getting up to had become encyclopae-dic, and was aired with authority in the village shop and at Eben-ezer chapel. If anyone questioned how she had come by all this information, she told them that the poor little evacuee she was caring for had gone to the house regularly, inveigled into helping with the baby, and had seen things going on that no child should be exposed to.

"Of course, I've stopped her going there, now," she would finish, remembering to cloak her voice in piety.

Of the few people in the village who refused to listen to such scurrilous gossip, Mr. Owain Owen was probably the most surprising.

"Perhaps you should pay another visit there," his wife suggested, as much in the hope that she might glean a titbit of information which would top the rumours Mrs. Preece was spreading, as in the desire for her husband to carry out his duties punctiliously.

"I don't really see as there is much I can do," he said. "Not hurting anyone, they aren't. They're not flaunting it, either. And we can't actually prove it. Not our business, I'd say. It would be different if any of the children I'm charged to oversee were in any sort of peril. But Mrs. Dawson wasn't even on my lists – so I can't see as how I'm responsible for anything that goes on between her and Doctor Eliot."

"She does things with the children, though, doesn't she?" Mrs. Preece said, when he repeated his stance during a visit from her. "A bad influence on them, a woman like that will be. No knowing what she could fill their heads with."

"Well I know I wouldn't want my children to be cared for by a woman with loose morals," Betty Owen said, folding her arms under her considerable bosom. She remembered now her own misgivings when Mrs. Dawson had been so brazen on that first night. She had briefly questioned her own judgement at the time, but later had felt reassured when the girl settled down so well into her housekeeper role.

"I'm sorry ladies," Mr. Owen said, with a firmness that he would doubtless be sorry for later. "Seeing a couple kissing in public doesn't mean they're getting up to anything else, does it? And I believe Dr. Eliot has stronger morals than that. He's a decent man."

His wife gave him the scornful look he expected. "Two people thrown together under the same roof?" she said, conveniently ignoring that she had been the one initially to do the throwing. "Can't expect a young man to turn down the advances of a woman if she throws herself at him, can you?"

"I blame her," Mrs. Preece said, recalling Lydia standing on her doorstep trying to tell her that she wasn't looking after Amy properly. "Probably easy to prey on the sympathies of a lonely man – and she's likely got her eye on the main chance. Nice little life in that house, after all."

"And we both went to see if she was getting on all right," Betty persisted. "She was on your list then."

"Ah, yes," said Mr. Owen, "but that was to make sure that the doctor was satisfied with the arrangement and that Mrs. Dawson had settled in well. There's been no complaint from either side, has there, so even assuming I am responsible for her, what can I do?"

He sat down, amazed with his own reasoning, but even more sure that he was not going to intervene. The truth was that he dreaded the thought of having to bring such a subject up with either the doctor or Mrs. Dawson, who would look at him with those large, challenging eyes. Incurring the wrath of the two women in front of him was preferable.

At first Lydia was oblivious to the whispering. She had returned from the day out in Swansea refreshed and invigorated, and more sure than ever that she and Andrew had something that could last. Their few hours together had flown by, punctuated by laughter and affection and shared dreams. Andrew had seemed a different man from the dour figure who had opened the front door on that first evening.

"The sea air has put some colour in your cheeks," he'd told her after a stroll along the pebble-covered seafront at the Mumbles. "When this war is over, we'll have a proper holiday at the seaside – the three of us."

During the drive home they had dared to start imagining what a peacetime life together could be like, and divulged more hopes and ambitions.

It was Andrew's certainty that they had a future together that Lydia daydreamed about for the next few days. The spectre of Billy was always in the back of her mind, but she steadfastly refused to let it come to the forefront. When the war was over, and nobody knew how long that would be, she would sort out the tattered remnants of her marriage. The way the war was going at the moment there was no certainty that the Allies would win, so Andrew was right – they should be content with what they had for now, and look to resolve it when this madness ceased, one way or the other. Perhaps by then, Billy, if he was still alive, would have met someone else and would be content to let her, and more importantly, their child, go.

A certain frostiness in the way Mrs. Thomas served her in the village shop first alerted Lydia to the fact that something was wrong. Her cheerful comments about the changing colours in the valley were met with stony-eyed monosyllabic answers that she hadn't encountered before. She wondered if Mrs. Thomas had had some sort of bad news, like the Parrys, but felt she didn't know her well enough to ask. She would check with Andrew later on, she decided, he would know of any misfortune.

"There's no-one in that family on active service, as far as I'm aware," he said when she mentioned it that evening. "Perhaps she'd just had a set-to with a customer before you went in, or was having an off-day. I know a lot of people are getting more scared now they can hear the bombers coming over – it brings the war so much closer, doesn't it?"

The next day began with fingers of mist which cleared to a pale blue sky and a smell of wood smoke in the air. It was Andrew's afternoon for playing rugby with the boys, so Lydia decided to wheel Grace along to the Red Shed field to watch. It was amusing to see the boys gather round the doctor, eager to be noticed by a man some of them would have been shy of when seeing him at the surgery.

At the end of the game Andrew trooped back to the school with the boys, so Lydia headed for home.

"I'm becoming very Welsh," she told Grace, who was sitting up well now and eager to take in all around her, "watching rugby games and then wanting to go home for a nice cup of tea."

She came across a couple of young mothers who also had babies in prams and she manoeuvred her pram into the road so that they could still walk abreast on the pavement. Normally they would have stopped to chat and admire each others' offspring. But today the other two seemed intent on going on their way.

"Been watching the doctor playing rugby, have you?" one of them asked, without stopping, in reply to Lydia's "Hallo".

The other mother nudged her friend as they went by. "She'll have seen it all before," she said in a giggled whisper just loud enough for Lydia to hear, "and more!"

She didn't tell Andrew about that encounter. She tried to tell herself that they were just being silly and she was equally silly to imagine that there was anything else behind their words. And she tried to quell the sensation that as she'd continued to walk home there had been one or two other people who had tried to avoid her eye when she had said "Hallo" to them.

But she didn't have to wonder for long. Next morning, after surgery, a subdued Rita came through to the kitchen behind Andrew.

"I need to have a word with you both," she said, "and I don't think you're going to like what I have to tell you."

"Not leaving us, or anything, are you, Rita?" Andrew asked. "You've been very quiet all morning."

Rita licked her lips nervously, quite unlike her usual bouncy self. Then it all came pouring out, the rumours and innuendo that were flooding the village.

"I only heard last night – well, there's not many that would say anything directly to me," she said. "Got it from my husband, I did, when he got home from the *Prince*. The men were talking about it in the bar."

Rita's husband, Glyn, was a collier, and *The Prince of Wales* was Penfawr's only pub, a Gothic-looking building stuck incongruously on the end of a terraced row.

"He was saying he wanted me to finish working here at first – stupid these men are when they've had a couple of pints, and my Glyn's no different. But I told him it was rubbish – that there was nothing between you and if there was I would have been the first one to notice."

Andrew spoke after a moment or two, while Lydia sat, white-faced, looking at her hands.

"Thank you Rita, for letting us know what's been going on. And you're right, of course, there is nothing untoward going on in this house." His voice held the formality that Lydia remembered from when she had first arrived, but hadn't heard for some time.

"There's something else, though," Rita said, her face contorted in an effort to hold back tears. "I think this is all my fault. That Mrs. Preece woman got me talking, see, the other day – and I told her that you had gone to Swansea together. And, well, it seems her sister saw you there, put two and two together and made five.

"I wouldn't have made trouble for you for the world," she went on, distress making her accent stronger. "If I'd never said anything she wouldn't have been able to start the rumours, would she – and I bet it was her, loves a bit of gossip that one does."

The tears had begun to flow, and she was clearly so upset that, forgetting her own distress, Lydia jumped up and put an arm around her.

"It wasn't your fault, Rita, truly it wasn't. Mrs. Preece doesn't like me because I told her I was worried about little Amy – she thought I was interfering, which I was, I suppose. And you warned me when I first came here that she was trouble, so I should have known."

"So if she hadn't started this rumour, she would have found something else," Andrew said, offering Rita a handkerchief.

It reminded Lydia of the day he had made the same gesture to her, when they had gone for the walk together. It was the day when everything between them had really begun. She had been a fool to believe that they could have continued as they were without something like this happening.

"But what are you going to do about it?" Rita asked.

"I'm not sure," Andrew said, "except keep our heads held high, because we are not having the sort of relationship that these rumours are suggesting, so we've nothing to be ashamed about."

Once they had sent Rita on her way, still sniffing and apologising, they stood holding each other quietly for a few moments.

"You know Rita only has to go away and think about your words to realise that you didn't actually say we aren't having a relationship," Lydia pointed out.

Andrew shook his head. "She'll repeat my words in her own fashion." He gave a slight smile. "You'll see – by tomorrow she'll be back to her old ebullient self and be defending us like a terrier."

Lydia sank down into the fireside chair. "That won't make it end, though, will it? All the time I'm here, people will go on thinking it now, even if they don't say it. And what will that do to your reputation?"

"Oh, hang my reputation! We're doing nothing wrong, except being two people who have discovered that they love each other. Narrow-minded people in a small place like this are always going to have something to say unless you happened to look like Miss Williams – I'm just surprised they haven't said anything before now, with or without just cause."

"That's because you're the inscrutable, distant doctor, and I'm supposed to be a widow, remember," Lydia said. "What if they find out that Billy's still alive? They'll have a real field day then!"

"There's no need for them ever to find out – although I do think we should perhaps do something more about it. But look – I really must go out on my calls now. Will you be alright until I get back, and we'll talk about it all again then?"

Lydia nodded. "I'm fine – just worried for you."

He kissed her tenderly. "Don't be. This will just be a flash in the pan until the next bit of gossip comes along."

She knew he had been right when he said that they should go about with their heads held high, but she was pleased that it was raining, which gave her the excuse to stay in with the baby for the afternoon.

A little while later, though, there was a knock at the back door, and for once Lydia didn't want to see who was the other side. But she made herself answer it and was relieved to see Edyth's cheerful face.

"Have you come to tell me the latest gossip as well?" she asked, picking up Grace and holding her almost defensively to her.

"'Fraid not. Don't go into the village often enough to hear anything, and then I'm always in too much of a hurry these days to stop and chat. Why? Is there something going on – oh, my dear, what's the matter?" Edyth had been busy putting her basket down and taking off her coat, so didn't see the stricken look on

Lydia's face until she straightened up.

She listened gravely while Lydia repeated the tales Rita had told them.

"Well, of course the so-called devout lot at Ebenezer chapel are all holier-than-thou," she said robustly. "It's still not that long ago that they used to drag a poor girl in front of the elders and have her drummed out, or whatever they used to call it, if she was in trouble – but it was never the man's fault, of course! Absolute nonsense, it was, and some still think like it now, which is why we only go on Sundays for the girls' sake and don't bother with them any other time."

"I thought I was being cold-shouldered a couple of times these past few days, but I told myself I was imagining it," Lydia said. "I don't really mind for me – as long as you and Rita are still my friends – but it bothers me for Andrew's… Doctor Eliot's sake. I don't want his reputation tarnished, he's too good a doctor for that."

Edyth was silent for a while, then looked Lydia straight in the eye. "Not entirely without foundation, these rumours, though, are they? Oh – I don't mean that you are getting up to anything together, though I for one wouldn't blame you if you were, and would regard it as nobody's business but yours. But I'm not wrong, am I? There is something between you?"

Lydia dropped her head for a moment then lifted it and returned Edyth's gaze. "We've developed… feelings for each other… but it's early days, Edyth, and there are complications, and I've been through a lot before I came here, so we're just treading carefully for now. At least we were – until this. I think we should probably nip it in the bud and I should find somewhere else to stay with Grace."

"What? And give these stupid old women the benefit of believing they were right all along? No you won't, my girl. Stare them out, that's what you'll do, and I'll be right there beside you! I'll give them what for if they say anything in front of me!"

Lydia couldn't resist a smile at Edyth's ferociousness and the picture of her as some sort of 'minder'.

"And I'll tell you something else," Edyth went on, barely pausing for breath. "Thrilled to bits I am that you and Doctor Eliot are making something of yourselves. Thought you were suited to each other for a while now, I have. I never liked the idea of him stuck in this house all on his own – him a young man, with all his life in front of him. I think you're made for each other."

"But you won't say anything, will you?" Lydia pleaded. "You're the only one who I've spoken to about any of this – even Rita has no idea, and I'd like it to stay like that."

"Of course I won't – not even to my Rhys, because these men can have a good old chin-wag when they get together too! Although, I must tell you he's already accused me of matchmaking on your behalf!"

Lydia was buoyed up by Edyth's stoic attitude, but still concerned for Andrew. "It's not fair on you," she told him. "You had trouble with that mad woman in your last practice, and now I'm causing you more problems."

He held her tightly. "I'll decide what's a problem for me – and this really isn't. Like I said earlier, it'll be a nine-day wonder and then there'll be a new piece of gossip coming along. We haven't done anything wrong, Lydia – whether Billy is alive or dead, your marriage is long finished, and you wouldn't be with him by now anyway. We just have to weather this little storm."

She kept hold of his and Edyth's words when she next ventured into the village, but, of course, it had to be that there were a lot of people in the village store, which she could see through the open door. She went to the butcher's first, instead, where there were fewer people, and managed to get what she needed without saying much to anyone.

But as she returned to the store several women were coming out – chapel women who had all been party to Mrs. Preece's rumour-mongering. She parked the pram deliberately, as if she hadn't seen them in the doorway, before straightening her back and turning towards the entrance.

The women ignored her, brushing past as if she weren't there. But there was a discernible "Tut" from one and, as another glanced at the pram, she heard a whispered, "It's the baby I feel sorry for."

Well, if that's the worst it can get, I can cope, she told herself as she stretched her mouth into a smile almost as wide as Edyth's when it was her turn to be served.

It was Andrew's day at the hospital, which Doctor Crouch

had agreed to cover completely. Morning surgery ran over time, but Rita stayed for a chat with Lydia afterwards.

Lydia told her of the encounter with Mrs. Preece's cronies and what she had heard said. "I don't see why they should feel sorry for Grace – even the most torrid affair wouldn't really affect a seven-month-old baby, would it?"

Rita reddened, which made Lydia look enquiringly at her and wait. "They're saying Grace doesn't have a father…" Rita blurted out, "and that you're not a widow, but a… *fallen woman.*"

The choice of such a quaint expression made Lydia laugh out loud, even though anger on behalf of her child was rising in her chest. How could people who had been so concerned for her and her baby just a few months ago be willing to think such bad things now?

"I think the war is making it worse," Rita said. "I know we're all supposed to be pulling together, but everyone's feeling the strain. There's so much bad news about, and they're talking of cutting rations again any day now, aren't they? A new bit of gossip to latch on to, like, gives them something different to think and talk about."

Two people had stopped Rita the day before to tell her that they wouldn't be staying on Dr. Eliot's list any more, but would be seeing a doctor in Maesteg from now on.

"That will be fine," Rita had flashed at them. "Worked his fingers to the bone for everyone in Penfawr, Doctor Eliot has, for the last couple of years. Do him good it will if he has a bit less to do. And I hope your doctor in Maesteg will get here quickly enough if you have to call him out in the middle of the night!"

Rita decided not to pass this snippet on to Lydia – she had enough on her mind already. "Will you be alright?" she asked as she rose to leave.

"I'll be fine. I'm going to take out my feelings on giving the hall and stairs a good clean through – and our *separate* bedrooms!" Lydia said, with an attempt at a proper smile. "You never know, I might have the Owain Owens round here at some point demanding to do an inspection!"

Not everyone listened to the gossip, though, amongst them the Parrys.

"Ridiculous fuss about nothing!" Delwyn told Rhys Llewellyn

the next time he saw him. "Been good to us, the doctor has, couldn't have been more understanding since our Lloyd went. Haven't had much inclination to go to chapel since we lost him, and I've even less desire now – except to go and tell them what I think of them! A glimpse of a man's shirt-tails would do some of those old biddies good. A lot of interfering busybodies if you ask me."

Edyth waltzed Lydia off to the weekly 'Make Do and Mend' afternoon, making sure that the women there appreciated the amount of sewing Lydia was getting through. Most of the younger women treated her no differently but there were some sticky moments when the conversation veered towards personal topics before trailing off into awkward silences.

"There now, that wasn't so bad, was it?" Edyth said, as they walked home, having met the children from school, who were trudging behind them.

"No – apart from my face aching from such determined smiling all afternoon," Lydia joked. "But thank you, Edyth, for your help – you're a good friend."

Amy was walking with the children, but when Lydia asked if she wanted to walk back through Amos's field with her, as they had been in the habit of doing, Amy shook her head.

"I'm not allowed. Mrs. Preece says I have to go straight home after school now that the evenings are drawing in."

She turned off, her steps slow and shoulders hunched, when they reached the turn-off for her terrace.

"Helping Amy was my main intention," Lydia told Andrew that evening. "But now I can't even do that because I've managed to upset Mrs. Preece so thoroughly. I'm certain Amy's unhappy in that house, but I can do less for her than I could before."

She rested her head on his shoulder. She was tired. All this fuss was making her sleep badly, and, ironically, making her even more aware that the person who could give her most comfort was just a few feet away across the landing.

The rumours finally reached even Dr. Crouch's deaf ears. He and Andrew didn't normally see each other because of Andrew's hospital work, but Dr. Crouch called in to see him a few days later, before the start of evening surgery.

"Might be better for you to make new housekeeping arrangements," he said. "It doesn't do, you know, in these parts, for a doctor to have any smirch on his character. If there's no foundation to the rumours, then you'll have no qualms about having someone else come and keep house for you."

"I think you're missing the point here, Dr. Crouch," Andrew said in his coldest voice. "Mrs. Dawson has behaved impeccably since the day she arrived in Penfawr and she's made a home here with her child. She had already gone through a lot in London since before the war began. Why should she be hounded out because of the gossip from a group of nasty old women who have nothing better to do?"

Dr. Crouch dropped his head so that his jowly chins hung over his starched white collar.

"Besides," Andrew went on, "I'm a great believer in loyalty – I don't let people down who have done nothing to deserve it."

Dr. Crouch eased himself to his feet. "I admire your sentiments, my boy, and I've nothing against the young woman myself. But at the same time I hate to see a bright young doctor's future be damaged – and it could be, you know – if it can be helped."

Andrew said nothing to Lydia about Crouch's visit. Nor did he mention that his surgeries seemed lighter than usual. Part of him felt disbelief that he could be going through this sort of thing again. But he was resolute this time. Had he been a more experienced doctor in London with a practice that owed more to his skill than a spoilt woman's whims he could have stuck it out then, too, and not left so hastily. But if he hadn't come here, of course, he wouldn't have met Lydia. And now the thought of letting her go was something he simply couldn't contemplate.

21.

Arfur and Rhian hurried up the farm drive and round the back straight into the kitchen, pausing only to kick their shoes off in the scullery. It had been raining all week and they were soaked from the long walk from school. They both headed for seats near the fire, whilst Edyth handed them a towel each to rub their streaming hair. Barney, who had been waiting for them to come in, immediately jumped onto Arfur's lap and tried to bite the ends of the towel, making both children giggle.

"Take those wet socks off as well, while I get you both some hot cocoa," Edyth told them, removing the puppy. They peeled off their long woollen socks, and rubbed their legs dry, the skin above their knees bright pink from exposure to the elements.

Edyth didn't sound as cheerful as usual, and wiped her nose a few times as if she were coming down with a cold.

"We'll have tea as soon as Bronwen gets in," she said as she spread their wet things on the airing rack suspended above the fireplace. She clattered about getting tea ready, but for once didn't issue instructions for them to help, so they stayed where they were, petting Barney who had again found his way onto Arfur's lap.

Bronwen wasn't so wet because the bus dropped her at the farm gates, but Rhys joined them with his hair plastered down from the rain, making his head look rounder and his ears stick out. He rubbed his head briefly with a towel, so that his hair now stood out in all directions, but he made no effort to flatten it. It seemed that both adults were anxious for tea to get underway.

When everyone had cleared their plates, and conversation about the doings of the day had petered out, Rhys walked over to the dresser on the other side of the kitchen, pulled a letter out from the drawer and returned to his seat.

He cleared his throat. "Um... there's something I have to tell you, children," he said. "It's to do with Arthur, but I'm telling all of you at the same time so you all know the situation."

He cleared his throat again. "I sent to London, Arthur, to ask the authorities if they could find out if your mother was back at home, and if she was alright. I had a letter back this morning. It seems... it seems that the flat where you used to live was bombed some days ago – but they've said that they have been unable to find your mother."

He put the letter down and looked tenderly at the boy sitting motionless opposite him. "Which is good news, actually, because the people from the other flats, who were in the shelter at the back – well, they all died, but your mother wasn't amongst them."

The two girls had become very quiet, Bronwen looking down at her plate, but Rhian's eyes, like her mother's, were fixed on Arthur.

"The man who wrote me this letter says that she may have left that part of London earlier, and headed out for the country – apparently lots of people have been doing that, to avoid the bombs. So perhaps when she's settled somewhere she'll get in touch. But it might also be that she left in a hurry and all her belongings were still in the flat, so she doesn't have your address with her."

Rhys waited for a few seconds to let Arthur digest all this information. "Do you understand what I've told you so far, Arthur?"

The boy nodded.

"The man also says in this letter, that they'll keep all your details clearly on their files, so if your mother turns up they'll make sure to pass them on. And I'll keep in touch with them regularly to check if they've spoken to her."

"I'm sure your mother is alright, Arthur," Edyth said quietly. "We would have heard if she wasn't."

Arthur nodded again.

Edyth bit her lip, quelling the desire to go round the table and wrap her arms round the forlorn figure. She still hadn't been able to show him any motherly affection, and she could sense from the set of his shoulders that he would reject any advance she made now, especially in front of other people.

It was Rhian who broke the silence.

"Come on, let's go in the front room and play some card games. No point sitting here and moping, is there? And you said you'd teach me Black Deuce."

"Don't want to," Arthur said.

"So what are you going to do instead?" Rhian asked. "Sit up in your bedroom? It's cold up there – and anyway if you do that, I'll only stay down here and teach Barney some more tricks, then he'll be my dog more than yours." She shrugged, while her mother held her breath at her brusqueness. "Your choice."

She picked Barney up and made for the door into the hall. After a moment's hesitation Arthur slid off his chair and followed her.

They sat on the floor with the cards between them, telling Barney off for trying to eat them until he gave up and spread-eagled himself across Arthur's legs. Rhian learned the game quickly, despite Arfur's reluctant, brief instructions.

"Beat you now, I will," she said. "Girls are always better than boys at cards – we've got better memories."

They played on until Arfur had won more games than her. "Let's play Newmarket instead," she said. "Bet you can't beat me at that."

"See!" she said some time later. "Knew I'd win this time! What do you want to play now?"

"Don't care," Arfur said with a shrug.

"Shall we do something else, then?"

Another shrug.

"Shall I ask Mam if we can have some more cocoa?"

No answer.

"We could go back and sit by the kitchen fire, now – and Barney might need to go out. It's a bit cold in here – be nice and warm in the kitchen."

Pictures of sitting with his Mum, huddled in front of their little fire, flooded his mind. Sometimes they'd have crumpets, holding them out to the fire on forks that weren't long enough, so that their hands and faces would feel scorched long before the crumpets were toasted. Sometimes it would just be slightly stale bread they were toasting, and then they'd spread it with dripping for their supper.

They wouldn't ever do that again, he knew. Even when he found his Mum – and he was determined to find her – they wouldn't be back in their little flat, cosy against the world, the two of them. Which meant that as well as his Mum being missing, he didn't have a home any longer.

He wiped his sleeve across his face, because now it felt as hot as when they were toasting crumpets, but it was wet too. The tears streaming down his face were beyond his control. They were part of a huge horror that threatened to engulf him, like pictures you saw in cartoons of people being flattened by a giant snowball that rolled towards them too quickly for them to get out of the way. Somehow, as he leaned forward onto the floor, making the puppy jump up with a squeal, and surrendered to explosive, chest-hurting sobs, Rhian was beside him, sitting as quietly as his Mum would sit on one of her 'off' days.

Rhian let him howl for a minute or two, before putting her hand on his shoulder and patting it softly. Her Mam always said it was healing to have a good weep, but Rhian also knew that crying on your own was the loneliest thing in the world. And she didn't want Arfur to be lonely.

"He's alright, he's had a long cry," she whispered to her mother when they finally went back through to the kitchen for their bedtime drink, making Edyth smile at her solicitousness despite her worries for the boy.

"You're a good girl," she whispered back.

But Rhian knew it was nothing about being good, not like the Good Samaritan they talked about in chapel. He'd refused to pass by a complete stranger, whereas she was comforting Arfur because he was going to be around for good, which meant, whether he realised it or not, he was already one of the family.

The next morning, the rain having eased, found Amy on the farmhouse doorstep before they'd finished their breakfast. It gave Edyth the opportunity to offer her some food as the child was looking painfully thin, but she would only accept a drink.

"You'd better play in the barn this morning," Edyth told them. "Give the ground a chance to dry off a bit, or Amy will be filthy going home."

Rhian was going to warn Amy against mentioning Arfur's mum, but he brought the subject up himself.

"Is your street still alright, Amy?" he asked.

"Me Mum takes Gran into the shelter at the bottom of the garden," she told him. "But she said lots of people go to the tube station – she would go too, 'cos she said that it's quite comfy down there and they all keep each other cheerful, but Gran can't get that far. I bet that's what your Mum did, Arfur, 'specially if she was out somewhere when the raid started."

When a pale sun began to shine Rhian went over to the farm-house to ask if they could play outside now. While she was gone, Arfur confided in Amy. "I'm saving up all the money Uncle Rhys gives me, you know, for working on the farm. I'm 'elping him this afternoon again. Then when I've got enough I'm getting the train back to London. Gonna look for me Mum."

"I wish I could go back to London," Amy said. "I really want to see me Mum too. I hate it where I am."

She looked so woebegone that Arthur stopped thinking about his own troubles. He knew from what all the other kids said that he had one of the best billets going.

"What's wrong with it exactly?"

Amy shook her head. "Can't tell you, but it's horrible. Mrs. Preece is a witch and… and Edwin… I just hate him, that's all."

"Tell you what," he said, "I'll save up even more, then we can both go together – I'll be able to look out for you then, won't I?"

The smile of gratitude she gave him made his heart swell with protective pride.

"How long do you think it will take, till you have enough?"

"Dunno – it's building up faster now I keep remembering not to swear, though. I'll work as hard as I can, I promise."

"Don't they ask you what you're doing with the money?" Amy asked. Mrs. Preece wanted to know what Amy did with every ha'penny of the money her Mum sometimes sent, even though it was very little.

"I've told Uncle Rhys I'm saving it for a present for Mum – I keep it at the back of the drawer in my bedroom, so no-one sees it unless I show it to them."

Rhian came back then, with pairs of wellingtons so that they could go off across the farm. "Let's see how deep the brook is today," Arfur said, taking the lead 'cos that was the only thing to do when you had two girls to play with.

Lydia was relieved when the rain stopped. She'd been warned during the warm summer weather that the valley usually saw more rain than sunshine, but she hadn't been prepared for it being so relentless. It had rained for almost two weeks without stopping. The river, shallow and so clear in the summer that every stone on its bed could be counted, gushed and boiled, a mud-brown torrent that threatened to rise above the curving stone bridge which linked the two sides of the village. Some days the cloud hung so low that the tops of the hillsides were completely lost to view.

Even when it wasn't actually raining the sky was heavy and grey, the air full of moisture. It matched her mood of weariness. As Grace grew bigger the old pram was harder to push, and for many days the path through Amos's field had been too muddy, so she'd had to go the long way round along the road, which was very steep as it approached the turning to the house. The leaves still on the trees drooped and dripped, whilst those which had already fallen gathered into a slimy mulch on the footpaths, making walking downhill even more difficult. So trudging to the village shops in the rain to try to eke out the rations – which, as predicted, had been cut – held no cheer when many of the faces she saw held hostility or downright dislike.

Once or twice she had seen Mrs. Preece scurrying along under a large, black umbrella. Like a loathsome beetle, Lydia thought, wishing that she could squash her underfoot and put a stop to her nasty ways. On one occasion Mrs. Preece had been walking towards her with Mrs. Owain Owen. Lydia made a point of standing still with the pram, so that they had to split up to go round her.

"Thank you so much," Lydia had said to Mrs. Owen, with the friendliest, almost conspiratorial smile she could muster, whilst ignoring the other woman, and had the satisfaction of seeing Mrs. Owen look uncomfortable. A small victory, but it made her feel a little cheered.

As a new week dawned, though, the weather changed again, becoming much colder, so that there was a crisp layer of frost on the ground in the mornings which a low sun peeping over the hill-tops managed to disperse by midday. Extra layers of clothes, with little regard to colour or style, were found to keep warm both indoors and out and the children excited each other by swearing that it was going to snow any day now. In the school there were fires lit in each of the classrooms and the children were given spoonfuls of cod liver oil and malt every morning.

By night the bombers kept coming. The people of Penfawr, safely tucked in their beds, could hear the drone of the aircraft as they passed overhead. With other big cities such as Birmingham and Southampton being hit, they knew it wouldn't be long before the cities of South Wales would be the target.

E arly one Wednesday morning the milkman knocked at the doctor's back door.

"Don't want to worry you," he told a surprised Lydia, who was expecting it to be an anxious relative summoning Andrew to an emergency, "but I know Dr. Eliot goes off to Swansea of a Wednesday for the hospital. Thought he should know that the bombing's started – Llandarcy oil works got it last night. You can see the smoke from here. Still burning it is, so there's talk that Jerry'll be back tonight, now he's got a landmark."

Lydia thanked him and hurried off to find Andrew.

"I'll take the car all the way, I think," he told her, "in case the trains stop. Could you warn Dr. Crouch when he comes that he may need to cover for me tomorrow as well?"

He saw her look of mute alarm and wrapped his arms around her. "If there's any hint of a raid tonight, I'll have to stay, you do see that, don't you? I couldn't come away again, just to be safe, knowing that I could be of some use."

She nodded. "Of course. It's just, now that we've found each other, I couldn't bear…"

"I know. Don't worry, I'll be back before you know it."

With a lingering kiss good-bye and a promise to phone if he could, he was gone into the sharp early morning air which still held more of the night than day about it. Lydia waited in the doorway until she heard the car engine start, and waved as it set off down the bumpy drive. The days when Andrew was in Swansea always felt different. On other days, even when he was at his most busy and she barely saw him until the evening, she knew he was never very far away.

It wasn't until he began his work in Swansea that she realised just how closely their daily lives were now interwoven and how aware of his presence she had become. Listening for his footsteps as he crossed the hall from the surgery, occasionally hearing the murmur of his voice as she went about her chores in the bedrooms above, the slam of the front door and her name on his lips when he returned from his calls, and anticipating the end of evening surgery when they could spend precious time together.

Grace now held her arms out to him whenever he came into the kitchen and he carried her about on his hip, as readily as if she were his own, talking in serious tones to which she appeared to listen equally gravely.

This particular morning Lydia found herself dwelling on these things more than usual. A new worry that Andrew's very life could now be in danger if the bombs fell on Swansea added to the nagging anxiety caused by Mrs. Preece, which underlay everything she did. Along with a third anxiety which had been troubling her recently.

"*I think we should do something about it,*" Andrew had said, referring to the dilemma of Billy's whereabouts. Despite his assertions that they could weather the hail of conjecture and tittle-tattle that was battering down on them, Lydia had occasionally seen the shuttered look again in Andrew's eyes and had wondered what attitude or innuendo he was having to face from some of his patients. Guilt that she was the cause of it continued to wash over her, especially on the days when Andrew wasn't there to hold her in his arms and convince her all over again that she should stay and fight it out.

So eventually she had agreed that they should make discreet enquiries as to the whereabouts of Billy's unit, within the limited amount of information that was available to anyone at the moment. The daily visits from Idris the Post now made her heart beat faster in case he brought news of Billy.

"I think we need some fresh air," she told Grace when the first post had brought no information, she'd finished her morning chores, and was already tired of the thoughts going round and round her head. "A nice walk out to the farm while the sun is shining would do us both good."

Bundling the baby into her thickest pram coat and bonnet, they set off down the lane from the house, where the sun sparkled on the remaining frost, and the tree branches were etched in silvery-white. Lydia pushed the pram at a fair pace to keep warm, so that the rasping feeling of cold air in her lungs was soon dispelled and she arrived at the farm with tingling skin and rosy cheeks. Rhys, lifting hay bales into the mangers in the front field, bade her a brief good morning as she walked up the drive. He stood watching her for a second, wondering why on earth, if the rumours were even only partly true, the doctor didn't snap her up and make an honest woman of her while he had the chance. And if the rumours *were* true, there were surely few men around who wouldn't have been equally tempted.

Lydia hadn't seen Edyth for a while, so she was soon regaled with the disappearance of Arthur's mother.

"And what about Amy?" she asked. "Have you seen her recently?"

"She spent about an hour with us yesterday," Edyth said. "The children were sent home from school a bit earlier because they were waiting for a delivery of coal to heat the rooms – ridiculous when you think we're surrounded by coal mines, isn't it? – but there you are."

The walk and her chat with Edyth lifted Lydia's spirits, which helped the rest of the day go quickly, and even Dr. Crouch's rather brusque manner at evening surgery, when she passed on Andrew's message, didn't bother her. She concentrated on preparing their evening meal in case he came home after all, and settled Grace down for the night.

The drone of planes in the distance could already be heard as she laid Grace in her cot. But this time they didn't seem to be moving across the country. She turned off the landing light and lifted up the blackout. In the distance, beyond the dip at the end of the valley, where two of the interlocking spurs met, could be seen a bright red glow. White searchlights were arcing across the sky above the red. *Swansea! They were bombing Swansea after all!* Maybe Andrew had left before it started. But even if he was on his way home, she knew he would turn back as soon as he realised what was happening.

Briefly, inconsequentially, she wondered what was being shown at the cinema in the city. There was a myth going about that wherever there was a showing of Chaplin's *The Great Dictator*, that's where Hitler would send his bombs.

The glow seemed to intensify as she watched. Maybe it was the docks they were targeting, rather than the town itself. Not that she would wish it to be anywhere, but there was likely to be less loss of life at the docks.

Suddenly she heard some voices coming from the lane that ran past the house. Fetching a coat, she went out through the front door to the gate. A number of villagers were making their way up the mountainside, some of them carrying tins suspended on lengths of string, with holes punched in the sides and hot coals in the bottom.

"Looks like the whole of Swansea is on fire," one of them told her. "Going up the mountain, we are, to get a clearer view."

It was impossible to settle to anything, but in the end she made herself go to bed, after looking once more at the red glow in the sky. The searchlights had ended, so the raid was over, but there was no way of knowing how much damage there was. She slept fitfully until she could bear it no longer and wandered down-stairs in the still-dark early morning, moving from room to room, praying, without even realising it, that Andrew would be home soon.

The message came through that German planes were heading in this direction just as Andrew was leaving the Casualty Department, and simultaneously the air raid warnings began to sound throughout Swansea.

He put his white coat back on, stuffed his stethoscope in his pocket and headed for the main desk. The senior registrar was already directing operations.

"Seems we're for it, this time," he told Andrew. "We're on red alert – need to clear this area of patients as quickly as possible. We'll send as many as possible up to the wards and send other people home, or at least to the nearest shelter, if we can. Soon sort out the malingerers, anyway!"

Nurses bustled to and fro, in orchestrated manoeuvres which had been practised since the outbreak of war for just this even-tuality. As many cubicles as possible were emptied of patients, and camp beds were set up in one of the waiting areas. Casualty Sister had emerged from her office, rolling up her sleeves and donning her cuffs, ready to work side by side with her nurses. A large, heavy woman, who had run the department since the end of the last war, she had a look of Winston Churchill about her and Andrew was in no doubt that, if called to do so, she would stand shoulder to shoulder with Churchill, equally unbowed, to the bitter end.

There were only a couple of patients still being attended to when the peculiar throbbing of Luftwaffe planes began to be heard in the distance, and as they grew nearer there came the sound of explosions, far off at first and then worryingly closer, and a couple of times the building shook. The faces of one or two of the younger nurses began to pucker with anxiety but the Casualty Sister found them a dozen jobs to do to keep their minds off it.

Just over an hour after the raid began the first casualties started to arrive, brought in from the First Aid posts by volunteer ambulance crew, who all continued to work despite the incendiaries and shrapnel falling all around them. By the time the all-clear sounded three hours later the department was already hectic, with more casualties arriving until they filled not only the converted waiting area, but all the corridors as well.

Andrew's first patient was an ARP warden who had tried to stamp out an incendiary, but it had blown up and taken off his foot. Despite being sedated, the man was swearing profusely, until Sister leaned over him and said, "I know you've had a terrible time, but I have young nurses here, so there's no need for language!"

There was no time to stop, with constant calls for "Doctor, over here please," no matter how organised they tried to be. Those with minor injuries would have been seen to at the various First Aid posts, yet the department was still straining at the seams, which made Andrew wonder just how much carnage there was beyond the hospital walls.

Some were announced dead on arrival at the hospital, some breathed their last within a few minutes of their canvas stretcher being laid down. Some seemed to have the strength of Goliath to be surviving despite atrocious injuries, and some went into spectacular decline very quickly from undetected internal injuries.

All of these Andrew could cope with, his training allowing him to work on automatic pilot and concentrate fiercely on each job in hand – until, having issued instructions for the further care of one patient, he was just about to move onto the next when a cry for help came from a large man who was running down the corridor, shouldering people out of the way like a rugby forward.

But instead of a rugby ball he carried in his arms a baby about the same age as Grace.

"Help her, Doctor, please," he pleaded, tears making rivulets in his blackened face. "I've laid my two little boys out on my front lawn – gone they are – but she was still breathing when I picked her up, I know she was."

There were no visible injuries on the baby, but she wasn't breathing either. She had probably died from the blast from an explosion. Andrew placed his stethoscope on her little chest anyway, and felt her neck for a pulse, for longer than was necessary while he steadied himself to look into the man's face and shake his head. "I'm… I'm sorry…"

The man let out a bellow that wasn't human, before scooping the baby up in his arms. He held her tightly to his chest, rocking backwards and forwards with the terrible grief of a man who had now lost everything that was dear to him. Andrew looked around for a suitably senior nurse who could help, but it was Sister herself who bustled over from the other side of the room, alerted by the man's cries, in the way that she seemed to pick up on everything that was going on despite the chaos and the noise.

She put her arms around the man's shoulders, and in a voice vastly different from the one she used to bawl out probationer nurses or swearing men, said, "There, there, my lovely. You come along with me. Hold her to you, that's it. You don't have to let her go."

Gently she led the weeping man away. Over her shoulder she said to Andrew,

"Time you had ten minutes, Doctor Eliot. There's tea in my office."

He was grateful that the office was empty so that he could get the slight tremor in his body under control before anyone else came in. He took several mouthfuls of restorative tea and closed his eyes for a few moments, but then opened them again because all he could see behind his closed lids was Lydia, sitting in the chair in her bedroom rocking baby Grace backwards and forwards, backwards and forwards…

By the middle of the next day most of the casualties had been attended to and work was underway to clean up the Casualty area and prepare it for any further onslaughts. Luckily the phone lines were still working, albeit erratically, and Andrew was able to put a call through to Lydia.

"I've been outside," he told her. "Everywhere's a terrible mess, lots of fires. I'm going to hang on here in case there's more tonight, if you and Crouch can manage for a bit longer."

The connection was poor, so he could hear her voice replying but couldn't make out the words. He wanted to say more, wanted to tell her how much he loved her, but the line crackled and spluttered before cutting off altogether and he couldn't get through again.

He managed a tepid wash followed by a couple of hours' sleep in an armchair in the doctors' quarters, and a meal in the canteen, where some of the women had come in to work even though they had been bombed out of their homes the night before.

The red alert came just after six, by which time he was back in Casualty. Within minutes there was a request from the senior registrar for Andrew to take the place of an ARP Medical Officer who had been injured the night before. A warden stood by to take him to his post.

"It'll be best if we walk, sir," the warden told him as they left the hospital. "Then we can dodge into buildings if things get a bit hairy."

Things were already looking hairy to Andrew's eyes. Amidst the devastation from the night before, hundreds and hundreds of incendiaries were dropping. Searchlights were playing their beams all over the sky to trap planes for the Ack Ack guns to aim at. Andrew watched as one plane became caught in the glare and the guns all opened up. Down came the plane, showering shrapnel like heavy rain. The warden pulled Andrew into a doorway to avoid getting hit by the debris. "Press yourself against a wall when stuff's falling," he said, "or we'll never get you to your post."

He passed Andrew a cigarette and told him that the bombs would start coming down any minute now.

"They drop them in salvoes of six, so we have to count them, then we know we've got a minute or two before the next lot. It also means we'll know if there's any not gone off."

They had almost reached the first aid post when they came across a young boy clinging to the one remaining wall of what must have been his house.

"You alright, son?" the warden called. "Come on, make your way across, over here by us. We'll take you to the shelter."

But the boy shook his head. "Gotta find my Grampy first."

"Where is he?" Andrew asked.

The boy pointed to the mound of rubble in front of him. "Under that lot."

The two men began to move bricks and pieces of wood from the top of the pile, the warden calling to some men further up the road to fetch a rescue team, while Andrew urged the lad to give them a hand. When the rescue unit arrived, the warden said, "We'd better leave them to do the digging, and see what's needed at your post. I'll give you a call if they find the old man needs your attention."

At the first aid post Andrew was immediately absorbed with a steady influx of casualties, many brought by the rescue teams battling through the blazing streets and buildings. Minor injuries were tended to by a tall, thin-lipped nurse who despatched them with ruthless efficiency, whilst more serious wounds were treated by Andrew, who decided who should be moved on to hospital.

It was over an hour before the warden appeared again in the doorway.

"They've reached the old man, doctor. He's alive – could you come and take a look?"

The rescue workers had dug a tunnel to reach the old man, who had been saved by a tall kitchen cupboard falling across the table he was sheltering under.

"His arm's trapped under a piece of brickwork, and we don't want to pull him out without him having a shot of something first for the pain," one of the workers explained. "Jack, his name is – Jack Hancock."

Andrew crawled through the narrow tunnel, his height proving a bit of a hindrance, until he reached the old man, who gave him a gummy grin. "Told them just to give me a big tug and I'd come out like cork from a bottle, but they wouldn't do it."

Andrew gave him a shot of morphine and waited for it to start taking effect. "There's no medals for being in pain," he told him. He shone his narrow torch on the arm, which was crushed but didn't appear to be bleeding, which was a relief, as it could have been that the bricks were the only thing stopping the man from bleeding to death and moving them would do more harm than good. Once the drug was doing its job he carefully moved some of the bricks and felt along the limb with practised fingers. The arm was undoubtedly broken, so he managed to slip a wide bandage under the man's body and strap the arm to his side. The old man was drowsy now, but still gave a groan as his arm was handled.

"I'm going to start sliding you out, Jack," Andrew told him. "It'll still hurt a bit, but I'll do my best to be careful."

He called to the rescue workers that he was bringing him out, then began to edge backwards, his arms under Jack's shoulders so that he could drag him out behind.

"That's it, Doc," the main rescue worker encouraged him, as he reached the mouth of the tunnel. "Ease him out and we'll get him on the stretcher by here. Soon have him to the –"

His words were cut short as a huge explosion erupted nearby. Andrew flung himself across the old man's body as those around him were thrown up in the air, and the remaining wall of the house crumpled.

A nother day had come and gone. Apart from his brief phone call, which she had barely been able to hear, Lydia had no idea of what was happening to Andrew. In the distance Swansea still blazed, a sure target for another night of conflict. She stayed in the house all day, not just to be near the phone, but also, burdened by a deep sense of foreboding, she didn't want to hear in the village any news of how bad it was in Swansea, or that the hospital, along with everything else, had been hit.

By evening, when the planes could be heard overhead again, she knew he wouldn't be home that night.

In the end, she sat in the rocking chair in her darkened bedroom, staring through the window at the war scene being played out just a few miles away. The same chair in which she had nursed her child so many times, the same window where she and Andrew had stood watching the storm on a sultry evening when he had murmured her name so longingly for the first time. She wished it would rain now. She wanted the heavens to open and put a stop to the raging carnage. She wanted Andrew to be on his way home to her in his battered car. She wanted to tell him how much she loved him.

What if the hospital had taken a hit? What if Andrew was killed? What if his heart murmur was more dangerous than he had led her to believe, and all of this put too much strain on him? Less than a year ago she had harboured the dreadful hope that the war would take away the man she had once thought she loved, to put an end to their horrendous marriage. Now she wanted the war to spare the man she *knew* she loved to the depths of her soul. Maybe this was her retribution for leaving Billy, for having such wicked thoughts and for claiming to be widowed.

But Andrew didn't deserve any retribution, she argued with the gods of destiny. Punish her if need be, not the man or child she loved. Doubtless, she realised, Mair Parry had said the same.

She wished now that she had declared her love for Andrew more passionately. What if she were never to see him again, and he died not really knowing how much she cared for him? What if he were already lying somewhere, injured… dying… ? It made a nonsense of the stupid gossiping and sniping from Mrs. Preece. How small those concerns seemed. Surely all that mattered in these dreadful times was that you made the most of what each day brought, and, if you were lucky enough to find love, you nurtured it and embraced it with all your being.

She didn't move from the rocking chair. She relived every moment she could recall of their brief months together, memorised every feature of Andrew's face, laughing, frowning, deep in thought, smiling in that special way that made him a boy again. Perhaps from now on memories would be all she would have. Her body became chilled from sitting so long, but she barely felt it. There was a greater chill of fear wrapping itself around her heart.

By the early hours of the morning she knew she wasn't going to see him again. His parents would be informed of their loss and they would take his body – if there was a body – back to Scotland and there would be nothing left of him for Lydia to grieve over. She would have to leave the house where all signs of him would be removed to make way for another doctor to take his place, and that would be it. Finished.

She must have dozed off in the rocking chair, exhausted by the thoughts that buzzed round and round her head, and the fit of weeping that she had been unable to quell. She wasn't sure what had roused her, and by this time she was so immersed in sorrow that it took a few seconds to register. She peered through the window. Daylight was just beginning to filter through. In the driveway, she could just make out a dark shape. It looked like Mr. Owain Owen's car... probably he would be the one responsible for taking bad news to people in the village...

She didn't want to answer the door. Just like Mair Parry, she wanted to hold onto the moment when everything was still the same. Slowly she put one foot in front of the other and went down the stairs. She could hardly bear to open the front door.

"*Lydia*"

With a sound half-way between a choke and a sob she flung herself forward.

"Thank God! Oh! Thank God!" she breathed, as Andrew's arms folded around her. "I was sure I'd lost you."

She led him into the kitchen and onto a chair before fetching hot drinks. She could see from the look on his face that the last two nights were ones he would prefer to forget but would probably be etched on his mind for years to come.

She placed a steaming mug in front of him before slipping into the other chair and taking his hand in hers.

"I could see it from here," she told him. "A big orange glow."

"Most of Swansea is on fire," he said at last. "They've gone straight for the town centre, not just the docks. Scores of bombs. So many people injured... I don't know how many dead. We lost a few – couldn't help them quickly enough, or just couldn't help them at all. Some we should have been able to save, but they just slipped away, no matter what we did. I should have been able to do more, Lydia... there were children... not everyone has shelters – some just hide under the stairs... how is that going to protect you from a bomb?"

She touched a large piece of sticking plaster on his forehead.

"And this – what happened to you?"

"I was helping to get an old man out from some rubble. The others all around... they didn't make it..."

He didn't need to close his eyes to see it all again. Coming to after the blast and trying to look around. Hearing a voice which sounded muffled at first, but gradually realising it was saying, "You're on my bloody arm!"

He'd carefully moved his weight and looked around. Across the road he could make out several inert bodies, two of them grotesquely back-lit by an incendiary which was still burning. He and Jack had been saved by being just inside the mouth of the tunnel, which hadn't collapsed, and the house wall had luckily toppled the other way.

He'd wanted to get back to the first aid post, but one of the stretcher bearers rescuing them told him it was gone. So he returned to the hospital in a makeshift ambulance van, and once the gash on his forehead had been attended to he'd been determined to help, but they wouldn't let him.

"Your clothes are filthy for one thing," the Sister told him, "and the worst of it is over now. I don't want you keeling over in my department."

"Why don't you have a bath and then try to get a little sleep?" Lydia suggested after she had persuaded him to eat a little soup. "I'll grab a couple of hours too, before Grace wakes."

He nodded his agreement and then, as he rose from the chair, he reached for her and kissed her more deeply, more hungrily, than ever before.

She heard him climb the stairs as she was undressing. Heard the creak of his bedroom door, could picture him sitting on the edge of the bed to undress.

She changed into her nightdress and brushed her hair with strong, swift strokes. She stared at her reflection in the dressing table mirror, remembering that early encounter, when he had been examining her and their eyes had met in the mirror. Looking back it seemed that they had both known, even then.

She stood up, checked the sleeping baby in her cot, then moved on swift, bare feet out onto the landing. Taking a deep breath she opened the door to Andrew's bedroom. He was sitting just as she had pictured, his tie in his hands, only the top buttons of his shirt undone. His hair flopped forward over the plaster on his brow, beneath which his eyes burned with an intensity that shone even in the shaded light of the room.

He was suffering, she knew that. As surely as she had been

physically hurt when she arrived at this house, he was now hurting in his soul. He had tended to her injuries. It was her turn to tend to his.

She stood beside him, where he grasped her round the waist, his head against the softness of her stomach. After a few moments she moved his arms from around her body and urged him to his feet. In two swift movements her nightdress was unfastened and fell at her feet, as she lifted her face to his. With a groan of desire, he pressed his lips to hers as his arms came round her naked body.

She had known the passion and want and excitement of love-making with Billy, but never before had she encountered such tenderness, or the joy of giving as much as receiving. The horrors of the night, the senseless gossip of the last few weeks, the uncertainty of the months ahead, all were put aside as they responded to their longing for one another. All that mattered was the feel of his body next to hers, exploring each other with their hands and mouths, teasing each other to respond; wave after wave of exquisite pleasure until his urgent need of her could wait no longer, making her cry out with love for him.

Afterwards, she lay in his arms as he slept, savouring the feeling of completeness, of helpless need for this man, of realisation that everything about their relationship had now changed irrevocably – and finding that she had no regrets.

22.

Whenever Arfur earned more money from Uncle Rhys he liked to count his stash, even though he knew to the penny the amount he had and could simply have added the next lot of pennies to the total in his head. There was something very satisfying in taking out the coppers, sixpences and shillings and counting them out every time.

Sometimes Uncle Rhys gave him odd pennies for doing jobs when there wasn't enough time to do a half-day or a full day. This evening he'd been given fourpence for going round the fields early in the morning to break up the ice on the drinking troughs, and helping to move the sheep onto warmer slopes after school.

But this time, when he opened his bedside drawer and slid his hand to the back to pull out the old sock he kept the money in, there was nothing there. No sock, no money.

He pulled the drawer out completely and emptied the contents onto the floor. It wasn't there. Frantically he searched through his other possessions, which didn't take him long, even stripping his bed, though he knew that he would never have left the sock anywhere else. It had taken him hours of graft over the weeks to build up the amount he had, and he reckoned he was pretty near to having enough to take him to London. With less for him to do on the farm after school because it got dark so early, it would take him months to get that much again.

But no matter how hard he looked, there was no sign of his money.

He sat down on the crumpled bedclothes. Who would have taken it? No-one in this house, he was sure – not even Rhian as a joke if she had found it. They all knew that Uncle Rhys paid him – and they'd all seen him troop upstairs and fetch pennies to pay back when he'd been heard swearing. He'd told them that he was saving the money to give to his Mum when he heard from her, and they were all too honest and understanding to have taken even one coin away from him.

But someone had taken the bloody lot! He thought back over the week. There was only one person, he realised, who had been in his bedroom during the past few days. Amy! Timid, shy little Amy! She was his friend, but she was also very unhappy. She must be feeling pretty desperate to steal from a friend – where they came from you stuck by your mates. He'd have to see her as soon as they got to school tomorrow and ask her what she was up to – although he had a pretty good idea of her intentions.

He wondered if he should tell anyone about it – perhaps a grown-up who could help. But then, if that Mrs. Preece got to hear that Amy had stolen something she would go mad and take it out on her, and that was the last thing Amy needed. No, he would wait and speak to Amy tomorrow. If she gave him the money back, then there would be no more to be said.

He surprised Rhian next morning at the speed with which he was ready for school and the pace at which he walked along the icy paths.

"I need to see Amy before school starts," he told her, when she asked him to slow down.

"What about?" Rhian asked, the familiar feeling of jealousy making her stomach squirm.

"None of your business."

It took him a while to find her in the playground. She was obviously trying to avoid him. But eventually he cornered her by the railings.

"Come with me," he told her, standing very close so no-one else could hear.

She refused to meet his eyes. "The bell will be going soon – we'll have to go in."

"Not before you tell me where me money is," he said. "Unless you want me to tell one of the teachers?"

He felt bad at the terrified look on her face when he said that, but she was right when she said there wasn't much time to talk.

"Come on," he said, and led her round the back, near the boys' toilets, where no-one lingered too long because of the smell.

"Why did you do it? Why did you take all me cash?"

"I want to go home," she whispered. "I would have given it back to you – honest! As soon as I'd got home Mum would have sent it to you – and a bit more if you needed it."

"Where is it?" he demanded.

"Still in the sock, inside my gas mask," she said. As she spoke a large tear rolled down each side of her face. There was no change to her woebegone expression, no acknowledgement of their presence. Arfur watched in fascination as two more followed the same tracks. He'd never seen a girl cry so silently, so desperately.

"What do you want to go home for so badly, anyway?" he asked her. "At least your Ma keeps in touch and you know everything's alright."

She didn't answer straight away. Then, speaking so quietly that he had to lean forward to hear her, she said, "If I tell you, will you keep it a secret, just you and me?"

"Alright."

"I mean, really a secret – you swear?"

"Course. I just said so, didn't I?"

"It's Edwin…" she paused, biting her lip.

"What about 'im? Apart from you hatin' 'im, which you've already told me."

"He does things to me… hurts me… at night. He – he comes into my bedroom and does things… you know… *down there.*"

Arfur flushed with embarrassment. You didn't talk to girls about things like that – not until you were a lot older, anyway.

"You'll break a few girls' hearts, you will, when you're older," his Mum had told him when she was in one of her gay moods. "But you leave them alone until you've left school – and then always keep your hands where they can see them."

Amy mistook his silence for a lack of understanding.

"*In my knickers,*" she whispered.

"Dirty bugger!" Arfur said. "Why haven't you told his mother?"

"Because he says that if I tell anyone he'll say that I made him do things – and then everyone will know I'm the one who's dirty and they'll send me away somewhere horrible. But I'm not, Arfur, I'm not dirty! And he also said he'd take my nightlight away and leave me in the dark. And I'm afraid of the dark. But I can't put up with it any longer, Arfur – I hate it, and I hate him, and I hate everything here! I want me Mum!"

She was properly crying now, tears gushing from her eyes and spittle running from her mouth. Arfur wondered if he should put his arms around her, but someone might see.

"Alright, alright," he said. "Look, I believe you, okay? And you can keep the money – I reckon you need it more than me at the moment. And I'll help you get home. Just stop crying now, 'cos we'll have to go into school in a minute."

"Will you really help me?" she asked, wiping her face with a scrap of rag Mrs. Preece always made her use as a handkerchief.

"'Course I will – we've got to stick together, ain't we?"

Her face looked a mess, but her eyes were shining at him through the tears. He felt the same urge of protectiveness he'd experienced when he'd told her on the farm that he'd save up enough for her too. It made him feel like a man, like a hero. He'd help Amy, definitely he would – and he'd sort out that bastard Edwin.

"Let me have a think about how you can get away," he said, as the bell went. "I'll see you at dinner time."

"Right, I've been thinking," he told her when they met again in the playground. It was the most thinking he'd ever done inside a classroom. "The best thing to do is to leave tomorrow, when everyone thinks you're at school. Mrs. Preece will think you've gone as usual, but you'll have to hide somewhere till after school starts. I'll tell Mr. Robinson that you've got a bellyache or something. Alright so far?"

Amy nodded, even though her heart was thumping in her chest because at last she was being given a plan.

"Then you'll have to walk to the station – don't get the bus 'cos someone might see you and send you home. You know the way to the station? – it's a good old walk."

Amy nodded again. She'd walk all day if it meant she could get away from Edwin.

"Right – when you're at the station, you don't buy a ticket, 'cos again the man there might send you back to the village. What you have to do is wait till the stationmaster is busy talking to someone else, then you sneak through onto the platform and get on the train to Bridgend – can you remember that? As far as I know, all the trains go to Bridgend."

"Yes – but why do I need the money if I'm not going to buy a ticket?"

"Cos if the ticket man comes along on the train, asking to see your ticket, you tell him you ran for the train and didn't have time to buy one, and then you give him the money, then he can't put you off at the next stop, see? If he asks who you're with, you tell him your Mum is further down the train, but you wanted to feel grown-up and sit on your own."

"Now – when you get to Bridgend you'll have to find the platform for the London train. You can buy a ticket at Bridgend 'cos they won't be bothered about you. Again, if the ticket man asks where your Mum is, you just point to some woman and tell him that's your Ma but she let you buy your ticket on your own, so you'd learn how to do it."

Amy's eyes were full of admiration once more. "How do you know all this? I could never have worked it out on my own."

"Been planning me own escape for months, haven't I? Asked Uncle Rhys what the places were we'd passed on the way down here, so's I'd know how to get back. And I often ride the trains in London – it's easy not to pay if you know how to give them all the slip, so long as you've got the money in your pocket so they can't do nothing about it when you offer to buy the ticket after all."

"Now – when you get to London, the train ends up at Paddington. So, to get back to your house, you're gonna have to find a copper or one of them wardens – anyone who's wearing a uniform, really. Tell 'em you're lost and they'll help you get home. If they ask how you got lost, say you got separated from your Mum in an air raid and you've been wandering about ever since. And if you're not sure what to say, just cry a lot."

"I wish you were coming with me, Arfur, It's a long way."

He nodded. "I know – but I don't think there's enough money there for the two of us. You make sure you manage it, okay? – 'cos I don't want that money wasted."

"I'll do my best, Arfur."

Amy wasn't the only one next morning who had something other than her gas mask in its cardboard box. Arfur left his mask under his bed and stuffed pieces of rope, cut from the fishing nets Morgan Grinder had given them, into the box instead. More pieces of thin rope were in his trouser pockets.

Once at school he gathered Kennie, Cledwyn and Meredith around him.

"Do you fancy a bit of an adventure?" he asked them. "A

proper one, not just messing about?"

Kennie immediately said to count him in, even though he didn't know what it was. But the two Welsh boys were a bit more cautious. They'd never been in so many scrapes as since Arfur and Kennie had arrived in the village, and had been threatened more than once by their parents that the friendship would cease if they couldn't behave.

"What sort of adventure?" Meredith asked.

"Edwin Preece," Arfur said. "Do you know him?"

"Sort of," Cledwyn said. "A bit tup, he is."

Arfur and Kennie looked puzzled.

"Tup," Meredith repeated. "Means he's a bit soft in the head, it does."

"Yeah, well, Amy's been billeted at his house, hasn't she, and he's been doing horrible things to her," Arfur said, "really bad things, only you're not to ask what they are, 'cos I promised Amy. Anyway, he needs sorting out, and we're gonna do just that."

"Why don't we just tell someone, like the Police?" Cledwyn asked, making Arfur and Kennie sigh.

"'Cos you don't never go to the police, 'cos they can't be trusted," Kennie explained in heavy patient tones, "'cept if you're lost, 'cos that's the only thing they're any good at."

"And if we told the police, it would only be our word against his, wouldn't it?" Arfur added.

"So, what we gonna do, Arfur?" asked Kennie, while the other two continued to look uncertain.

"He goes home for his dinner, right, from the sawmills where he works – about the same time as we have our dinner time here, Amy told me. So we're gonna nick off school then, catch him on his way back from his dinner – so's his Mum thinks he's gone back to work alright – and we're gonna teach him a lesson."

"How?" Meredith asked.

"I've got lots of rope with me – we're gonna tie him to a tree and leave him there. Somewhere where he won't be found too quickly, so he'll be there till it's dark and cold. Give him a bit of a taste of how Amy's been feeling when he's been bad to her."

"I don't know," Meredith said, shaking his head. "Mrs. Preece talks to our Mam in chapel, she does. If she found out it was us we'd be in terrible trouble."

"Yeah – and my Dad's handy with his belt when he's in the mood," said Cledwyn.

"I thought you wanted to be in a proper gang?" Arfur asked.

"We do," Meredith replied, "but... well... this is something we could get found out about, isn't it?"

"Well of course it is," said Arfur, his voice rough with impatience, "that's what makes it an adventure. Doing stuff and making sure you don't get caught. We get to be like... whassit called?... heroes sticking up for the good people..."

"What? Like Robin Hood?" asked Cledwyn.

"Yeah," said Kennie, "only we won't be doing no stealing, will we, Arfur?"

"'Course not – we'll just frighten Edwin – give him a taste of his own medicine."

Meredith still looked dubious. "I don't know, Arfur... Edwin's almost a grown-up – he could get us into a lot of trouble."

"But how would you like it," said Kennie, "if you came to stay with us where we lived in London, and didn't have any of your family around, and then someone was horrible to you? You'd want someone to do something about it, wouldn't you?"

"I suppose so... but why doesn't Amy just tell Edwin's Mam?"

"'Cos Edwin's told her that he'll put all the blame on her – and his Mum'll believe him first, won't she?"

"Can't we do something else, though, Arfur, other than tying him up?" asked Cledwyn.

Arfur sighed again. "Tell you what then, me and Kennie'll sort him out. You two can make sure you keep whichever teacher's on duty in the playground away from the gates so we can make our escape without being seen."

Not for nothing had Arfur spent Saturday mornings at the pictures – and many an evening too, if he could sneak in without being seen, or one of his 'uncles' had been generous with a sixpence.

The two local boys looked happier with this arrangement and spent the whole of morning playtime working out what they would say and do to keep the teacher distracted.

A*rabbit*, Mrs. Preece thought. She'd been told the butcher had some hanging in the shop and they were only 1/8d. She'd get a couple of meals out of one if she stewed it slowly.

"Trying to feed up that little girl who's with you, are you?" the butcher's wife said. "Sorry to hear she's poorly."

"She's not poorly," Mrs. Preece said with a frown. "Plenty of energy she's got to keep me on the go from morning till night."

"Oh – only our delivery lad saw her this morning, he did, out along the road. And when he asked her why she wasn't at school, she told him she couldn't go because she was poorly. Wondered about that I did when he told me, because I said to him, Mrs. Preece would have her in bed, I said, if she was ill, not out roaming the streets. 'Specially when it's so cold. Just the rabbit today, is it, Mrs. Preece? Mind, she doesn't look strong, that little girl, does she, but then you don't really know what their home life has been like, do you, poor little things…"

But Mrs. Preece wasn't listening any more. If Amy wasn't at school, where was she? Set off this morning, she had, as if butter wouldn't melt in her mouth. Sly little minx.

Which made her think of that other sly minx, up at the doctor's house. Still there, as brazen as anything, no matter that most of the village thought it a disgrace. Come to think of it, that was probably where Amy was right now! Instead of being at school she was sloping off to be with that Madam. She probably encouraged the child, just to get one over on her, Mrs. Preece. Well, she'd put a stop to that! March the child right back to school, she would, and let the teachers know who was to blame for her missing her lessons!

The hammering on the front door took Lydia by surprise. It couldn't be anyone wanting Andrew because he was in his surgery and Rita was there, so they could just walk straight into the waiting room. Her heart skipped a beat. Perhaps it was the postman with a special delivery – or even a telegram.

She didn't stop to tidy herself as her Welsh counterparts would have done, but went to the door as she was.

"Where is she?"

Mrs. Preece only came up to Lydia's chin, and she stepped forward so quickly when Lydia opened the door that at first Lydia saw little more than the top of the black felt hat rammed down uncompromisingly over her brow.

She took a step back and saw Mrs. Preece's angry face like

a boiled beetroot from a mixture of toiling up the hill and the righteous indignation which she had stirred up to a fine pitch as she'd walked.

"Amy! She's not gone to school this morning. Out along the road she was, she was seen. On her way here – you can't fool me! Told not to come to this house, she was – not with a hoyden living in it. But I know this is where she'll have come. So where is she?"

Her eyes were darting about as she spoke, trying to see past Lydia who remained resolutely in front of her.

"I don't know what you're talking about," Lydia said. "I haven't seen Amy for ages. If she's not at school, then I suggest you start looking for her somewhere else."

"And what if I don't believe you?" Mrs. Preece's mouth was working almost as furiously as her eyes.

"Then you can go into the surgery waiting room and ask to see Dr. Eliot. This is his house, and if he thinks it necessary I'm sure he would be happy to take you round it to prove that Amy isn't here.

" And," Lydia went on, "even if she were here, why do you think I wouldn't tell you so?"

"Because you think you know better than everyone else! Tried to take her off me before, you did, just to make trouble."

"Mrs. Preece," Lydia said, feeling her own temper beginning to rise. "If I wanted to make trouble anywhere, then the first person I would come to for advice would be you – you're an expert in the field."

"We were a God-fearing village, we were, until you and your sort came here," Mrs. Preece hissed. "Half the children have never seen the inside of a church, and most of their parents no better than they should be, judging by those who turned up the other week. Corrupting influence, that's what you are. Everybody says so. Hobnobbing with the doctor and the morals of an alleycat!"

"I think you'd better go, Mrs. Preece," said Lydia, keeping her tone as calm as she could, "or I'll have to call Dr. Eliot so he can see you off the premises himself."

Mrs. Preece glared at her for a moment, before turning on her heel. "And that's Miss Williams's apron you've got on!" she spat over her shoulder. "Besmirching her good character you are, by wearing it!"

"You needn't worry – I take it off when I'm seducing the doctor!"

Lydia could have bitten her tongue off once the words were out of her mouth. How could she have let herself be drawn into giving the woman more ammunition? But surely, she thought as she closed the door, no-one really could believe her spiteful attitude?

And Amy. Where was she? She hoped that now Mrs. Preece had released her venom on her, she would make an effort to find out where the child had gone to. Maybe she had gone to the farm. But why wasn't she at school? She couldn't come to too much harm in this place wherever she was wandering, but the thought came to Lydia again that she should have tried harder to get to the bottom of what was making Amy so unhappy.

She would ask Andrew to keep a look-out for her as he went on his rounds, she decided. And when Rita came through from the surgery she would ask her to stay for elevenses. If they could have a laugh together over the preposterous little woman, Lydia would feel a lot better about the encounter.

Except, she chided herself, *you'd better not tell Rita your parting shot, because seducing the doctor is now exactly what you've done.*

The *Prince of Wales* did a fair trade at dinner time. Several of the men still working in the village often popped in for a pint, and some of the seats around the shiny-topped tables in the bar were the acknowledged province of a number of elderly gentlemen who met for a game of dominoes or cribbage to break up the day.

Much of the talk today was still about the bombing of Swansea, and the damage to the town.

"Barely a shop left standing, by all accounts," a florid man standing at the bar said. "Don't know how they'll ever re-build it. Port Talbot next, I expect."

The others nodded in agreement and sipped their beer thoughtfully as the door from the street was flung open and a young soldier walked in. Through the door could be seen an Army motorbike.

"Pint of bitter, please," he said to the barman, as he fished some coins out of his pocket. He checked what he had before adding, "And a whisky chaser."

He took a long draught of beer before wiping his mouth with the back of his hand and looking around him.

"Stationed near here, are you?" one of the men asked.

The soldier turned piercing blue eyes on him. "No – come down from London. Got a few days' leave."

"Well, it'll be a bit of a busman's holiday for you, then," the florid man said with a smile. "Bombing us down here they are, too, now."

"Actually, I'm looking for someone," the soldier said. "Have you had many evacuees in these parts?"

"We've got a few – schoolchildren mostly," said the barman. "Fitted in nicely, most of them have."

The soldier knocked back his whisky and indicated for the barman to pour him another.

Then he took a photo out of his wallet.

"What about mothers with small babies?" he asked. "This one in particular."

He passed the photo round.

"Ah – that looks like the young woman up at the doctor's house, and she's got a baby," said the barman.

"Is it far from here?"

"No – go on along the road here a bit further, and then take the next right. A bit of a narrow lane, it is – the doctor's house is about halfway up. You can't miss it."

He handed the photo back to the soldier. "Nice young woman, she seems," he told him. He exchanged glances with the florid man. "Keeps house for the doctor. A widow."

The soldier caught the glance and looked at each of them solemnly for a moment before sliding the photo back into his wallet. He swallowed his second whisky in one go.

"That's funny," he said, slamming the glass down on the counter and turning towards the door, "her being a widow. Because last time I saw her she was my wife."

Cledwyn and Meredith did a sterling job of distracting Rhian's teacher, Miss Edwards, who was on playground duty during dinner time. Arfur and Kennie slipped out of the small pedestrian gate nearest the church and made their way along the river bank towards the track leading to the sawmills.

"If we've timed it right, he should be along soon," Arfur said, as they headed for a group of trees on a slope above the track.

"We can ambush him from here," Arfur decided, "and then tie him to one of these trees."

It was cold by the river. The boys tried stamping their feet and blowing on their hands but it was difficult without making a lot of noise.

Eventually their patience was rewarded.

"Look – I think he's coming," said Kennie.

Sure enough, Edwin's lanky frame soon came into view. To their relief he was on his own – the plan would have been scuppered straight away if he'd been walking with someone else.

"I don't think he's got any friends," Meredith had assured them after giving them a detailed description of him so that they could be sure of getting the right person.

The two boys had played cowboys and Indians so many times with various gangs along the canal bank in London, that swooping down on an unsuspecting Edwin was like a choreographed routine.

They waited until he was below them before charging down the slope with bloodcurdling yells, one slightly in front of him, one behind. Edwin had been walking along head down into the wind and had only time to see a mop of black hair and legs in short trousers before he was jumped on from both directions and hurtled to the ground. Kennie on his back and Arfur catching him around the legs in a rugby tackle Dr. Eliot would have been proud of.

"Aah! Get off me!" Edwin screamed. "Let go of me!"

But they took no notice, kneeling on him and swiftly grabbing both arms to bind rope around them before letting him move.

"Shurrup and listen to us," Arfur hissed in his ear. "You've been hurting our friend, Amy – so it's time you learned your lesson."

"I've never touched her! I don't know what you're talking about!"

He was stronger than he looked, struggling and kicking on the ground, so that they couldn't tie the rope as tightly as they would have liked.

"Leave me alone!" Edwin cried. "You stupid kids! You can't

do this!"

"Yeah, and Amy's only a kid – you were supposed to be looking after her!" Arfur yelled.

"I do look after her – whatever she's said, she's lying!"

They managed to drag him to his feet and pushed and pulled him up the slope towards the trees. The frosty ground gave way to softer grass under the trees, which caused them to stumble and lose their footing. Twice they slid down the slope, Edwin's squirming body between them. The second time he got to his feet before them and tried to run off, his hands still tied behind his back.

But they caught up with him, pouncing on him, Arfur's arms around his neck and Kennie round his legs, so that they all tumbled to the ground once more.

"I'm not going with you, you little ruffians!" Edwin's shouts were muffled as his head was thrust into the muddy grass. "Get away from me!"

But this time they managed to keep hold of him, hauling him up against a thin tree. Arfur's jacket pocket ripped on a low branch, but he took no notice. Auntie Edyth was used to mending his clothes even though he didn't usually get into big scraps any more.

"What are you doing to me?" Edwin's breath was coming in short bursts, as he struggled to free his hands, but the rope was starting to hurt the more he tried to force it over his wrists.

"We do this lots when we're playing cowboys and Indians," Arfur told him. "You're our prisoner and we're tying you to the totem pole."

"Yeah! And if it's real cowboys and Indians, we set fire to you!" Kennie added.

Arfur almost laughed at the fear on Edwin's face as he shouted, "Help! Help! Somebody help!"

He wished Amy could see it. They weren't going to set fire to him, of course, but he looked so scared that it was a shame they didn't have a box of matches to rattle in front of him. And good for Kennie for thinking of saying that.

He slapped Edwin's face to shut him up. "You needn't make such a row. We're not going to set fire to you – not at the moment anyway. But we might come back later," Arfur taunted him, "when it's dark and there'll be no chance of you being rescued…"

"You'll get in awful trouble for this, you will! I'll put the police on you – then you'll be for it!"

"They won't take any notice of what we've done – not when we've told them about you! There was a man in the next street from us who hurt a little girl, and they locked him up!" Kennie said.

They were tying him to the tree during this time, although it was a bit harder than they'd thought without the other two to help them and they only just had enough rope. Arfur pressed himself against Edwin's body to stop him getting away while Kennie ran round the tree with the rope. Edwin squealed and wriggled, even after a hefty kick on the shin from Kennie.

"With a bit of luck you'll be here all night! Think how dark and cold and scary it'll be!" said Arfur as he tried to secure a final knot. "Almost as scary as you've made Amy feel. There'll probably be some foxes about as well! And horrible, slimy things coming up out of the water…"

Unfortunately, just as he was beginning to get into his stride and thinking of really ghoulish things to say, Kennie said, "Ssh! I think I can hear someone coming!"

"Hah!" Edwin cried, "They'll set me free! Not so clever now, are you? You won't get away with it!"

Arfur answered him with another kick on the shin.

"Just think," he said. "Every time you walk along this path from now on, you won't know when or where we're going to be. But we'll get you again – I hope you're frightened every day, just like Amy's been. And next time there might be more of us. Next time you might end up in the river. That's if the police don't come knocking on your door first after we've told them what you've done!"

"Arfur! Come on!" Kennie hissed. With a couple of punches aimed at Edwin's middle, the boys ran off.

They headed round the back of the copse of trees, away from the path, so that they wouldn't be seen.

"If we leg it quickly enough we can be back at school before the end of play-time," Kennie puffed. They could already hear Edwin's high-pitched cries for help. Arfur felt cross with himself that he hadn't thought of gagging him.

"Hang on a minute," he told Kennie. He ran back through the trees, pulling his tie off as he went. A few seconds later he was back, with Edwin's cries no longer heard.

"You'll get in trouble now 'cos you haven't got your tie," Kennie said.

"Don't care," Arfur shrugged. "It'll be worth it. Come on, or we'll both get found out."

"Are we really gonna tell the police?" Kennie asked as they crouched near the school railings waiting for an opportunity to slip back in through the gate.

"'Course not! Wouldn't trust them buggers! Did you see the look on his face when I said we would, though? Frightened him good and proper, didn't we? He was squealing like a big soft girl! Come on, we can sneak in now. Let's find the others and tell them what we did."

"Something else, though, Arfur," Kennie said as the two Welsh boys caught sight of them from across the playground. "What if he takes it out on Amy, once he gets home?"

"He won't," Arfur said, with just a hint of swagger in his step as he walked towards the other lads, "'cos she's not there."

Kennie stopped in his tracks and looked at his friend with renewed admiration. Bloody marvel, he was, thought of everything. He was so pleased he was in Arfur's gang.

He ran over to join in the telling of the tale to the other two, just as Miss Edwards came round the corner ringing the bell for afternoon lessons.

23.

For the second time that day there was a hammering on the front door. Lydia was reluctant to answer it in case it was Mrs. Preece again, returning to spit more venom at her. But it could be someone needing the doctor sufficiently urgently that they had ignored the surgery bell. She picked up his visiting list so that she could tell whoever it was where they might find him.

"Hallo Lydia."

He said her name softly, but the periwinkle eyes glittered a threat.

"*Billy.*"

His face was thinner than the last time she'd see him. Sharper.

"What's the matter, love? You look like you've just seen a ghost! Oh, but then you probably have, haven't you? Seeing as I'm supposed to be dead."

"What do you want?" She struggled to get the words out through a throat as parched and raw as when she'd last had sight of him, lying amongst the rubble of their house.

"Don't you think you'd better let me in? Then you can give me a proper welcome, like a loving Army wife who hasn't seen her husband for months."

He was already pushing past her into the hall. Anxious that he wouldn't waken Grace who was still napping in her cot upstairs, Lydia led him into the kitchen. Already she was experiencing the same sense of anxiety and uncertainty over what he was likely to do that had coloured their last months together in Bermondsey.

"How did – how did you find out where I was?" she asked, keeping the table between them.

"Got friends, haven't I? Friends who told me that enquiries had been made about me and where they'd come from. I figured you'd probably gone off on one of the evacuee trains – reckon you'd had that in your mind all along. The obvious way to try to disappear. Didn't take much to piece it all together. I've been making my way along the railway stops, asking in all the villages.

They told me in the pub where you'd be."

"So what do you want?"

"I want what belongs to me, that's all." His voice was quietly menacing, his eyes on her face the whole time.

"I'm not coming back to you, Billy."

"Huh! Do you think I want you back, after you left me for dead?"

"*You* had just beaten me black and blue!" Lydia suddenly flared, her eyes blazing to match his. "There were boot prints on my body! Why should I have cared what happened to you?"

She was as lovely as he remembered, especially when there was fire in her eyes. She could still move him. Perhaps he should insist that she return to London and they could try again.

She had a look about her, too. Like she had in those first months, when he had awakened a sexuality in her she hadn't known she possessed. When they couldn't get enough of each other. There was a lustre to her hair and a bloom in her cheeks. He knew that look on a woman.

Perhaps this little set-up was more than just a cosy billet. The old jealousy, fuelled by the whiskies in the pub, and the ones he'd had before that, stirred in his belly, and with it the desire to hurt her.

"So what do you want here, Billy, now you've found me?" she was asking again.

Ignoring the question he looked about him before casually sinking into an armchair, stretching his legs out. "Nice place this, isn't it? Roomy. Good to you, this doctor, is he? Keeping you satisfied? I wondered why it suddenly mattered to you if I was alive or dead."

"I'm here as his housekeeper, that's all. It's a place to live."

But he had seen the tell-tale flush creeping up her neck, even though she tried to stare him out.

He sprang from the chair towards her so quickly that she jumped and stepped back. He liked the feeling of power, of seeing the bravery in her eyes turn to fear.

"Well he can keep my whoring wife," he said, "but you know what I want, Lydia. I want my daughter. Where is she?"

Lydia ran her tongue around her lips and took a step backwards, but there was only the wall behind her now.

"She's not here. A friend has taken her out for a walk."

Billy shook his head and moved closer. "Not good enough. Pram's in the hall. So where is she? Upstairs, maybe? Shall I go and look for her?"

Lydia quenched the desire to turn her head away from the stink of alcohol on his breath. It was important to look him in the eye.

"Leave her alone, Billy. She's asleep. If you disturb her she'll be frightened. That's not fair. Come back when you're sober – you can see her then."

He slammed her body against the wall and cupped her face in one hand, squeezing it hard. "What? And find you gone again? I'm not that stupid. She's my daughter!" The heel of his hand was pressing hard on her windpipe, making it impossible to speak. It was even harder to breathe. "She's my daughter," he insisted, "and I'm not leaving here without her."

She was choking. The edges of her vision were starting to disappear. In a few seconds she would black out completely, then Billy would be able to do what he wanted and she would lose her precious baby.

"Do you understand?" he was shouting at her, his face so close their brows were touching, but his voice sounded far away, fighting with a buzzing in her ears. "I'm not leaving without Grace."

Suddenly the buzzing stopped as the pressure on the her throat was released. She heard a voice say, "Oh yes, you are," as strong arms yanked Billy away from her. There was a crunch as Andrew's right fist made contact with Billy's jaw, sending him crashing onto the kitchen floor.

Lydia sank on to a chair, unable to control the rasping sound coming from her throat as she struggled to get air into her lungs.

"She's *my* wife!" Billy shouted as he staggered to his feet, wiping blood away from the corner of his mouth. He lunged at the man in front of him – the man who had taken his wife!

But the alcohol made him misjudge his timing and his punch fell short, tipping him off balance, so that he fell hard against Lydia who was still trying to breathe. They toppled over together, taking the chair with them.

Andrew grabbed Billy by the back of his army jacket and hauled him to his feet.

"Lydia stopped being your wife the first time you hit her," Andrew said. "Now get out of here before I have you arrested for assault!"

Still with his hand on his collar, he pushed him roughly towards the kitchen door. Billy brought his arm up ready to bring his elbow sharp into Andrew's solar plexus, but the taller man was too quick for him. He grabbed Billy's arm and twisted it behind his back, making it impossible for Billy to do anything more than be frogmarched from the room.

"I'll be back, Lydia! I'm gonna get my daughter– you wait and see!" Billy shouted. "Bloody whore! You're not keeping her! You're not having Grace!"

Andrew flung him through the front door, onto the gravel drive.

"You stay away from here," he warned him. "You're not fit to be anyone's father."

Billy picked himself up, his eyes on Andrew. He staggered forward a few paces as he wiped away the trace of blood from the side of his mouth. For a moment it seemed as if he was going to take another swipe at Andrew, but instead he got onto the motorbike and roared off down the lane.

As soon as Billy was gone, Andrew hurried back to Lydia. The sounds in her throat were getting worse, while her eyes implored him to do something.

"It's alright." Gently he lifted her up to sit in the chair again. He knelt down in front of her and took hold of her hands. "Your throat is in stridor. You have to breathe really slowly and carefully and it will return to normal. Come on, now, try. Nice and easy... that's it... and again. Relax your shoulders, everything is fine, Grace is safe, Billy's gone. Come on... another slow breath in... and out... that's it."

Gradually her breathing returned to normal under his hypnotic command, and with it the look of terror in her eyes began to fade. It was replaced by gratitude, trust and a deep abiding love which she saw returned in his eyes as she struggled to speak.

"I thought..." she gasped, "I thought he was going to kill me... and take Grace... if you hadn't come back..."

"I know, I know, but it's alright now. Here, have a sip of water."

It was some time more before Lydia could talk properly and her hands stopped shaking enough to be able to hold the glass herself.

Then the tears began. Andrew held her in his arms, stroking her hair as he murmured reassurance.

"It's all finished," she said at last, when there were no more tears left. "He told people at the pub that I was his wife – it'll be all round the village by tonight. We won't get over it this time. Your reputation will be ruined."

"We'll cope with all of that if and when it happens," Andrew said. "The main thing is that you and Grace are safe and we are together."

The shrill ringing of the telephone stopped him saying more. With a look of apology he went to answer it.

"It's an emergency – I can't ignore it," he said, coming back with his bag in his hand. "Look – I've made sure the surgery door is locked, and the front door. Now you lock the back door behind me, and I'll be as quick as I can."

Lydia stood up. It was best that he was going out on a call now, before she could be lulled into any feeling of security again. She knew what she had to do.

"I'll be fine," she said. "You go."

It took many minutes for Edwin to stop panicking. Arfur's tie was digging into the corners of his mouth and had become wet with saliva, making it chafe. The rope around his wrists was rubbing at the skin, too, as he twisted and turned his hands in an effort to be free.

It wasn't fair. What he did with Amy was nothing to do with those boys. Rough little tikes they were! Probably got up to all sorts in their East End slums. Treated Amy like his little sister, he did. Watched out for her when his Mam was in one of her bad moods. And now she'd told on him to these boys – when he'd made her promise not to.

Tears of self-pity began to roll down his cheeks, increasing the sogginess of the gag. What if no-one found him and he was here for the rest of the day, maybe round until tomorrow morning? He couldn't be seen from the path. And it was already bitterly cold – if he couldn't move he might freeze to death before he was found. Here, amongst the trees, it was colder than down on the path where the wintry rays of the sun gave a little warmth. Already he was aware of a whip of breeze around his ankles. And what would he do if he wanted the toilet? The very thought made him feel that he needed to go.

He knew he had somehow to extricate himself from this situation before more vilification, in the form of police officers if the boys carried out their threat, reigned down upon him. Or – and he couldn't decide which was worse – night would come early, when the benign surroundings of daytime would transform into a hostile environment, where the nocturnal habits of a score of different animals involved the stealthy pursuit of the helpless by the strong. And this time, he would be the helpless one…

The thought defeated him, so that he slumped against the tree, all writhing attempts to extricate himself abandoned. He remained still, his hot breath steaming above and below the gag. After a few minutes he moved his right hand and found that the rope holding it seemed a little slacker. Perhaps if he moved slowly, in less of a panic, he could continue to stretch it bit by bit until it was loose enough to release his hands completely.

He didn't know how long it took him before he was able to wriggle his hand around until his fingers could grasp the knot the boys had made. It felt like hours, by which time he no longer heeded the cold, so concentrated were his efforts. When, at last, he managed to free his hands, he could have shouted with joy had the gag not still been in his mouth.

He still had to get out of the ropes binding him to the tree, and until he'd done that he couldn't remove the gag. But, luckily, the boys had been running short of rope in the end, and, with lots of tugging and pulling at the lower-most binding, he managed to pull it loose.

By the time he had removed the gag and released his ankles from their ties he was exhausted. Every part of his body seemed to be in pain and all he wanted to do was to go home and have his mother tend to him and soothe his grievances, as she'd done all his life.

But he knew he couldn't do that. If the boys were intent on telling Sergeant Hughes, at the tiny police station in the village, whatever tale Amy had convinced them about, the Sergeant would definitely investigate. His officiousness had grown over the years in direct correlation to the paltriness of real police work that came his way in Penfawr. Edwin knew that he would make a big show of striding up to their front door, hammering hard on the knocker and then booming out, "Your Edwin about, is he, Mrs. Preece?" whilst looking to left and right to see if he had an audience. And Sergeant Hughes' wife, Olwen, was one of the biggest gossips in the village. Word would soon get about.

He had to leave the village. Now. Get as far away as possible. Otherwise he'd likely end up in prison.

Forcing his unwilling limbs to move, he began to run along the river bank, in the opposite direction from the sawmills. Past Morgan Grinder's filthy old caravan and along the lane behind the row of shops, which all had back yards mainly used for storage, with high brick walls and gates onto the lane. When he heard voices in some of the yards he ducked down behind the wall until they went into the shop again.

Then down the next lane at the back of his terrace. He had to wait at the corner of the row until two of his neighbours stopped gossiping and went through their respective gates before he could move on. Dodging past his own back gate in case his Mam saw him, he wished he could go in and have her exclaim over his torn clothes and tend to his sore legs where he'd been kicked, and the graze on his face which stung in the wind.

He wondered what she would be doing now. Probably cleaning something that didn't need it and planning what to give him for his tea. He wasn't hungry, but he would give anything for a drink. The picture of his mother bringing him a cup of tea, as she always did when he returned from work, with that look of love and admiration on her face, which had increased since his father died, made him sob aloud. What would she do when he didn't turn up? What would she say if anyone told her what Amy was accusing him of? What if Sergeant Hughes was already on his way to the house? Or perhaps he'd go to the sawmills first, and they'd find out why he wanted to see Edwin. The men there could take the law into their own hands if they thought a child had been hurt – there were tales passed down in village folklore where those considered to have overstepped accepted decency were dragged up the mountain and never seen again.

Fear continued to spur him on. He bade a silent farewell to his Mam and hurried along the lane, despite his aching body, until he was at the far side of the village and out on the main road.

He'd head for his Auntie Peggy's first, in Swansea. Get some money out of her somehow, and then take off further away. He knew his Mam would miss him, but he had no choice. Perhaps he could write to her from wherever he ended up, once any fuss those lads made had died down. Perhaps he should try to join up after all – it couldn't be worse than going to prison and he might get a desk job.

He'd heard the church clock strike so he knew there wouldn't be a bus for another hour or more. He was unused to exercise at the best of times, so by now his breath was coming in ragged gasps. Sometimes stumbling, he urged himself on along the verge of the road, where today the sun hadn't penetrated the frost even though it was shining quite brightly.

He was relieved when he heard an engine behind him. It wouldn't be anyone looking for him yet – they'd search his house and the village first. Maybe he could cadge a lift – concoct some story if it was someone he knew that he was on an urgent mission to his Auntie Peggy because her house had been bombed. People believed anything like that these days.

The engine could be heard just about to round the last bend. Edwin stepped out into the road and waved his arms up and down.

The road twisted and turned out of the village, but Billy took little notice, even when the bike began to swerve a bit here and there. His mind, clouded by beer and whisky and fury, could focus only on revenge and paying that bitch back for the way she'd treated him. As thoughts of her and the doctor together raced through his head, so the bike went faster and faster. Once or twice he skidded on patches of ice but took little heed, cursing aloud as, rounding a bend, sunlight surprised him with its winter ferocity. The road straightened, so he let the throttle out further, his fuddled brain gaining some consolation from the power of the machine.

A larger bend. He took it wide, straight into another patch of ice. As the bike skidded round the curve the low sun streamed directly into his eyes, blocking everything else out.

The brakes screamed as he struggled frantically to keep control. He had no idea what it was he hit, as the impact flung him over the handlebars.

Lydia heard Grace begin to cry as she finished writing the letter. She wasn't sure how she was going to get away or where she was going, but she knew she had to leave. She'd brought enough trouble with her as it was, and it was only going to get worse once word got about that her husband was still alive. Andrew had already been forced to leave one place because of a woman – she wasn't going to be responsible for that happening to him again.

She tried to blot out his look of loving concern when he had coaxed her into breathing properly again, and the memory of his body against hers when they had lain in his bed together. He would be hurt at her going, she knew that, just as she also knew that she would find it hard to survive anywhere else now that she had discovered what love was really about.

But she couldn't, *wouldn't*, be the cause of his downfall. He had told her of his determination from an early age to become a doctor and how fulfilled he was when he was carrying out his duties. What if, in years to come, when the first flush of love had died down, he held her to blame for spoiling all of that? How would their love survive if he was drummed out of this job through scandal and was unable to get another? No matter how exaggerated the reactions of the Welsh villagers might seem to those living more sophisticated lives in London, there was no getting away from the fact that a prejudice, once voiced, was relinquished with reluctance. She only had to think of her own father's persistent refusal to acknowledge his grand-daughter for proof of that.

The baby's crying had stopped, but she would give her some food quickly anyway, and then they would be on their way. Go to the farm and beg Rhys to take them into Maesteg from where she could make her own way to… she would decide that later.

Deep in thought, with her head down as she entered the bedroom, it took a second or two to register the reason why Grace was no longer crying. Kneeling by the bars of the cot was Amy.

With everything that had happened since, Lydia had forgotten her earlier concern for the little girl's whereabouts.

"Amy!" she cried. "Are you alright? What are you doing here?"

The child began to weep. "I'm sorry, Mrs. Dawson – I'm sorry. I didn't mean to come here. I'm sorry."

Lydia gathered her into her arms. "Oh, Amy, there's nothing to be sorry about! I'm not cross with you. You know I'd have you here every day if I could. But you must tell me what's wrong! Why didn't you go to school today? Whatever it is, we'll put it right, I promise you."

"I was – I was going home, to my Mum," Amy stammered, between sobs. "Arfur gave me the money he'd saved up and told me what to do, but in the end I got scared – he said I had to walk to the station so no-one would see me, but I couldn't remember properly what he said to do after that. So I came back here – I sneaked in the back door when you were at the washing line this morning."

"And you've been here all this time?"

Amy nodded. "I was in the bedroom at the back. I was going to hide there until tomorrow so I could try to go to home again. But I heard lots of shouting downstairs, so I came in here to make sure Grace was alright."

Lydia hugged her and felt her thin body relax a little. "That was so brave of you, Amy." She waited a moment before continuing softly, "But why didn't you go back to Mrs. Preece's house?"

Amy stiffened and pulled away from Lydia, but didn't answer.

"Whatever it is, I've already told you, I'll make it better, I promise," Lydia said. "I won't let any harm come to you – just like you were going to watch over Grace."

She waited while Amy struggled to overcome her indecision.

"It's Edwin," she whispered eventually.

Lydia waited again, but the child ventured no more information.

"Amy – a few weeks ago, I asked you if Edwin hurts you, and you said no. But look – look at my throat – you see those marks? They're from a nasty man who was here today and used to hurt me when we were in London. That's why I was sure Edwin has been hurting you – and I'll understand if you tell me about it."

Amy shook her head. "He doesn't hurt me like that," she said, through a fresh onslaught of tears. "If I tell you – you won't send me away, will you? You won't stop me playing with Grace?"

"I've already promised – cross my heart."

"He hurts me inside – in my tummy. At night, when he comes to tuck me up in bed, and when Mrs. Preece is out. He didn't used to at first – he told me he was being my big brother. But then he started to hurt – and I know Maisie's brother doesn't do things like that. But Edwin said it was my own fault, and that's what he'd say if I told anyone and... I was dirty... and..."

It was like pulling a bath-plug. To Lydia's horror the words tumbled out of Amy's mouth as if, now she'd started, she couldn't stop. Even the childish expressions she used to convey what had been done to her made it clear that she had suffered the worst sort of abuse.

When she'd finished she clung to Lydia, who rocked her back and forth in her arms on the side of the bed, whilst her own child, unsullied and innocent like this little girl would never be again, sat and played in her cot.

L ydia!"
There was no answer to his call as Andrew let himself into the house. Called to the accident scene, he'd done all he could for the injured boy whilst he waited for what seemed an age for the ambulance to arrive from Maesteg, all the time nagged by a sense of foreboding and a need to return home.

He headed straight for the kitchen.

Lydia's note was propped up on the table. He scanned the contents, his heart thudding so strongly it was reverberating in his ears. She couldn't have left, not now. And where would she have gone – why hadn't he seen her on the road?

The pram was still in the hall, so she couldn't have gone far. He called her name again, but there was no reply. Checked the rooms downstairs. Nothing. The whole house was still. As quiet as before she'd arrived. How could even the thought of her no longer being there affect the very fabric of the place?

Taking the stairs two at a time, he told himself that this is what it would be like from now on, if she was gone.

"*Sssh!*"

He stopped on the threshold of her bedroom. Lydia had her

fingers to her lips in warning as she laid a sleeping Amy in her bed and pulled the eiderdown over her.

He strode across the room as she moved towards him. The light through the window played on her ravaged face and high-lighted the pain in her eyes. She looked back towards Amy, opening her mouth to explain, but this time Andrew put his fingers across her lips.

"I thought I'd lost you," he whispered.

His lips found hers then. His kiss was passionate, urgent, as if by its very force it could persuade her to stay. As she found herself responding, despite her intentions, tears coursed down her face. Tears for Amy's ruined innocence, tears for the mess of her marriage, and tears for the love she and Andrew had found and were now going to lose. This would have to be the last time they would ever be so close and she didn't want the moment to end.

He was gentle when he released her. "You can't go," he said. "You don't need to go. Billy's dead, Lydia. He's dead. In a road accident. I don't know what Edwin Preece was doing there, but he was under the wheels of the motorbike. He's very badly injured – I did what I could, but I'm not sure he'll survive."

She stared at him for a moment, confused, uncomprehend-ing. She looked round the room at Edwin's victim, sleeping in her bed, at Billy's daughter playing in her cot. She turned back, raising her eyes to Andrew.

"I hope he dies," she said. "Then he and Billy will be going to Hell together."

24.

A h! Mrs. Preece!" The ward Sister's face was as serene as a nun's below the starched white wings of her cap. "Dr. Gilbert would like to see you before you go in to visit Edwin."

She followed the Sister's squeaking shoes into a half-panelled side room, gleamingly spotless like the rest of the ward, with a large clock which ticked loudly above the cast iron fireplace. It was a comforting little room, the sort kept aside for imparting bad news.

"I'll tell Doctor you're here," the Sister said, with a benign smile.

Mrs. Preece gave no indication that she had heard the woman's words, but scrutinised her face for any indication of other emotions hiding behind the professional authority which sat well on her shoulders.

Does she know? she wondered, as the Sister left the room with quiet swiftness. Almost immediately the doctor entered, wearing a dignified striped suit, a pocket watch chain strung across the waistcoat which struggled to contain his paunch.

"Mrs. Preece – please, do sit down."

Doctor Gilbert held his arm out to the chair behind her, his face bluff and good-natured.

Does he know?

It was the question that haunted her continually everywhere she went since the terrible day of Edwin's accident.

Do they know? she would ask herself of the young nurses who flitted backwards and forwards, attending to Edwin's needs with keen solicitousness whilst keeping a watchful eye on the whereabouts of the Sister whose benignity could change to acid sharpness if she thought any of them were slacking or failing to maintain the standards she imposed so rigorously.

Do they all know and treat him with contempt when I'm not here? she would wonder as she sat beside the inert form of her son. *Do they know what he's been so unjustly accused of?*

His pale, unconscious face, which she studied meticulously during each of her visits, looked no different from when he was a little boy and gave no clue as to how he had ended up being accused of such terrible things.

Dr. Gilbert was talking to her. She forced herself to listen.

"Edwin is coming round," he told her with a heartiness that she didn't know was his way of prefacing unwelcome news. "He's opening his eyes and even said a few words on several occasions, which is an encouraging development. You may find that he will now speak to you a little if he is awake while you're here."

He waited for some response from the impassive form in front of him. When there was none he made up for it with an increase of joviality. "Which I'm sure you'll agree is good to hear!"

He cleared his throat, preparatory to taking the bluffness down a tone or two.

"However, there is some news that isn't quite so welcome, I'm afraid. From what we can tell so far, there has been considerable damage to the spinal cord. I'm sorry to have to tell you that it seems unlikely that Edwin will ever walk again."

Still no response. The little woman who had always had a dozen words to everyone else's three or four had barely spoken since the afternoon that the knock had come on her door. Not the knock to tell her of her son's accident – words of anguish had poured forth in a torrent then. It was the knock on the door the next afternoon and the details imparted by Sergeant Hughes that had rendered her speechless.

"Of course, miracles do happen," Dr. Gilbert was saying now, "but, whilst we are sure that Edwin will recover consciousness completely, and will have use of his upper body, I feel that you must prepare yourself for the fact that he is likely to spend the rest of his life in a wheelchair."

He waited for a few seconds. He hated this sort of interview, particularly when it was received in this way. He could feel the acid indigestion, that times like this always brought on, churning in his stomach and longed to go home where he could have a glass of milk and words of comfort from his wife.

"Mrs. Preece?" he said when the pain was making him want to undo the lower buttons of his waistcoat, "Do you understand what I've been telling you?"

"Yes – thank you, Doctor," she said at last. "I'll go to Edwin now, if I may."

She made her way slowly down the ward to her son's bedside. She didn't look to left or right in case she saw someone she knew, or caught the knowing look in a young nurse's eye. She would show them, she vowed. Once Edwin was awake all this nonsense would be cleared up. They'd be sorry, then, that they had, even by a glance or an ill-considered word over his prone body, given her son anything less than his due as a patient on this ward. She would prove that it was nothing more than the malicious tongue of that madam who had stolen Miss Williams' rightful place as Dr. Eliot's housekeeper. Her and that child, who had had nothing but the best of care, had concocted these terrible tales between them out of sheer spite because she, Mrs Preece, had unveiled the true goings-on in that household.

These thoughts had spun round her brain continuously like fairground horses which refused to stop. Each visit to Edwin's inert figure had made them spin faster. But now they were going to stop.

Edwin's eyes were still closed, but he was moving his head from side to side as she approached the bed, which he hadn't done before. Leaning over him she laid a hand on his arm and whispered, "Son, son, it's me – your Mam – wake up now, there's a good boy, terrible time you've given me. Come on Edwin – wake up for Mam."

His head, turned away from her, became still. Slowly, as if with enormous will, it came back round to face her. He opened his eyes and stared into her face. Clouded with confusion at first, he blinked several times and closed them again.

"Edwin, come on, talk to me, son," she whispered once more. His facial expression didn't change, but suddenly his eyes shot open again. And this time she recoiled from what she saw there. She had seen it before, when he was a child and had been found doing something he shouldn't. Guilt, edged with the shame of discovery and a silent plea for her protection against his father's chastising belt.

She collapsed into the chair beside his bed as a voice inside her head screamed, *No-o-o-o!* Edwin had sunk back into sleep but she needed no further confirmation of what she had seen. The knowledge of the evil her own flesh and blood – her *only* flesh and blood – had perpetrated, possibly whilst she was in the house, unaware of what was happening, was branded onto her brain. She closed her own eyes, but could still see only Edwin's. She could even hear his childhood high-pitched whine which always accompanied a misdemeanour, *"It wasn't my fault, Mam, it wasn't my fault…"*

Eventually Dr. Gilbert's words came back to her. She had focussed so much on the news that Edwin might wake up that she had almost ignored the rest of his words. Edwin would never walk again. He was to spend the rest of his life in a wheelchair. It was, she knew, the action of the God of Retribution she so firmly believed in. It was no accident, it was Edwin's punishment.

There was a woman, Mabel Roberts, who lived at the other side of the village, whose daughter had a huge swollen head and a wasted body. Unfailingly cheerful, Mabel pushed her around in an invalid carriage and was met with nothing but compassion and sympathy by everyone in Penfawr.

But it wouldn't be like that for her and Edwin.

As she sat, as immobile as her son, she looked into the future with increasing horror. She wasn't to be spared God's wrath, either. Her Christian duty was to look after her son for the rest of his life, or until she was taken. And every day, every time she looked at him, every time she tended his body, she would be reminded of what he had done. Every time she left the house she would be cloaked in a mantle of shame, that the only fruit of her womb, on whom she had doted with a love that far transcended what she had felt for his father, had turned out to be a monster, to be shunned by every decent man and woman.

She had often wondered how she would bear it if Edwin met a young lady and got married, leaving her alone in the house with only the portrait of her husband and her bible for company. Now, she knew, she had him to herself forever. Already she could hear the childish cry turned into the aggrieved whine of a self-pitying invalid. "Mam!… *Mam!"*

And there would always be that look in his eye.

Most of the people in the village knew one version or another of how Edwin Preece met his fate on the main road out of the village when he should have been putting in an afternoon's work at the sawmills. Many of the details were embellished in the telling and some were omitted out of common decency according to where and to whom the tale was being told.

The Owain Owens knew the full story. A long interview with Dr. Eliot the next day resulted in Mr. Owain Owen offering to resign as the Billeting Officer and Mrs. Owain Owen becoming prostrate with shock that such acts could have been perpetrated by a member of her own family.

"Breaking her heart, our Elsie was, when the news came about the accident, and to think he was doing dreadful things like that! His father must be turning in his grave," she said when she could eventually string words together. "But I still don't see what he was doing out on that road."

"Amy had gone missing that morning," Dr. Eliot said. "He probably suspected that if she was found then she would tell everyone why she had left, so he was trying to get away."

"Of course," Dr. Eliot went on, "if the child hadn't sought sanctuary with Mrs. Dawson, then we could well have had an even bigger disaster on our hands – she could have ended up anywhere."

Mr. Owain Owen cleared his throat. "I've sent word to the mother – I'm hoping she will come down to see her daughter as soon as she can. Till then it's very good of you to take care of her."

"Well, that's due to Mrs. Dawson as well," said the doctor. "She's the only one Amy trusts at the moment.

"We have something else to thank Mrs. Dawson for too," he went on. "She's going to do her best to persuade Amy's mother that, with Edwin so badly injured, there would be little purpose in pursuing a court case. It certainly wouldn't do Amy much good. And if her mother agrees, then Mrs. Preece won't have to cope with any further ordeal – which, given the cavalier way she apparently treated Amy too, she should be very grateful for."

Mr. Owain Owen swallowed. "And I'm sure she will be sir, definitely. Very grateful."

The doctor looked steadfastly at Mrs. Owain Owen. "Well, of course, Mrs. Dawson knows only too well how it feels to be the subject of gossip – it hurts just as much when it's unwarranted. We can only hope that the right facts about her husband are put about now."

He paused without taking his eyes from Mrs. Owen. His voice remained clipped and precise, very different from the tone he used when talking to his patients.

"Having found that her husband hadn't been killed in action as supposed, was shock enough, but then for him to die on the same day that he reappeared has left her enormously distressed."

He waited.

Mrs. Owen had been looking down at her hands which were twisting nervously in her lap. Now she raised her head to return the doctor's chilling gaze. "I'm sure she'll get nothing but sympathy."

For a few days the village reeled with what had been going on its midst and that Mr. Owain Owen was wanting to give up his job. There was also talk about the soldier on the motorbike turning out to be Mrs. Dawson's husband. But Mrs. Owain Owen had done her job well. When Lydia eventually ventured into the village she met kind looks and nods from many of the same people who had previously shunned her, and the gossip about her and Andrew seemed to have been forgotten as quickly as it had begun.

Epilogue

Arrangements were made for Billy's body to be returned to his regiment, whilst Mrs. Preece, shrunken and subdued, ventured out only to catch the bus to and from the hospital, or to do a meagre bit of shopping before the village shop closed at night. The more compassionate members of Ebenezer chapel tried to visit her, but she refused to answer the door, preferring to sit by the light of the fire and stare into its depths until her eyes hurt.

Edyth had been told the full story by Lydia, including the facts about her marriage to Billy. Some days later, when they had mulled over the events yet again with the inevitable cup of tea, Edyth asked, in her brisk way, "So when are you going to do something about Dr. Eliot? Besotted by you he is, it's seeping out of his pores – and what's done is done now. The best way to get over it is to face the future, and make the most of it – too uncertain it is, for everyone, to hang about too long."

Lydia smiled, lifting the strained look around her eyes. "We want to wait until all of this dies down a bit. And I rushed into things last time, and look where it got me. But I do love him, Edyth, and he knows that. It's almost like I want to keep it to ourselves for now, though, after all the talk there's been. So maybe next spring, when a bit of time has passed and we won't start tongues wagging again too much.

"But don't worry," she added, "you and Rhys will be the first to know!"

It was nearly a week later before Lydia and Andrew found themselves alone in the homely kitchen that had become their sanctuary. Amy's mother had stayed with them for a few days, needing Lydia's kindness and Andrew's care to help her cope with the emotional fall-out of what had happened to her child. Mr. Owain Owen had had to remain as the Billeting Officer because no-one else wanted the job, so he reported to the doctor's house almost daily, about arrangements he was making with the authorities to find a safe place where Amy could be with her mother and her gran. Eventually a billet was found in Sussex, Amy's mother was released from her job on medical grounds, and mother and daughter returned to London to tell Gran that from now on they were all going to stay together.

"I'll miss her," Lydia said, after saying good-bye to Amy.

"I know," said Andrew. He drew her towards him, until their faces were close. "But this is our time now, Lydia, free from everything that's gone before. We can be a proper little family, you, me and Grace."

He smiled, that special smile that so few people saw, "And we can fill this house with as many children as you want."

His face became serious again, but his eyes glowed with warmth and sincerity, telling her yet again everything she needed to know before he said it. "I love you so much, Lydia."

For the first time she felt free to say it back. "I love you too."

Rhian knew there was something Arfur wasn't letting on about. All they'd been told by her parents about Amy was that she couldn't stay with Mrs. Preece any more because of the shock of Edwin's accident. But Rhian, finely attuned to everything to do with Arfur, had been aware of his reaction to this news. That sullen look he'd had when he first arrived had crossed his face, along with something else she couldn't pinpoint.

When she'd tried to ask him about it, he'd told her to "Sod off!" and then he'd had a long talk with her Dad. A couple of times at school, too, he'd gone off in a huddle with the other boys and hadn't wanted her to join in. It was a mystery.

It didn't matter too much, though. She'd find out about it eventually. There was plenty of time. Arfur wasn't going anywhere. In fact, he was going to be in her life forever.

THE   END

The Author

Julie McGowan is an established short story and feature writer for national and international publications, and has won numerous writing competitions over the years. Her writing credits also include educational features, pantomimes, sketches and songs and newspaper columns. Well known in her home town of Usk for her work in the community, Julie runs a theatrical group which performs variety shows and her witty pantomimes to sell-out audiences every year. She also co-directs *Is It?*, a theatre company which runs young people's drama workshops and tours schools in Wales with productions covering health and social issues.

Born in Blaenavon, Julie left Wales for Kent at the age of 12. She trained as a nurse at Guy's Hospital, London, and then as a Health Visitor in Durham, living there for 4 years after her marriage to Peter. The couple now have four adult children and have lived in Surrey, Lincolnshire and Hertfordshire before returning to Wales in 1992. Julie has had a variety of jobs including teaching piano and a stint as Town Clerk in Usk.

Julie's first two books, *The Mountains Between* and *Just One More Summer*, are also available, both in print and digital versions.

Julie loves to be in contact with her readers. You can visit her website at:

www.juliemcgowan.com

or email her at:

juliemcgowanusk@live.co.uk

The
Mountains
Between

Julie
McGowan

SAMPLE CHAPTER

The Mountains Between

by

Julie McGowan

ISBN# 978-1-907984-01-3

Despite a comfortable living, surrounded by lush farmlands, Jennie's life under the critical eye of her tyrannical mother is hard. Desperate for affection, she stumbles upon dark secrets and into the uncertain murmurings of love. On the other side of the scarred mountainside, and in the wake of a disaster that tears through his family and their tight-knit mining community, Harry finds the burden of manhood thrust upon his young shoulders. Through the turmoil of the Depression years, life for both Harry and Jennie takes many unexpected turns, with love won and lost. But the onset of World War II brings changes that neither could have imagined. This is the extraordinary tale of two young souls living in different worlds, yet separated only by the mountains between them.

A searing and powerful novel from one of Wales's best-selling authors.

Part One

1929

Jennie

Jennie heard Tom's voice calling her, but she ignored him and scrambled over the gate into the ten-acre field. She ran head down, forcing her legs to go faster and faster, her breath coming in great racking sobs, until she reached the corner of the field where the land sloped down towards the railway line, and she would be hidden from the house. As she flung herself face down onto the grass and the sobs became bitter, painful tears, Mother's words echoed in her head, refusing to be quelled.

You were never wanted! You were a mistake!... A mistake... a mistake!... Never wanted...!

The day had started so well. The Girls were coming home and Jennie had been helping Mother in the house – as she always did, but more willingly this time, excitement tightening her chest because her sisters would soon be here and the summer holidays would then have begun in earnest. Mother, too, seemed happy; less forbidding, and the crease between her brows that gave her such a disapproving air had been less pronounced.

Never wanted!... A mistake... Your Father's doing!

Eventually there were no more tears left to cry, but the sobs remained; long drawn out arpeggios every time she inhaled. And the more she tried to stop them the more it felt as if they were taking over her body.

She sat up and wrapped her arms around her knees in an effort to steady herself. A small girl dressed in a starched white pinafore over a blue print summer frock, with two mud-brown plaits framing a face whose eyes looked too large for it. She stared at the mountains – her mountains, her friends, keepers of her secrets. But today she wasn't seeing them, could draw no comfort from the gentle slopes of the Sugar Loaf which stretched out like arms to encompass the valley. Today the mountains were majestic and aloof, wanting no share of her misery. In her head the scene in Mother's bedroom replayed itself endlessly before her.

She'd been returning a reel of thread to Mother's workbox – a sturdy wooden casket kept in a corner of the bedroom. Inside were neat trays containing all Mother's sewing things, and one tray full of embroidery silks, the colours rich and flamboyant as they nestled together. Jennie had lifted the silks up and let them run through her fingers, enjoying their smooth feel and the rainbows they made.

Then, for the first time, she'd noticed that what she thought was the bottom of the workbox was, in fact, too high up.

She lifted the rest of the trays out and pulled at the wooden base, which moved easily to reveal another section underneath. There was only one item in it; a rectangular tin box with a hinged lid on which was a slightly raised embossed pattern in shiny red and gold. She traced the pattern with her fingers. It was an intriguing box. A box that begged to be opened.

Jennie had lifted the tin clear of the workbox when suddenly Mother appeared in the doorway, her face bulging with anger.

"What do you think you're doing? Put that down at once!"

Taken unawares by her mother's arrival and the harshness of her tone – excessive even for her – Jennie turned suddenly and the box had fallen out of her hands, the hinged lid flying open and the contents scattering over the floor. Had she not been so frightened by Mother's anger, Jennie would have registered disappointment, for the box, after all, held only a few old papers.

To Mother, though, they seemed as valuable as the Crown Jewels. With an anguished cry she'd pushed Jennie aside and scrabbled on the floor to retrieve the documents.

"I'm s-s-sorry," Jennie stammered, "I didn't mean…"

But Mother wasn't listening. She was too busy shouting.

"Why don't you ever leave things alone? This is mine! You had no business! You're always where you're not meant to be – always causing me more work! Either under my feet or doing something you shouldn't!"

Her voice had grown more shrill as she spoke, with a dangerous quiver in it, so that Jennie didn't dare offer to help – or to point out that the things her mother was accusing her of were grossly unfair. She'd given up doing that a long time ago. "… It's not right – I didn't want… Three babies were enough!"

Mother had been looking down, thrusting the papers back in the box, continuing to exclaim about the unfairness of her lot as she did so, almost as if she were no longer addressing Jennie. But then she'd snapped the box shut and swung round to face her daughter.

"You were never wanted, you know! It was all a mistake! All your Father's doing!" She turned back to the workbox, her shoulders heaving with emotion.

There was a moment's silence.

"What did Father do?" a crushed Jennie had whispered.

Mother's hand had swung round and slapped Jennie across the ankles. "Don't be so disgusting!" she'd hissed. "Get out of here!"

Jennie knew, as she sat on the grass, that Mother had meant it. She was used to her mother's tempers, her insistence that the house, the family, and at times the farm, were run exactly as she wished, but this was different. The expression on her face as she'd spoken the dreadful words was one that Jennie had never seen before. It had been full of a strange passion – and something else which Jennie, with her limited experience, couldn't identify. But it had frightened her.

Never wanted! A mistake!

It changed everything. Nothing in her world would ever be the same again. Her eight years thus far had been secure ones; lonely at times, being the youngest by so many years, and hard when Mother's standards were so exacting. But happy, too. Happy in the knowledge that she was well-fed, clothed and housed; well-cared for (didn't that mean loved and wanted? It appeared not). Happy on the farm, surrounded by her mountains, and in the company of her beloved father.

Father! Jennie's heart beat faster in alarm. Did this mean that he didn't want her either? That he too saw her as some sort of mistake? Her relationship with her mother always held uncertainty, but Father's affection never seemed to waver.

A kaleidoscope of images of herself with her father rushed through her mind. Making her a wheelbarrow all of her own, so that she could 'help' him on the farm, when she was only four. Holding her in his arms when she cried because a fox had got in and wreaked havoc in the hen-house; comforting her because she'd been the one to discover the terrible decapitated remains. Letting her help to make new chicken sheds, safely off the ground – not minding when she'd splashed creosote on the grass. Urging the cows to milking, his voice kind and gentle, calling each cow by name and helping her to do the same until she could recognise each one.

Surely he loved her! He had to love her!

Panic was rising inside her and she wanted to run to her father and beg him to tell her that it wasn't true; that she wasn't simply a mistake. But fear stayed her. There was the awful possibility that he might tell her even more dreadful things that she didn't want to hear. It would be the same if she asked The Girls, and as for Tom, well! – he had never disguised the fact that a sister six years younger than himself was fit only for endless teasing.

The words were still playing in her head when suddenly the panic eased. What else had Mother said?… *All your Father's doing!* She didn't know what her father had done, but surely if he'd done it then he must have wanted her?

She lay back on the grass and closed her eyes. Perhaps if she went to sleep she would wake up and everything would be just as it was. She could go back to the house and carry on as usual and the lead weight in her chest that was making breathing so difficult would be gone.

The hot July sun soothed her. Mother would be cross if her skin burned, but Mother being cross about such a thing didn't seem quite so important at the moment. Convincing herself that her Father loved her and wanted her was, she instinctively knew, the only thing that would help her to push her mother's awful words to the back of her mind.

Katharine Davies sat on the edge of her bed, her shoulders sagging uncharacteristically, her breathing rapid and shallow. The papers were safely stowed away again but the episode had unnerved her too much for her to return downstairs just yet. Jennie was too young to have understood the implications of what the papers contained, but what if she told the older children of their whereabouts? A hot flush spread over her anew as she considered what they would think of her. She tried hopelessly to calm herself, but memories of nearly seventeen years ago refused to go away.

"Edward! Oh Edward!"

The voice was her own, urgent, pleading as his hands caressed her, explored her; and she wasn't urging him to stop. Oh no! To her everlasting shame she wanted him to go on, to satisfy the craving that had taken over her whole body. And he had: gone on and on until she felt she was drowning; until she had screamed her ecstasy.

I love you Katie. I'll always love you! Edward had held her afterwards, murmuring into her hair, promising to take care of her. And he had. But it hadn't been enough.

The memories sent prickles of shame up her spine until her neck was on fire. Yet, unbidden, the feeling was there again; that same burning physical wanting that had gnawed away at her in those early years, trapping her with its demands, its insatiability.

She stood up abruptly, angry that her body should be betraying her after all these years when she'd thought she had it firmly under control. She clenched her hands tightly in front of her. She must, she would, maintain that control.

She forced herself to think of what must still be done, which chores in the dairy or in the garden would best exercise her treacherously unreliable body.

She thought fleetingly of Jennie as she moved swiftly out of the bedroom. She shouldn't have spoken to her as she did, but doubtless the child would get over it – would probably look at her with those sheep's eyes for a day or two and then it would pass.

But you meant it, nagged the mean voice of Conscience.

She clutched the crucifix hanging round her neck, as if gathering strength to push the voice away. *I'll pray about it tonight,* she vowed, making for the stairs.

"Bessie! You'd better see about scalding the milk or it will turn in this heat! Then come and help me clean the dairy."

The girl, plump and homely, turned from the large stone sink where she was peeling potatoes, ready to make a cheery remark until she saw the expression on her employer's face. Best not look in the churn, madam, she thought, or the milk will turn never mind the heat.

Jennie saw her mother in the dairy as she entered the back of the house and tiptoed up the back stairs. She didn't want Mother to see the grass stains on her apron.

She'd thought long and hard once she'd finally stopped crying, and had reached the conclusion that if she tried, really tried, not to let Mother see her doing anything wrong, and not to argue with her ever again, then perhaps Mother would forget that she was 'a mistake' and decide that she was the best-loved and most wanted of all her children.

She sighed as she reached her room. It would be hard work. There seemed to be so many things that Mother had definite and immovable views on. Take her apron, for example. Aprons weren't meant to get dirty. Mother's aprons always stayed spotless – except for the apron she wore over her apron to do 'the rough'.

Not that Mother ever did the really dirty jobs. They were done by Bessie, the latest in a long line of girls who stayed until they could take Mother's demands for perfection and her sharp tongue no longer.

She put on a clean apron and went to the recently-installed bathroom to wash her hands and face, careful to wipe the basin clean afterwards and replace the towel just so. The bathroom was a sufficiently new addition to be treated with exceptional respect. Then she returned to the kitchen by the front stairs so that Mother would think she had been in the house all along.

"May I go now, please – to meet The Girls?"

Jennie didn't want to look Mother in the face; instead she fastened her gaze on the shiny gold crucifix.

The crease between Mother's brows deepened as she surveyed her daughter. She opened her mouth as if to speak, but closed it again. Then her shoulders dropped a little as she appeared to relent from whatever it was she had been going to say.

"Very well. But wear your sunbonnet – and keep your apron clean!"

Jennie went meekly to the little room behind the kitchen and fetched her sun hat before letting herself out through the back door, forcing herself to walk sedately in case Mother was watching her as she crossed the farmyard – immaculate as ever because the cows weren't allowed to cross it lest they make it dirty.

Once round the corner of the barn she ran again to the gate of the ten-acre field. But she didn't climb over it this time. Instead she divested herself of her apron and sunhat and hung them on the gatepost before turning to a smaller, iron gate which led to the lane running parallel to the field.

She began to skip along the lane, sending up little clouds of dust as she went. It was impossible, somehow, to walk once you were out-of-doors and alone, even when you were feeling pretty miserable. Had she been feeling happier she would have tucked her skirts up into the legs of her knickers and tried a few cartwheels. But as she thought this, the awful words bounced up at her in time to her skipping... *Not wan-ted... not wan-ted... not wan-ted...*

The engine hooted as it pulled out of Nantyderry Halt, diverting Jennie. No need to think about anything else now The Girls were home! She broke into a run as they appeared at the end of the lane. They were each wearing their school uniform and carrying a small case; Tom would take the van down later for their trunks. Their uniforms bore the badge of the convent school at Monmouth, which they attended not because they were Catholic but because it was the best school in the area, and they boarded, not because it was far away but because that was what the best families did.

Jennie threw herself into the arms of her eldest sister, sure of a rapturous response.

"Steady on!" laughed Emily, swinging her round. "You nearly knocked me over! Let me look at you! You've grown again while we've been away! Laura! Don't you think she's grown?"

Laura, a year younger than sixteen-year-old Emily, but inches shorter and already more buxom, hugged Jennie more steadily.

"At least an inch taller," she agreed.

"Does that mean I can use your tennis racket this summer?" Jennie asked excitedly, turning back to Emily. "I've been practising like mad against the barn wall with the old one, and you promised me yours when I was big enough."

"We'll see," came the reply. "You'll have to show me how good you are."

But Emily's eyes held a merry promise and suddenly she caught hold of Jennie and danced round with her again.

"Isn't it wonderful? I've finished school for good! My very last day! I can hardly believe it!"

"It won't be so wonderful if we're late for dinner," Laura reminded her, picking up her bag and beginning to walk up the lane. "Jennie, your dress is terribly dusty – Mother will have a fit!"

"It's alright," said Jennie, "I can cover it up with my apron – I've left it on the gate."

But as they reached the gate, there was Tom, Jennie's sunhat perched ridiculously on his head, and the apron held aloft.

"Give it back, I mustn't get it dirty!" Jennie cried, hers arms flailing wildly as Tom held her easily at bay with one gangly arm.

"Please, Tom!" Laura sounded as urgent as Jennie, as the gong for lunch sounded from the house. "You know she'll get into trouble."

Emily sauntered through the gate behind her sisters. "Give her the apron and the hat, Tom, and carry these bags in for us." Her voice sounded almost lazy, but Tom was aware of the authority behind it. He was taller than both his sisters, but Emily always managed to make him feel small.

He relinquished the garments to a relieved Jennie, tweaked each of the long brown plaits hanging over her shoulders, and then grinned. "Better not spoil the homecoming, I suppose."

But he didn't move to embrace his sisters. Instead they all hurried in for dinner.

Come along! Come along!" said Mother as Father stopped to kiss and hug his two elder children. "This dinner will be getting cold."

Jennie contrived to sit between Father and Emily and at once felt happier, although tears threatened again when Father asked her in his gentle voice what she'd been doing all morning. Fortunately Mother began speaking to Emily, and as it was unwise to talk at the same time as Mother she didn't have to answer.

Edward Davies surveyed his family with a degree of pride as they sat round the large, scrubbed kitchen table. All four children well-grown and healthy – no mean achievement when you compared them to the malnourished rickety children over in the valleys, many of whom would be lucky to survive infancy. He would have liked another boy, for the farm, but he loved his daughters nevertheless.

Not that Katharine would have been happy with another boy – there'd been enough fuss as it was when Jennie came along, so he'd thanked God that He had seen fit to bless them with another girl. For some reason Katharine saw girls as a blessing and boys as a kind of blight. *Poor thing,* she would say whenever she heard of a mother being delivered of a son, no matter how longed-for. She treated Tom well enough for all that, Edward allowed, although he never saw the look of pride in her eyes that he had seen other mothers bestowing on their sons. But then, he reflected, Katharine was not like other mothers in a good many ways.

He watched her now, talking to Emily. She was still a handsome woman, despite her nearly forty years, with no hint of grey in the coils of rich brown hair which she wore piled high like Queen Mary. She'd kept her figure too, which was petite, with delicate wrists and ankles, but her body had always curved in and out in the right places.

Beautiful she'd been, when he first met her; beautiful with no idea of her beauty, which was what he'd found so appealing. Large grey-green eyes, more green when stirred to anger or passion, had beguiled him, and a relentless determination to set the world to rights according to her own view of things had been particularly attractive in one who looked as if she should languish and be pampered all day.

They first met when she was only eighteen, and had returned home from being a children's nanny to care for her younger brothers and sisters following the death of both their parents –

her father having discreetly drunk himself to death after losing his wife from septicaemia.

Edward had watched her over the next few years as she struggled valiantly to prepare her siblings for adult life, while he himself was struggling to make a go of his first smallholding. But it had been some time before he'd plucked up courage to court her formally; there had always been an elusive quality about her that held him back, whilst at the same time tantalising him. She was twenty-three before the demands of her family had ceased and she had begun to take Edward seriously and allow him any degree of familiarity – and then, to his joy, what sensuality had been unleashed! And he had loved her! Oh, how he had loved her!

And I still love her now, he mused sadly. But it had been many years since the passion which had simultaneously driven and mortified her had been given rein. The determination which had enabled her to take over successfully from her parents had been channelled into 'getting on' in the world – or at least in the important bits of the society in which they moved, while the passion had been supplanted by a strange mixture of worldliness and godliness.

And, he thought with a sigh, *if cleanliness really is next to godliness, then she'll have a special place reserved for her when she gets to the other side.*

"The Talbots are expecting you from the beginning of September," she was telling Emily now, "so you will be able to have the school holiday here as usual."

Emily nodded, her mouth full. She was to be employed by the family who lived at The Manse in Llanfihangel Crucorney, to care for their two young children while Mrs. Talbot recovered from the imminent birth of their third child. Emily had mixed feelings about staying at home until September. She seriously doubted whether she could survive six weeks of Mother without sparks flying. The most confident and headstrong of the four children, and with a finely-honed sense of humour, she was aware every time she came home of the growing urge to kick against the restrictive rules of 'proper' behaviour by which their lives were governed.

The others all seem to have found ways of coping with it, she thought. Laura, stolid and naturally more placid, was the most easily convinced by Mother's edicts and could be quite shocked if it was suggested that they should be disobeyed, or even mildly distorted. Tom, mischievous and loud, had already escaped by allying himself with Father and spending all his time out on the farm, the only place where Father's word was law.

And what of little Jennie? Emily looked down affectionately at the small girl sitting docilely beside her. She, more than any of them, bore the brunt of Mother's abrasive tongue. How would she cope during the next few years as she became increasingly the only one under Mother's domination? She seemed happy enough out on the farm, playing and running free. But indoors she was a completely different child; withdrawn and somehow more solitary than when playing for hours on her own outside. Judging by her pale face and heavy eyes she'd probably been in some sort of trouble already this morning.

A wave of protective love for her baby sister swept through Emily. *I'll give her a good time this holiday,* she vowed, *and come home as often as I can to see she's alright.*

Emily's own future was already mapped out for the next few years. She was to spend the time until she was eighteen with the Talbots – approved by Mother because, although they lived in a thoroughly Welsh village, they were of English stock and very well-connected – and then she was to fulfil her long-held ambition and begin her nurse training. This had also met with approval, as she was to go over the border to Ross-on-Wye, and nursing as a career for genteel young ladies had gained a lot of ground since the war. Emily felt excited and impatient for the next two years to pass every time she thought about it, and no dire warnings of how hard a life it could be would deter her. The rules and regulations governing every aspect of a probationary nurse's life could be no more confining than those she'd lived under for the past sixteen years.

"I'll help you unpack," Jennie told The Girls after dinner, hoping that Mother had heard her being helpful, "and then there might be time for some cricket. I want to show you how I can bowl over-arm – Tom taught me!"

Ever since she'd discovered the range of sport to be played there, Jennie had longed for the day when she too would be attending the convent. She'd wondered at first how the nuns managed to run in their long habits, and had imagined them tucking their skirts up into their knickers like she did for cartwheels. Emily and Laura had shrieked with laughter when she'd mentioned this and explained between chuckles that special mistresses were brought in for games. But Jennie preferred the image of the nuns running to and fro, their black wimples flying out behind them, and refused to replace it with the more prosaic picture of a sturdy-thighed young woman in an Aertex shirt.

"Did Mother get cross with you this morning?" Emily asked casually. The three of them were sitting on the hay bales in the shady Dutch barn after half an hour's cricket in the hot sun.

"N-no," faltered Jennie, aware of Laura's concerned mother-hen gaze upon her. "Well, not really… She was a bit worked up about getting things ready for you both coming home." She sought to change the subject. She didn't want to tell them what had really happened because everything they did together after that would be done out of pity for her – she knew they already felt sorry for her being so much on her own – and more than anything she wanted them to love her for herself. "Mother says we can all go to the market on Tuesday," she said with desperate inspiration. "Will you both come?"

Laura reached over and hugged her. She'd seen the pain in the large grey eyes that were so much like Mother's. "Of course we will. Come on – I need a drink of water. Then we'll try you out with Emily's tennis racket."

Sunday was as hot as the day before, but airless and humid. It was a relief to go to Holy Communion and sit in the cool, dark church at Nantyderry. Unless it was pouring with rain Mother preferred to walk down the narrow winding road from the farm, she in front with Father, her back ramrod straight, and the children in miniature procession behind.

They left the house sufficiently early to enable them to pass the time of day with their neighbours, done in strict accordance with the neighbour's prominence in the community. Thus, Ced Griffiths, from the next farm along, who sat on the parish council, would be greeted with considerable warmth, and Mrs.

Protheroe, widow of Major Protheroe of Nantyderry House, with conspiratorial respect meant to convey equal standing. The vicar's wife, always referred to at home as 'poor Mrs. Simmons', received a smile of pitying condescension, due to her inability to make her unruly children behave in a manner fitting for a Reverend's family, while the farm labourers' families received not a glance, unless it was winter and the children were sniffing with colds, when Mother would glare at them and 'Tut-tut' very loudly. At such times Mother's own children would stare steadfastly ahead so they could pretend not to see the rude gestures directed at Mother once her back was turned.

For once Jennie was eager to go to church, desperate to engage the Almighty's help in the seemingly impossible task of keeping Mother happy and becoming a favoured child.

"Come *on!*" she urged her eldest sister, dragging her away from the bedroom mirror. "Mother will start shouting at us in a minute."

Emily, too, had been looking forward to the morning, because she'd put her hair up for the first time and wanted Ernest Gronow, whom she knew was sweet on her, to see how elegant she'd become. Not that she had any intention of returning his interest: had no intention of becoming involved with anyone for at least ten years – and who would want to be called 'Mrs. Gronow' anyway? But it was amusing to turn her head from time to time during the interminably long service and see his round face glow like a beacon because she'd caught him watching her.

"Emily! Sit round!" her mother hissed the fourth time. Tom craned his neck to see what had interested his sister and caught the tail end of Ernest's blush. He smiled. He could have some sport with Ernest next time they met.

Tom himself had no desire to be in church. He felt uncomfortable in his starched white collar and flannel suit, already getting too small for him so that his bony wrists protruded too far from his sleeves and his turn-ups were too high up his boots to look right. He and Father had been up since four-thirty, milking the cows, feeding the animals, and delivering the milk, more hurried than usual so that they could get back and rush around even more to be washed and changed and ready for church and the remainder of their so-called day of rest.

Laura sat next to Mother, holding herself taut in an effort to prevent her stomach from making indelicate gurgling sounds which she couldn't help but would get blamed for nonetheless. Only Father and Tom were allowed a light breakfast on Sundays because of rising so early, but the girls and Mother only had a weak cup of tea so that there was nothing in their stomachs when they took Holy Communion. And by the time they returned home it was too late, as food would then 'spoil their dinner'.

Mother stood, sat and knelt at the appropriate times, her face pious and rapt throughout. *She still notices everything, though,* thought Jennie, receiving a frown and a "Keep still!" for fidgeting. She must have eyes in the back of her head!

The prospect of Mother with another pair of eyes intrigued her, and she spent several minutes imagining where they would be and how Mother would manage to brush her hair without hurting them. Lost in contemplation, she was surprised to receive a sharp poke in the arm from Tom as the congregation rose for the final hymn.

Oh, damn! She hadn't spent enough time beseeching God to help her, and now it was too late! *And now I've sworn as well!* she thought in rising panic. *And in church, too!...* Perhaps it didn't count if you only thought it, but then God was even worse than Mother for knowing everything you did, including what you thought.

She tried to pray as well as sing, but it was impossible and she got another nudge from Tom because she kept missing the note. *I'll say extra prayers tonight,* she vowed, trying surreptitiously to rub her arm – *and next week I'll remember not to sit next to Tom.*

"An excellent sermon, Reverend Simmons," exclaimed Mother as they shook hands in the porch.

"Yes, excellent," echoed Father cheerfully. Glad of the opportunity to sit down, he hadn't listened to a word of it. Leaving Mother to exchange social niceties with the ladies of the parish he strode over to Ced Griffiths to indulge in fifteen minutes of farming talk, while The Girls stood shyly but provocatively eyeing the young men from under the wide brims of their straw summer hats.

Jennie saw Tom amble over to Ernest Gronow, nudge him – Tom was a great one for using his knobbly elbows – and nod towards Emily. She watched in fascination as a deep red flush spread above the white of Ernest's shirt collar, until his whole face looked on fire.

"He's taken a real shine to you," Tom told Emily with a grin as they walked home. "Breaking his poor heart, you are."

But Emily tossed her head, pleased with the feel of her hair tucked up under her hat, and looked haughty. "He can mind his own business," she said, "and so can you, Tom Davies."

"I'm sweating!" announced Jennie, remembering Ernest's red face and feeling hot for him.

"Animals sweat, men perspire, but ladies *glow!*" Mother immediately reproved, but she didn't sound too harsh. She'd enjoyed the outing to church and was feeling particularly satisfied because Emily's prettiness and ladylike appearance had been commented on by several people. Not that it would do to let Emily know that, and risk her becoming vain, but it reflected well on herself to have such a personable daughter. She didn't think that Laura would impress with the same qualities, but she was undoubtedly going to become striking in her own way and could make an excellent marriage.

She glanced at Jennie, walking hand-in-hand with her father, and could feel no emotion at all, except perhaps a faint irritation. She'll have to improve greatly if she's going to match up to her sisters, she decided, taking in Jennie's rather sallow complexion and deep-set eyes that permanently had dark shadows under them. But then, it wouldn't matter too much, as she'd already marked Jennie down as the daughter who would stay at home and help care for her parents as they aged. Mother was a great fan of Queen Victoria, and she'd kept her youngest daughter at home.

"Ced Griffiths is thinking of giving up Pontypool market for a while," said Father over dinner in the pleasant well-proportioned dining room. "There's so little money about that people will only buy vegetables when they're nearly going off, so you're practically giving them away."

"And that certainly wouldn't suit Ced Griffiths," observed Tom with a chuckle.

Mother gave a disdainful shudder. "I don't know why anyone would want to go to that dreadful hole anyway."

"Now, Katie," reproved Father in his gentle tones, "it's not their fault if there's no work to be had."

He realised his mistake as soon as he'd finished speaking. Mother hated to be called by what he considered the pretty diminutive of her name.

"They may not be to blame for their idleness, but they don't all have to be so dirty!" she snapped. She rose and began to clear the dishes, indicating to the girls to help, effectively curtailing further discussion.

Pontypool was about nine miles away from the farm, in the opposite direction from Abergavenny, the nearest of a string of mining and industrial towns in the Welsh valleys for whom this second decade of the twentieth century had been disastrous. Repeated strikes for better pay and conditions had only resulted in demoralised men crawling back to jobs for less instead of more, and now shrinking world markets and steel production being moved to more favourable coastal sites made their prospects even bleaker.

Mother, however, could only see sloth in their enforced idleness, and had a deep mistrust of their chapels and public houses which seemed to spawn each other on opposite corners of every mean little street. She much preferred Abergavenny, with its air of bustle and purposefulness as a little market town, proud of its place as the gateway to the beauty of the Black Mountains and Brecon Beacons. Here, life might be tough if you were a struggling hill farmer, but at least more people were Church, and the Blorenge mountain separated you from the awfulness of the mining communities.

And that's the best part of the day over, thought Jennie as she put away the clean cutlery while The Girls washed and dried the dishes. Mother took herself off for her afternoon nap, claiming that she would never rest properly in this sticky heat, but nevertheless everyone would be expected to be as quiet as possible until she arose.

"You can play with your dolls in the parlour," she told Jennie before mounting the stairs, "and then later on we can look at the Big Bible."

"Thank you, Mother," Jennie responded dutifully but dully,

and went to fetch her dolls.

She sat on a tapestry stool in the parlour with the dolls on her lap and wondered, as she did each Sunday, what she was supposed to do with them. She'd been told repeatedly that they were very expensive and she was lucky to have such beautiful dolls, and she was sure if she was a doll-type little girl she would be thrilled with them. But there was something sinister about their bright staring eyes, while their rosebud mouths, which Mother claimed to be the epitome of beauty in ladies as well as dolls, seemed petulant and cruel.

Not that Jennie had ever analysed their features to this extent; all she knew was that she couldn't cuddle them and croon to them the way she could to Mopsy, the old rag doll she'd pushed around the farm in her wheelbarrow when she was younger and which was now tucked safely away in the back of a cupboard in her bedroom, lest Mother should find her and deem her too old and tattered to keep any longer.

Jennie thought of Mopsy now and wished she could fetch her to cuddle. She felt in need of the comfort that the familiar feel and smell of her old friend – a mixture of mustiness from the cupboard and old dirt from outside – would give her. But to go upstairs now would be to make the floorboards creak and incur Mother's wrath.

Jennie gazed around the room, hoping for diversion, but everyone was occupied. Laura was busy with her embroidery, which she did exquisitely, and, to Jennie's amazement, with great enjoyment; Emily was writing a letter, while Father and Tom were reading the local papers. They were both back in their working clothes – and thus seated on hard chairs – attendance at church being Father's only real concession to the Sabbath.

Jennie thought about undressing her dolls and then dressing them again but it seemed a rather pointless exercise and their frilled and flounced clothes had so many tiny buttons. The oppressive stillness and heat began to overwhelm her and her head began to ache faintly, but she wouldn't admit to it because that would mean a dose of Syrup of Figs, which she detested and which always left her with a gripey stomach-ache.

"Can I go outside, Father?" she asked, her voice high and loud in the quiet room.

"'Mmm?" he replied absently, his mind still on the newspaper.

"May I go for a walk around the garden? It's very hot in here."

He put the paper down and looked across at his daughter. He noticed her pinched, solemn countenance and smiled kindly. She looked a bit off colour and the room was very warm. "Of course you may," he said.

Jennie laid the dolls on the stool and left the room hurriedly, before Father could remind her about taking a hat. As long as he didn't tell her, it wasn't so bad to pretend to forget.

She was only allowed to walk around the paths edging the formal gardens when wearing her best clothes, and besides, running and shouting would be totally inappropriate on a Sunday. She ventured along the drive until it became too dusty, and then turned and followed a path that led to the side of the house and the part of the garden which the parlour overlooked. She could see her mountains now, except for the very tops of them which were hidden by a shimmery heat haze.

At the bottom of the garden was a large rhododendron bush where she'd discovered a blackbird's nest in the spring. The baby birds had flown, but the mother bird was hopping agitatedly about nearby, hoping to distract her away from the nest.

"It's alright," she said, "I won't hurt you or your babies," and then she laughed as the bird stood still, its head on one side, as if considering what she'd said.

The thought of the mother blackbird's concern for her family brought back all the feelings of yesterday. Jennie probed at them like she did with her tongue at the gap made by a tooth falling out. They felt much the same; raw and faintly bloody, and much too big ever to be filled properly again.

She made her way back the way she'd come, keeping a lookout for one of the farm cats to distract her away from her thoughts and pausing to lean on the garden gate and gaze at the front of the house, feeling a rush of love for its solid beauty. She liked the way the windows each side of the front door seemed to wink at you in the sunlight, and the large cream stones making a pattern up its gable ends. The woodwork was picked out in Father's favourite apple green and cream, except for the front door, which was heavily varnished, with a gleaming brass knocker and letter box.

I never want to leave here, Jennie thought fervently, not even sure in this mood whether she wanted to board at the convent. *Even if Mother doesn't love me, I can't stop loving the farm and everything about it.*

There was something so comforting in the rhythm of its day-today activities. Very soon Father and Tom would be back outside for afternoon milking, the pigs and chickens would be fed and preparations made for the beginning of a new working week, each day with its clearly prescribed tasks, varying only slightly according to the seasons.

The best day this week would be Tuesday, Jennie decided, because they were all going to the market. But first, the worst day of the week had to be endured; Monday Washday. Mother would be in a foul temper all day, exclaiming constantly that she didn't know how a family could get its clothes so dirty – although as it was the same every week you'd think she'd be used to it by now.

The large boiler in the washroom between the kitchen and the dairy, from which Father and Tom would only extract a small amount of water for washing and shaving since they never used the bathroom, would be lit at first light. The Girls would strip and change the beds before breakfast, after which everybody tried to keep out of the way as much as possible until they all sat down to dinner – always cold meat from yesterday and re-heated vegetables, because Mother wouldn't have time to cook as well and The Girls, when home, would not be allowed to do it as Mother wouldn't be able to oversee their activities in her kitchen.

"Come along! Come along! I'll never get done at this rate!" was Mother's constant cry to anyone who happened to be in the same room as her and dared stop to take a breath.

By this time Bessie would be red-faced and breathless from her exertions with the dolly, and her arms reddened and sore-looking from hot water and soda, and even Mother, who scrubbed the collars and dealt with the underwear, would, true to her edict, be 'glowing'.

I'll get up early tomorrow and see to the chickens and collect the eggs, Jennie decided, as the first step of her plan to become indispensable to Mother. She conjured up a picture of Mother smiling benignly and crooning words of praise and love – which, in truth, Jennie had never heard in her life – as her youngest child became the mainstay of her existence. *And I'll strip and change my bed myself, and then...*

Her plans were interrupted by large drops of rain plopping purposefully on her head as, in the distance, the first rumblings of thunder could be heard. Jennie hurried up the front path and entered the house just as Mother was bustling down the stairs, issuing orders.

"Turn the mirrors round! Laura! See that all the cutlery has been put away! Leave that front door open, Jennie, and go and open the back door!"

Jennie scuttled off to do as she was told, relieved that her mother was too preoccupied to question why she had been outside. A flash of lightning illuminated the now dark kitchen, followed closely by a burst of thunder that seemed to be right above the roof, making Jennie jump as she opened the back door but filling her with excitement rather than fear.

Mother, though, was frightened by thunderstorms and insisted the doors had to be left open so that a thunderbolt coming down the chimney could find its way out again, and all precautions had to be taken so that lightning shouldn't hit metal or glass.

"Why don't you put your crucifix inside your dress until the storm is over?" Tom had once suggested, and had had his ears soundly boxed, as apparently he should have realised that the wearing of the crucifix automatically protected Mother from the risk of electrocution and it was blasphemous to suppose otherwise.

The storm was heavy but brief. Afterwards Jennie stood at the front door breathing in the scent that the rain had unleashed from the rose bushes lining the path, and watching the early evening sun – released now from the oppressive clouds – making the raindrops sparkle on spiders' webs. The evening was still but fresh, the air sweet, with that indefinable quality of Sunday restfulness and peace, and for a while her mother's recent malevolence was forgotten.

END OF SAMPLE CHAPTER

ALSO BY JULIE McGOWAN :

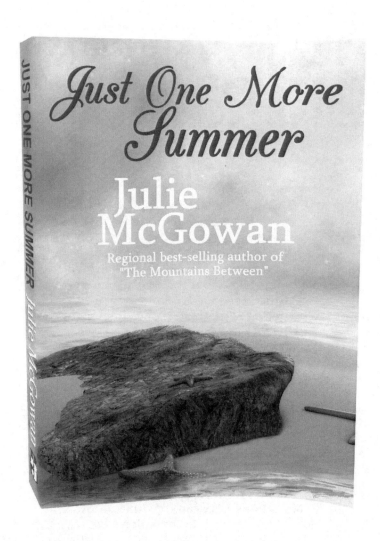

ROSE & CROWN, BLUE JEANS, BOATHOOKS, SUNBERRY, CHRISTLIGHT, and EPTA Books

MORE BOOKS FROM the SUNPENNY GROUP
www.sunpenny.com

A Flight Delayed, by KC Lemmer
A Little Book of Pleasures, by William Wood
Blackbirds Baked in a Pie, by Eugene Barter
Blue Freedom, by Sandra Peut
Brandy Butter on Christmas Canal, by Shae O'Brien
Breaking the Circle, by Althea Barr
Bridge to Nowhere, by Stephanie Parker McKean
Dance of Eagles, by JS Holloway
Embracing Change, by Debbie Roome
Far Out, by Corinna Weyreter
Going Astray, by Christine Moore
If Horses Were Wishes, by Elizabeth Sellers
Just One More Summer, by Julie McGowan
Loyalty & Disloyalty, by Dag Heward-Mills
My Sea is Wide, by Rowland Evans
Someday, Maybe, by Jenny Piper
The Mountains Between, by Julie McGowan
The Skipper's Child, by Valerie Poore
Trouble Rides a Fast Horse, by Elizabeth Sellers
Uncharted Waters, by Sara DuBose
Watery Ways, by Valerie Poore